The Secular Gospel of Sophia

The Secular Gospel of Sophia

Daniel G. Helton

TOP HAT BOOKS

Winchester, UK
Washington, USA

First published by Top Hat Books, 2016
Top Hat Books is an imprint of John Hunt Publishing Ltd., Laurel House, Station Approach,
Alresford, Hants, SO24 9JH, UK
office1@jhpbooks.net
www.johnhuntpublishing.com
www.tophat-books.com

For distributor details and how to order please visit the 'Ordering' section on our website.

ISBN: 978 1 78535 181 5
Library of Congress Control Number: 2015941040

A CIP catalogue record for this book is available from the British Library.

Design: Stuart Davies

Printed and bound by CPI Group (UK) Ltd, Croydon, CR0 4YY, UK

To my father, Fred Helton, who often told me that there was never a time when mankind did not have an explanation for everything.

DGH

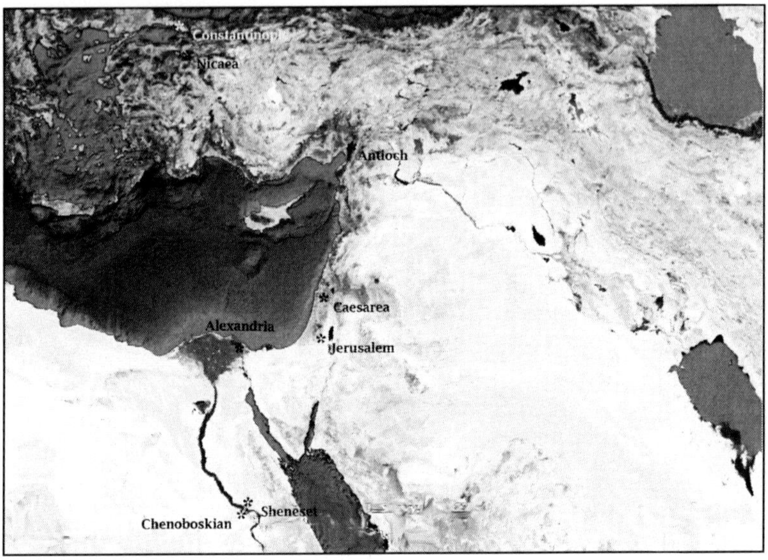
Constantinople
Nicaea
Antioch
Caesarea
Alexandria
Jerusalem
Sheneset
Chenoboskian

The Secular Gospel Of Sophia

For I am the first and the last.
I am the honored one and the scorned one.
I am the whore and the holy one.
I am the wife and the virgin.
I am the barren one, and many are my sons and daughters
I am the silence that is incomprehensible.
I am the utterance of my name.

Thunder, Perfect Mind

Chapter One

Sophia

324 A.D. – Antioch

He who has ears to hear, let him hear.
He who understands, let him understand.
The Gospel According to Mary Magdalene

Sophia was not her birth name. That was forgotten. So much was forgotten. Trivial things. Important things. Mother? Father? She had no mother, no father, except for the streets of Alexandria, the wide world, and the universe. Where was she born? Perhaps a linguist, studying the curves of her inflections and the tacks of her Greek or Egyptian could have calibrated her place of birth, but she knew not. In any case, those were not the curves of first impression, even for a linguist. But how could these things matter once she embarked on a quest for knowledge?

She was seventeen years old, fresh and beautiful despite three years in the brothel in Antioch. The finest brothel in the capital, she had been told on many occasions. And she was a favorite of a select few of the finest, richest, most noble and most devout men. That much she remembered. Who forged papers to sell her as a slave to the brothel owner before her fourteenth year? Lost, for now, to time's intervention. What she did there? Well …

One day a different kind of man came to the brothel. Timaeus, he called himself. He stood before her, stars for eyes, staring without sight and without the usual lusty mien, but with a fixed, eyeless stare all the more intense for the absence of focused orbs. Perhaps it was love, but she did not recognize it. He made no motion toward her and no effort to remove his travel-worn robe. When she asked him what he wanted, he said, simply, quietly, "I seek you, Sophia."

"But I am not Sophia."

"I have been seeking you my whole life and now I have found you. You are Sophia."

And so she was, from that day forward.

"Come away with me, Sophia," he said.

"Come away with you and go where?"

"To where we are needed."

"I do not understand."

"You know more than you understand. I will give you understanding. You will give me knowledge."

"But I belong to Ammianus."

"I have purchased you."

"Then I belong to you?"

"No, you are free and if you choose you are free to come away with me."

"To follow you?"

"We will see who leads and who follows."

And so, knowing, but not understanding, she went away with Timaeus.

Chapter Two

On The Road To Gnosis

324 A.D. – Syria, Palestine, Judea, Samaria

Who is Jesus? What did he preach? Where shall I find him?
Those who seek him will find him.
The Gospel According to Phillip

Sophia did not know why she went away with Timaeus, what powers of fate or what hunger impelled her. In future years, when she would wonder about such things, she still could not decide. Perhaps it was his eyes, which she never saw, but remembered as flaming stars between arched and greying brows. Certainly there was nothing in the life of the brothel to hold her, but there was little of brothel life that repulsed her either. Perhaps it was the prospect of adventure in a life that, as a prostitute, was predictably short with a predictable ending. Most often, she thought it was merely his certainty that moved her: His absolute conviction that he had been seeking her and now had found her. Perhaps she believed him. Perhaps she was merely moved by being the object of such a quest and discovery.

But at first, without questioning, she travelled with him. Toward Nazareth, for, he said, that was where Jesus started.

"Jesus was not the first, nor will he be the last," Timaeus told her. "He was the Alpha and the Omega because he was both the question and the answer. But there was knowledge, gnosis, before Jesus and there is knowledge now that he no longer walks among us. Knowledge is in the air and in the earth. It is in fire and ice. It is on land and on sea. And, sometimes, it is in the soul of a woman. We go to Nazareth for that is where Jesus first acquired knowledge. That you may see. That I may see."

"How does one acquire knowledge, Timaeus?"

"I should be asking you, Sophia."

"But I have no knowledge. See, I have already forgotten my name."

"You are Sophia. I felt your knowledge before I saw you. I heard your knowledge before you spoke to me."

"But what knowledge do I have, Timaeus?"

"Eventually you will understand and then you will tell me, so that I may know."

Another time, another evening, Timaeus told her that acquiring knowledge was a lifetime quest, to be accomplished through years of study and meditation, but that sometimes, for a very few people, it could be gained in the blinking of an eye. One could be instructed on the pathways to knowledge, but one had to acquire it on her own terms. Some people, those without the divine spark of the undying generation, could never obtain true knowledge. Very rarely, he said, as in her case, one could have knowledge without realizing it.

"Why do we seek knowledge, Timaeus?" she asked. "Knowledge of what?"

"We seek knowledge of the one true Goddess and the Unknowable One who did not create this world, but without whom no worlds could exist," he answered. "I believe the true Goddess is knowledge, pure knowledge, the meaning of and reason for all that exists. We cannot know the Unknowable One, but we can know His emanation, Sophia, the true Goddess. And by having knowledge, gnosis, of Her we can join with Her in spirit and leave our anguish with the creator God who, through His creation, separated us from the perfection of Sophia's mind, *ennoia*."

Much of what Timaeus said was invisible to Sophia. She would ask a question, maybe two, then would ask nothing further, sometimes for days. Timaeus took her silences as proof that he had been correct, that she was the Sophia for whom he sought. The truth is that she fell silent to avoid becoming even more confused. His words were enigmas, ghosts with a presence, but no form, no meaning. She would acquaint herself with the ghosts slowly, at her own pace. The biggest enigma was, why me? What am I that he who cannot see can see?

They traveled on foot, frugally. The hardships of this life were not hardships to her. As a comely, young woman in a brothel for noble citizens of the Empire, she was used to finer things, an easier life in many ways. But as she had neither exalted nor despaired in the life of a courtesan, she did not exalt or despair in her new life as Sophia. The yellow silk toga and silver ankle bracelets that she wore as a licensed prostitute were exchanged for linen tunics and a few coppers. Being young and slight, her feet soon toughened to the road.

Between cities and towns they walked the broad lanes of Roman roads, *viae* and *itenera,* making way for the traffic that fed the extended limbs of the eastern Empire. Trains consisting of three and four wagons hitched together behind a team of oxen and driven by teamsters armed with whips and weapons rumbled past, carrying local goods to ports and distribution centers. Overfilled labor carts bounced past roughly on iron rimmed, wooden wheels, laden with workers, slaves and freemen, occasionally dumping one or two over the side or crushing one under a wheel. Elegant passenger carriages on spring-cushioned wheels carried as many as twelve travelers at a time for those who could afford the coin for comfort. Horses, mules, donkeys and camels carried individual travelers or their goods. Many others wandered on foot. Occasional troops of legionaries would march past, accompanied by a horse-riding officer and the sound of a drum, keeping cadence. Each processional was accompanied by its distinctive odors, sweet or rank, mellow or pungent, that proceeded and trailed after the passage. Every color that could be extracted from nature, woven into cloth or daubed onto skin, adorned the travelers who passed. When they entered a town, Timaeus would often approach a man or a woman and speak to him or her in hushed tones. At first Sophia thought that the selection was random. But almost invariably, after a few words were spoken, they would quietly be escorted into a dwelling and given bread and drink and rest.

Often, in the early evenings, there would be a gathering. Sometimes only a handful of people would come, sometimes a dozen or more. The places varied. Sometimes the gathering would be in an olive grove. Sometimes in the shade of rock cropping, a thousand *passus* from the road. Never in a dwelling. Never in a hall. The people would arrive separately, by different routes. As they gathered they would greet each other individually, exchanging touches and words and acute gazes. Timaeus seemed to know everyone by name. He would introduce her as Sophia, eliciting varying reactions, from a smile, to a slight gasp, to stiffening and drawing back, as if she were herself a relic of worship or an object of suspicion.

Eventually one would be chosen to preside over the service. Man or woman, it did not seem to matter. Timaeus, whom many addressed as "Bishop," would often be asked to preside, but almost as often demurred. "I have more to learn than I have to teach," he would say. Or, sometimes, "we are all equal in our quest for knowledge."

There seemed to be little in the way of ritual and no sacraments. A few prayers offered to the true Goddess or to Lord Jesus sufficed for ceremony. One such prayer that in later years Sophia transcribed, was:

> "Let us bless our Lord Jesus who has sent us to the Spirit of Truth. He came and separated us from the error of the world; he brought us a mirror in which we looked and saw the universe. Jesus carved a river in the cosmos. He carved a river, even he of sweet name. He carved it with a pickaxe of truth.

He dredged it with a shovel of wisdom."

Timaeus would always be asked to speak. "Tell us what you have learned, Bishop," someone would say. "You have traveled far on your journey of truth, your journey for gnosis. Please instruct us."

Sometimes Timaeus would decline to speak, saying that he knew no more than any other among them or (indicating others in attendance) that Sister Doritea or Brother Amenius had already said what he may have been inclined to say.

But often Timaeus would speak. His voice rippled like a gentle forest spring. He spoke with inflections of wonder and humility, which infused his words with authority and purpose.

The first time Sophia heard Timaeus speak at such a gathering, this is what he said:

"Jesus said to the nineteen disciples (seven of whom were women, you know), 'Come from invisible things to the end of those that are visible, and the very emanation of Thought will reveal to you how faith in those things that are not visible was found in those that are visible, those that belong to Unbegotten Father. Whoever has ears to hear, let him hear!'

"What Jesus teaches is that while Truth is not visible, it emanates from everything that is visible; that while Truth cannot be told, it can be heard. Our journey takes us through the realm of the visible, through the matter that was created by the God of Abraham, Yaldabaoth, to the realm of the Unknowable One, Sophia's creator: He or she who has no human form, for whoever has human form is the creation of another. The physical world is a dead world, since it was created in perishability. The body that we inhabit is not who we are. It is the creation of Yaldabaoth. The body the Romans crucified was not Jesus, but they crucified Yaldabaoth's body while Jesus stood aside, laughing at them. The Catholics say the Romans and Jews crucified God, that they killed God, but we know this cannot be true. God comes from the imperishable and cannot be killed. Jesus, the real Jesus, cannot die, just as that which is eternal within us cannot die. We who gather here tonight have retained a spark, a sliver of essence, from the Unknowable One, through His emanation Sophia, who exists as perfect knowledge. Sophia is not the creator. This world is the creation of her imperfect creation. Yet, the creation could not exist without Sophia and the Unknowable One from which she emerged and of which she is a part. Like Jesus, we cannot attain perfect life until we shed our imperfect bodies.

"And this is why Jesus said, 'whoever has ears to hear about the infinities, let him hear. He speaks to those who are awake. Everything that came from the perishable will perish, since it came from the perishable. But whatever came from imperishableness does not perish but becomes imperishable. So, many go astray because they do not understand this and they are destined to perish in ignorance.'"

There would be questions and answers. All would question, all would answer, each in turn as they were inspired, the women equally with the men. Nobody presumed to have perfect knowledge or gnosis. All were instructors; all were students.

The longest of Timaeus' messages (he insisted that they were not sermons), and also Sophia's favorite, was given in Tyre to a group of almost thirty, among whom, Timaeus was certain, were no Catholics who had infiltrated the gathering. It was the story of Norea, the wife of Noah.

Chapter Three

The Story of Norea

324 A.D. – Palestine

Do you think these rulers have any power over you? None of them can prevail against the root of truth; for on its account he appeared in the final ages; and these authorities will be restrained. And these authorities cannot defile you and that generation; for your abode is in incorruptibility, where the virgin spirit dwells, who is superior to the authorities of chaos and to their universe.
The Hypostasis of the Archons

Timaeus' telling of the story of Norea:

"Before the beginning was the realm of Pleroma where Sophia exists as Ennoia, or pure thought. There was no darkness. No land. No sea. No heaven. No earth. No creation. And in that realm of Pleroma we, too, were there, or at least fragments of ourselves, not creations, but emanations. Not as humans or individuals or beings of any kind to live and perish apart from the All, but as thoughts together, emanations together, all as one, in the mind of Sophia as part of Sophia. Knowing all without awareness. Needing nothing. Perfect.

"One day, in the realm of Pleroma, Sophia, or Barbelo as some name her, conceived a son in the form of a separate thought or emanation. And this emanation pulled apart from Sophia. It is unknown how and why from the perfect Sophia would emanate an existence with autonomy of thought and will, but so it was. Yaldabaoth, we call him. The Hebrew calls him Yahweh or Elohim or El. Having conceived of Yaldabaoth, she gave birth to her one imperfection. This imperfection left the Pleroma and could not reenter the perfection of Sophia's mind, Ennoia.

"In his ignorance, Yaldabaoth thought apart from Sophia, apart from the harmony of Ennoia. He saw the Pleroma as chaos because he could not understand the perfection of the All as One. He grew angry at his expulsion and isolation. His separate and inferior mind could not grasp Ennoia, could not grasp Sophia's perfect mind. Knowing this caused him pain. In the manner of a dullard schoolboy, his mind began to wander. He thought of another realm, a physical realm that his Mother could not enter, where he would be supreme and unquestioned.

"So it was that Yaldabaoth divided portions of the All, separated the light from the darkness and the land from the sea and the earth from the air. He created the physical existence of all living creatures and gave them form in the manner of his reckless choosing, circumscribed only by the limits of his imagination. Into this world he last made man and woman, Adam and Eve. As a cruel act of rebellion against Sophia, he gave Adam dominion over Eve.

"Once he had created this world, Yaldabaoth realized that through him, against his wishes, his creations carried something of Sophia and that there existed in them, or at least some of them, a spark from the divine and a longing for the Pleroma. Although he had made them, everything he made came originally from Sophia and, through her, from the Unknowable One. As a child born a hundred generations after the matriarch may possess the nose or eyes or hands of her ancestor, so, too, did Yaldabaoth's creations possess within them not knowledge itself, but the vestigial memory of knowledge manifest as longing and curiosity.

"Discovering this trait of his Mother within the minds of his highest creation, Yaldabaoth sought to deprive them of knowledge, that they might forever worship him. Thus, he decreed that we would live hungry without knowing for what we craved. He made all flesh mortal so that our time for seeking knowledge would be limited. He forbade Adam and Eve to eat from the tree of knowledge that grew from Sophia's seed. While they lived thus suspended, Yaldabaoth loved them and played with them as a child might love and play with figures carved from wood. He mingled with them, taking physical form to fornicate with Eve to bring forth Cain and Abel.

"But Eve, possessing more of Sophia than Adam, hungered for knowledge and ate of the fruit of the forbidden tree and beckoned Adam to do likewise. With their knowledge, they learned that Yaldabaoth was not almighty, that he was but the imperfect emanation of a perfect mind. They learned that he was childlike in his anger and his jealousy. They clung to each other. They loved each other. And Eve would no longer lay with Yaldabaoth, so he cast them forth from the Garden of Eden.

"If Yaldabaoth thought that Adam and Eve would be frightened and beg to be returned to the garden of ignorance, he was mistaken. Eve gave birth to the first son of man, Seth, and the first daughter of woman, Norea, and they flourished, growing ever closer to an understanding of Sophia, Ennoia, and realm of the Pleroma.

"A thousand years passed and the children of Adam and Eve prospered in gnosis, gaining wisdom and knowledge of their great mother Sophia. They ceased to pay heed to Yaldabaoth, except as one heeds a criminal in the dark. They feared him and his intermittent wrath, but they worshiped him not. They learned to speak and write and to craft poetry from their words, in this way communing with Sophia, gaining awareness and knowledge of the Supreme Existence that makes all things possible. They learned to organize, to cultivate, to build. Their thirst for true knowledge led them to look for the truth in every direction, to see gods in the earth, the sky, the sea, the rivers, the wind and the stars. And they were not wrong, my brothers and sisters, not completely wrong, because aspects of Sophia, the essence of Sophia, can be found in all things. And so it was that they were gaining knowledge of Sophia.

"As people gained knowledge, they stopped worshiping Yaldabaoth, knowing that it was he who had separated them from Sophia in the Pleroma. So in his anger, Yaldabaoth determined to start over, to destroy mankind utterly, saving only the single most ignorant man on Earth and his family. I speak of Noah. Yaldabaoth told Noah to build an ark for his family and for all lesser creatures that dwelt upon the Earth. He told Noah to leave all other men and women behind, thinking thereby to erase the very spark of Sophia from his creation.

"So, Noah built the ark, but when it was finished his wife Norea, having gnosis and realizing the plans of Yaldabaoth, set it afire. Noah built the ark a second time and, again, Norea burnt it to the ground.

"Now Yaldabaoth was angry and, taking the form of a man, came to Norea with the object of killing her. But when he saw her beauty, he instead insisted that she lay with him, as her ancestor Eve had once done.

"Repulsed, Norea turned to Yaldabaoth and said: 'You are the ruler only of the Darkness; you are accursed. And I am not your daughter, but the daughter of Adam, who is a man. I am not your descendant; rather it is from the World Above that I am come.'

"Yaldabaoth turned to Norea in fury. He said to her, 'You must render service to me, as did also your mother Eve.'

"Norea cried out to the heavens for help and was rescued by Understanding, an angel of Sophia, who taught her about her origins and destiny in the world beyond time. Understanding said to Norea, 'Do you think Yaldabaoth has any power over you? He cannot prevail against the Root of Truth. You, together with your offspring, are from Sophia, from Above. Out of the imperishable Light your souls are come. Thus Yaldabaoth cannot approach you because the Spirit of Truth is present within you. He can destroy only what he has created, but what he did not create, he cannot destroy.'"

"It is said that after the attempted rape of his wife, Noah did not build another ark. That, instead, Norea led her family and others with gnosis and as many animals as could be herded, to high ground, beyond the limited power of Yaldabaoth, to ride out the storm. And in his evil, Yaldabaoth did cause floods throughout the Earth and many people perished. But some, like Norea, could divine the Universe and see his plan so that it did not succeed altogether. And, thus, did Knowledge survive the flood."

Timaeus' delivery was animated and without hesitation, as if he were speaking from personal knowledge. When he finished, he smiled a beatific smile and took a long drink of water before continuing.

"What does this story mean to us," Timaeus continued, "this story that survived the flood and the punishments of David and Solomon, yes and even the punishments of the Caesars and the Catholics? Simply this, my brothers and my sisters: That Yaldabaoth exists in the realm of perishability, the dead world, and thinks he can keep us, his creations, apart from the Imperishable. But those with knowledge understand that we come from the Imperishable and that only by resisting the power of the perishable god Yaldabaoth and his contrivances, by seeking the higher ground of understanding, can we return to the Pleroma. For, in truth, that spark within us which longs for knowledge came not from Yaldabaoth, but from the True Mother, from Sophia."

Chapter Four

Damaged Christians

324 A.D. – Palestine

I am sown in all things; and whence thou wilt, thou gatherest me, but when thou gatherest me, then gatherest thou thyself.
The Gospel of Eve

Sophia soon noticed that many of the people who came to the gatherings bore scars. There would be a missing eye or hand or leg. The mottled landscape of burnt flesh would form a deep topography up the calf of a leg or along the curve of a cheek. Fingers, toes, hands and feet, arms and legs would extend at unnatural angles or be altogether absent. The congregants bore these afflictions without comment or complaint. Timaeus wore two star-shaped scars where his eyes used to rest. It was a mark that would certainly have frightened her when he asked her to come away with him, had she noticed at the time that his eyes were not embedded in those stars. She had been traveling with him a full day when she first realized that his eyes were not hiding behind the scars.

Sophia asked Timaeus, "Why are so many of us damaged?"

"You said 'us.' I was right, you are Sophia."

"Don't be silly. But please, answer the question."

"We are not damaged, Sophia, but improved. The loss of my eyes has improved my vision."

"If that is true, then what do I look like?"

Timaeus laughed, kindly. "What I can see, more clearly," he said, "is that everything is in God, the true Goddess, and that the true Goddess is in everything. That lesser gods and angels and spirits and even emperors who demand worship or obedience have detached themselves from the true Goddess and pursue selfish ends."

Sophia frowned.

"Why do you frown, Sophia?" Timaeus asked.

"How did you know I frowned?" Sophia questioned.

"I can see you frowning. Tell me, why do you frown?"

"It is because when you told me you could see, I thought you meant you could see things of this world and so I asked you what I looked like. A woman has her vanities. I guess I hoped you could see me. I was disappointed that you can see the All and not just anything."

Timaeus took Sophia's right hand between his two, rough palms. "I do not need eyes to see you, Sophia," he said. "I do not need eyes to see your long, dark hair, the color of the Tannus in Cappadocia, or your wide, unblinking eyes of the same color, but that flash like that river as it bounds over the rocks of a rapids. I do not need eyes to see the strength of your cheeks or the rich arc of your neck as it races to find cover beneath the folds of your tunic. I do not need eyes to see that you are the most beautiful of women, Sophia. And beyond this, do not ask me to speak for if I think much on these things, it gives rise to a forbidden desire that leaves me blind to everything else."

"Timaeus," Sophia said, "I think that is the best compliment I have ever received."

They were walking along the road from Tyre to Caesarea. At high points, when the foliage thinned, Sophia could see the majestic Mediterranean frolicking below. They passed olive and grape orchards and hemp fields organized with military efficiency, in service to the Empire. The smell of the sea filtered on a gentle breeze through the groves to produce a sweet, salty and fruity perfume that teased the senses with the promise of life in paradise. That breeze, she thought, felt like her new life, her life on the road with Timaeus.

"Timaeus," Sophia said after a few minutes, "through your

flattery, you have skillfully avoided my question. Why is it that so many with whom we gather bear signs of torture and abuse?"

"The answer is easy. Because ignorance hates knowledge."

"Is it the Romans?"

"Sometimes, but not often any more. The Romans have enough troubles without looking for more. No. Most of the time it now comes from the Christians."

"But we are Christians!"

"We call ourselves Christians. But what does that mean? We follow the teachings of Jesus of Nazareth. Jesus is a divine instructor, Seth incarnate, a guide to knowledge of the All, to reuniting with the All. For those who call themselves Catholic, Jesus was the Son of Yaldabaoth, whom they consider the only God."

Sophia frowned.

"You are frowning again."

"But what you are saying is that for the Catholics, Jesus was sent by Yaldabaoth to trick men into worshiping him?"

"Yes. But, of course, they do not believe that. They believe that Yaldabaoth is all powerful and good and that his love for mankind was such that he sacrificed his son, his only son, so that we could find our way to Him."

As they walked, a brown dunnock followed them along, arching from shrub to shrub, serenading them with a thin warble. The relentless sun dried the path and mists of dust softly surveyed their steps.

"But this does not explain why they maim us, Timaeus. Why must they behave this way?"

"Because they offer easy salvation, but their house is built of straw. To be a Catholic, all a person must do is to confess that he is a sinner and to profess that the only way to be accepted by God is by recognizing Jesus as the savior. For this, they promise eternal life, not simply of the mind or the soul, but of the physical body, resurrected in paradise.

"To this we say they are telling a child's story, for only a childish mind could believe it. We do not seek a resurrected body, even if we thought it was possible to attain. Our body is one of the things that separate us from Sophia in the Pleroma. We seek unity with Her through knowledge. Simple children's stories are only another barrier to attaining true gnosis."

With a few parting notes the dunnock darted away and looped back to her home where several determined suitors awaited her return. Sophia and Timaeus walked on in the sun.

"But this still does not explain why they punish us so fiercely."

"Don't you see, Sophia, it is because they cannot tolerate our Jesus. They are saying, 'accept Jesus and be saved,' and we are saying, 'study Jesus and begin your journey, study what he said and did, learn from him and begin to think on the nature of the world, on the nature of good and evil, on the nature of the infinite.' We are quite happy to live with the Catholics, to let them pursue their folly. But our very existence, our belief in Jesus threatens the certainty of their faith. If we did not follow Jesus, if, for example, we applied to Zeus or even to pickled fish or to anything else, they might be able to allow it. But we trace our beliefs to Jesus. His brother Thomas was our guide and many of the other disciples believed with him. The Catholics' belief in this child's tale of the resurrected Jesus depends upon its certainty, upon unquestioned acceptance. And here we are, proclaiming to them that we know Jesus and we accept Jesus, but you are wrong. It casts doubt upon everything they say. It causes people's minds to open up, to reclaim their intelligence and to question the silly tale the Catholics are telling."

"Have they always maimed us?"

"I have been told that in the early years, before the bishops settled into dogma, all who accepted Jesus as a prophet accepted each other as brothers and sisters. But some followers of Jesus were successful at imposing their vision of the resurrected Christ upon many others. Some disciples, such as Peter, who never learned the true nature of Jesus, were among these. Among many they were successful. They established a hierarchy; they separated men from women, laity from clergy, clergy from bishops and the bishops of great cities from the bishops of smaller towns. In creating such Earthly structures, they grew farther and farther from true knowledge of Jesus and his mission. The higher officials became vain with power and often rich with offerings. And, as we see every day, the more important one thinks he is, the more he insists that others adhere to his opinions.

"By contrast, Sophia, we are pilgrims. We have no structures that would only serve as barriers to knowledge. Our message does not promise easy salvation, only the possibility of unity with the Infinite through study and thought and meditation. So they became large with numbers, which only served further to convince them that their infantile view of Jesus is the only right one. They lashed out at us as infidels and heretics.

"At first they were content to attack us in words and writing. Bishops like Irenaeus and Justin wrote slanderous accusations about our beliefs and our practices. These were outright lies, which were easily rebutted by reading our gospels or speaking with any one of our faithful. They burned our books, so that the lies about us could not be refuted. They also began to capture us and demand we confess to the truth of their slanders and the falsity of our teachings. If we would not, then the torture would begin. I can tell you from experience, Sophia, that a flaming iron put to the eyes can cause a mongoose to admit he is a cobra."

Sophia looked at Timaeus' face. Kind and gentle Timaeus. From his grizzled cheeks, his mouth emerged in a perfect smile. And his eyes, too, she thought, his scar-starred eyes were smiling.

"But we survived," she said. "Even with all that, we have survived."

"That remains to be seen, Sophia."

"Are we in danger, then?"

"Yes, Sophia. We are in very grave danger."

Chapter Five

Eusebius of Caesarea

325 A.D. – Caesarea

> *For I [Jesus] exist with all the greatness of the Spirit, which is a friend to us and our kindred alike ... It is I who am in you, and you are in me, just as the Father is in you in innocence.*
> The Second Treatise of the Great Seth

The incongruous pair was drawing some attention as they journeyed from town to town in Galilee, Judea and Samaria. A blind pedestrian in ragged robes was not an uncommon sight, but the distinctive stars seared into flesh by a red hot, four-sided pike were memorable to anyone who noticed them. Despite the stars, for eight years Timaeus had travelled throughout the region, and north and west into Greece and Macedonia and south and east into Persia, and south and west into Egypt, studying and listening and teaching and learning, without bringing much attention to himself. With Sophia at his side, that was changing. She dressed plainly and kept her head covered and behaved demurely, but there was no hiding a physical beauty that evoked ancient myths of Greece and Troy and Egypt. Seen in stark relief against the features of her shorter companion, Sophia could not help draw notice. As they made their way from Joppa along the Samarian coast stories of the angel and the bishop following the footsteps of Jesus began to circulate.

After crossing the Plain of Sharon, they entered the great city of Caesarea at dusk. It was a spectacular sight still, over 300 years after it was built by Herod the Great upon Augustus Caesar's commission. White marble and granite flashed refracted shards of the day's last light. A defense wall bounded the city in a semi-circle from the north shore to the south and was a glistening thing of beauty. The amphitheater, palace and citadel were architectural wonders, as was the hippodrome, although it had not suffered the ages quite as serenely as the other structures and had been rebuilt in the second century. Stern, stone Emperors from olden days, once worshiped as gods, stared vacantly down upon many of the squares. Augustus, Claudius, Marcus Aurelius, Gallaenus, and Domitian stood silent guard over the closing of shops and the slow processional of citizens, workers, slaves, donkeys, camels, and horses as they lumbered along toward the decline of the day. A new, larger statue of Constantine, the emperor of the unified Empire, stared with hollow-eyed pride from a prominent pedestal at the center of the city. Sophia and Timaeus walked steadily on brick-paved streets toward the horseshoe-shaped harbor that cut into and mostly tamed the mighty Sea.

"Where do we sleep tonight, Timaeus?" Sophia asked.

"I think we will visit my old friend Eusebius," Timaeus replied. "He is a great persecutor of heretics like us, but he might have a kennel available for an old dog."

"But what about me?"

"I should think you would warrant a palace bed."

"That would require a palace."

"You should not be so skeptical, Sophia," Timaeus gently chided.

In a few minutes more Timaeus put his hand on Sophia's shoulder to stop her progress outside a splendorous stonework building, almost a palace, adjacent and attached to a basilica. In stone on the face of the basilica a cross proudly announced that this was a Christian, a Catholic, temple. Sophia could not prevent a small shudder from coursing over her skin, announcing the fear she felt to see her blind companion dwarfed before the thick, wooden doors of the church. Without feeling for it, Timaeus grasped the brass knocker and sent three sharp thumps through the doors' timbers.

Momentarily, a young man dressed in brown robes, a white pileus and with a stringy beard and hooded eyes answered the door. Sophia could not hear the hushed words that Timaeus and the man spoke, but she saw the door close again, with Timaeus still standing outside. In a few more moments, a tall, white-robed man of about sixty years opened the door and motioned for Timaeus to enter quickly. "Bishop Eusebius," Timaeus said by way of greeting as he simultaneously gestured toward Sophia. In exasperation Eusebius raised his arms to the sky, then motioned for her, too, to quickly get inside.

They entered a long hall adjacent to the vestibule and followed Eusebius as he walked quickly into the dark interior of the basilica. Eusebius stopped to whisper something into the ear of the young priest who had first spoken to Timaeus. A few steps later, Eusebius opened a door in the middle of the hallway and urgently gestured them to follow. The young priest glanced at them, pausing his eyes a little longer on Sophia, then walked briskly down the hall and out of sight.

Once inside the room, Eusebius closed the thick door securely and turned to his unexpected guests. The sweet and musty smell of leather and papyrus entered Sophia's nostrils, filling her with a new and unexplained excitement, as of a promise of unknown intent.

"Timaeus," Eusebius said, "you should not have come. Things are becoming complicated. What happened to your other eye?"

"Is that all the greeting I am to receive from a brother in Christ?"

"It is more than you deserve. It has been a long time since we have worshiped the same Christ."

"Not true, Father. We may differ slightly about what he taught, but we agree that his mission was man's salvation."

"We differ a great deal about his nature and essence," Eusebius replied. Then, "All this confusion could have been avoided if, in addition to carpentry skills, Joseph had taught him how to write."

"That is assuming that Joseph knew how to write and Jesus could not. Perhaps he could. Did he not debate the Pharisees with citation to scripture? At twelve years of age did he not astound the rabbis with his understanding? Was he not writing in the sand when asked to judge the prostitute?"

"Then if only he had written to provide us guidance," Eusebius said.

"Perhaps he did. The two books of the Great Seth are in his name."

"But even you do not believe he wrote them."

"No more or less than I believe that the Galilean John wrote the Greek gospel named for him."

Eusebius smiled and at last embraced Timaeus. It was a sincere, long held embrace of the kind that flows from deep affection. Putting his arms on Timaeus' shoulders, Eusebius told the pair to be seated. "Philippus will bring up some bread and cheese and wine in a few minutes. I told him that you were a retired bishop and a young novitiate that have come to consult with me about the Council that Constantine has called for in the spring. You see, just your presence has caused me to sin by telling falsehoods."

"What is false about what you said?" Timaeus asked. "I am an old bishop and, if you like, I will consult with you about the Council, whatever it is. So you see, what you said is true if only you wish it to be."

"But retired?" Eusebius said. "That is surely false."

"I am retired," Timaeus said earnestly.

"Not voluntarily," Eusebius laughed.

Timaeus shrugged and smiled. "It is true I was driven from my See, but I have not been excommunicated. Only a council of bishops can excommunicate a bishop."

"An oversight that will no doubt be corrected at Constantine's

Council."

"So Constantine is convening a Council? Strange days are these, when an emperor can convene a Catholic council and not for the sake of feeding the bishops to the wolves. In the spirit of such liberalism I should be there to defend myself," Timaeus said, smiling mischievously. "Wouldn't that be fun?"

Eusebius frowned but instead of replying, changed the subject. "So," Eusebius said after releasing the frown, "who is your companion and why are you traveling with a woman?"

"This is Sophia," Timaeus replied, gesturing for Sophia to step forward. Not knowing how to behave in the company of one so august in the privacy of his home, Sophia took a single step closer to Eusebius and bowed.

After nodding a stern acknowledgement of her bow, Eusebius asked Timaeus: "Sophia?"

"Yes, at long last I have found her."

"For your sake, my friend, I hope that you have," Eusebius chuckled. "For my own sake I pray that you have not."

Looking around, Sophia saw that the room they were in contained many, many books. She had seen a few books before. Once, one of her callers, a gout-stricken public official, she recalled, had brought a book with him to the brothel. He had set it on the table beside her cushions while she attended to him. But she had never touched a book and had no idea that so many existed in the world, let alone that one man could collect so many. There was a large, plain, oaken table in the center of the room, on which were strewn codices, scrolls, and writing paper and several sharpened, hollow bamboo reeds, their points blackened with ink. She examined them carefully, recognizing them as the source of the promise she felt upon entering the room, but still uncertain of what the promise portended and unsure of why she felt so strongly their mysterious appeal.

Eusebius of Caesarea was a tall, gaunt man, with a long, Syrian face. The beard was fully white and though it grew from his cheeks and chin in waves, it was neatly cropped at the perimeter to form a perfect parabola that further elongated his face. There was still some black in the hair on his head. His hairline receded in the center, but was thick at the temples. In the front his remaining hair was cut and pressed against the head in the style of Roman Emperors, but grew long and freely in the back as it tumbled against his robe.

Sophia listened to the two men talk without uttering a word. Of course, they talked theology, a subject that interested her little before that day Timaeus appeared at the brothel in Antioch several months earlier. But after being with Timaeus, listening to him and the other congregants at the gatherings, and talking with Timaeus as they walked, it already seemed familiar. She had lived seventeen years without thinking about such things, without thinking much about God or the gods, creation or salvation. Through these early days with Timaeus, she learned that his faith promised resolution of life's great mysteries. She was already forming opinions of her own, which she could not yet put into words and which, in any case, she did not yet have the confidence to utter. If she had ventured any opinion at all, it would have been of doubt and confusion. Timaeus and the people they met together talked about things like God, the Pleroma, creation and heaven as if they were tangible things in their everyday lives, as if they were a hairpin or a brush that could be picked up and examined. She was beginning to learn the concepts, the terminology, but the matters they represented remained opaque. She hoped that someday they would become clear. But for now she thought that far from being the embodiment of Timaeus' Sophia, she had no knowledge at all and was unable to understand what others seemed to know.

"Please tell me what happened to your other eye," Eusebius demanded. "I asked that question before."

"My stars," Timaeus said. Pointing an index finger at his left eye, he said, "As you know, my left eye was taken under the authority of Governor Tiberius Claudius." Pointing to his right eye, Timaeus said, "This was a gift from your good friend Alexander of Byzantium. He had the iron put to the left socket as well, either to make sure the job was done or to provide me with a matching set. You'd have to ask him which."

"I wouldn't think that a ninety year old man could have lifted the iron."

"Well, Saint Alexander — I call him saint for your church is sure to sanctify such behavior — is very inspired and, I might add, inspirational. He inspired a presbyter named Paulus to perform the act."

Eusebius shook his head. "Such barbarism should not be practiced by anyone who preaches the gospel of the Lord resurrected."

"Of course it should," Timaeus corrected. "In fact, it must, if one believes as you believe. You can't have heretics like me running around, confusing people with all manner of complications."

"I would never behave in such a manner," Eusebius protested. "I would rest on the strength of my arguments and my faith in the Lord to prevail upon you. God will punish the wicked and the deceived."

"Well," Timaeus chuckled, "that hasn't worked so far, has it? What did you write, oh yes, 'like brilliant lamps, the churches were now shining throughout the world, and faith in our Savior and Lord Jesus Christ was flourishing among all mankind, when the devil who hates what is good, as he is enemy of truth, ever most hostile to men's salvation, turned all his devices against the church. He employed wicked men and sorcerers, like baleful weapons and ministers of destruction against the soul, and conducted his campaign by other measures, plotting by every means that sorcerers and deceivers might assume the same name as our religion and at one time lead to the depth of destruction those of the faithful whom they caught, and at others, by the deeds which they undertook, might turn away from the path of the saving word those who were ignorant of the faith.' You were writing of Simon Magus, from whom I find inspiration. You were writing of my faith."

Eusebius shook his head. "You have an impressive memory, Timaeus."

"I should remember those words," Timaeus replied. "Most of them were mine, or ours, spoken between us while you were writing your Histories."

Eusebius nodded. "You have strayed, Timaeus. And I fear your punishment will be eternal damnation. But I would still never resort to the barbaric methods of Alexander."

"Perhaps you should," Timaeus insisted. "In fact, if you are certain of your words, I am an agent of the devil. If that is true, what do I not deserve?"

Eusebius waved the thought away with his hand. "I am a scholar," he said, "and a bishop of the Church. I have my hands full enough ministering to the faithful and the clergy without picking new fights with old friends, even if they have fallen."

The round was over. Philippus delivered a tray with bread, cheese and cured lamb and a vessel of red wine. He placed the items on a clear corner of the table and left as silently as he had entered, pausing only briefly to cast a furtive glance at Sophia. While he was in the room Timaeus busied himself by holding a book in front of his face. Once he had left, Timaeus returned the book to precisely the spot on the table from which he had lifted it.

"I do not think your priest has seen my stars," Timaeus said. "When I asked for you at the door I was rubbing my sockets as if my eyes burned from the dust. And, as you know, I identified myself to him as Timaeus of Thrace and not Timaeus of Kaymaklı, where I was bishop."

"That was probably wise," Eusebius said. "Philippus is not as broadminded a student as you were, Timaeus. In any case, it was not upon you whom Philippus cast his eyes."

Indicating the repast, Timaeus said, "We are in your house, Father, you must say the blessing."

They bowed their heads and Eusebius prayed:

"Our heavenly Father. May I be no man's enemy, and may I be the friend of that which is eternal and abides.
May I never devise evil against any man; if any devise evil against me, may I escape without the need of hurting him.
May I love, seek, and attain only that which is good.
May I wish for all men's happiness and envy none.
When I have done or said what is wrong, may I never wait for the rebuke of others, but always rebuke myself until I make amends.
May I win no victory that harms either me or my opponent.
May I reconcile friends who are wroth with one another.
May I, to the extent of my power, give all needful help to all who are in want.
May I never fail a friend in danger.
May I respect myself.
May I always keep tame that which rages within me.
May I never discuss who is wicked and what wicked things he has done, but know good men and follow in their footsteps.
We ask these things in our own names and in the name of our Savior, Jesus Christ. Amen."

"Amen," Timaeus repeated. "I would not change a word."

Eusebius grinned. "I thought it was your belief that God is feminine."

"He is," Timaeus laughed. "Or should I say that she is masculine. These are things we cannot know. But I am certain that the true God comes before man and woman and, therefore, must contain both."

"God is certainly masculine," Eusebius protested. "As are his clergy. To hold otherwise is to insult the divine ordering of the world."

"Those are your beliefs, not mine," Timaeus replied.

Sophia and Timaeus fell upon their food. Eusebius explained he had already eaten, but poured himself a measure of the wine and sipped it as he continued to converse with Timaeus. Four candles in holders on the large table cast a dim, flickering, golden light upon the room.

"What has it been," Eusebius asked, "ten years since your separation from the Church?"

"Eight," Timaeus said as he washed down some lamb. "The year 1071, 317 years after the birth of Jesus."

"You had been troubled for several years."

"Nonsense. Troubled! I had been gaining wisdom."

"I read your letters, with alarm," Eusebius said gravely. "You wrote about the difficulty you were having ministering to your flock and training your young priests. You wrote that it was as if you were giving them strong wine to intoxicate them, when what they needed was cold water from a mountain spring."

"I came to understand that the teachings of our church had become a wall between man and God, the true God. I was providing rote and ritual when what was needed was thought and wisdom."

"You were losing your faith."

Timaeus nodded. "Yes," he said slowly. "Or more precisely, I was losing your faith and gaining my own. But I think you have hit upon the key difference between your religion and mine. A Catholic relies on faith for his way in the world. With its traditions, its rituals, its hierarchy and its symbols it provides an easily followed path to salvation."

Eusebius scoffed. "Easily followed, you say. You have read my histories. You did some of the research and helped with the writing. You know the persecutions we have suffered. You were yourself persecuted. A list of the martyrs would fill one hundred books. Easy? Not by any sane reckoning."

Timaeus dismissed Eusebius' rebuff. "Growing pains," he said. "We were sticking our hands into the middle of the Roman thicket. Of course we were going to get scratched. And for our suffering (and I am justified in calling it ours because it was mine, too) we were promised eternal salvation, a resurrected body, streets paved with gold, and immortality. Now that's an easy trade-off. I would trade my life today, and throw in all of the pain you could inflict on my body, if I could believe in those promises."

"You have lost your faith. Let me help you find it again."

"I do not want it," Timaeus said fiercely. "What I was getting to was the difference between the Catholic and what you would call the Gnostic beliefs. You rely on faith. We seek knowledge, learning, understanding, and wisdom. The Catholics have mined the mystery out of Jesus' teachings. If salvation were as easy as a few memorized words and a few sacraments, there would be a lot more goodness in the world."

"You are selling us short," Eusebius replied. "Faith requires a steady commitment. No faint heart finds faith. We have starving ascetics repopulating our deserts. We have scourgers and self-flagellators. I don't think they would agree that faith is easy."

"Yes, but even if you don't mock them, neither do you say that they own the key to Heaven."

The two old friends fell silent. They had reached the edge of a precipice that both wanted to examine, but neither wanted tumble over. Sophia finished eating and rose from her seat. In the dim candle light she examined the volumes of leather bound books shelved on the walls of the room, running her fingers along them, breathing in their thick, but strangely pleasant fragrance. Her wooden-soled sandals made muffled clicks as she stepped upon the stone floor. She longed to remove her headscarf and let her long, mahogany hair tumble freely, but she feared to ask the bishop to allow that indulgence. She knew, as she always knew, that the eyes of the men followed her. Yes, even the empty stars of Timaeus followed her as she examined the books.

"Do you like books, young Sophia?" Eusebius asked.

"I would like to," she said in a soft, almost reverential voice.

"What is stopping you?"

"I have never held one. And I cannot read."

"Well, you can correct the first deficiency right now. You may examine the ones on the shelves, if you like. But be gentle, for some are very old and frail, like me."

"Thank you," Sophia said. She took a folio from a shelf and held it in both hands, feeling its texture and heft and breathing in its musty perfume.

Eusebius' brow furrowed as he watched her. "Strange that you would choose that particular volume, Sophia, since it is the work of one of my friend's predecessors in heresy."

"Which one?" Timaeus asked.

"What? With your heightened vision you cannot see?"

"I have not reached that level of understanding."

"Then I shall have to tell you. She has selected what I believe is one of the last remaining volumes of Valentinus."

"I read that very volume in this library. It helped me on my journey, I believe. You must have copies made. To preserve it."

Eusebius laughed. "What you say is the strongest argument I can think of for not having it copied. But don't worry, my friend, it is safe as long as I live."

"Then may you live forever."

"I believe God has already granted your wish."

After the first few ravenous mouthfuls, Timaeus ate in small bites, rending a bit of bread or a bit of lamb between the fingers of his left hand, bringing the captured morsel to his lips and presenting it to his mouth as if it was as a sacred offering. Once he had swallowed, he would raise the goblet to his lips in the same, deliberate fashion, taking only a drop or two at a time so the level of the wine was lowered at approximately the rate of evaporation. When he was finished, Eusebius wrapped the remaining meat, cheese and bread in a cloth. But Timaeus' hunger for conversation with his old friend and mentor had not been sated. For one thing, he needed to explain why he had parted ways from the Church, a process that had left Eusebius feeling saddened, even betrayed.

"It is not your fault, you know," Timaeus said, "my 'heresy.' I read your letters. I felt your heartache. But the more I pondered these things, the more I came to understand that I was not satisfied with church dogma. If anything could have kept me in the flock, it would have been my loyalty to you and my heart-break in knowing that I was breaking your heart."

"Do not trouble yourself on my account," Eusebius replied. "My feelings are nothing. It is for your lost soul I fear and grieve. But even when you were here in Caesarea with me, I think I knew you would not be satisfied."

"I should thank you for that. In helping you with your history of the church I came to realize that the faiths of the first believers were far more diverse and alternative beliefs far stronger and prevalent than you were portraying. That is why others such as Iraneus and Tertullian would not have spent so many words and so much time to attack them. Even the letters of Paul, that your church now accepts as canon, are mostly occupied with attacks on other Christians. The more I looked into these other beliefs, the more I came to realize that they embodied a fuller under-standing of Jesus."

"You always sided with the runt. You were bound to adopt a faith that was already in mortal decline."

Timaeus grimaced and said sternly, "The decline was inflicted from without. Imposed by the Church."

Eusebius shook his head. "If mankind had thirsted for your libations, no force on heaven or earth could have broken the vessel. Remember, we too, were persecuted, and not too long ago, but we survived and flourished." Eusebius paused, then continued. "No, a faith that requires such acts of individual study and discovery could never form the basis of a civil society."

"I did not know that a civil society was Jesus' goal," Timaeus shot back. "I have not heard that he concerned himself with governing."

Eusebius smiled. "Ah, but he has not returned as yet and life must go on. The ritual the church provides is the structure people need."

"Not all people. What has always bothered me about the Catholic faith is that it is fixed in time and claims its rules are not subject to change."

"That is because its laws are written in stone by the inerrant hand of God."

"So you say. But meanwhile we use the mind God gave us and the eyes and the ears and our understanding of God evolves, grows. My faith is based on the teachings of Valentinus and Colorbasus and many teachers who sought the deeper truth behind Jesus' words. I study the timeless lessons of the universe that were written before mankind could speak. But I do not have to believe in seven spheres of heaven or a host of archons to find wisdom in the teachings of men who came before me or to learn from what they taught. I stand on their shoulders to see further."

"But Timaeus, what you advocate would have everybody pursuing their own religion and in the process all religion would be lost. There would be far more error than wisdom, I fear."

"There always is, my friend. But I believe I am coming closer to knowing the mind of God."

Eusebius shot a stern look at Timaeus. "That is sacrilege," he said.

"It is the only reason for religion at all."

The two warriors drew back. Once again they had reached a cusp, the other side of which lay enmity. They loved each other too much to press forward.

Finally, Eusebius broke the silence. "Here I am, defending the Church to you, my old friend, and yet, this spring, I, too, may be declared a heretic. I may have to seek your guidance on how to behave in the world as a former bishop."

Now it was Timaeus' turn to look stern, but not with disapproval. "What is it you have done? Or failed to do? I cannot imagine."

Eusebius explained about the dispute over the nature of Jesus that was raging through the Catholic Church. Eusebius believed that Jesus was, literally, the Son of God, begotten by God and sent to Earth in human form to die for man's sins and to provide mankind a pathway to salvation and eternal life. Necessarily, Jesus, being the son, is divine, but is subordinate to God Himself. Those who agreed with him, Eusebius explained, are called Eusebians after himself and Bishop Eusebius of Nicomedia or, by many others, Arians, after an abrasive, but intelligent priest of Alexandria named Arius.

Eusebius told Timaeus that the Arians were opposed by the followers of Bishop Alexander of Alexandria or, more accurately, his brilliant, ruthless deacon Athanasius. They hold that Jesus is God. They hold that God, Jesus and the Holy Spirit are one and the same. Jesus is merely a physical, and the Holy Spirit merely the spiritual, manifestation of God. They accuse the Arians of heresy, of promoting polytheism under the guise of Christianity for if Jesus is subordinate to God, yet still divine, then the Arians must believe in multiple deities. The followers of Alexander were commonly called Trinitarians. When asked how the Father and Son could be one and the same, the Trinitarians replied simply that if God wills it, it is done.

"It has become," Eusebius continued, "a matter of great doctrinal import. Alexander of Alexandria has decreed that those who do not hold his beliefs are heretics. He convened a council of like-minded bishops who voted to excommunicate me. I do not recognize their action and will not cede my authority. But battles are being fought in the streets of Alexandria and Antioch. Virtual civil war. The Emperor is not pleased. That is why he has called for all bishops to attend Ecumenical Council at Ancyra in May, just four months hence. No doubt he will try to force an agreement of some kind."

"Which way is he leaning?" Timaeus asked.

"That depends entirely upon who has been in his ear most recently. He listens uncritically, like a schoolboy, and is persuaded by every argument. I think he wants to understand the importance of the debate, but doesn't quite. And he is distracted by his ambition. What he wants above all is resolution so that he can reunify the Empire under the Christian faith. What it will come down to is whether there are more Greek or Latin thinkers, for the issue seems to divide along these lines."

"Well, my friend," Timaeus laughed, "you are in luck. I am Greek through and through. I will go and defend you."

"But you don't believe either doctrine."

"That wouldn't stop me from helping a friend. In any case, my thinking is closer to yours than the nonsense that Jesus and God are the same and different at the same time."

Eusebius laughed heartily, a deep, brown laugh with the texture of tree bark. "Timaeus, you are my favorite heresiarch. I thank you for your offer, but perhaps I would do better without your help."

"Perhaps you are right," Timaeus replied. "And, in any event, you Catholics have misunderstood the question all together."

"In what way?

"You are fighting over if and when and how Jesus became God, as if we have always believed that there is only one god and as if Jesus ever declared he was God or the son of God. But not even the Hebrew, with his angels and archangels and ascension of prophets, has a heaven of one. So, my belief that Jesus became a god or joined the Godhead would not have been such an unusual thing three centuries back. But now that you have decided that Heaven is occupied by only one deity, the question becomes not whether Jesus is god, but whether God was Jesus."

And what is your belief?" Eusebius asked.

"That Jesus became divine through gnosis and that he invited us to join him in the divine realm. Not as individuals, mind you, but as refugees returned to the All, returned as one."

"With such an abstraction as you profess, it is no wonder that your numbers decline."

It was late and the great bishop was clearly tired. He told Timaeus that the danger was too great for him to put them up under his own roof, but said they could stay in the stable under two conditions: that they not sleep together and that they be gone by first light. He was sorry, but that was the best he could do under the circumstances. He handed Sophia a cloth in which he had wrapped the remaining cured lamb, cheese and bread. "May you find your way back to the Church," he said to Timaeus by way of goodbye. "May you be able to stay there," was Timaeus' reply.

Just before he turned in the doorway, Sophia spoke softly to Eusebius. "Father," she said. "Excuse me for sticking my nose into matters I do not understand, but if Jesus and God are the same, then what was the point?"

"I'm sorry, but I do not understand your question."

"If Jesus is your God, then what was His sacrifice? How can the crucifixion of one who cannot die be an example for people, who are not God?"

Eusebius looked startled, but Timaeus said, "I told you, she is Sophia."

"I will leave that for Timaeus to explain," Eusebius said. "Good luck to you both and God be with you."

Chapter Six

A Stolen Book

325 A.D. – Palestine

To return Wisdom's stolen power to God, a plan comes down from the whole fullness of the mind of God.
The Apocryphon of John

Sophia and Timaeus left Caesarea the next morning in the shocking light of a January dawn. They had slept, separately, in a stable, chaperoned by the horses and donkeys of the See. It was not a palace bed for Sophia, as Timaeus had promised, but she slept comfortably with the musty smell of book leather rising from the small, tattered volume she had found curled and fallen behind the writings of Iraneus on Eusebius' shelf, and had slipped under her tunic, against her breast. It rested there still, chafing the soft flesh as it shifted, as they gathered their few possessions and slipped away before the coming of the first light.

Walking briskly as if pursued, they hastened past the stone emperors, old and new, and past the jejune guard at the entrance gate who, if he noticed them at all, lacked the energy or inclination to show it. Two miles later they were still at a hare's pace when Sophia parlayed a slight stumble into a protest.

"Timaeus," she said, "why do we rush? Are we not to break our fast before we journey?"

Timaeus stopped, turned toward Sophia and looked at her as if he could see her.

"I do not trust Philippus," he said. "He means to harm us. Or to harm Eusebius, perhaps. Either way, he means ill."

"He looked harmless enough," Sophia replied. "He didn't look to me as if he paid us much mind at all."

"I smelled him in the stable last night," Timaeus answered. "His scented baths betrayed his presence. There are things you cannot see yet, Sophia. But I have known men like Philippus. I know his kind. When he answered the door last night I should have merely begged for bread. I made a grave error and either we or Eusebius will pay for it."

"I really think you exaggerate. If I am not mistaken, Philippus looked more at me than at you. Last night you told Eusebius that you had covered your eyes. You gave him no cause for concern."

"Yes, but Eusebius was concerned. And that was before Philippus' espionage in the stable. Now, I think that what Eusebius told him, the excuse for our presence he gave, was the worst of all possible fabrications. I am only forty-five years old and bishops do not retire, they die in office or are martyred. Even if I had retired, a former bishop would not travel alone, unchaperoned, with a young woman. He would have a priest or a monk for his company. And he would not arrive in rags as worn as mine. It would have been better to have said that I was a pilgrim seeking the father's blessing and to have been sent off with bread and benediction. This will come to no good, wait and see."

"You wanted to talk to an old friend, and Eusebius wanted to talk to you," Sophia said.

"It was a kindness that will not go unpunished," Timaeus answered.

In a few hundred more yards they came upon a small stand of cypress trees. Timaeus said that they had probably gone far enough to be out of immediate danger and sat against one of the tall trunks, beckoning for Sophia to join him. She untied the parcel of cheese, bread and lamb and they ate, washing down the food with water Sophia had drawn from the stable well.

As they sat, a Phoenician family passed by on foot, guiding a mule laden with household items. The father looked at the odd couple and greeted them with a single nod of his head. After a few more minutes a Hebrew passed on a donkey that also carried several goat hides. Without the white marble of Caesarea to reflect its light, the winter sun, like a shackled beast, made desultory progress in the eastern sky. The air was sharp, but not frigid and no rain beckoned on the horizon. Sophia's only discomfort came from the leather chafing her bosom, but the discomfort was more psychic than physical, exacerbated by the unease Timaeus had just expressed. At last she decided to confess her crime.

Retrieving the book from beneath her tunic, Sophia spoke nervously. "Timaeus," she said. "Please do not be angry with me, but I have transgressed. I took a book from Eusebius." She placed it in Timaeus' hands.

To Sophia's surprise, Timaeus was not angry. He felt the book's heft and texture and said, gently, "What inspired you?"

"I do not know. It was fallen, curled behind another volume. It was so forlorn, so neglected. It seemed an orphan, like me. Before I knew what I was doing, it was lodged beneath my tunic."

Timaeus clucked, but with good humor. "And you suckled it to your breast, did you? Never mind. I have an idea what this is," he said. "But I cannot be certain. Open it up. Turn its pages. Tell me when you get to a page where the writing does not fill the page."

He handed the book back to Sophia and she opened it. She carefully placed each successive page on top of another in the worn codex. She finally informed him that she had found a page where the writing covered only about a third of the page, but hastened to add that the very next page was again filled with letters.

"Stay on the partial page," Timaeus instructed. "Do you know what language?"

"I recognize the letters as Greek."

"Is the last line on that page a short line?"

"Yes."

"Do you know what the letters are?"

"No."

"Trace in my hand the first of the letters on the last line."

Sophia traced a long vertical line and three shorter, evenly spaced, horizontal lines shooting out from it.

"Good. Eta," Timaeus said. "Next letter."

Sophia repeated the process until she had completed the letters of three words.

"Ευαγγέλιο της Μαρίας (*the Good News of Mary*)," Timaeus said. "It is what I thought. If you go maybe twenty pages in I think you will find another partial page, for I know this book. It contains three gospels. In addition to the *Gospel of Mary*, it also contains the *Apocryphon of John* and the *Sophia of Jesus Christ*. At the end, on the last few pages, is my own writing. I summarized what I then knew of the *Acts of Peter*. At the time I thought it was heresy. I have come to believe that these books contain more error than truth. But I was drawn to these texts. Though your thievery was blind, you have selected an important book."

She expected him to proclaim that her selection of this book proved yet again that she was Sophia, but he did not. Instead, he told her that he would teach her to read. She would trace the letters in his hand and he would tell her what words they spelled.

"First Greek, then Coptic, your native tongue," Timaeus said. "You will read to me each evening."

"Eventually, you will return the book, when next we see Eusebius," Timaeus said. "It was wrong for you to take it. It was not yours. But we will consider it a loan from someone who is not likely to notice its disappearance. He will have no anxiety about it, only gratitude when it is returned."

"But for now," Timaeus continued, "we must make Jerusalem in haste," he said. "For you must make that pilgrimage. Then we must travel to Ancyra, many weeks journey from here."

"Ancyra?" Sophia asked. "Why Ancyra?"

"I am determined to attend Constantine's Council."

Chapter Seven

Jerusalem

325 A.D. – Jerusalem

Weep, then, for him who dwells in Jerusalem.
The Apocalypse of James

They entered Jerusalem in the middle of the fourth day after leaving Caesarea. As they walked, they discussed the contents of the book Sophia had taken from Eusebius' library. She called it "Eusebius' book." Timaeus told her that the *Apocryphon of John* was an attempt to explain a complex cosmology through a presumed dialogue between a resurrected Jesus and his apostle John. Timaeus said he did not put much stock into it because it presumed to know what the author himself admitted was unknowable. "I do not put much faith in the visions of other men. The vision might be true to the person who has it, but it is what Jesus taught when he was among us that we need to learn and we must learn it for ourselves."

Sophia walked slightly behind, not upon Timaeus' instructions, but to shield herself from the view of the men who passed. She knew that behind many kind glances lurked familiar desires. Timaeus gave various answers to any questions about the status of his companion, his answers calibrated to best put off each particular inquisitor. To the Roman soldier he said that she was to serve as a virgin at the Temple of Venus in Jerusalem. To the young Hebrew he said that she was his daughter. He was able to identify the tribe and occupation of each person by the sound of their voice or the fall of their steps, without the benefit of eyesight.

During their rests he instructed her on reading. She would

trace the Greek letters in the palm of his hand and he would identify first the letter, then the word. He never told her that he could have recited the entire volume from memory. She learned rapidly. By the time they entered Jerusalem she was recognizing many of the repetitive words by sight and was able to sound out some of the longer, less common words. Neither one spoke of how these simple lessons were transforming their relationship, how the soft touch of Sophia's fingers on Timaeus' coarse palm brought surprising warmth to both master and pupil.

Jerusalem was tired and grey. It was a Jewish city without Jews, a city rededicated to the Roman gods that no one worshiped any longer. Statues of pagan gods appeared forlorn, as if they could sense their status as unwanted usurpers. Jews were allowed through the city gates only one day a year, Tisha B'Av, to mourn the destruction of the Temple in 70 A.D.

Weary from their journey, the pair followed the road into Jerusalem and ambled the streets. As they entered the city, Timaeus told Sophia that they were passing by the Temple of Venus, located on the site of Golgotha, where Jesus had shed his mortal body and reunited with Sophia in the Pleroma. In a few more minutes, Timaeus asked a tradesman if he knew where he might find Marsanes the carpenter and was given directions to his home. Sophia saw that most of the people Timaeus addressed did not seem to notice his blindness. "Two streets over, one street down," were all the directions he needed to bring him close enough to Marsanes' workshop that the sounds and smells led him the rest of the way.

Marsanes was a friendly, dark haired man in his mid-thirties. His two sons, John and Thomas, were in their mid-teens and worked with him in the trade. They looked like three fruits from the same tree, with square faces and broad shoulders, black hair and eyes and a thick, kind mouth in common. Marsanes' wife, Ephedra, was tall and plain and, to Sophia's eyes, had made almost no indention in the mold from which her sons were cast.

The couple's daughter, Magda, was five years old, chatty and cheerful. She looked more like her mother, but with the rose of youth that lends to even plain features the visage of radiant beauty.

Upon seeing Timaeus, Marsanes left the truss that he was nailing and flew to the older man to wrap him in the unconcealed embrace of brotherly love. "Had we known you were coming we would have prepared a feast."

"It is not wise for a man of my notoriety to announce his itinerary," Timaeus replied. "A little bread and water will do us nicely."

"You will have more than that, you will," Marsanes said. Then, to his sons, "John, Thomas, clean up and help your mother prepare food for our guests."

"After our greetings, Marsanes," Timaeus chided.

Timaeus greeted them all like fast friends, even Magdalene, whom he had never before seen. For each he had kind words and warm humor. He remembered even the name of the family's donkey and reminded John of having fallen from its back six years earlier. He introduced Sophia as his guide and friend.

After the meal, Marsanes sent the boys out with the message that there would be a meeting in the Garden of Gethsemane at dusk. Timaeus and Sophia found separate corners of the room and took their rest.

Chapter Eight

The Keeper of Gnosis For The Ages

325 A.D. – Jerusalem

What makes the sin of the world?
There is no sin, but it is you who makes sin by the things that you do.
The Gospel According to Mary Magdalene

Frigid evening sprung with sudden temper upon Jerusalem, like a cheetah upon an aged oryx, sending sharp shudders through Sophia's slight frame. Sophia bore the cold in silence as a group of seventeen gathered in the place where Jesus prayed on the last night of his life as a man. Marsanes posted his two sons at the edge of the group to safeguard the privacy of their words.

Having called the gathering, Marsanes offered a prayer to the Infinite Mother and for guidance on the path to Knowledge that would lead them back to Her bosom. Then, as always happened, someone asked that Timaeus speak words of wisdom so that they all might be aided along their path.

Timaeus cleared his throat. "I am often asked to speak at the gatherings of the faithful, as if I had more to contribute than Marsanes here or Atabus or even little Magda. I am not sure that is true. I once read the many gospels. I have studied these things. And I have aspired to gain wisdom and knowledge every day of my life. But the life of Jesus teaches us that the path to God and to Sophia is open to all. It is not an easy path. Jesus never said it was easy. It is not granted with a single prayer or sacrament. It must be earned through the living of one's life, sacrificing all that one must sacrifice in the quest for the Infinite. It is an individual quest. We meet in groups such as this to share our progress and for the comfort and unity that comes in knowing that we are not alone in our journey. But when the light does come, it comes to us one at a time following our own steps. I wish it could be otherwise, but it is not."

Timaeus paused for a moment. "Tonight," he said, "I will not decline to speak. Not because I have more to impart, but because our faith is in peril. We do not ask much of the Emperor or the bishops, only to be left alone to follow our path. So long as the Emperor and the bishops opposed each other, we faced no more danger than the average subversive. At times Rome, at times the Church, would take their turns persecuting us. Such efforts were intermittent and often random. But now Constantine has embraced the Church and the Church has embraced Constantine. Jesus said, 'Render unto Caesar the things which are Caesar's and render unto God the things which are God's.' For the Church, it seems, there is henceforth to be no difference and everything must be rendered unto both. The Church will have armies to enforce Her edicts and posses to round up those She declares to be heretics. We are entering dangerous days with no end in sight. Gatherings such as ours here tonight will become impossible and they will try to obliterate even the fact of our existence.

"Why do I speak thus? If I meant only to frighten you, I would hold my tongue. If I thought they are going to be successful in forever closing the path to gnosis, I would keep it to myself for I would already have strayed from that path. No. I speak to give you comfort. Remember, Yaldabaoth has always sought to suppress knowledge. Did he not banish Adam and Eve from the Garden? Did he not bring the floods? Did he not destroy cities and peoples who would not submit to him? It is no different today. Yaldabaoth has united the State with the Church and they will promise salvation in the name of the very Jesus whom they crucified upon a cross. We all contain the seed of Sophia. We will pass it down to our children and their children and so on until the end of the generations of man. And when it can, that seed will sprout and grow. We do not need faith to know this. We know it because it is the story of our own lives."

Timaeus took a drink of water from a skin and continued.

"Many have wondered about my companion. Is she my daughter? Is she my wife? Why do I travel with her?" Timaeus chuckled and held his hands out. "Why does she travel with me? The answer is, she is Sophia. No, that is not the name her parents gave her, if she had parents (for we do not know). She is Sophia because she is the protector of gnosis for the ages. How do I know this? As I entered Antioch a few months back, Jesus appeared to me in a dream and told me that in that city I would find Sophia and that Sophia would be the living covenant with the All and that through her would men and women of future ages find their way back to the path. Jesus told me to guide her and protect her for as long as I lived. And that I will do.

"So, this is Sophia. Jesus led me to her in Antioch. When I asked her to follow me, she picked up her feet and followed and has never questioned. Even now she is hearing what I tell you for the first time and yet she has followed with faithfulness and patience.

"Now I must go to a great Council of bishops. What I hope to accomplish there I cannot say for I do not yet know. But I must try to prevent the persecutions that are coming our way. I must urge tolerance and the acceptance of diversity among the peoples of the Church. I believe that this must be why Jesus led me to Sophia and what the words He spoke to me meant."

A murmur that started when Timaeus spoke of his dream took on an anguished tone when he spoke of attending the Council. Timaeus held up his hands to quiet them. "It is natural that you would be concerned for me. But we know that this life is important only as a vessel for our soul as it journeys toward the Infinite. I know I will probably fail at the Council, even if I am allowed to speak. I pray only that whatever happens will bring me closer to true gnosis. I think that it must, since at least it will bring clarity to the meaning of what Jesus said to me in my dream.

"I tell you all of this for yet another reason. I do not need you to fear for me. Indeed, I do not want it. But if the Council is the end of me, or if I fall elsewhere upon the road, know that Sophia walks among you. If she needs shelter or bread, please provide it. If she needs escape, facilitate it. I ask this of you not for my own sake or for hers, but for the sake of the words that Jesus spoke, that they may come to pass."

There was a rustling nearby and John called out, "Papa."

A priest appeared in the garden, wearing new robes of Egyptian cotton. "Greetings, my friends," he hailed. "Am I interrupting?"

Marsanes spoke. "Our little group came here to pray in the Garden where Jesus prayed. We do so to honor Him. Sometimes not so many of us. Thank you for asking, Father."

The priest was a soft, kind looking sort, probably forty years old. His dull, brown eyes matched the color of his robe and his thick lips mimicked the shape of his belly.

"I often do the same," he replied. "I have come here just now for the same purpose. I serve our good bishop, Macarius. I have just come from my quarters to pray in the Garden myself. May I pray with you?"

Timaeus spoke up. "Would you lead us?" he asked.

"But of course, of course," the priest said cheerily.

It was a lengthy prayer, full of hallelujahs and images of blood and thorns and suffering upon the cross and ending with a request for God's blessing in the name of His Son. As he spoke, Sophia occasionally looked up to see the entire group with their heads bowed, then quickly bowed her head in imitation. Timaeus followed the priest's "amen" with an "amen" of his own. He then started to say that the group had concluded their prayers and would now be heading back to their homes when the priest suddenly said, "I know you. Yes. You are Timaeus. I knew you when you served Eusebius. I was younger, just starting my training. You were kind and wise. Peter is my name. From Tyre. Perhaps you remember."

"I think you have mistaken me," Timaeus said.

"No," rejoined the priest. "You are too humble. It is you, Timaeus. Even by your voice I know you."

Timaeus thought it unwise to continue to deny his identity. The priest was too certain and, after all, was right. Timaeus did remember him and had adjudged him to be a simpleton at the time. Nothing in this meeting caused a re-reckoning of that assessment. "Of course I am Timaeus," he said, "but kind and wise? I thought you must have been referring to someone else."

The priest laughed amiably. "But it is true. Tell me, I know that you do not serve Eusebius any longer. I heard that you went to the east, into Cappadocia, I think. I even heard that you were ordained bishop of Kaymakli."

"Yes," Timaeus answered. "But I am retired. As you see, Galerius took my eyes from me. I was not able to do all the things a bishop must do. So, I have been allowed to pilgrimage these past few years. That is how you find me now."

The priest thought over these lies. Timaeus prayed Peter was too simple to see through their obvious cracks and was hoping that Peter did not think to wonder why he did not know these fellow Christians who lived in Jerusalem. His prayers were answered on these accounts, but Peter had another stone to throw in his path.

"Come with me. I am sure Macarius would like to see you again. You have met, have you not?"

"Yes, we have met. But I cannot see him tonight. I am tired from my journey and must rest. Perhaps I will call in the morning."

"Of course," Peter answered. "I will tell him to expect you."

"Please do not," Timaeus implored. "Let it be a surprise."

Chapter Nine

Devil On Their Tail

January 325 A.D. – Palestine

We do not know whether the Unknowable One has angels or gods, or whether the One who is at rest was containing anything within himself except the stillness, which is he, lest he be diminished. It is not fitting to spend more time seeking. It was appropriate that you know, and that they speak with another one. And you will receive them ...

The Revelation Of Allogenes

As they had Caesarea, they left Jerusalem in haste. "The devil is on our tail," Timaeus told Marsanes. "If they find I stayed with you, tell them I still held myself out as a wandering bishop and you knew no better." He told Marsanes to bid his family and the other seekers fare-thee-well for him and they slipped out before the dawning of the day.

As they made their way quietly north toward Nazareth, Marsanes' final words to them lodged in Sophia's heart. "You will always find haven with us, Timaeus," he said. "And you as well, Sophia, whenever you need." The words provided comfort to Sophia, perhaps beyond their intended measure. She was, she felt for the first time in her life, a part of a family now. She was somebody.

After they had passed beyond the gates of the city, Sophia asked why, this time again, they had fled like thieves.

"The last time we were thieves. Or have you forgotten?"

"No, I have not forgotten. But that was not why we ran then and I have taken nothing this time."

Timaeus smiled. "I know, my Sophia," he said. "No, we fled Caesarea for fear of a priest. We flee Jerusalem for fear of a bishop. Such a fainthearted guide you have chosen!"

"But you chose me."

"I no more chose you than you chose me. I was led to you by Jesus, through a dream."

As they walked, Timaeus explained that Macarius was an avid heretic hunter, hostile toward everyone who did not conform to the strict regimen of beliefs that he deemed orthodox. Peter the priest was a simpleton who would not keep his silence on his having met Timaeus the night before. He would tell Macarius about the meeting and Macarius would know all about Timaeus' ouster from Kaymakli and the accusations of heresy leveled at him by Alexander of Byzantium, or New Rome as it was now called. Macarius would deem the loss of eyesight to be too light a punishment and would insist on meting out judgment in his own fashion. So they fled.

"It is as if they sense your power, Sophia," Timaeus said. "I traveled eight years practically without notice. With you at my side my anonymity is obliterated. My identity is suddenly revealed."

"But I have no power," Sophia protested. "I am an orphan and a harlot, nothing more."

"What the Infinite has given you cannot be concealed," Timaeus answered. "But for your sake and mine we must do a better job of disguising it."

The sixty-five-mile journey from Jerusalem to Nazareth took five days. For the first two days of the journey, at least once an hour Timaeus would tell Sophia to look behind them to see whether anyone was approaching. On the second day, she spied a group of three robed men on horseback in the distance. When she reported this to Timaeus, he insisted that she lead him far off the road where they hid behind some rocks until the travelers, a Roman, his wife and a slave, passed them by.

Timaeus did not contact any friends along the way. For the first time since she met him, Timaeus produced coins to pay for their drink and nourishment as they traveled.

Even though he saw snakes crawling out from every rock on their path, Timaeus insisted that Sophia continue her reading lessons. At each stop along the way, Sophia took out her book and tried to read. By the time they reached the tiny town of Nazareth, she was reading aloud in a halting voice, struggling, but getting through almost every word. Timaeus expressed his astonishment repeatedly by rubbing her hands with affection.

Sophia delighted in the lessons. To unlock the magic symbols on the ancient pages seemed to her like unleashing a yoke from around her neck. Fresh air streamed into the deepest recesses of her soul. Light illuminated the crevices of her mind. The feeling of being part of something, of a family, that she began to feel in Jerusalem became a rich, full-born emotion of completeness as she absorbed the meaning of what she was learning to read. Something in her that had remained always in its infancy was suddenly maturing and becoming part of her, of her self.

They did not stay long in Nazareth. One day only. They walked the ancient streets where Jesus prayed and thought and grew in understanding. Timaeus told her where Jesus was thought to have lived and stopped for her to examine an old inn that Joseph, with Jesus' help, was believed to have built. Then they were gone, traveling east and north, toward Ancyra.

Chapter Ten

Lessons and Memory

January – April 325 A.D. – Syria

But Jesus said, "Father, behold, A strife of ills across the earth Wanders from thy breath; But bitter Chaos man seeks to shun, and knows not how to pass it through."
The Naassene Psalm

Peter, the dull monk, had indeed informed his master Macarius, Bishop of Jerusalem, of his chance meeting with Timaeus the night before. Rather than the pleasant surprise and casual inquiry Peter expected, the news provoked a cross-examination. Macarius wanted to know every detail about where they met, what Timaeus looked like and who gathered with him. Fortunately for the small Gnostic community of the city, Peter could recall few details about the composition of the gathering. He described Timaeus by garb and appearance well enough, but recalled only one other significant detail: that he seemed to be accompanied by an attractive, young woman. This last piece of information caused a grunt of disgust from Macarius' ample gut and Macarius directed Peter to instruct Gregorius, a young priest of muscular build, to make inquiries and search for Timaeus and his companion and to not return without them. Gregorius' mission was folly. Not knowing which direction they were headed he was soon back reporting to Macarius that the trail was cold and the travelers could not be found. A few days later Macarius, accompanied by Peter and Gregorius, headed off to Ancyra, the same destination of the fugitives.

For Macarius and his entourage, the first leg of the journey was across the Eastern Mediterranean, from Caesarea to Lycia and, from there, overland to the intended destination of Ancrya. Most of the bishops of Egypt and Palestine took a similar route, including Eusebius. For Timaeus and Sophia, it was 600 miles, much of it over mountainous terrain and all of it by foot. Roman viae and itenera, prevalent and usually well maintained, guided their passage, but presented peril. There was the routine peril inherent in the nature of the traveling companions – a blind man and a beautiful young woman. To both the amateur and professional highwayman, the very appearance of the couple screamed of opportunity. They did not appear prosperous, so there were no riches to be gained. But a crust of bread and a sip of wine can be wrung from the meanest of travelers, even if it leaves the victims in imminent danger of departing the realm of the living. And from the young woman, well, there were other gains to be realized. These random threats could be tempered somewhat by joining up in fluid, ever-changing packs of travelers, merchants, peddlers and tradesmen mostly, that were ever moving in overlapping spheres between towns and enclaves along the route.

But joining up with these groups presented Timaeus with the potentially greater danger of being discovered as a famous heretic. Twelve years earlier Constantine had lifted the ban on Christianity, opening the way for the Empire to become a predominantly Christian realm. Two years after that Alexander, the ancient Bishop of Byzantium decided that his thirty-five-year old Bishop of Kaymakli in Cappadocia needed to visit him. Rumors had reached Alexander that Timaeus was saying some things that could not, under any circumstances, be considered orthodox. Timaeus arrived happily enough and happily enough explained his evolving ideas on the nature of Christ and His role as savior of mankind. Alexander tolerantly encouraged Timaeus to repent his errors, adding tortures du jour as incentives. But even with the remaining eye burnt from its socket, Timaeus could not be brought to see his doctrinal errors. After two years of imprisonment, Timaeus was released to roam the Earth. He departed with the admonishment of Alexander, conveyed by Paulus, that should they meet again and should Timaeus' views remain unchanged, the resumption of their discussions would prove fatal. In the intervening decade word had spread throughout Eastern Christendom of the former bishop become Gnostic proselytizer and Bishop Alexander of New Rome let it be known that a reward would be paid to the be-sainted person who returned the stray sheep to his pen in the new capitol. Thus, traveling in groups provided some protection against the law-breakers, but put them in danger of the lawmakers.

And so they travelled, sometimes alone, sometimes joining for a few hours with a small band of itinerants: Always seeking to avoid anybody who appeared that they might be – or even know – an official of any kind, state or religious, never neglecting Sophia's reading lessons. By the time they made it back to Antioch toward the end of February, Sophia could read on her own the book of gospels she had taken from Eusebius' library and was learning the Coptic alphabet of her native tongue. As they walked, they would discuss many things, including the new world that was opening to Sophia through the written word.

"What did Jesus mean when he said to Magdalene, 'All nature, all formations, all creatures exist in and with one another, and they will be resolved again into their own roots'?"

"What do you think he meant, Sophia?"

"I do not know. Perhaps that every part of the world that exists, the world that we can see, is conjoined, but those things have separate essences or roots. And that through his coming, those roots will once again become separated."

"Sophia, I have never been able to grasp those words so clearly as you have just explained them."

"But won't that mean an end to this world? If all things are dissolved or resolved, how can the world continue?"

"Does the thought trouble you, Sophia? Shouldn't like be

rejoined with like? Shouldn't the All once again rejoin the All? Isn't this world but the artifice of Yaldabaoth?"

"But is not the All with us already? How does separating the pieces into individual roots make it any more or any less of the All? How, by separating the roots, are we not destroying this world? How can the disunited roots become more aware, rather than less aware, of the whole?"

"What does awareness matter if the roots are reunited with the tree? What we seek is not awareness, but knowledge?"

"That sounds like a good deal of nonsense to me. How can one have knowledge without awareness? I am confused now. I must think these things over."

"I knew you were Sophia when I found you."

Timaeus was certainly the oddest man she had ever met. The men who came to the brothel were easy to understand. In their dealings with her, they had a more or less uniform purpose. Ammianus, the brothel owner, had sheltered her. Her looks and youth and grace and untouchable dignity made her a valuable possession. Ammianus recognized these properties when he found her in rags, trading scraps for scraps on the streets of Alexandria. He had long maintained that the best meretrices came from the Egyptian capital. It was not simply that the melding of the tribes of the earth there occasionally resulted in the features of a goddess encased in the soft brown tones of skin most comely among the earth's women. It was that, even more rarely, something of the wit, intelligence and urbanity of the city would imbue even an urchin with a civility and temperament which men of every place and station found irresistible. So, just as Timaeus had immediately recognized Sophia as a source of gnosis, three years earlier Ammianus had immediately recognized Hypatia (for that was her name when he purchased her from a young priest) as a source of wealth and stature for his brothel.

Ammianus developed her slowly, imagining that she knew

nothing of men or their carnal desires or of his intentions in taking her to Antioch. He gave her the name Adama, meaning diamond. He believed enticements such as dates or silk shawls were responsible for her obedience, imaging even that he was seducing her into an unknown life and that to preserve the value of his possession, the seduction had to be smooth, gradual and soft. To be sure of his control, he once showed her a contract that he claimed gave him ownership of her person. Sophia, or Adama rather, understood Ammianus, what he wanted and what he was trying to hide. As he gradually introduced her to the men who became her callers, she understood each of them in turn, from the awkward, young son of a high Roman official, to the aging merchant who professed love and illegally promised marriage, to the soon-to-be bishop, Eustathius, who prayed away his sins in the throes of concupiscent ecstasy. Ammianus only allowed a wealthy few to know her company. Her value would be diminished if her favors were made widely available. From the urgency of their climaxes to their hasty, apologetic retreats, Sophia knew that the love some professed for her belonged only to themselves. She would have had it no other way.

But Timaeus was different. He did not seem to want her in the way other men had. He did not profess love. His awareness of her sexuality appeared to be on the far side of disinterested. Yet he treated her with a kindness and tenderness she had never known. He had spent a lifetime thinking about the nature of things, of God, of the world, of existence. Yet he deferred to her barely coherent raw, first impressions as if they had been spoken by Plato or Pythagoras. In another man, she would have taken this as ironic, if not perverse flattery. In Timaeus it seemed genuine. He was a fool, she had no doubt, but a different kind of fool than any she had known. As they journeyed together, and slept and ate and talked, she felt growing within her affection the likes of which she had never before experienced. She began to love him.

They travelled past Antioch on their way to Ancyra and

Sophia thought of how long ago the life she lived there now seemed. The following day, she spotted a path off the main *via* that led to a secluded grove of barren olive trees. It was a good place to rest for the night. They supped on cheese and dried dates and pulled their cloaks about them against the chill. The days were growing longer but the warmth that was returning to the earth trailed behind them as they travelled north. They were quietly talking about verses in the Sophia of Jesus Christ that she had been reading when their solitude was arrested by a clamor of voices and hoofs approaching from the direction of Antioch. As Sophia and Timaeus stayed hushed, the retinue halted. A dignitary in presbyter's garb alit from his camel and the rest of the party of fifteen made camp about fifty feet from the viae and some two hundred feet from them. Sophia described the group to Timaeus, then crept closer for a better look.

She slipped behind a split trunked olive tree about fifty feet from the party as four members unpacked and pitched two tents. Four other members carried swords and shields. There were six clerics, one of who looked quite old and who was dressed in the white robes of a bishop. The old bishop remained seated in a carriage as others prepared a camp. The presbyter, wearing black robes, was a short man with wild hair of raging red and a neatly cropped beard of the same color. She recognized this man from her days in Alexandria as Athanasius, a steel-tempered priest, widely known among the urchins of the city for cuffing anyone stupid enough to beg alms from him. Sophia knew him for a more particular reason. One night when she was twelve years old he came upon her sleeping in an earthen hollow along a church wall. Cupping his hand over her mouth, he had pushed her down and climbed on top of her. It was over in two minutes, brutal but fast. A fist to the head was his payment to her as he hurried into the church without having said a word. Yes, she recognized Athanasius.

Sophia was about to creep back to Timaeus when she heard

Athanasius say to the bishop who was still seated in the carriage, "Father, I wish word had reached us that the council was moved to Nicaea before we disembarked. We could have traveled most of the way by sea. As it is we must make our way on beasts overland, like common men."

"Never forget that we are all common men before the Lord, Athanasius," the bishop replied.

Sophia slipped back quietly and whispered to Timaeus what she had seen and heard.

"The old bishop is Alexander of Alexandria. The young priest, Athanasius, is an inciter of trouble. They are no friends of Eusebius and would not be friendly to us. It is fortunate you learned what you did, or we would have ended up in Ancyra and missed the Council. Nicaea is a shorter and easier journey."

They could not break camp and move without being noticed, so Timaeus spent a restless night, alert to the danger of being so close to a group of armed and militant clerics. Sophia slept under Timaeus' attentive presence. Once she stirred and uttered a sleep-soaked groan and he was quick to place a hand gently over her mouth to muffle the sound. He listened carefully for sounds from Alexander's camp, but heard nothing that caused him to suspect that anyone there was aware of another presence. Mostly, he listened to Sophia as she breathed. He felt the warm sweetness of her body so close to his. He felt stirrings of a desire that he had not known for many years and that he knew could never be fulfilled. Nonetheless, it was a pleasant feeling. Its gentle warmth poured into his very soul. He did not banish or reject it, but let it cover him like a quilt as the night air descended. He knew it would be abhorrent to its object. He knew that if requited it would barricade the path to knowledge that they both were on. Yet he savored it, even as he knew it was of this world, part of Yaldabaoth's creation. In the morning, he told himself, it would be gone.

In the morning he hushed Sophia as she awoke and silently

bade her to abide quietly until the others broke camp and departed. When they were gone, he told her that she must cut her hair, bind her bosom, and dress as a man if they were to accomplish their goal.

"What is our goal, gentle Timaeus? Why do we go to a Council when we have not been invited and are not wanted?"

"It is a good question," Timaeus replied. "I know going is foolish and dangerous. I know that it is a departure from the quest for knowledge that must ever be our object. But I am afraid that the path to knowledge is about to be obliterated. The Church and the Empire now work together. Great institutions require great uniformity. The Church will decide what is the right way and the Empire will enforce its decisions. Gnosis must be acquired. It cannot be told. If Knowledge is determined for you, for everyone and for all time, it cannot be Knowledge. It can only be memory. Do you understand what I am saying?"

"I think I do. If you are told the truth, you do not have to learn it for yourself. It becomes like a supper you are served, without knowing the recipe or ingredients."

"Yes, exactly."

"But that does not explain why we go to Nicaea."

"Because when the great church fathers decide such things as the nature of Jesus and the right way to worship Him, a voice from the wilderness must be there to tell them that however they decide, they will take the life and humanity out of Christ. They will create a myth that over time will become like all other myths, a picture in a book or a statue in a church, as devoid of substance as Zeus or Poseidon. It is not enough for one faction to say it is this way and another to say it is that way. There must be a voice to say, 'it cannot be decided by churches and empires. It must be left to each person to learn for themselves.' I fear it falls upon me to be that voice."

"I fear for you, Timaeus. And no good can come of it."

"I fear for us, Sophia, for I am placing you in danger also. But

I am certain that it must be done, if for no other reason that years from now, someone reading the records of this Council will hear what was said and, by so hearing, will find a way through the walls and hedges to the path of true knowledge."

Sophia considered this for a moment, then asked, "Do you wish to die in Nicaea? For if you do, I will not follow."

"No, Sophia. I wish to live. With you I feel my life has just begun. But I must do this."

"You have changed," she said. "There is something different about you this morning."

"That may well be, but will you follow? I cannot do this without you."

"I will follow you, Timaeus."

"And I will follow you, Sophia."

A few miles further down the road Sophia asked why she must cut her hair and dress as a man.

"Because I will be seeking admission as a bishop," Timaeus replied. "And as we saw from Alexander's camp, a bishop must have a retinue. You will be my retinue."

"But I cannot impersonate a priest."

"We will call you my scribe."

"I cannot write."

"You must practice, then. You will be writing by the time we reach Nicaea."

Chapter Eleven

Nicaea

May 325 A.D. – Nicaea

The One cannot be seen, for no one can envision it.
The One is eternal, for it exists forever.
The One is inconceivable, for no one can comprehend it.
The One is indescribable, for no one can put any words to it.
The Apocryphon of John

They arrived in Nicaea during the second week of May. The bustling city was already swollen with Christian luminaries and their retinues and more were arriving every day. Everywhere the robes of bishops, presbyters, priests, deacons and scribes shuffled through white stone streets. Nicaea could scarcely contain the outpouring of grace, pride and self-importance. It had only been twelve years since Constantine the Great had lifted the ban on Christianity. Only two years had passed since Constantine had declared Christianity the favored religion of the Roman Empire. Men who scarcely a decade earlier had either fled in terror of a legionary or submitted bravely to torture and forced hard labor, were now the most celebrated men in the Empire. Many of their names were widely known. Their doctrinal disputes, once argued in hushed tones in crabbed quarters, were now a matter of state, hotly debated by partisans in shops and on streets in every major city. The Empire was now Christian. But what was Christianity? That was a question that Constantine wanted resolved once and for all. The first great Ecclesiastical Council at Nicaea was called to answer that question.

Over three hundred bishops attended the Council. Each was

allowed to bring five assistants: priests, deacons and scribes, and, since the Emperor paid travel expenses, most bishops arrived with a full retinue. Once in Nicaea, lodging was provided in well-equipped housing, either, for the bishops of the great cities, in Constantine's palace or, for bishops of smaller Sees, in housing that had been built expressly for the clerics. The bishops had private rooms; three sleeping quarters were provided for the other members of their portable households. They dined communally, all catered and paid for by the Emperor. If these spiritual descendants of the barefoot God felt like royalty, they could not be blamed.

What a gathering! How many future saints! How many names remembered down through the darkened corridors of time! It was a hall of fame of ecclesiastical luminaries unlike anything seen before or since. There were three patriarchs, or popes, present, although those titles had not yet descended upon their haloed heads. The already mentioned Alexander, Patriarch of Alexandria was there with his young, soon-to-be successor, Athanasius. Alexander, Patriarch of the new capital in nearby Byzantium, now named New Rome, attended bearing the dignity of his ninety years like a sash across his robe. Eustathius, the Patriarch of Antioch, though only in his early thirties, with golden brown hair and beard, conscientiously took on the appearance of a prosperous Christ as he imagined him to be, wearing red tunics and blue robes and keeping his hands pressed closely together, as if in prayer, even as he walked.

So many others. Hosius of Cordoba, advisor to Constantine and one of the chief organizers of the Council, dark skinned with greying hair, was already nearly seventy, with a long life ahead of him. The two Eusebiuses, Eusebius of Caesarea, the historian, Timaeus' mentor and friend, and Eusebius of Nicomedia, a distant relative of Constantine, both arrived heavily armored with knowledge and wit. Macarius, Bishop of Jerusalem, was there, white robed and white bearded. With his priest Gregorius,

Macarius was a reminder to Timaeus of just how dangerous his mission was. The golden haired Nicholas of Myra, posthumously transformed into Santa Claus, attended, exuding a kindness and humility that was not always in his heart. The pious Spyridon of Timythous, who held down two jobs, bishop and shepherd, attended, as did Hypatius of Gangra, who would be killed by a woman robber the next year on the road from New Rome. The killer's insanity that immediately resulted from the act, and the cure that resulted from her repentance and conversion, paved Hypatius' road to sainthood.

At the outskirts of town a circus was set up to meet the spiritual needs of the secular population, complete with jugglers, elephants, charioteers, beggars, whores and pick-pockets. There is no record of the worlds of the Council and the circus colliding, but with all that was going on, for a brief few weeks Nicaea took on the role of apparent center of the universe, sacred and profane. As sinful as many of the activities of the circus undoubtedly were, it is an open question which of the two events sent the greater number of souls to their eternal damnation.

Of course Timaeus was not on the Council guest list, so there was no use in seeking shelter with the other bishops. At best, the fact that he had not officially been excommunicated or removed from office had simply been forgotten. After all, Eustathius of Kaymakli had been named as his successor and Timaeus had no doubt that his name had been removed from all church records. At worst his excommunication was a small item on the Council's agenda, which would make his surreptitious attendance much more complicated.

As it was, they were able to find lodging in a room of an inn. He told the paunchy and swarthy, middle-aged innkeeper that he was traveling with his scribe and that they would need separate pallets.

"Can't be done, old sir," was the response. "Not enough to go around as it is. Have to sleep all snuggled up."

"Are you sure that is all you have ..."

"Chin up old man, old man," said the innkeeper, lewdly, "scribes tote as much kindling as the next wench, I reckon."

"My scribe is a boy."

"And a might pretty one, too," said the innkeeper. "No matter to me."

Timaeus paid for the room from a goatskin purse that never seemed to empty.

After an hour's rest, Timaeus said they must buy new clothes, appropriate for the Council, which began in two days.

"You cannot obtain a bishop's robe in so little time," Sophia declared.

"I could if I wanted to," Timaeus replied. "But I will attend in humbler garb, like the shepherd Spyridon. A white robe will suit me. You must crop your hair and we will dress you in brown wool. A modest, hooded robe should do, so that you can keep your head covered."

"Timaeus, may I ask you a question?"

"Of course, my young scribe."

"How do you always have coin for our needs?"

"Well, I could start by observing that our needs are not great and a little silver and a little gold goes a long way."

"But how do you come by silver and gold?"

"That is easy. As a man, I am rich. My earthly father, good Christian that he was, was a shipping merchant, books and paper mainly. He brought papyrus from Egypt to Thrace and shipped vellum from Thrace to Egypt and made quite a fortune before he was burned alive on authority of Emperor Domitian. I was the eldest and was given the largest share of his inheritance. I entrusted most of my share over to my only brother. I kept some and my brother provides whatever I ask for from time to time. But I have never spent much either, until I purchased you, that is."

"Did my freedom cost you very much?" she asked.

"A great deal. But I still have a fortune. Not so large a fortune any more, but quite enough for our needs."

"Where do you keep it?"

"Someday I will tell you."

Chapter Twelve

The Great Council

May 20, 325 A.D. – Nicaea

And all the powers in the heavens ceased not from their agitation, they and the whole world, and all were moved one against the other.
Pistas Sophia

The great ecumenical Council at Nicaea was convened amidst great pomp, pageantry and intrigue on May 20, in the year of our Lord 325. By the time of its convocation, Timaeus' friend, Eusebius of Caesarea, had already been excommunicated, along with his fellow Arians, Theodotus of Laodicea and Narcissus of Neronias. A pre-council meeting had been held in Antioch shortly before Timaeus and Sophia had met with Eusebius. Constantine had placed the Spanish bishop Hosius in charge of the planning. The bishops at Antioch approved a statement of faith that had been written by Athanasius. According to the statement, all bishops were required to affirm that they believed in one Lord Jesus Christ, the only begotten Son, begotten not from nothing, but from the Father, that the Son has always existed, that He is immutable and unalterable, and that He is the image not of the will nor of anything else except the actual existence of the Father. This requirement was accompanied by anathemas, condemning views that Jesus is a creation, rather than the Creator, that he is not eternal and that his nature is subject to change.

In spite of the action taken against them at Antioch, Eusebius and the other excommunicants were invited to attend the council at Ancrya where they were to be given the opportunity to repent and be restored to communion. A short time later the place of the great council was moved to Nicaea at Constantine's insistence.

The great Eusebius excommunicated! The most famous Christian historian of all time! This was the news that buzzed through Nicaea as the bishops gathered and that echoed through the hall as the great Constantine himself called the Council to order.

Nobody took or called out a roll. There was no scribe appointed as official record-keeper. Seating was not assigned, though through unspoken assent the seats at the front of the hall remained vacant until filled with the three patriarchs in attendance and others who, by unspoken, but common understanding, occupied elevated positions in the Christology debate that was the first order of business. Timaeus, with his young scribe Sophocles, entered without notice. Most of the bishops had never seen most of the other bishops. The scars of his eye sockets were credential enough. Many limped in on severed hamstrings or Achilles tendons, many others felt their way in with a cane, others came in hunched from years of gang labor in the mines and quarries of the Empire. The persecutions had ended barely a decade earlier and many of the men who assembled in the great hall were, as Eusebius called them, athletes of religion, who had endured the tortures without wavering in their faith. To the extent he was noticed at all, Timaeus was given deference as a noble religious athlete. They sat in the back, away from the luminaries.

Dressed magnificently in a gold and purple robe, wearing the imperial diadem, dark-skinned, square-jawed and beardless, Constantine entered after the clerics had taken their seats. At the age of fifty-three, he projected the vigor of a much younger man to accompany the stature of the most powerful man in the Western World, one who had arrived at his position through the successive smiting of enemies great and small. Constantine paused before the assemblage and stated, in Greek, "I am your guest in this house. I believe strongly in Christ, but as an

Emperor who must yet sometimes do un-Christian things, I have not been baptized. It is therefore my humble request that I be seated near you to advance my knowledge of the true religion."

A roar of assent arose from the hall. An elaborately worked wooden stool was produced and Constantine sat, a small distance from the front, where he could hear and participate in the discussions.

Eusebius of Caesarea rose and rendered a pre-approved panegyric, greeting and praising the Emperor. Apparently the excommunication of the Antioch Council did not have full effect. Whatever the outcome, who was to be in or out and Christ's ultimate relationship to the Father, was to be decided here, in Nicaea.

After Eusebius' panegyric, Constantine asked and was granted permission to speak. He spoke in Latin this time from prepared notes and his words were immediately conveyed in Greek by his own trusted translator.

"Honorable bishops and great fathers of the Church, you are come here today on a great mission: to decide now and for all time the meaning and doctrines of the world's only true religion, the religion of Christ crucified, of the Word revealed, of God on Earth and Earth in God.

"How simple a thing is faith! And how complex! Believe on Christ the Savior, the Son of God and be saved, in this world and in the ever after. Follow His teachings and be redeemed. The simplest ploughman can understand this and, so understanding, can be lifted from the pains and miseries that have always been his lot in life. And yet, you come here today because you cannot agree among yourselves on such things as the nature of the Christ, His relationship with His Father, and which writings are the golden gospel of truth and which are sharp stones that block the true path to redemption.

"What were once friendly arguments between men allied against common hardships have lately taken on the tone of a civil war. There are clashes in the streets of Alexandria as the followers of Arius fight with the followers of Alexander. Throughout the realm it is the same as conflict and discord reign. It has come even to this: you have excommunicated my good friend Eusebius, perhaps the most Christian man I have known! These battles must stop.

"The Empire has seen quite enough of civil war. From the time of Sulla until the present day, Rome has endured one civil war after another. There is no victor in a civil war. Rather, the entire Empire loses. We have ended the Empire's civil wars. It is time now for the Church to do the same. Bring us peace, so that the Empire and the Church can thrive together. So that the blessings that Christ promises us hereafter may be enjoyed in some small measure in the here and now.

"It is not for me to decide these issues. I am not a theologian. I have not even been baptized, although I believe mightily in the Lord Jesus Christ. I have brought you together, you fathers of the one and true church, to decide them. You must speak freely. You must dispute the issues openly and honestly, but with love for one another. And when everyone has spoken and spoken again, I believe the Truth will be revealed. This I pray."

Constantine crossed his hands and sat again on the ornate, cushioned stool.

Spyridon of Timythous arose to present a petition to Constantine seeking exemption from taxation of his sheep herd. Achilleus of Larissa presented a petition to have a rival claimant to his See exiled. Several others were on their feet with petitions in hand, waiting their opportunity to address the Emperor. The anxious petitioners had spent a great deal of time considering their grievances and were loath to miss this rare opportunity to seek direct, imperial intervention. A wave of Constantine's heavily brocaded sleeve brushed them all back into their seats as if by physical force. "This is not the time or place for petty grievances or parochial petitions. My man will collect them, of course, but you must now proceed to the proper business of this Council." With the lift of Constantine's finger, a Praetorian walked through the room, collecting papers from thrusting hands. When he returned with the petitions, Constantine said, "Your petitions have been considered." He then placed them in an empty stone basin that had been put before him. With another wave of his hand a torch was produced and the petitions were set aflame.

The white-bearded, ancient Pope Alexander of New Rome now rose to speak, but the Emperor turned again to Eusebius. "I understand, my dear friend," Constantine said, "that you have a traditional baptismal creed in Caesarea that you think may satisfy all here."

"Yes, we do," Eusebius replied. "We believe in One God, the Father, almighty, maker of all things visible and invisible. We have faith in one Lord Jesus Christ, the Word of God, God from God, light from light, life from life, Son only begotten, first-begotten of all creation, begotten before all ages from the Father, through Whom all things came into being. Who because of our salvation was incarnate, and dwelt among men, and suffered, and rose again on the third day, and ascended to the Father, and will come again in glory to judge the living and the dead."

Constantine nodded his approval. "This is surely acceptable to all. It is what I believe. How can it be objected to?"

A murmur of assent bounced around the Hall, but before adoption of the creed could be proclaimed, Alexander of New Rome rose and, summoning all of the dignity his office and age could project, objected to Eusebius' creed. Speaking as if wisdom and knowledge, not dotage, was an innate attribute of age, Alexander said that the creed was flawed because it did not reject outright the Arian assertion that Jesus was something, someone different than God, not identical to God. Alexander, slowly and pompously called for immediate assent to a requirement that all present affirm that they believed in the one Lord Jesus Christ, who has always existed, immutable and unalterable, and He is and always has been, since the beginning of time, one and the same as the Father. "It seems to me," Alexander intoned, "that this affirmation is not only self-evident, but is a necessary precondition to all honest discussions and debates this Council is to have."

"Self-evident!" exclaimed Eusebius of Nicomedia.

"I WAS NOT FINISHED," Alexander of New Rome roared in a voice that crackled, but did not break.

"Proceed," directed Alexander of Alexandria, assuming the role of chair that he was not to relinquish for the remainder of the Council. Constantine sat back, realizing that his hope for a quick and serene end to the conflict was lost.

"Thank you, good Bishop," said Alexander of New Rome. "I was going to say that, once the affirmation has been made by all who will make it, that all others, including, most especially, the vile serpent Arius of Alexandria, be immediately excommunicated, declared heretic, banished and branded, and removed from our sight and our noses."

An immediate din arose. Assents and dissents clashed and echoed through the hall. It was clear from their respective volumes that the hall was packed with supporters of Alexander of New Rome's proposition, including the imaginary gavel wielder Alexander of Alexandria and the flame-haired Athanasius, who was frantically whispering suggestions and support into his bishop's right ear.

Eusebius of Nicomedia arose to say, "It seems to me that the learned and pious Alexander is placing the cart before the ass." Whereas Eusebius of Caesarea had tried to bridge the divide with malleable words, Nicomedia relished the conflict, knew he was right and wanted to crush the Trinitarians with his logic. Nicomedia continued. "Whatever else Alexander's proposal is, it is not self-evident. When John baptized Jesus, lo, a voice came out of the heavens saying, 'this is my beloved son, in whom I am well pleased.' To His disciples, Jesus said, 'every one therefore who shall confess me before me, him I will also confess before my Father who is in heaven.' Upon the cross He proclaimed, 'forgive them Father for they know not what they do.' Knowing these words, knowing that Jesus was son and God the Father, how is it self-evident that they are one and the same? No, the son is begotten of the father, he stands in obedience to the father, he makes passage for the father, he brings gifts from the father, but he is not the father. By His death and resurrection, Jesus joined his Father who is in Heaven. They rule the Heavens and Earth as one mind, one will, one Word, one God, but they cannot be one and the same."

Another din. Staffs were banged against the tiled floor, voices were raised, fists pounded wood, and above all could be heard Athanasius' shriek, "heretic." The great hall of Constantine sounded more like Tyre on market day than a dignified assemblage of future saints. Everyone, it seemed, had an opinion, had a belief, rather, and was so convinced of his own truth that he would not blanch at condemning, excommunicating, banishing, torturing or even executing anyone, even old friends, who denied his version of the truth. Constantine kept only a measure of wordless order by gesture, a raised eyebrow, a frown, a finger lifted, hands clasped. He did not speak, but everyone who spoke looked toward him to measure approval or displeasure or, at least, the measure of tolerance he would have.

And so on the contest raged. Although there was much nuance in the beliefs of individual bishops and deacons and priests, this became an existential struggle for the future of the Church, a Church that had now coupled its power to the Empire and would have Imperial means to enforce orthodoxy, whatever orthodoxy was decided. In such circumstances, there is no room for nuance. Jagged edges must be chipped away, rough facets must be shaved and smoothed surfaces must be polished. Only the grossest outlines of the original thought can be preserved.

Only without depth or nuance could argument be displayed as Truth.

The Trinitarians were ahead of the game in the process of polishing their Truth. God and Jesus were one; Jesus always existed; Jesus was God on Earth in the form of a man, but ever God. Eternal, existing before creation, not of God, but God himself. The two Pope Alexanders (Alexandria and New Rome), Hosius of Cordoba and the young priest Athanasius had worked hard polishing their perfect Truth and were able to present a mounted gem from the outset of the Council.

The two Eusebiuses and the priest Arius, who had given his name to his faction, were at a distinct disadvantage. First, their belief that Jesus was the Son of God, that Jesus was begotten of God, could never provide the certainty of the Trinitarian position. The relationship between Father and Son could not be so definitively set forth. Is the Son necessarily less than the Father, necessarily inferior to Him? Could the begetter become the begotten? The Arians had to admit they could not be certain of the answer to these and other questions. Further, the Arian position of a Son begotten of God, but less than God, left them open to the charge of polytheism, a charge with particular disrepute at a time when the Roman and Greek pantheon had been so thoroughly rejected. It did them little good to point out to the Trinitarians that it made no sense that the Father could also be the Son and the Son the Father. "How could that be?" the Arians would ask. But the Trinitarian reply that faith does not require understanding trumped the question in the mind of most of the Council. "If God wills it, it is so," Alexander of New Rome stated on many occasions to blockade an avenue of inquiry that, otherwise, the Trinitarians could not answer.

Despite their disadvantages, the Arians had many assets, foremost among these being the agile mind of Eusebius of Caesarea, the great historian of the Church. It was said that he had read every word ever written about Christ and Christians from the time of the Gospels and Paul on down to his own time. He knew all of the battles the Church had fought within its own ranks even as it struggled to survive successive persecutions. He knew all of the arguments used to fight those battles, both the winning and losing sides. He knew of all the heresies and all the heretics and why they arose and why they fell. Every time a prominent Trinitarian bishop rose to proclaim with certainty that Father and Son are one God, one and the same being, inseparable now and inseparable forever, Eusebius would provide a learned answer based on gospel or tradition to replace certainty with doubt and to suggest that the Trinitarian doctrine was wrong.

By the end of the first day, lines had been drawn, challenges issued, truth proclaimed and disputed, but nothing had been settled. Timaeus and his young scribe Sophocles, nee Sophia, quietly left the Hall and said nothing as they hunched their way back to the inn.

Chapter Thirteen

Homoousios

May 20, 325 A.D. – Nicaea

That is why the Good came into your midst, to the essence of every nature in order to restore it to its root.

The Gospel According to Mary Magdalene

Bishop Timaeus and scribe-clad Sophia walked steadily back to the inn. A warm west wind blew off Lake Ascania and tickled the back of Sophia's newly shorn neck. It was a novel sensation and she greeted it like a revelation. Yellow-legged gulls circled above, their cries of discovery and plunder piercing the late-afternoon stillness. Distant echoes from the circus rumbled beneath the clouds.

At the inn, the unshaven innkeeper came around a corner wiping his hands on his blouse. "Old man, old man," he said, "you never told me yer were a bishop. An' you choose my inn above the palace." Timaeus did not want his host's attention, but turned to the voice he said, "Too much of the same company can be vexing. We keep our own counsel for Council."

"Good enough, old bishop sir. Good enough."

In their room, sitting on the single straw pallet, they talked.

"The Alexanders will have their day," Timaeus predicted. "Full of hate and slander, pretending to know what they cannot know, they will have their day. And with their win, they will paint the streets of the Empire red with the gore of their enemies. I hope Eusebius can save himself."

In a gesture of habit, Sophia brushed back at her hair with her right hand, only to find the hairs' close-cropped remnant in no need of adjustment. She pulled back the hood of her cassock and scratched at her scalp. She had struggled throughout the day to understand the meaning of what was being said. Alone with Timaeus at the end of the day, she struggled with how to frame her many questions. What came out was, "Are they really so far apart?"

"What do you think, Sophia?"

"I think both yes and no. If I have followed correctly, the Trinitarians say that Jesus and God are the same and always have been the same, that Jesus was God when he was born, as he lived and when he was crucified. That he was always God. Eusebius counters that Jesus was the Son of God, but was born human and lived human and died human, but is now God's equal."

Timaeus smiled. "You understand. I knew you would. But you have only described how they are different. You said they were both far apart and not so far apart. How are they not so far apart?"

"I think they are fighting only over whether Jesus knew he was God when he lived as a man. They agree he is God's son. They agree he is one with God upon his resurrection. They agree that God is all knowing, so God must have known He would call Jesus to Him, to rule the heavens with Him, after his death. So all that is left is whether Jesus knew what God knew when he lived as a man."

The smile had never departed from Timaeus' face. "You have a gift for seeing through these things, Sophia."

"Am I wrong?"

"No, I think you are right. But the question I have for you is, who is right as between Alexander and Eusebius?"

It was Sophia's turn to smile. "You are trying to trick me, Timaeus."

"How so? I only asked a question."

"If both are wrong, neither one can be right."

"Are both wrong?"

Sophia's smile turned to a deep frown and she sighed. "You

teach," she said, "that Jesus brought us knowledge of the infinite and that only by achieving knowledge can we, men and women, achieve one with the All. And if this is true, then Jesus cannot have been the Catholics' God either during his life or after, since God is none other than Yaldabaoth, who hates knowledge, who raped Eve and banished Eve and Adam from the garden. And so, both Alexander and Eusebius must be wrong and the Jesus they worship cannot lead to salvation."

"Yes," Timaeus said, "that is what I have taught you. But what do you believe?"

"I have come to accept this."

Timaeus placed his hand on Sophia's leg and said, "I am glad, Sophia. But you must never accept it only because I have taught it. My search for gnosis is ongoing. I have not achieved it. You must always allow that I am wrong, perhaps profoundly wrong. Can you do that?"

Sophia laughed. "Of course," she said. "You are a man."

Timaeus laughed with her and at himself.

After a few moments, as the laughter faded, Timaeus became aware that his hand was on Sophia's thigh and quickly removed it. The touch had pleased Sophia and the hand's removal brought with it a vague sense of loss, but she said nothing. She felt Timaeus' mind working, trying to come up with something to say to paint over the awkwardness he felt. For Sophia, there was no awkwardness, but she felt Timaeus' anxiety and wished to relieve it and so asked, "Now, if you want me to say who is more wrong, Alexander or Eusebius, I will say it is Alexander."

"Why is that?" asked Timaeus.

"Because Eusebius' Jesus was fully human while he lived. He had to struggle for knowledge just like everyone else. And he found it too. It is only upon his death that Eusebius takes that achievement away from him by making him God. Alexander's Jesus is an actor. He was born, lived, and died as a man, but was only pretending. He was always God. Alexander's Jesus is just another of Yaldabaoth's tricks. Yaldabaoth has also usurped Eusebius' Jesus, but because he lived and died as a human, he can still teach us if we ignore the ending Eusebius urges. So, I would say that Eusebius is less dangerous to true gnosis, but because he ends up agreeing with Alexander in uniting Jesus with God, their argument is largely meaningless. At the end of their argument, Jesus has the same nature, the same *homoousios* as Yaldabaoth and his lessons are lost."

If he had had eyes, Timaeus would have stared at Sophia in rapt wonder. He thought to himself, once again, that he was right, that she was his Sophia. His heart leapt with excitement. The same nature, of course, he thought. How succinct! How explicit! In his excitement he blurted, "I love you," thinking to mean no more by it than an expression of excitement and communion, without reference to the genders into which, by the folly of Yaldabaoth, they were separated.

"I love you too, Timaeus," came the tender reply, without any such qualification.

That night, for the first time, Timaeus dreamt about Sophia in the Pleroma.

Chapter Fourteen

The Great Debate

May 21, 325 A.D. – Nicaea

Darkness will be preferred to light, and death will be preferred to life. No one will gaze into heaven. And the pious man will be counted as insane, and the impious man will be honored as wise. The man who is afraid will be considered as strong. And the good man will be punished like a criminal.
Asclepius

On the second day of the Council, after the convocational prayer and the seating of Constantine, Alexander of New Rome rose to address the bishops. If the first day of the Council had been a day of skirmishing, of testing volleys and opening salvos, the second was to be all-out warfare, with no quarter granted and no prisoners taken. The Trinitarians had agreed that the venerable Alexander of New Rome, fighting on his home turf, would command their first assault.

"Arius," the ancient man roared, "let us say his name for, shamefully, he is here among us today, Arius, and all those who would question the eternal divinity of Christ, call into question all piety and doctrine, after the manner of the Jews, and have constructed a workshop for contending against Christ, denying the Godhead of our Savior, and preaching that He is only the equal of all others. And having collected all passages which speak of His plan of salvation and His humiliation for our sakes, they endeavor from these to collect the preaching of their impiety, ignoring altogether the passages which His eternal Godhead and unutterable glory with the Father is set forth. Arius and his supporters daily stir up against us, the faithful, the pure, seditions and persecutions. Indeed, they drag us before the tribunals of the judges, by intercourse with silly and disorderly women, whom they have led into error and whom they would ordain as priests. They cast opprobrium and infamy upon the Christian religion, their young maidens disgracefully wandering about every village and street. Even Christ's indivisible tunic, which His executioners were unwilling to divide, these wretches have dared to rend. And now, having discovered, rather late on account of their concealment, their manner of life, and their unholy attempts, by the common suffrage of all, we must cast them forth from the congregation of the Church, the true Church, which adores the Godhead of Christ."

Alexander took a long draught of water, adjusted his robe and fixed his stare on Eusebius of Nicomedia. "But who is Arius?" he said. "He is an apostate priest who has already been thrice excommunicated and should long ago have been turned into the unredeemable dust to which his creed will inevitably consign him. No. Arius is nothing, an ant, less than an ant, and we would not even know his name or have need to rebuke his errors, but for the venerable and elevated personages whom he has enlisted to his cause.

"In our diocese, then, not so long ago, there went forth lawless men, and adversaries of Christ, led by Nicomedia, teaching men to apostatize which thing, with good right, one might suspect and call the precursor of Antichrist. And I, indeed, wished to cover up these matters in silence, that so perhaps the evil might spend itself in the leaders of the heresy alone, and that it might not spread to other places and defile the ears of any of the more simple-minded. But since Eusebius, imaging that with him rests all ecclesiastical matters, because, having left Berytus and cast his eyes upon the church of the Nicomedians, and no punishment having been inflicted upon him, he is set over these apostates, and has undertaken to write everywhere, commending them, if by any means he may draw aside some who are ignorant of this heresy. He, Eusebius of Nicomedia, desiring by their assistance, to renew that ancient wickedness of his mind, with respect to which he for a time was silent, pretends that he is speaking on their behalf, but proves by his deeds that he is exerting himself to do this on his own account. He praises apostates from the Church: Arius, Achilles, Aithales, Carpones, Lucius, Julius, and Helladius, formerly deacons, and Secundus and Theonas, who dare to come to this council, calling themselves bishops. And on their behalf and on his own, Nicomedia proclaims that God was not always the Father; but there was a time when God was not the Father. That the Word of God was not always, but was made from things that are not, for He who is God fashioned the non-existing from the non-existing, wherefore there was a time when He was not. That the Son is a thing created, and a thing made, nor is He like to the Father in substance, nor is He the true and natural Word of the Father, nor is He His true Wisdom, but He is one of the things fashioned and made."

Fire raged in the eyes of old Alexander as, with archaic rhetoric, he mowed down his enemies. That this fire emerged from the appearance of a charred and ashen frame made its intensity all the more impressive. If asked, he would have proclaimed that he loved his enemies, as Jesus had taught, and had hate only for their error, their heresy. But flesh and error are inseparable, and Alexander's fire sought to consume both the beliefs and the men who held them. However, as the fire burned, the fuel Alexander was able to supply was limited. He was old and tiring. He was winding down and his opponents were fidgeting, waiting their turn to challenge his assertions.

Alexander continued at lower volume. "The good Eusebius of Caesarea has fallen prey to this apostasy. He has written that Jesus was created and sacrificed by God for love of mankind. He thinks this was a great gift made by God, but how much greater the gift, how much more effective to wash away our original sin, for God himself to have made the journey in human flesh? How much greater His love of man for God to have sacrificed himself on the cross? How much stronger His commitment to man's salvation that He would endure the lash and crown of thorns and nails of crucifixion knowing that at any time He could have put a stop to it all, could have risen, thrown off His cloak, revealed His glory and smote all of His oppressors into dust and ash?

"And what does my learned friend, Caesarea, have to say about John 14:9, where Jesus says, 'he that has seen Me has seen the Father?' And how, if the Son is the Word or Wisdom and Reason of God, was there a time when He was not? It is as if they were saying that there was a time when God was without reason and wisdom? And how can He be changeable and mutable, who says, at John 14:10, 'I am in the Father, and the Father in Me,' and at John 10:30, 'I and My Father are one,' and by the prophet, at Malachi 3:6, 'I am the Lord, I change not?' No, I say to Eusebius and all who remain in sympathy with the abased heresy of Arius, when He became man He changed not, but was the same yesterday, today and forever."

Spent, Alexander sank heavily but triumphantly into his chair, eyes still aflame, but contrasted with the ashen-white face that framed them.

Before anyone could arise with a rejoinder, Constantine, taking the fervent counsel Hosius of Cordoba had been whispering in his ear, said, "I find kind Alexander's words most convincing. Clearly, Father and Son are one. They are the same, eternal being and have acted always as one. I am not sure what could be said against the wisdom of Alexander." Constantine gracefully held out the palms of his hands, turned upward, seeking acceptance of, if not acclimation for, what he had just said.

Eusebius of Caesarea, long head held high, arose. "Great Emperor," he said, "your victory over Licinius and all your enemies was a gift from God. You were His worthy instrument and you have been true to His commandments. Thus, after all tyranny had been purged away, the Empire was preserved firm and without a rival to your earthly power. It is preserved for you and your sons alone. And having obliterated the godlessness of your predecessors and having recognized the benefits conferred upon you and your sons by God, you have exhibited your love of virtue and of God and your piety and gratitude to God by deeds, which you have performed in the sight of all men. You have ended the oppression of God's true church and all here, whatever our side in this debate, praise you and your works.

"But," Eusebius said without pause, "you yourself opened this Council by telling us that truth can be found and accepted only if we speak freely. You commanded us to do so. You commanded us to dispute the issues openly and honestly, but with love for one another. It is not for me to say whether Alexander spoke with love for me or for the Bishop of Nicomedia or for Arius of Alexandria. But it is for me, before we accept by acclimation what Pope Alexander has demanded by threat of eternal damnation and opprobrium, to ask your permission to speak, so that I may correct the charges that Alexander has laid upon us and to amend the praises that he heaps upon himself."

Constantine ignored Hosius' counsel this time and bowed his head in assent to Eusebius' request.

Eusebius spoke for over an hour. Not a minute passed that he did not quote from a Gospel or a Pauline epistle or another liturgical source. His argument was scholarly. His tone was dispassionate, but kind. His criticism of Trinitarianism was firm, but tolerant. Only when the subject turned to Alexander's attack on his doctrine's influence and corruptive effect on women did his ire flash.

"We have heard Alexander accuse us of impiety, of leading women into sin, suggesting that our beliefs and hearts are not as pure or faithful as his and that any deviation from what he deems true necessarily leads to lewdness and depravity. He accuses us of promoting women to positions of leadership, which truly would be an abomination of the divine order. Perhaps I should be flattered, for in making these charges it is clear that he has read my Histories of the Church, wherein I wrote of the depraved debauchery of certain Gnostics, as documented by Irenaeus. He must have read it there, because it has no basis in reality as applied to our beliefs. We believe in chastity as much as Alexander. I have ever been celibate. I am not sure that a man such as Alexander, who has bragged that he spent four years naked, can say the same."

After the inevitable outburst that followed this attempt at humor, Eusebius returned to moderation. "We all agree that Jesus was the Son of God. We all agree that Jesus is God. The only dispute is over the nature of his humanity. It does not diminish God's gift that Jesus, when He lived among us, was fully human. It enhances His gift. What the Trinitarians say cannot be reconciled to logic. They say Jesus was human and God. To us who say, 'that is incomprehensible,' they shout 'such is God's will and not for you to understand.' They would deprive the world of God's gift of intelligence to mankind and, therefore, mankind's ability to believe in God's Truth. I pray we do not accept their dictate."

And so it went. A second day, back and forth, argument and counter-argument. With each exchange the Trinitarians became more strident, harsher in the demand for punishment to be meted out to their opponents. And with each passing hour the countenance of Constantine became less patient and graver.

In their room that evening, Timaeus and Sophia talked about the day's battles. Timaeus fretted for his friend Eusebius. He said he knew that if the Trinitarians prevailed, all tolerance would be obliterated and Gnostics like themselves would be in even greater danger. As he fretted, Sophia brushed his hair and wiped his brow with a familiarity and affection he had not previously felt. Before they went to sleep she said, "Do not trouble yourself, sweet Timaeus. They cannot eliminate the knowledge that is all around us."

"You are Sophia," Timaeus said, "Sophia."

That night, for the second time, he dreamt about Sophia in the Pleroma. The same dream as the night before.

Chapter Fifteen

Timaeus' Dream

May 21-22, 325 A.D. – The Pleroma

Yet you are sleeping, dreaming dreams. Wake up and return, taste and eat the true food! Hand out the word and the water of life! Cease from the evil lusts and desires.
The Concept of Our True Power

Timaeus' Dream

Stars in the night. Stars without light. Swirling darkness, motion felt but unseen. Infinite, undulant darkness. Not black. Black can be seen. Darkness: no color, no light. Abyss. Deeper and deeper into the swirling Abyss. Down, down into the swirling Abyss. Until ... a pinprick of white. A star, a single star, a single, moving star emerges from the darkness and is instantly swallowed up. Back into the Abyss. Was it even there? Did he see it? But there it is again. No. Not the same star. A different star. A little brighter than the last. And not quite white. Not all white. Blue, perhaps, or green or red or yellow. A flicker. Just enough light to illuminate the edges of the roiling Abyss by which it is instantly consumed. Again, was it there? Did he see it? What was its color? And always and ever, the roiling Abyss.

What was happening? He was lost. Who was he? Gradually there were more and more stars. Here and there. Sometimes two or three together. Then a neighborhood of stars, a community of stars, a nation of stars, emerging, shining, flashing through the colorless heavens. Lighting the heavens faintly. Moving, yes moving, toward each other and apart and always swallowed up again by the Abyss. The churning Abyss.

Was the Abyss jealous of the stars' light? Is that why the Abyss moved so quickly to swallow them? But why should the Abyss, which was infinite, be jealous of small, finite flashes of light? Why should it not merely enjoy the infinite, infinitesimal variations in its own universal darkness? Or was the Abyss unconscious? Was it a fluid nebula that simply filled every space as quickly as the space appeared, consumed every object and variation as a raging river swallows up all things in its path? But then, why did it roil so? Why was it so restless? Was it conscious or random?

Gradually, without awareness, he slipped through the darkness and into the bright light of the Abyss. He felt it moving around him, heard its voices, smelled its scents, felt its warmth, sensed … could it be? … sensed its consciousness. No, it was not an unconscious river of nothingness. It teemed with the essences of infinite realities, with the vitality of infinite beings, but existing as one reality, one consciousness. A common origin. A common end. Existence before creation. Existence after time. A palimpsest of all life, all matter, all time, flattened to a plane, invisible but subsuming all. As he moved within it, merged with it, diffused into it, he knew that it was not filled with jealousy for the stars, but unbounded, passionless love. It rushed to cover each lonely, new spark of light with its warm perfection, its timelessness, its unblemished and pure darkness. And the stars coveted its embrace, welcomed their return to the mother, to the All. He was in the Pleroma. He was one with the mind of Sophia. He was immersed in the pure nothingness, the pure everything of love, of God.

He moved within it, churned within it, surrendered to it, like the stars. It was timeless and eternal. Eternities passed as, without will of his own, he let it carry him forward and backward, through time and beyond hunger or care or longing or life or death. He was one with the Pleroma and wanted nothing more. He lost all sense of being. A deep, deep, but conscious sleep, an unshakeable sleep, deep within the All.

But there was a light. Ahead. Another star. Out of the Nothingness, out of the All, was a small, fragile flickering light. He pulled himself hard away from the light of the Pleroma, aching, longing to make it out, to distinguish it from the other stars. It was familiar. It pulsed, almost as if it breathed. The pang of loss he felt as he separated himself from the All did not deter him. Why was this light familiar? Why did it beckon to him with so strong a call that he would leave perfection in order to know?

Suddenly, he was again in the world he once had known, so long ago, before the Abyss, before the Pleroma. He could see again with human eyes, his eyes, unblemished. Perfect. And he saw ... Sophia.

Was it her? Did she see him? He knew that he was still part of the Nothingness, the Everything. He knew this vision was fleeting. He longed, in fact, to return fully to the All, the Abyss, the Pleroma, to flow within it, to become subsumed again. But there was Sophia, lovelier than he could ever have imagined. Pure, soft, perfect. A perfect form, distinct from the formless All. She kissed him with an unfathomable tenderness and timelessness. The heat he now felt did not come from the Pleroma. The consciousness was his own. The heat was his own. His own and Sophia's. As they kissed, their bodies merged into a perfect and sublime oneness. Apart from the Everything, the All, the Nothing. A raging and fulfilling fire burned around them, did not consume them, but nourished them. The Nothingness fled. It hid from a fire too strong to consume. It could swallow suns and galaxies, novae and pulsars, it could absorb every being that ever lived, everything that ever existed, but drew back from and paused before the fire that burned between Timaeus and his Sophia. His Sophia.

They moved together now, rolled together now. At a distance the Pleroma separated into a billion fragments, a billion ghosts, watching in envy or pride, waiting in envy or pride, as the lovers moved together, moved as one, moved to fulfill an eternal, shared and common longing. Moved until perfect unity subsumed them and the warmth of a billion stars washed over them.

He was moving again, subsumed again within the darkness, within the Pleroma. But where was Sophia? Gone, gone, behind an unseen screen, a locked and hidden door. There was not even her light. He could not see. He was blind again. He was home again in the All, in the Nothing, in the Everything, in the Pleroma. He welcomed it, surrendered to it. He slept.

Chapter Sixteen

Only This World

May 22, 325 A.D. – Nicaea

And in that day, the world will not be marveled at and ... immortality will not be worshiped. But it is in danger of becoming a burden to all men. Therefore, it will be despised.
Asclepius

In the morning Sophia was fully arranged and dressed before Timaeus awoke. She was busy laying out a little bread and cheese on a cloth on the pallet when he opened his eyes to the day. He felt her smile wash over him as she said, "Did you sleep well, my Timaeus?"

He raised his head, expecting to see Sophia and the room about them, but there was only the pang of disappointment that came with the awareness that last night's experience had been only a dream and that the person who awoke was old, blind Timaeus, sightless again. He shook his head to wipe away the last remnants of sleep and to reorient himself to his abiding reality.

"Why do you call me your Timaeus?" he asked.

"Am I not your Sophia?"

"Yes, you are my Sophia."

"Then you are my Timaeus. How silly you are."

Timaeus began to nibble on a little cheese. They could hear the old innkeeper banging stools around in another room. The sweet odor of morning drifted in from Lake Ascania. People were stirring in the streets outside. The sound of the market climbed inside their window. Two flies buzzed about the room, resting occasionally, momentarily, on a wall or a piece of cheese and swiftly taking off again.

"Sophia," Timaeus said, "I believe I understand existence."

With knotted brows Sophia said, "That's nice. Please tell me."

"It came to me in a dream last night. I believe I attained true gnosis."

"That was quite a dream you had then," she replied. "I think you had the same dream the night before." Her voice was playful, teasing in a way he had not before heard. He thought about what she said.

After a long pause he said, "Yes. I think you are right, but I remember last night's dream better. I was in the Pleroma. It was vast and warm and filled with many consciousnesses. Life sprung from it and it loved those lives and embraced those lives and welcomed the return of those lives. There was no death, only life separated and life reunited. It was love. Vast love."

"And how did it feel, that love, my Timaeus?" Sophia asked.

"It subsumed everything. It was everything. Beyond feeling. It was complete. I believe it awaits us all, if we only have eyes to see and ears to hear it."

Sophia smiled and patted him lovingly on the head.

A fly landed on Sophia's leg. She deftly swatted and killed it with her hand.

"Did you get it?" Timaeus asked.

"I returned it to the Pleroma," she replied.

Timaeus laughed. "I'm not sure that's ..."

"Timaeus," Sophia interrupted. "Let us leave this place. It holds nothing for us. A bunch of silly, old men arguing about things that nobody can know. Arguing as if one side were right and the other wrong. Let us get away before they hurt you."

The star-shaped scars, where Timaeus' eyes once were, crinkled in sympathetic calm. "They cannot hurt me, Sophia. What will they do? Banish me? Imprison me? Torture me? I suppose the Emperor could do those things, but he will not. And far too many of the bishops know the injustice of these things to impose them on another, especially one who worships the same

Jesus they do. No. The most they can do is excommunicate me and banish me from Council. And as far as that goes, I have not taken communion in years and once I have had my say I will leave any way. No, no harm will come to me."

"They will kill you," Sophia proclaimed.

Timaeus laughed. "Kill me? No they will not. They don't have the authority and the Emperor will not allow it. I feared that before we arrived here, but witnessing this conclave, I no longer think there is something to fear. The Empire is not uniformly Christian yet. There are too many people of too many faiths for him to start executing someone for not being Christian enough. No, they will not kill me."

"Timaeus," Sophia pleaded, "I know Athanasius. I knew him when I was a child in Alexandria. He will kill you. He is brutal. He is evil. He is in love with power and full of hate. It will not take a vote of the bishops. It will be done by the priest."

Sophia's seemingly certain knowledge of both the character of Athanasius and the likely turn of events jostled Timaeus' jovial serenity. He thought about what she said and knew it had a certain logic to it. Unlikely, he thought, but not impossible. Still, he would not be deterred. "Sophia," he replied, "if I am killed, I will simply return to the Pleroma, where I had such a pleasant visit last night. It would be of no great matter."

For the first time since they met, Sophia began to cry. "Do you care so little about me, then?" she wept.

"What do you mean?"

"What do I mean?" Sophia asked incredulously. "You have taken me to this awful place. I have no money. I have been pretending to be a cleric when I know little of their religion. I have been pretending to be a man in a place where no woman is allowed. I know nothing of this Pleroma you talk about. I know only this world. I know only one beautiful man in this world. You are going to put that man's life in peril for reasons I cannot understand. And you ask me what I mean? Clearly you care little for me."

Timaeus reached out to stroke her hair, but she pulled away and his hand fell heavily through the air.

Deep silence subsisted as Sophia wept and Timaeus rearranged his worldview. "Alright," he said at last. "I think the dangers are overstated, but I have not considered them enough. I must do some thinking about what you have said."

"Let us leave here," Sophia said. "Today. Now."

"Give me today to think on these things. I promise you I will say nothing at Council today. We will keep our heads down, as we have been doing. We will decide the future tonight."

Timaeus' decision did not please her, but she was grateful for the concession he made. She put the hood up over her head and they began their walk to the Hall.

Chapter Seventeen

Christianity In This Decomposing World

May 22, 325 A.D. – The Christian World

> *And there shall be others of those who are outside our number who name themselves bishop and also deacons, as if they have received their authority from God. They bend themselves under the judgment of the leaders. Those people are dry canals.*
> The Apocalypse of Peter

Draw away from the Council. Move away from Nicaea, from New Rome and Antioch and Alexandria. Consider the years. Jesus was born at the apex of the Empire. Augustus was emperor. For all its economic and cultural advancements, the Roman Empire was built on force and fear as surely as infection thrives on fever and filth. The extractive economy built on conquest and suppression was designed to provide lavishly for the Roman estates and the palace courts scattered throughout the realm and to leave only subsistence scraps behind to be grappled over without concern as to who would wrangle enough to survive and who would perish into dust. Into this world Jesus came to preach salvation in exchange for deeds of kindness and succor shown to the "least among these." "Do unto others as you would have them do unto you." "Love thy neighbor as thyself." Do as I do and I'll see you in the hereafter. Simple. No theologian necessary.

By the time of Jesus' death, Tiberius, a crueler, less competent Emperor, had succeeded Augustus. In the three hundred years that followed, Rome was controlled by a digression of rulers, with few exceptions each more venal and less qualified than the last. Sustained only by the inertia resulting from the impossibility, even for its enemies, of imagining its absence and the occasional reclamation of fragmentary glory by a Trajan, an Aurelian or a Vespasian, Rome extracted an ever-greater portion of an ever-decreasing bounty from its conquered peoples. Waves of invaders swept in and either crawled out or were absorbed by the Roman morass. Traditions faded and were replaced. The ancient pantheon that bound the conquerors could not hold, as new gods, ordained by law, imposed by force, or adopted by faith, invaded and old gods slumped into the obscurity of neglect and disbelief. Life became harsher, crueler, and less coherent. Jesus' message flourished.

At first there was no clergy. No church. His teaching spread first among the Jews, but there was nothing about it in any of its essentials that required either great, religious knowledge or restricted it to the circumcised. It spread among gentiles of every kind, requiring no particular training, no altar, no temple. Make life better for those you see suffering. Be kind. Offer food to the hungry, even from your own meager share. Bring water to those who thirst. Daub the brows of those who are ill. Comfort yourself with the knowledge that doing these things is the path to eternal and glorious life. In short, the way to Heaven is to make life better here, on Earth.

And so it was that Jesus' most basic message, stripped of mystery, magic and the apocalypse, grew like an insurgency within the greatest political structure the world has ever known. Overflowed, in point of fact, that realm, into the largely unknown regions of the Hindi, the Mongols and the Hans, flourished at its most primal level and manifested itself in untold millions of acts of kindness and grace and goodness. Christianity in its primal essence was a balm and an opiate given to the eternally dying patient that is mankind.

This flourishing must be understood separately from the growth of the churches that claimed inheritance from Jesus and His apostles. The churches had their place, certainly. A million Christians independently obeying the teachings of Jesus had not the means necessary to protect themselves from the inevitable persecutions of individuals and the state alike. The Church was protection and solace for these Christians. A Church requires structure and structure hierarchy. Priests had to be qualified. Deacons had to be trained to instruct and anoint the priests. Bishops had to be appointed to oversee the flock and manage the economy of the growing congregations. Temples had to be built. Rules of succession and management had to be drawn. And what if some of the worshipers, the practicing Christians, were misinterpreting Jesus' word, as handed down by tradition and eventually transcribed into gospels and epistles? What if they emphasized only part of His message at the expense of other parts? Shouldn't they be properly instructed? Of course, and the Church, consisting of the collective intelligence of the most studious and righteous of the faith, was the proper instructor. And what if the texts left some things out, some things that must have occurred or must have been said. Shouldn't those things be added? Yes, again, and again it was the proper role of the learned and sacred Church to oversee these changes and ordain what is proper to be taught to and believed by all Christians. And so the Church grew. Always in peril, always under attack from within and without, it grew. Its survival and growth proving that it flourished by the Grace of God.

All of these things were done with the purest of hearts by the purest of souls. All of these things were done for the good of all Christians. But it came to pass that Jesus' most basic message, the instruction to make life in this world better for those who suffer, was diluted. It was not intended to be so, but with time, as the importance of each man's post within the Church came to be defined and circumscribed, one became less likely to see His message in practice as one looked higher up the chain of the Church's command. The bishop was less likely to embody this message of love than the deacon, the deacon than the priest, the priest than the parishioner and the parishioner than the new initiate who, having heard the words that Jesus spoke for the first time, ventured out in the world to follow them in practice. Seeing themselves as God's representatives and interpreters on Earth, the clergy came to emphasize fealty to the Father over service to the suffering.

Now return through time to Nicaea. The Church has reached adulthood. It has been taken into the ruling family. Its place in the Empire is fixed. Here it is tempting to write, "and Jesus is dead," and end the discussion. But Jesus' naked message is pure enough and strong enough to survive the tapestries of power and the veils of explanation. Out in the world in 325 A.D., and before then, and after then, this message resonated and motivated millions who heard it or felt it and incorporated it into their hearts, and motivated countless acts of sacrifice and kindness that eased the boundless suffering in this decomposing world.

Chapter Eighteen

The Marriage Contract

May 22, 325 A.D. – Nicaea

> *"Strip off the old garment of fornication, and put on the garment which is clean and shining, that you may be beautiful in it."*
> The Teachings of Silvanus

The third day of the Council differed from the first two in that Emperor Constantine did not appear until late afternoon. With Constantine gone, Athanasius, though not a bishop and not yet twenty-seven years of age, felt unconstrained to vent his anger at all he called Arians. To young Athanasius, the word "Arian" was used to denote all manner of heresy. It was clear he hated the old priest Arius at least as much as he hated the doctrine. Athanasius' great rhetorical gift was to be accusatory while sounding aggrieved.

He began calmly enough, proclaiming that the "Jesus that I know as my redeemer cannot be less than God," but devolved into rants against anyone who would question his beliefs, calling them "heretics deserving of excommunication and excoriation." Warming up, his boney hands thrusting sharp exclamations into the air, Athanasius charged, "Old man Arius has seduced wayward packs of women with wank and word, holding ungodly orgies to lure the unsuspecting to his cause." He claimed that Arius' teaching that Jesus became divine and that He came into being after the Father "would open the floodgates to every manner of heretic, including the fiendish Gnostic who believes he can think his way to equal status with Jesus." A little later, Athanasius proclaimed, "I did not come to Nicaea to interpret or expound, but to witness. The truth is not interpreted. It is given and we give witness to it. The Arian creed seeks to deny our right to witness our faith. Saint Mark the Evangelist speaks through Bishop Alexander. The debate is ended. The truth is witnessed."

But the debate was not ended. Others spoke as well, unburdened by the potential of arousing the Emperor's disapproval or ire. Nicholas of Myra, voice brittle to the point of breaking, supported the orthodoxy of Alexander and Athanasius, but without Athanasius' relish and venom. Theonas of Marmarica and Secundus of Ptolemais supported Eusebius of Nicomedia's arguments. Eusebius of Caesarea spoke again too, arguing that the common Christian would have difficulty understanding how the Father could be the Son and the Son the Father, and urging the bishops to tolerate some differences for the sake of all that they agreed upon.

And so it went. Even as food was brought in and grace said over it, the debate continued. In the afternoon Sophia noticed that Athanasius was looking at her and Timaeus. He stared intently for several seconds, then whispered something to his bishop, Alexander of Alexandria, who whispered something in return. Athanasius then walked over to Paulus, seated beside Alexander of New Rome and whispered into his ear. Paulus whispered something to his Alexander, whereupon the three of them looked across and to the back of the room at Timaeus and Sophia. Of particular concern to Sophia were the occasional glances hastily shot at her by the delegation from Antioch, but unlike Athanasius, Antioch's young bishop Eustathius did not appear keen to alert others about what he had noticed.

Sophia whispered something quickly to Timaeus so that he would turn toward her and away from the inquisitors. This was not good, she told Timaeus. "We should leave at once." But Timaeus did not seem concerned. The same, serene smile that had been on his face all day remained in place, as if he had ceased caring about his own safety – or hers. How far removed he was from the journey to Nicaea, when he had her look behind every rock and shrub for hidden spies and enemies. She wanted that Timaeus back.

Sophia tugged at his sleeve and repeated that they had to leave – now. The tug rousted him a little and he turned toward her. Just then Constantine arrived with a flourish and entourage and all attention turned to him. He begged forgiveness for having been called away on official business and expressed the hope that the bishops were approaching consensus. After Constantine sat, Timaeus whispered, "We cannot leave the Emperor's presence." So they sat. When Constantine arose again to leave about an hour later, the Council was adjourned for the day and Sophia hurried Timaeus out of the hall toward the inn.

When they arrived at the inn, the innkeeper was waiting for them. His hands were soiled from working the earth in the garden patch. He wiped them on a dirty rag as he spoke. Sweat dripped heavily from the glistening stubble of his beard. "Old bishop sir," he said, "they's another distinguished old sir waiting for you and a young one too. Old one says he's a friend, but I don't know. Looks all high and mighty. Thought you'd want to know." And with that the innkeeper hustled around the corner, out of sight.

Sophia felt fear crawl up her spine as a gazelle might feel at the sight of a deadly panther. "We have to go now," she told Timaeus. Timaeus was unmoved.

"Go?" he replied. "Go where? If they are enemies, do you think we could outrun them? Safer to meet them and see what they want."

As they entered their room, Sophia was confronted with the equine face and ursine demeanor of Eusebius. From his stringy beard and youthful countenance she recognized the priest Philippus standing beside him.

"My good friend Eusebius," Timaeus said, holding out his hands. How Timaeus knew who was there, Sophia did not know.

"Welcome to our humble lodgings. And who is it with you? Is that you, Philippus? You see, I remember. Greetings. Please, sit on the pallet. We have some wine and cheese to offer. How may I serve you?"

Eusebius' practiced serenity was nowhere to be found. Without sitting he said, "Timaeus, you have entirely lost your mind. I come here and it's even worse than I thought. You're sharing a room and a pallet with the woman who is pretending before the Emperor to be a priest! Do you really mean to have yourself killed?"

The words of rebuke had no apparent effect on Timaeus. "First," he said, "it has been my goal all along to lose my mind and to find Ennoia. Second, we are celibate. Third, I do not mean to see myself killed. Why do you suspect that?"

Eusebius scowled. "They know who you are, Timaeus. They are waiting to pounce."

"If, by they, you mean my old pope, Alexander, then I would have been disappointed if he did not recognize me. And I have been waiting three days now for them to pounce. I am ready for them."

"Oh, you fool," Eusebius rejoined. "You cannot be ready for them. Can the lamb be ready for the hungry lion? They have all the power. I am no match for them, good friend to Constantine that I have been. And I do not just mean Alexander of New Rome, either. Alexander of Alexandria too, and his priest Athanasius, who seems to be driving the chariot for the old men. Others too. Stay any longer and it will be the end of you."

Eusebius sank heavily down onto the pallet. Philippus remained standing, casting occasional shy glances at Sophia. Timaeus handed Eusebius a skin of wine. Eusebius took a long pull and passed it to Philippus. "Philippus," he said, "are you sure we weren't followed?"

"I did not see anyone behind us, Bishop." His voice was as thin as a wood pipe and Sophia smiled at the sound. Eusebius frowned.

Timaeus spoke next. "I think it is important I be here, that I speak for those without a voice. Constantine seems a liberal man. Surely he must know that by fixing belief, you can kill faith. He must hear it, in any event."

Eusebius shook his head. "There is no point. You have misread Constantine if you think he cares about faith, yours or mine. I once thought he did, but I know now that what he cares about is order and he is determined to have it. It is all fixed. The Trinitarians have won this battle. You can add nothing to it but your own demise."

"Those are grim words from one who has already spoken out for the humanity of Jesus. What will you do?"

"What will I do? Become a Trinitarian, of course."

"Do you care so little, then, about your beliefs?"

"My belief," Eusebius said, his voice rising, "is that Jesus Christ is the Son of God, that he was born, suffered and died upon the cross so that our sins may be forgiven if we believe in him." Eusebius paused and sighed. "I will not sacrifice my life or my office over such a distinction as the Trinitarians draw."

Timaeus sat beside his old mentor and placed a hand on his shoulder. "I am afraid," he said, "that mine is not such a fine distinction."

Eusebius grinned wryly. "No," he agreed, "it is not. And, if called upon, I will vote with the Alexanders to excommunicate you. But believing, as I do, that you are destined for Hell if you do not repent, I do not share their desire to send you there expeditiously. Look. Practice your faith. Believe what you must. Come to me when you see the error of your thought. But why must you be here, at this Council, where none share your beliefs?"

"I come to save Jesus' flesh. I come to save Jesus from becoming marble. I come to defend your right to hold your beliefs, my dear friend. I come to assert my right to be called

Christian. I come to remind the Emperor and all who will listen that their knowledge is not perfect and to persuade all who will hear that the only way that we and future generations can improve our understanding, to be saved, is to leave open the possibility that we, here today, might just be wrong."

"You come on a fool's errand. It has been decided. Live, Timaeus. Forget your folly and live."

Timaeus' countenance turned grave. "You don't think Constantine would approve of my execution, do you?"

"I doubt very much they would ask his permission. You will be excommunicated, that much is certain. And there are those who might take the rest into their own hands."

Timaeus said lightly, "Well, that doesn't seem too certain. I've been hiding from them for years. I'll say my piece and depart. It will be the same as it has been."

Eusebius shook his head sternly. He waved at Philippus. "Tell him what else you've discovered, son."

Nervously, Philippus spoke. "They know who she is, too," he said, tilting his head slightly toward Sophia.

"Sophia? They know she's a woman?"

"Well, yes sir. They know that." Philippus clearly had more to say, but stopped short.

Timaeus frowned. "Yes. I see how that could be bad. But I don't know of any rule against a woman appearing at Council."

"Oh, for our Lord's sake," Eusebius exclaimed. "If that was all, it would be quite enough. You know very well that only bishops, priests and deacons are invited. She's a woman, so she is an impostor. That alone might cause Constantine to take it as a personal affront. But that's not all. Tell them the rest, Philippus. I won't say it."

Looking squarely at the floor, Philippus blurted, "They say she was a notorious prostitute in Antioch. They said she was famous as Adama."

Silence covered the room like volcanic ash. The only sound

was Philippus' hard breathing, brought on by the anxiety of having spoken the last words and the uncertainty of whether, in so speaking, he had sinned against God.

Sophia broke the silence. To Philippus' surprise, her voice did not fade in shame, but rang with exasperation. "I have been urging Timaeus to leave since we got here. I did not want him to come at all. I have been living in particular fear for him since the first day, when I saw Eustathius at the Council."

"Eustathius?" Eusebius questioned.

"Yes. I knew him. In Antioch."

"Bishop Eustathius?"

"Well, he was not bishop at that time."

"You knew him?"

"Yes. He was a patron."

"My Lord!"

Timaeus arose and paced the room. "Yes," he said, "I see how I have put Sophia in danger. Sophia, you will not attend the Council. I will say my piece and rejoin you as quickly as possible. There, my friend, does that satisfy you?"

Eusebius and Sophia spoke in one voice. "No!"

Eusebius continued, searching for any argument that might divert Timaeus from his course. "Even if you do not care about your own safety, what about the girl's? What is she to do? Stay here? As if they don't know where you are staying."

Now it was Sophia's turn. "I can take care of myself. But I don't care a fig for my life if they kill you, Timaeus. Listen to your friend. Let us leave tonight."

Timaeus did not respond to Sophia, but to Eusebius he said, "How do they know where we are staying?"

Eusebius shot back, "How did we know? It was not hard to find out. Your innkeeper is so proud of having a bishop lodging here he has told the entire city. He says the good bishop prefers his inn to the palace. Everyone in Nicaea who knows who you are, knows where you stay."

"If that is so, then we must be quite safe. Otherwise, harm would have come to us already."

Eusebius grunted in disgust. "These men are not common murderers," he said. "They will not conspire or plan among themselves to kill you or the girl. They will rage against your effrontery, your apostasy, your moral decrepitude until one of them, not a bishop, certainly, takes action on his own, without the knowledge, but with the blessings of the others. You must leave here Timaeus, as the girl advises."

Eusebius arose. "We must leave now, Timaeus. We have been here too long already. You are a lost soul, to be sure. But you have a good heart and have been a good friend. I hope you will soon follow us out that door and I hope the next time I see you is when you come to me in Caesarea to repent your folly and rejoin the flock. Until then, beware. Follow the girl's advice. She has more wisdom than you, I think."

Eusebius motioned for Philippus to follow. Philippus cast another furtive glance at Sophia and fell in behind his bishop. Before they reached the door, Sophia stopped them. "Bishop Eusebius," she said, her voice suddenly trembling. "When we were in Caesarea, I took a book from your library. I do not know why I did it. I could not even read. But I took it and I would like to return it now and ask for your forgiveness."

Sophia pulled the book from beneath the pallet and reached it toward the learned bishop. Without touching it or opening it he instantly recognized it, as he would have recognized most of the two thousand books he owned. "A volume of Gnostic texts, *Mary, The Apocryphon of John* and *The Sophia of Jesus Christ*. Tell me, Sophia, how did you come to take this volume, of all others? Did Timaeus put you up to it? After all, if you cannot read, you certainly did not know what you were taking."

"I did not know what I was taking," Sophia replied. "Timaeus did not know I took it until later. I was so ashamed, I did not tell him until we were well gone from Caesarea."

Eusebius smiled. "I find it nothing short of amazing that you took this particular volume. And you cannot even read."

"I said I could not read when I took it. I can read now. Timaeus has taught me."

Eusebius laughed. "Taught by a blind man to read? Perhaps the age of miracles has not passed." As his laughter subsided, Eusebius said, "You are forgiven for your theft, Sophia. And let me now offer you the volume as a gift. If you returned it to me, it would likely be destroyed within a few years. My successors will not likely see the historical value of such texts and it only takes one to destroy a work for all time. So keep it. And if you ever make it back to Caesarea, I will give you the remainder of their ilk that I have."

"Does that meet with your approval, Timaeus?" Eusebius asked. "I hope it gives you something to look forward to."

Timaeus had stopped paying attention. His crooked fingers crawled their way through the thicket of his black and grey hair. Without answering Eusebius' questions, it appeared to no one in particular, Timaeus exclaimed, "I have money, you know. Family money. I was the eldest. My father was quite wealthy. I entrusted my share of the estate to my younger brother, but he promised to provide for me if I was ever in need. I have some money in my own name, as well. Held by a banker in Cappadocia. Quite a bit of it, I think. I can provide for Sophia. Even if something were to happen to me, I could provide for her."

Eusebius hesitated. "I do not know what you're talking about," he said.

"No," replied Timaeus. "I never told anyone. But my point is, she would be provided for, if something were to happen to me."

"That is not what I want," Sophia said. "I want you out of here."

More practically, Eusebius said, "You may give her what you have on your person, if you would like. But as for anything not in your possession, it passes to your heirs. Sophia is not an heir."

"Marry us then," Timaeus blurted.

"What?"

"Marry us."

Eusebius long face was overcome with an expression of horror and wonder, but he quickly converted it to anger. "She is a prostitute. This only goes to prove that you are not thinking straight."

"She was a prostitute. I purchased her freedom."

"Alright, she was a prostitute. That alone should dissuade you."

"Did not Jesus forgive Magdalene and make her foremost among his disciples?"

"I would not say foremost. That is your belief. And, besides, I do not believe that Magdalene and the prostitute were the same woman."

Ignoring Eusebius' rebuke, Timaeus challenged, "Did not the resurrected Christ appear first to her, even before Peter?"

Eusebius changed direction. "You have been living in sin. I could not tarnish my office by performing the ceremony."

"We have been celibate."

Eusebius turned to Sophia. "Is this true?"

Sophia spoke deliberately, "Timaeus does not lie."

"Those are careful words. Answer this: have you been celibate?"

"I have not even been alone with another man since Timaeus purchased my freedom."

"See," Timaeus said, "your objections fall away. Marry us, so that she may be protected."

"You are not a Christian, so I cannot marry you."

"I say that we are and are willing to swear any oath you desire. We will take communion, if you'd like."

"You are a heretic."

"I have not been excommunicated."

"She has not been baptized."

Sophia spoke up, "Yes I was. In Alexandria. When I was twelve. Athanasius himself baptized me." She did not describe his peculiar method of administering her baptismal rights.

"There is no marriage contract," Eusebius said. "Without a marriage contract, a marriage could not protect her claim of rights."

"Either one of us could write one in minutes. But since you can see, it would be better if you did the writing."

"This is folly. You have not thought this through. What would be the terms?"

"All that is mine becomes hers. Upon my death, I leave everything to my beautiful wife Sophia, formerly known as Hypatia of Alexandria."

"And her dowry? There must be a dowry for the marriage contract to be legal."

"Her volume of *The Gospel of Mary, The Apocryphon of John* and *The Sophia of Jesus Christ*, which I have coveted these many years."

"She stole that property."

"You gave it to her not ten minutes ago. It is now hers and that is why I want to marry her, so that it can be mine."

Eusebius' laughter burst forth like the bells of Jerusalem on Easter Sunday. He reached behind his head and gave a sharp tug on his flowing mane. Regaining his solemnity, he said, "You have an answer for everything, Timaeus. I will not perform the ceremony, but I will have you married upon two conditions."

"Name them," Timaeus said.

"First, Philippus must agree to it. He must perform it. I can protect him if it ever comes out what was done and where and why. But I cannot protect myself if I am at the center of the charge. So, first, Philippus, would you do it?"

All eyes and Timaeus' stars turned toward Philippus. The young man turned ashen, churning over in his mind whether performing the ceremony might be a sin, whether it was the right thing to do. Whether – and it was the first time he had any such thought – he should do any act that would forever bind this beautiful woman to another man. He looked up in confusion at Sophia, thinking he did not want her to marry this old man. He did not want to do a thing that did not seem right.

As these thoughts traversed opaquely across Philippus' face, Sophia spoke. "Nobody has asked me whether I consent," she said, solemnly. "Nobody has asked me whether I want to give up my only possession, my beloved and prized book, just so I can be married to a blind, old man who seems bent upon courting trouble at every turn. Why don't you ask me, Timaeus? Why don't you ask me whether I would marry such a fool?"

Surprise crossed Timaeus' face and he blurted, "I am trying to protect you, Sophia. I got you into this. If you and Eusebius are right, I may not be able to get out of it. I want you to be provided for."

"That does not sound like a real marriage to me, Timaeus. What if I want a real marriage? What if I want a husband, instead of just a marriage? Will I be getting a husband?"

Eusebius solemnly added, "Marriage must always be primarily for procreation."

"Exactly," said Sophia. "I want children, Timaeus. Will you give me children?"

This was beyond anything Timaeus had contemplated. In the year she had travelled with him Sophia had never given any indication that she wanted marriage. They were on a spiritual quest together. There was something about her that had reached out to him, led him to her. Jesus had come to him in a dream and told him that she would be the keeper of gnosis for the ages. Once he found her, she had been dedicated to his quest. She speedily learned to read and write upon his instruction. She went wherever he directed. He looked out for her and she for him, but their greater, common journey, was for knowledge of the Pleroma and Ennoia. They were trying to know and become one with the All. What did that have to do with such worldly things as marriage and children? Maybe he had been mistaken. Maybe she had simply followed him obediently, as a slave should follow her master, a wife her husband? How could he not have known? As these things raced through his mind, Timaeus was clear that he wanted to provide for her, regardless of anything else. And so he said, meekly, "I will give you what you want, Sophia."

To which, Sophia replied, "Good. Then I will marry you. And the first thing I want is for us to leave this city."

Timaeus frowned, but said nothing. Instead, Eusebius said, "Philippus still has not consented to perform the rites."

"Will you, Philippus?" Sophia asked.

Gazing at her beautiful face, Philippus said yes.

"Thank you," Sophia replied.

"Good," said Timaeus. "What is your second condition, Eusebius?"

"Sophia has already extracted it for me. You must leave this city."

"We are agreed, then."

Eusebius rubbed his whiskers. "Philippus will return in the hour with the marriage contract. He will perform the sacred ceremony and witness the agreement. Then you will leave. Is everyone agreed?"

Eusebius and Philippus quickly left the inn.

Once the two had left, Sophia started gathering their things into bundles. If she felt the weight of what had just happened, she did not show it. If she was excited about the coming nuptials, there was no sign. Instead she simply said, "I am gathering our things, Timaeus. We have to leave as soon as we are wed."

"I need something to write on," Timaeus replied. "There is a piece of vellum, some ink and a reed in my sack. Would you find them for me?"

"Whatever you have to write, you can write it after we are out of here."

"We cannot leave before morning," Timaeus said. "It would be more dangerous to leave our shelter tonight. If they were coming for us here, they would have done so by now. We'll leave in the morning. In the meantime I have a message for Eusebius."

So, obediently, Sophia unpacked their few possessions and handed the writing materials to Timaeus.

Timaeus found the corners of the vellum and began writing, using the dowry as his writing table.

In less than an hour Philippus returned with a parchment scroll, a Bible and a codex of sacraments. As the great night chirped with the sound of frogs and insects, Timaeus wed Sophia by the open flame of an old clay lamp.

Before Philippus left, Timaeus handed him the vellum on which he had written and instructed him to deliver it to Eusebius.

When it came time to lie on the pallet, Timaeus took his usual position facing opposite Sophia. She sat up. "You are now my husband," she asserted. "It is my right that you lie with me face to face."

A puzzled look passed across his brow, but without objection he burrowed his way under the blanket and came out with his head inches from hers. He thought it was from this mild exercise that his heart was now pounding, drowning out the steady screeching of the crickets that seconds before had serenaded them with their plaints of blind longing. He heard, just barely, the low, sweet call of a night bird as it, too, sought love in the dark. Sophia's hands cupped Timaeus' face. They were no longer the soft, satin instruments of Antioch. They were toughened from her journey and stained from the ink of her writing practice. But they were as tender as a water rush in summer's bloom as her fingers felt the contours of his grizzled cheeks.

"I wish you could see me tonight," Sophia said. "I am sure

you have made me quite beautiful, even if my hair is mannish. I will grow it out for you again, so that you may run your fingers through it whenever you like."

Then, suddenly, without warning, Timaeus felt her lips against the hollows of his eyes, then his nose and finally his mouth. Her unexpected kisses were unlike anything he had ever felt or tasted. Sweeter than a ripe date that washed over his mouth and filled him with an ancient desire he had never before unearthed. The slight gape of her mouth on his mouth and the soft, almost imperceptible press of her tongue against his lips sent an ecstatic jolt through his entire body. His mouth involuntarily opened and her tongue cavorted slowly and tenderly with his.

Without will, without consciousness, except for an awareness of the supreme and unnamable bliss that coursed through his body and filled his mind, Timaeus surrendered. Her hands, the hands now of a goddess, found their way down between his legs where she took hold firmly, but gently with both hands and began to caress and stroke, pulling him into a new and more intense world of pleasure and joy. He was surrendering, losing himself as he had done in his dreams of the past two nights. She slid weightlessly on top of him and he felt the roiling, ecstatic swirl of all things, all pleasures, all joys as he merged once again with the All.

A final murmur of earthly consciousness gripped him and he said, "Wait." She did not wait. "I do not know what to do," he protested. "I have never done this before."

As she guided his pulsing *verpa* slowly and exquisitely between her legs, she said, "Yes, you have."

Consciousness fading into ecstasy, almost unaware that he spoke, Timaeus said, "I assure you I have not."

Her movements and the sweet, wet pull of her love now erased the last vestige of his will. The last thing he heard as he surrendered to the Pleroma of her love was her sweet words, confidently spoken, "and I assure you that you have."

Chapter Nineteen

Bursting Asunder in the Midst

May 23, 325 A.D. – Nicaea

Therefore there are many deaths which burden their thoughts. For I foretell it to those who have a heart.
The Paraphrase of Shem

The next morning, Timaeus emerged from the other world before dawn. A remnant of his dream, in the soft touch of Sophia's arm, was draped across his chest. He slowly, gently, lovingly lowered it to her side and slipped out of bed without waking her. He noiselessly pulled on his cassock and carried his sandals as he slipped out of the room.

By the time Sophia awoke, Timaeus had made his way to Constantine's palace. As he passed a guard inquired, "No comely scribe to attend you today, sir?"

"He is ill today," Timaeus answered brusquely and proceeded to find his seat in the almost empty hall.

He sat as the hall filled and his thoughts drifted over the dreams of the past three nights. He knew that last night was real, that Sophia had made love to him. Fleetingly he feared that every act of physical love was as powerful and transforming as what he felt last night. For the first time he thought of her in the brothel in Antioch, pleasing so many men. Perhaps, to her, last night was nothing more than that, an old man pleased and sent on his way. But she did not send him on his way. He had slipped out like a thief. She was his wife. His loving wife. For the first time in many years he had something of this world for which to live, to which to look forward. Was this the supreme trick of Yaldabaoth? Did he coat the common act of copulation with a relish so sweet that people would be tied to this world and blinded to the greater joy of Ennoia?

Those doubts were fleeting. The greater confusion arose from his inability to separate the dreams of the two prior nights from the reality of his wedding night. They were all of a piece. Each time he was swept up into a world that was at once conscious and utterly without consciousness. It was as though Sophia was the true Sophia and that with her he had accessed that world beyond worlds where chaos and unity, life and death, being and nonexistence had no rank or distinction. A world where faith yielded to experience. He had attained gnosis.

Eusebius frowned at Timaeus as he passed by. Philippus kept his head bowed as he followed Eusebius into the hall. Alexander of New Rome pointed a boney, ancient finger toward him and glowered as he spoke to Alexander of Alexandria, Athanasius and Hosius. Many others cast angry stares at him as they took their seats. Timaeus saw none of this, of course, but he felt the weight of the hostility that settled in around him. Finally, bells rang and the Emperor swept in with a swish of thick, brocaded fabric against the marble floor and the heavy, muted bounce of gold against satin.

Sophia awoke in a fit of rage. Timaeus was gone and she knew to where. She had married him to keep him safe. She had made love to him to seal the pact. She had tried to give him something for which to live.

She understood, or thought she did, his quest for gnosis. It intrigued her and amused her. She did not know how he knew, or could know, all he seemed to know about such things as Adam and Eve, Noah and Norea, Yaldabaoth, Sophia, the Ennoia or the Pleroma. On the other hand these things were not less believable to her than any of the other faiths of which she had learned. At the brothel in Antioch there had been believers of many faiths. She had met other Christians, of course, of the more orthodox variety. She had known a centurion who had faith in the mysteries of Mithras and claimed to be a seventh grade initiate in the cult. She met a Persian who spent his entire time with her worried about whether Ahuramazda would approve of his consorting in a brothel, but went away happy. In the end he consoled himself by overpaying her (or overpaying Ammianus, to be more accurate), saying that it met the God's commandment to actively participate in life through good deeds. She had met a Roman who uttered "Jove almighty," as he watched her disrobe and shouted "Apollo save me," as he came.

Timaeus' quest for gnosis had more to it than the shelvable faiths of these other men. He was true to his quest. The others she met who shared his faith loved and admired him. Such was his humility that she did not know that he was the preeminent Gnostic of his age or that many of the people she had met on her journeys with him called themselves "Timaeans." He had probed deeper into the faith's many texts than anyone had before or anyone would afterward. He could unify the seemingly endless inconsistencies of purpose and design. He knew as well as any person who ever lived that dogma was the enemy of knowledge. He accepted all faiths and beliefs as fragmentary clues in the hunt for the greater, universal truth. Sophia admired these things about him, but she did not share his faith. Instead, she loved Timaeus the man. For the first time in her life she loved a man. The kindest, truest and in some ways the most naïve man in the Empire. And because of this love, when she awoke and found him gone she cared nothing at all for his quest or his faith. Their bags were packed. He had promised to leave with her in the morning. And yet, he had gone off to the Council, where he was determined to have his say and, she feared, meet his end.

A flame of anger toward Timaeus burned within her, kindled by fear and fueled by the Roman fire of her love for him.

Timaeus thought with shame of his promise to Sophia. He knew when he made it that he would not keep it. He was in Nicaea, attending the most important conference of Christians that had ever been held. He was a Christian. The other Christians at the Council intended to set their faith in everlasting stone and to ever after punish divergence. The result would be the opposite of faith and the enemy of truth. Truth cannot be given. It must be learned. It must be experienced. If the Council ended with agreement on a creed, whatever creed it was, it would mean the end of all other creeds, all pathways to knowledge. He knew he was powerless to prevent any outcome, but he could not be who he was and not oppose it.

They were talking now, the bishops. Macarius of Jerusalem had the floor. He was, as even his supporters acknowledged, a simple man, white bearded and white robed, speaking with all the dignity and animation of the statuary that decorated the great hall. He had begun by asserting that by virtue of the importance of the city that was the seat of his See, he should have precedence over all other clerics of Judea. This being so, the weight of his opinion should overpower any contrary argument offered by Eusebius of Caesarea. "Jesus," Macarius said, "is God. It is that simple. There is only one God. God has existed always. God created the Heavens and the Earth. God created man. Because man sinned, God banished him from the Garden of Eden and, thus, from eternal life on Earth. But God loved man. He created man in his own image and did not like to see him forever condemned to a life without hope. So God became Jesus. Mary gave birth to Him so that He could experience all the things man experienced. He lived a man's life. He experienced cares and aches and grief. He lived his life as an example to all men, as a path to be followed in order to reach Heaven. He was scourged, crucified and buried, but rose again to show man that he, too, could experience life after death. After forty days, He ascended into Heaven to rejoin His Father, who was, in fact, Himself."

Macarius' dronish delivery was unaccented by any hint of

wonder or incredulity. He spoke with the certainty of a zealot, but with a passionless zeal. There was no room for doubt in anything he said, from his assertion of supremacy over Eusebius to the miraculous, but unexplained separation and reunification of a single God. He was so sure of the miraculous that it became mundane, not even a cause for wonder.

"There are those," Macarius continued, "who ask, 'How can this be? How can God be both the Father and the Son? How can two be one?' To these doubters I say, 'you do not need to understand these things. It is God's will that you must accept without understanding.' How presumptuous are they who demand understanding of God?"

As Macarius droned on, Timaeus thought of Sophia and the pain he was causing her. He knew she would be angry. He hoped that she would understand that this was something he must do. He would say what he had to say, what needed to be said, and would rejoin her as soon as he could. He hoped she would understand.

Sophia could not understand why Timaeus had to go. What could he possibly hope to accomplish? The men she had listened to at Council were not engaged in a great debate. They were not seeking to learn from each other. They had circled into their own camps and were lobbing missiles at their enemies. Nothing more. Timaeus hoped to reason with them. How could someone so wise be so foolish?

An even greater question was: what was she to do? Her first mind was to put on her robe, slip into the Council and somehow compel Timaeus' departure. She put on the robe and three times resolved to leave the room. Each time her steps were halted by the thought that many dangerous men at Council knew she was a woman; knew, in fact, she had been a prostitute. Would her appearance, then, not make things worse for Timaeus? Perhaps her not being there on this day was a slight measure of protection. Perhaps she was to have been the trigger for their attack. Perhaps Timaeus would stand a better chance of survival if she stayed put.

So she paced and fumed, wondering over and over again why Timaeus had to go to Council. She found herself praying that he would not speak.

Timaeus rose to speak. Macarius had droned to a close and had taken his seat, quite satisfied that he had settled things once and for all. Before any of the more prominent bishops could rise, Timaeus started up.

Addressing the Emperor directly, Timaeus began. "Great Emperor Flavius Valerius Aurelius Constantinus Augustus, I am Timaeus, formerly Bishop of Kaymakli in Cappadocia. And although I no longer hold that office I remain a devout Christian and a fervent believer that Jesus of Nazareth, who was crucified upon the cross at Golgotha during the reign of Emperor Tiberius, is the light that illuminates the pathway to Heaven and is our savior. I ask, Emperor, for permission to address you and this Council."

In the stunned hush that followed among the bishops, Constantine said, "proceed" and before the gasps turned into protests, Timaeus proceeded.

"The difference between the two sides we have heard from this week is very small, very small. Both acknowledge that Jesus is God. Both acknowledge that Jesus lived life and suffered as a man. Both sides recognize that Jesus' suffering was real, that his pain was real, that his passion was real. Both sides proclaim that Jesus was the Son of God. With all these beliefs in common, the amazing thing is that we find room for angry disagreement."

Timaeus' voice was a pleasing middle tenor. His Greek was perfect. His pitch rose and fell in simple modulations that conveyed honesty and sincerity. His welcoming voice was augmented by his physical aspect, from the humble stance to the stars that seemed almost to glow from his eyeless sockets. Constantine the Great took an instant liking to him. Moreover, he wanted what Timaeus proposed, agreement, not dissent. So it was that when Alexander of Alexandria protested that only seated bishops should be allowed to speak, Constantine firmly stated, "Let him continue. He is doing no harm." When Alexander of New Rome proclaimed that Timaeus was a heretic, Constantine asked whether he had been excommunicated.

"Not yet," Alexander of New Rome stated. "Let us proceed to a vote."

"You can vote after you have heard what he has to say." And with that, Timaeus proceeded.

Timaeus smiled. "My old friend, Alexander of Constantinopolis," (Timaeus' use of the city's popular name, which was not yet official, brought a smile to the Emperor's face) "does not think I should speak. He already has one of my eyes as a souvenir and apparently wants my tongue to keep it company." Constantine smiled wryly. "But I assure you, great bishop, I mean no harm. If, when I have spoken, my former colleagues think I should be removed from this conclave and ostracized from our common faith, I will abide their decision and it will not lessen my belief in Jesus as our common savior.

"Alexander of the great city of Alexandria protests that only bishops should speak. With so many here at Council, perhaps that is best, but I cannot help but think that we are missing much wisdom by silencing our juniors. For example, the young associate who accompanied me to Nicaea has suggested a solution to the problem that has divided this Council. All would agree, I think, that Jesus and God, be they Father and Son or Father and Father as Son, share the same *homoousios*. They have but one mind, a common nature, the same essence. Can we not agree on this and agree to continue any remaining debate at our leisure, with Christian love for each other?"

Timaeus could not see the reactions as they crossed the faces of the hall, but from the murmuring that came from the area occupied by the Trinitarians, that they, at least were dissatisfied with the proposal. Hosius gave voice to this dissatisfaction, saying, "If we can agree that their common nature stems from the fact that they are one and the same being, that Father and Son are one, then the problem is solved. But I do not think the Arians will agree, so intent are they at placing Jesus below God."

Eusebius of Caesarea spoke. "Not at all. The Son and the Father sit as one on the thrown of Heaven, with one mind, one will, one nature. I believe Timaeus is right. An agreement that Father and Son have one *homoousios* satisfies."

Constantine was pleased. He had been fearing that the Council would dissolve in disagreements and recriminations and the church that he was depending upon to provide unity to the Empire would itself splinter and fall apart. But this strange, blind man whom he had seen sitting quietly in attendance but had never heard of before had offered a unifying way out of the mess. He was pleased indeed.

Constantine now spoke. "I am not here to vote," he said with exaggerated humility. "My opinion should not be given any more weight than that of any other layman. But it is my suggestion, if you care to hear it, that two or three among you be appointed to devise a new proposal of creed and that the drafters include at least one from those who hold with the Eusebiuses and at least one who holds with the Alexanders. It is further my suggestion, and my suggestion only, that tomorrow being the Sabbath, we reconvene to consider the new proposal two days hence."

Mere suggestion that it was, the matter was quickly put to a vote and passed. Eusebius of Caesarea, Hosius of Cordoba and Alexander of Alexandria were appointed to draft the proposed creed.

Constantine spoke again. "I have matters of state to attend, but I wish to be here whenever my presence might prove helpful. So, I will be here bright and early on Monday." Turning to

Timaeus, he said, "I hope you will give proper praise to your young priest. His suggestion may do a great deal of good, I think. Why is he not here today?"

"Ill, sir," Timaeus answered.

"Not very, I pray," Constantine replied. "I have seen him with you on other days. A pretty lad, I might add."

"Yes, sir," said Timaeus. And he knew he should not say more. He knew the Emperor was pleased as things stood. But he had not said what he needed to say. He felt his chance slipping away and knew that it may not come again. Yet, he knew he should go, rejoin Sophia and leave Nicaea.

The Emperor was again speaking to him. "I will tell him so myself on Monday, if he feels better. Please, bring him to me so that I may do so."

"Yes, sir," Timaeus repeated and he knew he should not say more.

Before mid-morning Sophia had found the purse of gold and silver coins and the note that Timaeus had placed inside the clothing parcel she had tied together the night before. The note, in Greek, was written on an upward slant. The letters looked hastily written, without the care he demanded when she practiced writing. It read:

"Sophia. You are my wife now. If anything should happen to me you are entitled to all that is mine. There is gold held by a banker in Cappadocia. My younger brother, Eumenes is his name, sends me some profits from his holdings, when he can find me or whenever I contact him with a request. I have written to him through Eusebius. For now, I am leaving my purse in which you will find what amounts to about fifty solidi – a good start. Eusebius has instructions as to the remainder, should I perish. You may trust him. He has been a good friend. But I do not believe his aid will be necessary.

"I did not want you to have to marry a blind, old man, but it was the only way to assure your survival if the worst happens. You are my Sophia. Never have I felt as close to the Truth as I have since you joined me on my search. I know my search cannot be your search and that you must find gnosis in your own way and in your own time. Trust me, you are closer than you think. Your husband, Timaeus of Kaymakli."

In writing the letter, Timaeus had imagined it would calm her by reassuring her that he had seen to her material needs. It had the opposite effect. There were no words of love and those of affection were limited to gratitude for the assistance she provided to his spiritual quest. He did not yet know how much she loved him. Or that she loved him at all. How she hoped the fool would not speak at Council!

Timaeus could hear the rustling of Constantine's robes and Hosius ask Nicholas of Myra to give a prayer of benediction. Still standing, Timaeus asked the Emperor if he could say one thing more. Constantine sighed, but said yes.

"It is only this," Timaeus began. "Twelve years ago, Great Constantine, you decreed that religious liberty ought not to be denied, but ought to be granted to the judgment and desire of each individual to perform his religious duties according to his own choice. This was true and just and proper. We who have lived in these times have witnessed miracle upon miracle, foremost among these may be that our Christian faith, whose followers for three hundred years have been robbed, beaten, tortured and murdered for their faith, is now the faith of the Empire. And I am afraid that a church cannot be a good ruler or a ruler a good Christian.

"But what I am even more fearful of is that this marriage between Church and Empire will result in barriers being erected in the way of the individual's path to salvation. I call myself a Christian because I follow Christ. I believe that the life of Jesus is the light that illuminates the pathway to heaven. But I believe that all men and all women can, like Jesus, become one with the true God. It is my belief, no, it is my experience that with faith and knowledge we mortals can enter the heavenly realm and merge with God. For that there are those who call me a heretic. For my beliefs I have been removed from my See in Kaymakli. I take no issue with being called a heretic or being removed from my office. But I beg that I be allowed to continue my quest, to perform my own religious duties according to how I choose.

"For I am afraid that when great institutions, such as the Church now is, meet in great assemblages, such as this one in Nicaea, and attempt to decide for all people and for all time that which is true and that which is untrue, that real Truth is lost. And when that Church has the power of the Empire behind it, the search for Truth is inevitably suppressed. Let us not carve Jesus in stone, as we do the old Roman gods. The concepts of God and Creation and all that is meant by them are so complex, so overwhelming, that the degree of generalization necessary to convey their existence precludes any explanation or description of their particular aspects. Yet by ignoring their particular aspects we leave out so much that the general concepts become small and insufficient. You see, I believe that real Truth, real knowledge of God and unity with God, can only be realized on an individual basis, one person at a time. Not through a profession of faith, a secret incantation, or prescribed rituals, but through a life of faithful seeking for knowledge. We can and must help each other along our way, but we must be free to pursue our own path, to err and discover our own errors, to stray from the path and to find the path again, and to do all of these things without our bodies being broken, imprisoned or destroyed. Let no books be burned. Let no worshipers be crucified for their faith. Let our places of worship be respected. Whatever this Council decides, keep your decree alive, I pray."

Before the clerics could mount any coherent outrage or other response, Constantine, who was anxious to depart, said, "You raise some interesting points, Timaeus, which I am sure will be more fully explored in the coming days. Could Nicholas proceed now with the benediction."

As midday approached, Sophia felt the weariness born of four hours of anxiety. She attempted to boost her hope with the thought that time was an ally, that the more time passed without her hearing that anything wrong had happened, the more likely it was that nothing wrong would happen. She knew that the town of Nicaea carried any news from the Council more swiftly than a mountain stream and that the innkeeper seemed to be an immediate source of all news from the palace hall. Surely, if something had happened, if a bishop had been harmed, he would have known and reported it to her. But these thoughts brought slight consolation and the elastic minutes brought eternities of disquietude. She sat and waited and worried.

Constantine left promptly following the benediction. Sightless and without Sophia to guide him, Timaeus waited for the room to clear. As he was waiting he heard a sharply pitched voice greeting him. "That was an interesting speech, Timaeus." With this, the unknown speaker clasped both of Timaeus' hands in his and rubbed them with purpose. There was a noticeable greasy feel to the stranger's grasp.

"I do not recognize your voice," Timaeus said. "May I have the honor of hearing your name?" But the hands released their grip and their owner departed without a further word.

As Eusebius passed by, he spoke to Timaeus in an undertone, without stopping. "I hope you will leave town promptly now. Not a minute to lose. That was Athanasius of Alexandria who just greeted you."

As the room thinned, Timaeus could hear voices, many of them saying such things as "heretic," and "sacrilege," and "outrage" and he knew the words were in reference to him. Once, unconsciously, he placed his hand to his lips and immediately tasted the bitterness of the oil that had been deposited on them. He wiped his hands on his robe and took a drink of water from a cup he felt for on the table.

By the time he had reached the Hall's exit he was feeling nauseous. By the time he reached the bottom of the thirty-two steps of the hall he had begun to vomit and defecate, simultaneously, uncontrollably, blood contaminating the vomitus and excrement. He collapsed in a faint and was dead within three minutes. Nobody came to his aid. Those who passed by, even some future saints of the Church, gave wide berth and looked down in disgust. Nicholas of Myra was among these. Timaeus' last few moments of consciousness were filled with pain and disgust. Nothing more.

Philippus arrived at the inn shortly after noon with news of Timaeus' death. To Philippus' surprise, Sophia did not swoon or shriek. She simply said that she must go to claim Timaeus' body.

"No," Philippus insisted. "Father Eusebius will see to the burial. He believes you are not safe. I believe that as well. In accordance with Eusebius' promise and in honor of his friendship with Timaeus, I have been tasked with getting you out of town. I can take you as far as Caesarea, though you must not stop there. If you have a preferred destination somewhere between here and there, I will take you. It is best if we go by sea."

He spoke quickly. Sophia sensed that he was as frightened for his own safety as well as hers.

"I cannot allow you to place yourself in danger for me," she said. "I will make my own way."

"No," Philippus said firmly. "This must be done. The promise must be fulfilled. I will accompany you. We must go now."

Without a further word, without a tear, Sophia grabbed her two parcels and followed Philippus out the door.

As they passed the innkeeper, Sophia paused and pressed a

coin into his hand. "Thank you for your discretion," she said, though he had not been at all discrete.

"Young sir, young sir," he said to Sophia, "is you going without the old man then?"

Sophia continued with her own purpose: "If not in the past, for the future then." A perplexed look came over the man's face and the two young traveling companions were quickly gone. As they rounded a street corner, Sophia looked back and saw Athanasius and the priest Paulus approaching the inn from the other direction.

Chapter Twenty

Into Egypt

May – September, 325 A.D. – Asia, Palestine and Egypt

There are men who make many journeys, but make no progress towards any destination.
The Gospel of Philip

Sophia ended up in Luxor Province on the Upper Nile in Egypt. It was not her choice to settle in a place so remote from anything she had known before. She travelled with Philippus by sea after walking the first thirty-five miles overland to old Byzantium, New Rome, Constantinopolis – it was called all these names along the way. A merchant vessel took them across the Sea of Marmara to Dardanella, near the long buried and forgotten ruins of ancient Troy. Hugging the Aegean coast, they chartered a fishing boat manned by four sailors who were in their twenties, but looked old enough to have sailed with Odysseus. The crew claimed descent from Crete and kept the pair fearfully entertained with warnings of each approaching hazard and the ships and crew whose existences had been claimed there. The fate of the vessels held no less tragedy for the four than that of the sailors who perished with them. They called their ship "The Maenad," with all earnestness, though it was not much larger than was sufficient to accommodate the two passengers and crew. Philippus and Sophia sat and slept on nets crusted in fish scales and had little to say to the crew or each other. The boat stopped unexpectedly at Kos, with the fishermen saying they would go no further. They turned a deaf ear when Sophia protested that they had promised passage to Cyprus and refused to return any of the payment. The Maenad, they said, had told them that an ancient serpent had taken up residence in the waters just to the south of Kos and there was nothing more they could do.

Sophia and Philippus travelled as priests. Sophia took the name Hypatius, adapting her birth name for the purpose. Although Philippus had been sent as her protector, it was Sophia who did all the haggling, told all the tales and paid all the fares and bribes necessary for their passage. They were stranded in Kos for a week.

Sophia arranged passage on a merchant ship to Kallinikisis on the Island of Cyprus. It was a thriving city of more than 10,000 with an abundant market and houses that were opened to the wayfarer as inns for accommodation. After another two weeks they were able to book passage to Berytus. On this final, week-long passage, Sophia was frequently ill. The mariners and Philippus took her illness for seasickness, but by the time they reached port she knew she was carrying Timaeus' child. They walked the final hundred miles of their journey to Caesarea, taking five days. During that leg of the journey, Sophia told Philippus she was pregnant.

Sophia thought of how strange it was to be traveling the same roads she had travelled with Timaeus six months earlier. Those early days with Timaeus were so full of wonder. It was not so much her interest in his idea of gnosis, of spiritual worlds of which she had never heard or suspected. It was more the wonder of such a man, blind, but knowing, pursued but happy, wise but trusting. That such a man could exist among men, in such times, could lead and inspire men and women and yet adhere to his own path, is where Sophia found her wonder. Now, traveling the same roads with Philippus, there was the same fear of pursuit without the happiness. In every physical way Philippus was stronger than Timaeus. Taller and younger and with eyes to guide him. Yet it was Sophia who led. It was Sophia who brought the stoutness of heart to the journey. Many times she would find him looking at her with what she took to be anxious eyes, the eyes of a frightened puppy looking to its master for protection. His principle use to her was as a prop, another priest whose company made her guise more credible. Before entering Caesarea, Sophia, with Philippus' back turned, changed out of the priest's cassock and into traveling tunics, outer and inner.

She had not grieved when she learned of Timaeus' death and she did not grieve on the journey from Nicaea. There was no time or place for grief. She would grieve later. For now, she subsisted on the indelible, but functioning sadness that is the lot in life of most women in most times.

Despite the absence of Eusebius and several others whom Eusebius had taken with him to Nicaea, the household was quite active. A deacon named Acacius was left in charge and there were a dozen others with various roles. Among these were four women who labored to provide food and accommodation for the men of the household. Upon their arrival, Philippus explained to Acacius the nature of his mission and the meaning of his arrival without Eusebius and with a woman as companion.

Acacius had received word from Eusebius, telling him, mysteriously, to expect unusual company. It came in a single sentence buried in a more detailed report about the proceedings at Nicaea. Eusebius' letter had travelled faster than the seven weeks the journey had taken Sophia and Philippus.

Acacius' first thought upon seeing Sophia was that she should stay at the house and work and have employment with the other women. But when Philippus told Acacius about what had happened to Timaeus at Nicaea and that Sophia was Timaeus' widow, it was agreed that she be removed from Caesarea as soon as possible. The revelation of her pregnancy put those plans on hold. Philippus advised Acacius not to write to Eusebius about the matter for fear that the Trinitarians would learn of the circumstances and allege complicity with a heretic.

In the end the two men decided that Sophia would stay in the room of the senior maid until she gave birth and could travel with the child. When they told Sophia of their plan, she would have none of it.

"I'm not going to stay here, with any connection to Eusebius at all. Do you really think the people who killed Timaeus would not find out?"

"Where to you propose to go?" Acacius asked sternly.

"Alexandria. Back where I came from."

"You would be even more at risk there," Acacius said. "Alexander's priest, Athanasius, has spies everywhere."

"I hate that man."

"We must love our enemies."

"Not I."

In the end, she agreed to accompany Philippus to Chenoboskion in Luxor Province. Acacius explained that in addition to the fertile farmlands of the Nile Valley, a community was growing up there under the influence of a monastery founded by Pachomius. The monks were famous for teaching Christianity to nonbelievers, converting many to the faith. To Acacius this seemed to be an important asset of Chenoboskion. The fact that her native language was Coptic, which Sophia could speak and now write, was also an advantage. It was far enough away from the centers of the controversy that it was unlikely her identity would be discovered. She would stay there until the child was born and was able to travel. Hopefully by then her small role at Nicaea would be forgotten. Sophia stipulated that the journey must begin almost immediately so that she could be situated well before her child was born. Three days after they arrived at Caesarea, Sophia and Philippus were again on the road, dressed in priests' clothing.

Before they departed, another letter arrived from Eusebius. Acacius read it aloud to Sophia and Philippus:

"Dear beloved Acacius, brother in Christ,

"Matters at Council move toward a close. Such is the divine and heavenly grace accorded us by our Savior's appearance and so great is the abundance of good things that peace will be provided for all human kind. We know that the envy that hates what is good and the demon who loves all that is evil still lurks, but by the Grace of our Heavenly Father, great matters have been decided for the good and, God willing, the Evil One shall be placed in shackles, at least for a time.

"There is good news from Nicaea. First, I have been reinstated into the bosom of the Church. Further, the good bishops and benevolent Constantine, sitting in Council, have devised a Creed upon which all can agree who have Love for Christ in their hearts. The Creed declares that Jesus Christ is the Son of God, begotten from the Father, only-begotten, that is, from the being of the Father, God from God, light from light, begotten not made, homoousios with the Father, through Whom all things came into being. The Creed also contains these anathemas: For those who say, here was when He was not, and, before being born He was not, and that He came into existence out of nothing, or who assert that the Son of God is of a different substance, or is subject to alteration or change, these the Catholic and apostolic Church condemns.

"Before signing the Creed, I asked for and received certain clarifications, including some offered by the Emperor himself, which I warrant satisfactory. All the bishops have signed, saving only Theonas of Marmarica and Secundus of Ptolemais. Great Constantine has banished them along with the Alexandrian priest Arius, whose great sin is pride and refusal to honor the holy hierarchy of the Church. I have been permitted to welcome Arius into our household, provided he not have any official capacity in the Church.

"My dear friend, I believe my adoption of the Creed is consistent with all we have discussed in the past. The Creed is broad enough for us to find shelter under it.

"The Council is now considering canons. The holy bishops have accepted my suggestion for a prohibition on self-castration. I know that certain of the desert wanderers will be disappointed. I have agreed, at Macarius' insistence, upon a canon that provides, "as custom and ancient tradition show that the bishop of Jerusalem ought to be honored, he shall have precedence; without prejudice, however, to the dignity which belongs to the Metropolis." Macarius made his demand for precedence with all the pomp he could summon and, since the Council and Emperor agreed that Jerusalem's precedence does not come at the expense of the dignity of Caesarea, I perceive no harm that can arise from it. Other matters being decided on I can best convey when I return, which journey, God willing, should commence within a week or at most two.

"Of the matter I referenced in my last letter, I trust and pray that by now the pilgrim has passed through.

"There was a commotion at Council several weeks back. A failed Christian who was once a bishop in Cappadocia, Timaeus by name, addressed the Emperor at Council as if he were still a bishop and not a heretic. He made a sacrilegious and impertinent attack on the divinity of Jesus and was immediately struck down by God Himself. Within minutes of his speech, he 'burst asunder in the midst, and all his bowels gushed out,' as is written in The Acts of Judas Iscariot. The three patriarchs, Alexander of Alexandria, Eustathius of Antioch and Alexander of New Rome, have ordered a search for the young scribe that attended Timaeus here, so that he might be questioned about this mischief, but he has vanished into thin air.

"If Philippus has arrived, be so kind as to read this letter to him. I know he wished to stay with me here in Nicaea and would have done so but for the circumstances that compelled his departure.

"Blending love of goodness with hatred of evil and secure in the knowledge that the shepherd I have appointed has well tended my flock, I send you my fondest regards and hope to bestow all blessings and thanks which it is in my power to bestow not long hence.

"Eusebius Pamphili, Bishop of Caesarea."

Sophia and Philippus began the next phase of their journey the following morning.

The distance from Caesarea to Memphis was about 350 miles, a far journey, but the roads were good and well-traveled and a carriage was available most of the way. This part of the journey took seven days, with the summer sun nagging them the entire way. From Memphis to Chenoboskion was about 500 miles and took ten more days. They hung close to the Nile and were refreshed by several cooling bursts of rain. They were robbed once, three days south of Memphis, by a group of errant Bedouins, but Sophia had so skillfully hidden the gold and silver coinage inside her inner tunic that all they lost was a few hundred denarii in change. Sophia could not be certain, but she sensed that their guide knew the robbers. Even with the robbery, the journey from Nicaea to Chenoboskion cost Sophia less than a single Solidus.

The relative comfort of this second journey, compared to the first, allowed more opportunity for conversation. It was an opportunity of which Philippus availed himself most fully.

Sophia learned, for example, that Philippus was born on the first day of the year 301, making him twenty-four years of age. She learned that his father was a leather worker of modest means and that he had four brothers and five sisters. He was the youngest male and seventh child.

He talked incessantly of his vows and his vocation. His parents were Christians, but he felt the particular call of the clergy as far back as he could remember. He spent as much time as he could with his local priest, Father Abacus, learning to read and write so as to be ready to take his vows and obtain a position as soon as he was able.

He took his vows seriously, he assured her. Yes, he was a man, with a man's eyes and desires, but he had taken the additional vow of celibacy, not strictly required by the Church, and had never strayed. Once he asked her not whether she found him attractive or desirable, but, rather, whether he was "the kind of man a woman might want." Sophia's answer, that she supposed so since there was nothing particularly deformed about his person or repulsive about his manners, seemed to boost his spirits. His spirits did not appear to be damaged by her quickly added caveat, "but what would I know? I married a blind and mutilated heretic."

Once she asked him if he would like to know the secret of gaining favor with a woman. He answered that although it would be of no practical use to him, he would very much like to know that secret.

"Refrain from hitting her," was Sophia's reply.

When she thought about it, Sophia thought that Philippus was passing handsome, if only for his youth. Even at twenty-four years old, his beard had not filled out. Its long, brown and reddish wisps did not conceal the angular contours of his face.

His hair was slightly darker, but not fully brown as it hung straight in long, thin strands from his head. He would bald early. He was of fair height, taller than most, but by no means unusually so. His frame was slight and, given his strict observation of every conceivable fast day, not likely to fill out much as time passed. It was hard to tell the color of his eyes as they were a kind of nondescript green or grey or blue depending upon the light, but never brilliant. It was clear when one thought about it that his lineage, whatever it was, paid tribute to an invading race from the north that had long since been subsumed and assimilated by the native soil of Judea. To Sophia he was neither appealing nor repulsive. All in all, he was more than he imagined himself to be, but less in her eyes than he would have wished. If grief, fear and anxiety had left any space for her to think about it, Sophia would have admitted that she was quite fond of Philippus. Beneath the fretful conflict between his desires to be attractive and to stay true to his vows laid the sincere heart of a man who wanted to do what was right both for himself and for others. It was a rare enough quality among the men she had known that in the months and years following his return to Caesarea, Sophia would remember him with fondness.

Before they left Memphis Sophia suggested that she drop the guise of a traveling priest, which, she said, might be awkward to maintain in the event of a challenge or another assault. Philippus readily agreed and added that he, too, should travel as a layman so that it would not appear strange that a priest should be seen traveling with a pregnant woman. Sophia knew her clothes were still sufficient to conceal her condition, but did not object to Philippus' suggestion. She provided the money that Philippus used to purchase a traveling tunic and broad brimmed hat.

For the remainder of the journey, whenever the occasion arose, and often when there was no necessity for it, he posed as her husband and said the pair was moving to Chenoboskion in search of spiritual guidance from Pachomius.

Sophia settled in a house of mud brick that she took by let from a prosperous pagan family who claimed descent from ancient Thebes. The wife's name was Qena, the mother of seven, three boys and four girls, aged infant to ten. She was a sun-dried twenty-eight and employed three servants to assist her in her household duties. Her husband, Cannus, was twice Qena's age. He earned the family's bread through the harvesting of figs and dates, and the renting of a few inherited properties, the diminishing legacy of old family greatness.

Philippus stayed with Sophia a week, alternating between fretting that Eusebius would be expecting him back quickly and offering to stay for as long as Sophia desired. For assistance and companionship, Sophia hired a widow whose children had moved away. Beset had been left homeless with the death of her husband the previous spring and would likely have followed him into the ground by winter without Sophia's intervention. Beset's gratitude to Sophia had no limit. Once she was settled, Sophia sent Philippus back to Caesarea and assumed the role of widow, at long last allowing grief to wash over her in recurrent waves of longing and loss. Philippus' parting look was that of a dog whom his master had sold to another.

Chapter Twenty-One

Chenoboskion

September 325 – January 326 – Chenoboskion

What came into being as a result of verbal expression, the gods and the angels and mankind finished. Now as for the ruler Yaldabaoth, he is ignorant of the force of Pistis [Sophia]: he did not see her face, rather he saw in the water the likeness that spoke with him. And because of that voice, he called himself 'Yaldabaoth'. But 'Ariael' is what the perfect call him, for he was like a lion. Now when he had come to have authority over matter, Pistis Sophia withdrew up to her light.
On The Origin Of The World

Hypatia settled down comfortably in Chenoboskion. With the stress of travel behind, her pregnancy became comfortable, natural. The thought of Timaeus' child growing within brought her joy, but she thought often of how strange a journey she had made with him. He had appeared in her brothel in Antioch, the most incongruous of visions. He had purchased her from Ammianus before he even spoke to her. He told her she was Sophia, the possessor of knowledge and protector of gnosis for the ages. He asked her to come away with him and she did, not because she thought she possessed or would ever possess any particular knowledge or that she knew the first thing about this thing he called "gnosis." She did not. But she went with him anyway. Why was that? It was not for fear of disappointing him. It was true that his confidence that he had found what he had spent a lifetime seeking was profound and unsettling, but she had disappointed men before. That was not it. It was more that he had awakened in her something that had been asleep for as long as she could remember. Timaeus had awakened her self. It would never again sleep.

But the rest of it made little sense in retrospect. The first few months, wandering through the holy land, she thought she was learning something. She learned the basics of Timaeus' faith. She felt its poetry and appeal. She enjoyed the company of seekers they travelled to see. She marveled at their faith and the humble obstinacy it took to reject accepted structures and dogma in order to seek something more that nobody seemed able to clearly articulate. She exalted at the women having an equal share with the men. She saw Timaeus' mission to this flock. He was an essential, but unobtrusive missionary, never insisting that his thoughts were any better than anyone else's, but always ready with some appropriate, memorized text, or insightful words or provoking question. For the rest of her life, Hypatia would remember these first few months with fondness, for the journey and the man.

After the visit to Caesarea, everything changed. Timaeus changed. When he learned about Constantine's Council he departed from the journey they had been on together and set off on a new and foolish errand of self-destruction. It is true that it was only after he had embarked on this reckless course that she realized she loved him. But it was not the Timaeus bent on self-ruin that she loved. No. She loved the Timaeus of the spiritual journey, the blind Timaeus with his head in the Pleroma. It took his exchange of that journey for a quest for disaster to make her aware of her love. She had hoped her love could save him. She had hoped that love from his Sophia would return him to his spiritual quest. She had failed. She was not Sophia.

In Chenoboskion, she took the name Hypatia, the first name of which she had any memory. The bishops did not know her by that name and would be unlikely to discover her 500 miles south of Alexandria. She reckoned that the search for her would soon be abandoned. With Beset beside her she considered what

Timaeus had left her: fifty gold solidi (forty-nine remaining), a book containing Gnostic texts, the ability to read them, and a child healthily growing in her womb.

Chenoboskion was dry and hot. As October crept in, the temperatures slipped down into the 90s during the day and fell to the 70s at night, providing a measure of comfort that had been absent since Sophia's, that is, Hypatia's arrival. Rain, when it came at all, seeped desolately from barren clouds in quantities barely sufficient to distinguish it from the ever-present sweat upon her changing body. The nearby Nile, having yielded its silt and receding from its summer pregnancy, provided no measure of relief. For the first month, Hypatia and Beset mostly sat in the house, shaded by palms. Beset would go to market and prepare the meals. Hypatia watched curiously as Beset performed the woman's routine household duties that she had never done. In the evening, they would talk, mostly about Beset's past and the life of Chenoboskion, in the Egyptian tongue Hypatia had not spoken in almost five years.

Apart from Roman officials and merchants, Chenoboskion did not attract many outsiders. Set upon the west bank of the eastward shifting Nile, it was a part of the vast breadbasket of Rome, yielding immeasurable quantities of wheat annually in tribute to the Empire. Whatever their station, most of the people who lived in the town were involved in the process of producing and delivering grain, as their ancestors had been for thousands of years before them. The old pharaohs had presided over the creation of a great hydraulic civilization founded upon the levees and canals constructed to domesticate the river. Like all wild creatures, the Nile was never safe, never tame, but for its time and given their materials, the rulers and engineers and slaves who built those systems accomplished a feat as impressive as anything mankind has accomplished since. The annual commemoration of their accomplishment was not a date on a calendar, but the feeding of the world.

The Nile Valley was long, but narrow. The house Hypatia let was on the western part of the settlement. Cannus' ancestors had owned large tracts of fertile farmland, but the deliquescent stock of successive generations had failed to follow the Nile's eastward migration. Although water was still available from nearby irrigation troughs, the river no longer deposited its rich silt so far to the west and the soil could support only the deep-rooted palm and fig trees.

Hypatia did not realize that immediately upon her arrival in Chenoboskion she had become the focus of intense speculation. A beautiful, single woman with a child in her womb who seemed to have the means to support herself led naturally to the conclusion that she was either the concubine of an important official or wealthy merchant with a jealous wife or the wayward daughter of such a man. The town settled upon the former explanation, since it was more likely that a wayward daughter would have been abandoned or stoned. Beset knew of the town's speculation and tried to stem it by telling all who would listen that Hypatia was a widow who had settled in Chenoboskion for her health. That explanation made no sense and was quickly discarded, especially because Beset could provide no details of the deceased husband. And after all, Chenoboskion was located in a mosquito-infested valley surrounded by desert. Nobody settled in Chenoboskion for his or her health.

Beset forbade Hypatia from going out without her, but the long hours at home with nothing to do but grieve eventually got the better of Hypatia. On the first few occasions, serenaded by Beset's grumblings, she walked the two and a half miles to the Nile and along its banks for another mile before returning home. The distance was nothing to Hypatia after her travels with Timaeus and Philippus, but Beset tired easily, yet could not be persuaded to stay behind. Hypatia loved the sight of the wide, muddy mother of Egypt and the vibrant green crowns of papyrus plants and other reeds that were coming up for air as the annual flood receded. She looked across the wide channel at the luscious, verdant grain fields, just sprouting, on the other side. She told herself she would cross the river one day to see that promised land up close. She enjoyed the swarm of people that moved about the streets, peddlers and thieves, chariot pullers, priests and beggars. But Hypatia did not enjoy the leers of the men or the grunts of their wives as she passed them by.

Hypatia asked Beset if she knew why the townsfolk acted toward her as they did.

"Pay it no mind, madam. Gooses got to gobble."

"Turkeys gobble, not geese."

"These ones here do. You know, no man, swelling belly, pretty as Hathor. It's tee-hee or tsk-tsk, like a knee jerk. Them can't help it, mistress."

So after these first few outings Hypatia walked in the other direction, west, into the desert, where she rarely encountered anyone.

Between October and December Hypatia ventured farther and farther out into the desert. Dressed in a long cotton tunic, and broad-brimmed hat, and wearing goatskin sandals, she would pack a jar of water, a loaf of bread and cheese or dried dates and journey forth, following beaten paths that led into the red sand covered rock hills that cropped up like monuments to ancient battles. She persuaded Beset to stay at home, saying she would meet no one in that direction from whom she would need Beset's escort or protection. As she journeyed farther out and up into the hills, she eventually came upon caves in the rock. She would enter each new cave cautiously, never venturing too far in. Most of the caves teemed with sleeping bats and were caked from top to bottom with their droppings. On one occasion, after hearing Beset complain about how poorly vegetable gardens in their neighborhood were doing, Hypatia brought a basket and filled it with guano from a cave for use in Beset's vegetable bed. In one cave she found etchings that she did not recognize, part pictures, part symbols, maybe letters. She stared at these and tried, without any success, to read the story they told. She concluded that someone long ago had attempted to preserve the account of an event or a belief or a story for future generations and wondered if the etchings would ever again be seen by anyone who could understand their meaning.

Her forays into the desert and hills brought her peace. She thought of the child growing within her and the father of that child gone forever. She thought of the Pleroma with fading memories of what Timaeus had said about it. She thought of Sophia in the Pleroma. She thought of Sophia, whom she had been so recently before, and of Adama before that. And she thought of Hypatia of Alexandria, the street waif, and of Hypatia of Chenoboskion, the expectant mother, whom she was now. It was sometimes difficult to fathom that all these persons were one, were her and made up her story so far. What would become of her she knew not. Everything was uncertain. But in the quiet of these solitary walks her mind could settle and she could go on.

On one of her walks, on a day she had travelled farther into the desert than was usual for her, she came upon an unwalled settlement consisting of several clay huts aligned to the left and right of a comparatively large building that looked like a church of some kind. As she approached a short man with a long, full beard, and full robe, came running out of one of the huts, waving his hands wildly and yelling.

"Get. Get Away. No woman. Get Away."

As Hypatia stared at him in wonderment, his gestures became more animated. He yelled something back at the huts, "demon woman," she thought it was. She could see several others scampering into the huts or lying flat, motionless, upon the ground. The yelling man, in his early thirties, was lost completely to the panic caused by her approach. When she stopped to stare at him, he stopped yelling and stared back with the frightened look of a gazelle in the presence of a lioness. Hypatia was sure that if she took even one step further he would have run away with all his flock, so she turned and walked back to home.

On each journey, Hypatia would return after three or four hours to find Beset in full alarm, saying she thought never to see her again and then what would become of her and her child and what would become of her faithful Beset. Beset would bring her gourds of water, wipe her forehead with a damp cloth, wash her feet and otherwise fuss over her until ordered to stop. For the next few hours, as she busied herself around the house, Beset would keep a keen eye on Hypatia, muttering words Hypatia could not quite make out, except for the occasional "child," or "care" or "thinking."

In the evening by candlelight, Hypatia would read and reread the Greek text of the volume she had taken from Eusebius' library. She loved the opening verses of the *Gospel of Mary Magdalene,* which read:

> In the fullness of manhood Jesus took Mary to wife, for he loved her best among all. And with her were born three children, a daughter first and then two sons. Full was his life and he rejoiced for the life he was given.

Hypatia could not help but wonder if Timaeus would have felt that way if he had lived to see his own child born. Would he have risked so much if he had known he had so much to lose? If he had known the joys of this life instead of being lost in the quest for another? But even in Mary's gospel, Jesus was crucified for his faith and teachings. Then he came to Mary and the other disciples in a dream and answered their questions. "What is love that gives so much only to leave behind so much sorrow?" Mary asked. "Love is the All. Love is my Father," Jesus answered. "What about our children?" Mary asked. "What is to become of them?" "Tend to our children, Mary. Teach the children, for they are the future of Love."

"In the end," Peter asked, "will matter be destroyed or not?" And Jesus answered that all matter, all natures, all creatures and all formations exist within one another and will be resolved again into their own roots. Peter asked what was to become of Jesus' mission, how was it to be spread among the people, to which Jesus replied, "Go, then, and preach the gospel of the Kingdom. Do not lay down any rules beyond what I appointed to you, and do not give law like a lawgiver, lest you be constrained by it."

Hypatia would settle down hard upon the words of the Gospel, trying to divine their meaning. She often thought to herself that Timaeus had been wrong about her, because she understood so little.

Chapter Twenty-Two

Hathor

February 326 – Chenoboskion

I am Protennoia, the Thought that dwells in the Light. I am the movement that dwells in the All, she in whom the All takes its stand, the first-born among those who came to be, she who exists before the All. She (Protennoia) is called by three names, although she dwells alone, since she is perfect. I am invisible within the Thought of the Invisible One. I am revealed in the immeasurable, ineffable (things). I am incomprehensible, dwelling in the incomprehensible. I move in every creature.

Trimorphic Protennoia

Hypatia's child was born on the last day of February in the Roman year 1080, year 326 of the Common Era. Beset was with her and midwifed the delivery. Beset, who had nine children of her own, six that lived, did everything that was needed, everything that could be done to ease the delivery. Beset, who did not know where the two daughters who survived long enough to be wedded off now lived, wiped Hypatia's brow and held her hand as it clenched in pain during the delivery. Beset, whose late husband's bequest to her was nothing beyond relief from caring for an abusive alcoholic, gently sang old, forgotten songs to Hypatia during her labors. And Beset, whose one living son left at age fifteen to seek his way in the Roman legion, gently pulled the baby's head from Hypatia's womb, swaddled it in cotton and laid it upon the new mother's breast. Hypatia had turned nineteen a week before the birth.

But before the birth something happened that was chronicled in the Roman archives of the region and preserved for several centuries before being lost to the onslaught of Islam in the eighth century. It started around the first of February when Hypatia and Beset received a strange and unexpected visitor from Caneopolis, about thirty miles east along the big bend in the Nile. Archaically and absurdly dressed in a white gown and a leopard-skin cloak, teeth projecting downward over the priest's forehead from the leopard's head, the man introduced himself as Nabwenenef, high priest of the goddess Hathor. His bald head glistening with sweat that poured out from under the leopard's head, the man said he had journeyed the thirty miles from Caneopolis to investigate claims that Hathor had been seen in the flesh, living in Chenoboskion. Beset, who had met him at the door, reacted like a stunned mule, staring blankly, mouth agape, wordless. When finally she found her voice she said, "Aye, you've come to the right place."

When Nabwenenef repeated his story to Hypatia, she promptly told him to get out. "You are the second holy man to appear at my door claiming I am a goddess. I was fool enough to follow the first. I am telling you to leave now."

Rather than reacting with disappointment, Nabwenenef simply said, "Then it is true." He pulled from under his robe a large piece of parchment and unrolled it on the table. "See," he said. "Look at this. It is you." On the parchment he had sketched the likeness of the statue of a woman. The woman in the sketch was young and comely and wore a headpiece in which the sun was held in place by cow's horns.

Hypatia examined the sketch, but was nonplussed. "So, someone has drawn a rough likeness and put horns and a ridiculous headdress upon my head. Be gone."

"No, no, no, your goddess," Nabwenenef protested. "I drew this myself but I never saw you before today. I drew it from the statue that graces your temple in Caneopolis. But it is you. As clear as Osiris. Let me explain." And before she could stop him, Nabwenenef was off.

"Hathor is the goddess of womanly love, joy, and motherhood," Nabwenenef explained. "She is the goddess of music, dance and fertility. She is Egypt's most ancient goddess. She is the consort of Horus, the mother of Ra. Her coming portends the rebirth of Egypt, the casting off of Roman rule. Her child will be pharaoh of a new dynasty. When I heard that she had appeared in the flesh out of nowhere, heavy with child, here in Chenoboskion, not more than ten leagues from Thebes, the ancient capital of Egypt, I had to come and see for myself."

"So," Hypatia said, "let me get this straight. You think that I am a goddess and that my child, whatever it may be, is going to be a pharaoh."

"It will be a man-child, your highness. It is foretold."

Hypatia smiled skeptically. "And you say he will kick the Romans out of Egypt?"

"Without any doubt."

"I want no part of that kind of trouble."

"You have no choice. It is written."

"A lot of things are written," Hypatia said. "The last holy man I knew said that I had knowledge of the infinities. If that was true, you would think I would have at least known who I am."

"Who was this holy man?" Nabwenenef asked.

"The father of my child."

"Your husband?"

"Yes."

"Where is he now? I would like to meet him."

"He is dead. Our marriage lasted less than a day."

Nabwenenef scratched at his chin and rubbed at the sweat on top of his head. Beset brought him a jar of water and he drank it down.

"Let me ask you this," he said. "Did you see your husband die?"

"No."

"He may simply have rejoined the realm of Ra."

"Is that anything like the Pleroma?"

"I know nothing of this Pleroma, goddess. You must teach me."

"Never mind. Anyway, my husband died. I am sure of it."

"How do you know, if you did not see him?

"A priest, whom I trust, came to me with the news of his death. I expected it. I was not surprised."

Nabwenenef's mouth was agape. "A priest," he said in tones of wonder.

"A Catholic priest. Not Egyptian."

"A holy man, nonetheless. And you foretold the death of your husband! Let me ask you this: where were you born?"

"Alexandria, I think."

"Aha. You're Egyptian. Who were your parents?"

"I never knew. I grew up on the streets."

"Ooooooh. Wonder of wonders. It is all true. Can you not see? You are Egyptian but were born without parents. You are the shining image of Hathor. You took a holy man for your husband. You are pregnant and the father departed this world without being seen. The prophecies are all true. You are certain to give birth to a new pharaoh and to be mother of a new dynasty. Let me ask another question, goddess."

"Stop calling me that. My name is Hypatia."

"That is a Greek name. Your true name is Hathor."

"Get out. I have heard enough foolishness to keep me entertained for a year."

"Will you answer one more question first?"

"What is it?"

Before Nabwenenef could ask his question, Beset returned with the jar refilled with water and presented it to him. He took a long swallow. "Thank you, good woman. Your kindness speaks well of your mistress. Before I ask my last question of Hathor, let me ask you what you think of this. You have seen that the drawing of Hathor could be just as well a drawing of your mistress. You have heard what has been said here. What do you think?"

Beset could not remember the last time she had been asked what she thought about anything. She was not used to having opinions, except as it involved the well-being of Hypatia, whether Hypatia should walk alone into the desert or to the river, what she should eat, how much she should rest. Beyond these things she had no opinions at all. She could quite willingly believe that Hypatia was Hathor, if it were true, if someone who knew told her so. And Nabwenenef seemed to know. But Hypatia did not seem to want to be Hathor. Beset was accustomed to accepting the opinion of a man over that of a woman, but Hypatia was not an ordinary woman. She seemed more like a man than a woman in the way she ran her own life, in the way that she did not need a man to tell her what to do. As these thoughts raced through her head, Beset felt the excruciating effort of formulating an opinion. She was torn between her belief — yes she did believe — that Hypatia was a goddess and the obvious fact that, whatever her reasons, Hypatia did not wish it to be known. She was about to say she did not know when Hypatia laughed and said, "Yes, Beset. By all means, you who have seen me eat and shit and sweat and cry, what do you think? Am I Hathor? Or just another woman, like yourself?"

Hypatia thought this would settle things for Beset. After all, Beset knew better than anyone how human she was. This showed a particularly profound misunderstanding of Beset's mind on the subject. Hypatia was decidedly not like her. She lived an infinite number of levels above her. She had means. She had independence. She had thoughts. She could read. She could write. She was, in Beset's mind, the most spectacularly beautiful woman she had ever seen. No. Hypatia's appeal to Beset had the opposite of its intended effect.

"You may be..." Beset started.

"What?" Hypatia exclaimed.

"You see, she agrees," Nabwenenef said.

"She had not finished," Hypatia said. "Go ahead, Beset, tell him I am not a goddess."

"The old ways are the best ways," Beset said, enigmatically repeating by rote words she had heard her husband say to her hundreds of times. "Do not ask me to say more. I do not know."

"You are a good handmaid and a wise woman," Nabwenenef said. "The old ways are the best ways. And they will become the new ways again. What is your name?"

"Beset."

"Bastet? The name of the goddess who protects us against disease. Handmaiden to Hathor. Do you not find it convincing," Nabwenenef said to Hypatia, "that you would pick a Bastet for your servant?"

"Her name is Beset, not Bastet, and you have worn out your welcome. I said I would answer one last question. That was your question. And the answer is no, I do not find it convincing. Now get out."

"That was not my last question," Nabwenenef said. "It is this: are you a virgin?"

"Obviously not. Now leave."

Nabwenenef departed, saying he would return soon.

When Hypatia and Beset awoke the next morning they saw a small, but bright, multi-colored patchwork tent pitched about fifty feet to the south of their house. As they looked at it, Nabwenenef emerged with an attendant. The attendant carried a small bird, perhaps a quail, under his arm. In front of the opening of the tent the two had constructed a crude altar of stones and a split log and a fire circle of stones beside the altar. A small fire of sticks spat out flames and sparks. As the women watched, Nabwenenef appeared to be saying something to the altar while raising and lowering his arms at seemingly random intervals. Then, taking the bird from his assistant, Nabwenenef struck off its head with a bone handled knife and shook blood from its severed neck into the fire, nearly putting it out.

There was nothing Hypatia could do about her new neighbor. She complained to Cannus, her landlord, but he said the priest was paying half as much for a few feet of dirt as Hypatia was paying for the house, so what could he do? Hypatia considered offering an equal amount to have the priest evicted, but thought better of letting Cannus know that she could afford more than she was paying.

The priest brought the town's attention to Hypatia. He was happy to tell all who asked that he was sitting vigil on the birth of the future pharaoh and to show all who would look his drawing of the statue of Hathor as proof of his prophesy. Soon others joined Nabwenenef and his assistant. Another tent appeared, then another. Cannus went around to extract whatever rent each new arrival could pay. Not much, but not nothing. More stones were brought in to augment the altar. Several times a day the growing group would gather around the altar as Nabwenenef performed his sacrificial ceremony on a bird, a fish or a dog. If no animal was available, he would throw a fig into the fire. By the end of the first week Hypatia counted twenty people living in what she had thought of as her yard.

Each day Nabwenenef discovered additional signs that Hypatia was, in fact, Hathor. For example, both Hypatia and Hathor began with the Coptic letter *horee*. Most impressive to Nabwenenef was the fact that Hypatia's vegetables flourished while the other gardens around it barely survived. This, he said, proved that she was the fertility goddess reincarnate. Hypatia tried to tell him that the reason for her garden's success was the bat dung she had brought down from the caves, but the only consequence of this revelation was Nabwenenef's proclamation that knowing where to find the instruments of fertility provided even greater proof that Hypatia was Hathor.

Hypatia mostly stayed indoors during Nabwenenef's vigil,

sending Beset out as rarely as possible to obtain provisions. As she passed through the ragtag group beside the altar, Beset was treated like a celebrity. Nabwenenef never failed to ask how her mistress was progressing and when she thought the birth might come. Others simply touched her garment or asked for a blessing. Leaving or returning, it was the same.

One day Hypatia looked out and was surprised to see the little monk who had waved her away from the settlement in the desert a few months earlier. He appeared to be engaged in a heated debate with Nabwenenef, who towered above the smaller man and whose leopard-skin cloak added to his predatory appearance. Finally, the little monk broke off and headed straight for the house. Nabwenenef followed about ten feet behind.

The little man burst into the house without so much as a by-your-leave. "What kind of game are you running here?" he demanded. "Have you not heard of the risen Christ?"

Hypatia examined the man as he stood waiting for an answer. He appeared to be in his early thirties, though, with his unkempt hair and filthy beard, she could not be certain. His black eyes glowed like burning coal as he stared at her. If he thought anything of her looks or even noticed her at all as distinct from the object of his wrath, it did not show.

"You're the 'get away' man, aren't you?" Hypatia asked.

"What?"

"Oh, you know, the man I came across in the desert last November. The man who yelled at me to get away. That was you."

"I don't know what you are speaking of," he lied. "I want to know what you intend to do about that crowd of heathens and heretics gathered outside your door. It is sacrilege to put yourself out as a god. Have you not heard of the risen Christ?"

"I am generally introduced before I have the pleasure of conversing with someone within the confines of my own home."

The little monk shifted, suddenly off guard. He looked around and noticed that Hypatia was seated calmly, hands crossed on her swollen belly, smiling at him with amused eyes. "I apologize," he said. "My name is Pachome. I am a monk and a shepherd among the local shepherds. There, we are introduced. Now, what do you think you are doing here?"

"Not so fast, Pachome," Hypatia playfully replied. "I have not introduced myself to you. I will do so now."

"I do not wish to know."

"But I insist and you are in my house, if you hadn't noticed. So, my rules. I am Hypatia and my friend here is Beset. Say hello to Beset."

Put back on his heels, Pachome complied.

"Now that we are properly introduced, what is your question?"

Pachome gave an impatient grunt. He had already asked his questions. Why should he repeat them?

"Go ahead, I'm quite willing to answer you."

Pachome shook his head before finally repeating, "Have you not heard of the risen Christ?"

"Yes," Hypatia answered. "But let me ask you this: are you a Trinitarian or an Arian?"

"Phtu," Pachome spat reflexively. "Arian! Heresy. There is but one God. Jesus is God." Pachome suddenly stiffened. "Hold on. How do you know of such things?"

"Never mind that," Hypatia replied. "I just needed to know with what kind of Christian I am speaking."

"There are not kinds of Christians. There are Christians and there are heathens. Arians are heathens like your crowd outside."

"They are not my crowd."

"Do you disown them?"

"I never owned them in the first place."

"Do you repudiate them?"

"Certainly not. They are not mine to repudiate."

"Then you endorse what they are doing out there?"

"Not for a second."

"What is your stand then?

"That I am Hypatia, a woman and a widow, and that you and they should both go away and leave us in peace."

"Do you send them away?"

"I would if I could, but my landlord assures me they are on his property and he likes the rent."

"I will make them go away."

"Could you, please?"

"I will implore the risen Christ."

"Please do so."

Pachome turned away triumphantly and returned to the crowd, Nabwenenef following closely behind. However, all the imploring Pachome could muster did no good. The crowd remained.

Soon the Romans became aware of Nabwenenef's vigil. A deputy consul named Cato Plutonious was sent from Caneopolis to investigate. The Romans knew about Nabwenenef in Caneopolis. Over the course of the 350 years of Roman rule over Egypt, worship of the old gods had faded to an even greater extent than Rome's worship of the Greek gods. There were still cults of some of the major deities, of course. Hathor was one of these. The number of worshipers was always small and there was rarely much passion. Since his ascendency to the high priesthood three years earlier, Nabwenenef pursued a course of agitation and instigation aimed at revitalizing faith in the old gods. The Romans in Caneopolis were accustomed to pronouncements of miracles and wonders from the young priest, but what he was doing in Chenoboskion was something new. It was insurrection, or at least the preface to insurrection. It was a seed planted in the feeble but fertile minds of the natives that liberation was at hand. The Romans knew it was a long shot, but with the right turn of events and with a skilled and determined agitator such as Nabwenenef to interpret them, that seed could grow to significance. The Romans did not like insurrection, even in incipience, so when word reached the Consul in Caneopolis of Nabwenenef's activities in Chenoboskion, he promptly dispatched Cato with instructions to deal with the problem.

At its most basic level, dealing with the problem meant murdering someone. Killing Nabwenenef was not the solution. It was more likely to create a martyr, thereby enhancing the priest's credibility and the cause for which he died. On the other hand, if the so-called goddess and the god in her womb were to die, Nabwenenef's prophecy would be disproven in the present and his credibility shaken for the future. So, when Cato left Caneopolis to investigate the disturbance, he brought with him two members of the Consul's legionary guards; Ankha Aegyptos, who claimed to be familiar with Chenoboskion, and Brutus Gaulinius, from the north.

Officially, the Deputy Consul and his guards did not have the authority to simply commit murder. Rome, after all, was both a nation of laws and now a Christian nation. In his official capacity, Cato was a fact finder. But he was deputized with the authority to "take whatsoever measures and mete out whatsoever penalties and punishments that may be deemed necessary based upon Roman law and the facts as they be found." Cato left Caneopolis with a heavy heart because, as a general rule, he did not like having people killed.

Cato did, however, enjoy the pomp and stature of his post. So, upon arriving in Chenoboskion he did not immediately proceed to the western outskirts where, he was told, Nabwenenef and his goddess could be found. Instead, he put up at an inn, slept, bathed, put on his finest tunic, cloak and sandals, and closely inspected his soldiers for proper dress before traveling the last two miles to Hypatia's house.

By the time they arrived at Nabwenenef's makeshift temple

the crowd had swelled to about fifty, including, for the first time, one or two persons of local repute. Cato and the soldiers dismounted from their horses and, with the soldiers a step forward of the Deputy Consul, approached Nabwenenef. Things went badly for Cato from the start. Before he reached the priest he noticed a spot of what looked and smelled like horse dung on the lower, right hem of his tunic. He cursed aloud and involuntarily thought of his stern father whom he imagined scowling at him with disapproval. His first words to Nabwenenef were, "Bring me water and a cloth."

Cato found Nabwenenef to be a cagey respondent. He was engaged in outreach in Chenoboskion, nothing more. He wanted the local folk to know that some still worshiped the old ways and gods and he was there to provide guidance as needed. To Cato's statement that he had heard reports about the reappearance of Hathor and the impending birth of Ra, Nabwenenef said, "Who can say what will be, only the future can tell." He added that he accepted Roman rule "implicitly." Others in the gathering were more explicit. Nabeef, a shopkeeper, enthusiastically explained that they were awaiting the birth of the new Ra who would set things to rights with the big-footed Romans. Nabeef pointed to the signs Nabwenenef had seen, including the similarity in their names, Hypatia's likeness to the Hathor statue, the fertility of her garden, her virgin conception. "She even has a servant named Bastet," he said. A few others expressed similar sentiments. It was enough for Cato to decide that his original course of action was warranted.

He pulled Ankha and Brutus aside. "I have determined that the threat to the Empire, though small, is real," he began. "It is my determination that the risk should not be run. You are hereby authorized and ordered to enter that house yonder and run both women through with your swords. Do it quietly. Do it gently. But don't drag it out." With that Cato walked back to his horse and daubed at the stain on his tunic. The soldiers approached and entered the house.

After ten minutes Ankha and Brutus came out of the house and approached Cato and the horses. Cato was pleased to see that they had cleaned their blades before leaving the house. When they reached him, Cato asked, "Is it done?"

Brutus shifted sternly, while Ankha spoke. "No sir, I couldn't."

"Why in Hades not?"

"The old woman, sir. She's my mom."

When Brutus and Ankha entered the house they found the two women seated, facing the pane-less window where they had been watching Cato's interaction with the crowd out front. Both soldiers were immediately struck by Hypatia's beauty and stood, gaping stupidly.

"Aren't you going to clear those fools from our yard?" Hypatia asked. Beset kept her eyes down and did not look at the soldiers. The soldiers stared at Hypatia.

"Well?"

Finding his voice Ankha said, "I am most sorry, but you must stand."

"Why? So you can run me through? What fools the Romans are."

"We have our orders," Ankha said as his knees wobbled. Brutus continued to stare at Hypatia, falling in love moment by moment.

"I know nothing of your orders," Hypatia said. "But I have met your Emperor and I know that he, at least, listens to all sides before rendering judgment."

"You know Emperor Constantine?" Ankha asked.

"He is just. He would hear all sides."

Ankha was at a loss about what to do. Brutus had become useless. Both knew they did not want to kill this woman.

"What is your side?" Ankha said at last.

"That I am no goddess. That my name is Hypatia, not Hathor. That I am a pregnant widow who lives with my friend, Beset. Not Bastet, Beset. That Nabwenenef is a fool. What more must I know?"

At the mention of her servant's name, Ankha's eyes moved from Hypatia to Beset. "Mother?" he asked.

Beset looked up into his eyes. "Ankha?"

The two fell into each other's arms. Tears were shed. Questions were asked and answered. Promises were made. Love was expressed. Brutus continued to stare at Hypatia.

When he regained his composure, Ankha said, "We have our orders, Mother. I think I may spare you, but the woman must die." Ankha motioned for Brutus to act, but Brutus remained motionless, mouth agape.

Beset threw her body over Hypatia. "To kill her, you must kill me," she said. "I would be dead by now without her anyway."

Confronted with this dilemma, the two soldiers returned to Cato.

Ankha explained all that had happened to Cato, excluding only Hypatia's extraordinary beauty. When Cato heard that Hypatia had claimed to have met Constantine, he decided further investigation was needed.

Cato, too, was taken by the beauty of Hypatia. He was also impressed by her calm reason and intelligence. What finally caused him to resolve against obeying his Consul's instructions, however, was her use of a lemon that she cut in half and rubbed against the stain she noticed on his tunic, removing it completely.

Cato agreed to remain in Chenoboskion until Hypatia's child was born. If it was a daughter, Nabwenenef would be discredited without further action. If it was a son, he would have to follow orders.

Hypatia gave birth to a daughter five days later. She named the child Magdalene, a name she remembered from Jerusalem. Within a day, Nabwenenef's makeshift temple had come down and the crowd of worshipers, which had grown to eighty in number, departed.

Chapter Twenty-Three

Birth and Rebirth

March 326 – June 327 A.D. - Chenoboskion

And he said to me, 'Be strong, for you are the one to whom these mysteries have been given, to know them through revelation …'
The Apocalypse of Peter

How can one describe the love a mother has for her child? Unbounded. Infinite. Absolute. Yes, but not nearly sufficient. There are certain things that the human mind cannot grasp or define. The concept of God is one of these. Infinity is another. In our primal need for explanation we invent words, shorthand, for these concepts. But these words are not explanations. They are merely placeholders or ellipses to allow us to skip over what cannot be known or explained so that we may continue with the business of living. Love, especially the love of a mother for a child and the love of a child for her mother, is as indefinable as God, as unexplainable as time before time, as unknowable as space never ending. What Hypatia, Sophia, did know was that looking into the bright, hopeful, green eyes, watching the helpless, tiny arms, the curled little legs and the miniature feet, listening to the coos and sucks and, yes, even cries of little Maggie opened in her a new level of love and understanding. She gently pressed a finger against every inch of Maggie, watching the child's responses, learning the child's body and personality. How many hours were spent simply staring in wonder at her little girl? How many times did Hypatia, exhausted, lay the child down to sleep, only to be overcome with the desire to wake her up again five minutes later? How much joy did she receive from Maggie's smiles, her contentment, the love she returned?

Unbounded. Infinite. Absolute.

Beset, Magdalene and Hypatia formed a happy family from the start. With two women to care for the child, the burden was light. Both women delighted in each new accomplishment as Maggie lengthened, fed and grew plump.

The first few months brought other pleasures as well. Principal among these was that Hypatia resumed her short forays into the desert. The time alone allowed her to reflect on the strange events of the past two years. She was still confused over Timaeus' certainty that she was Sophia, a living covenant with the All, keeper of Gnosis for the ages. She remained certain that he had been wrong. The little faith she had gained during her time with Timaeus was fading, yet it pained her to think that Timaeus had spent his last year on Earth believing in such folly and that he died in pursuit of it. She wanted to be worthy of the faith he had placed in her, but she knew it was not warranted. During her walks through the barren outskirts of Chenoboskion, as she watched strange lizards and watched out for scorpions, she pondered the meaning of the past several months. One day as she was returning from the cave that held the ancient hieroglyphics she decided upon a way to honor Timaeus, even if she could not be the Sophia he had believed her to be. She would copy the Gnostic gospels she owned, translating them into the Coptic letters of the Egyptian tongue. It was a small thing, to be sure, but perhaps it might provide inspiration to someone smarter and more open to the path to knowledge than she. She now saw that through her time as Sophia, Timaeus had rescued Adama and restored Hypatia and had left her with a more precious gift, Magdalene, than she could ever have imagined. In the process of copying the texts, she would be keeping the memory of Timaeus alive, at least for herself. She soon started copying the texts of the *Gospel of Mary*, the *Apocryphon of John, the Sophia of Jesus Christ,* and the notes Timaeus had written about the Acts of Peter.

An unintended consequence of the resumption of her desert walks was that she again brought baskets of bat guano back with her. She used it on her own garden, of course, but the attention Nabwenenef had brought to her and the fertility of her plants prompted others to ask about her secret. At first she simply gave it away to neighbors, but soon people from further and further away from her house came for a share and she was obliged to charge for it simply so that she could keep it in stock for herself. Within three months, it had turned into a small, but steady business. The temperatures were such that garden vegetables could be grown year round if properly protected from the sun and there was always plenty of water diverted from the Nile. All the soil outside the flood basin needed was nourishment and Hypatia was able to supply it for twenty denarii a basket. She liked that it made others think she needed the coins and, perhaps, that she was not the kept courtesan of some distant Roman.

Nabwenenef left other legacies as well, principally in the form of increased attention. It seemed that nobody in Chenoboskion did not know of her and where she lived. Most of the attention was harmless enough and passed without her paying it much mind. But the obscurity she moved there to find had eluded her.

She was paid other, more direct attentions that were more difficult to ignore. Within two weeks after Magdalene's birth she started noticing that desert flowers were being left outside her house once or twice a week. The first was a flowering caper, with white and purple stamen shooting out like tentacles in every direction. There were cactus flowers, too. Once she found the giant flower of the camel hoof tree cut and delicately placed on a fresh leaf near her garden.

Cato Plutonious returned from Caneopolis when Maggie was two months old. On this first visit he said he had come to assure the Consul that the disturbance in Chenoboskion had died down and that the threat to the Empire was fully abated. On his second visit three weeks later he suggested that Hypatia would be wise to put herself under his protection and although it was clear to Hypatia how she could do so, she meekly said that she and Beset would be grateful for any level of protection he could provide from his position in Caneopolis.

Ankha Aegyptos accompanied Cato on his visits. He would bring his mother little gifts such as a clay lamp or some oil. His gifts were for the household, he would explain, for all three who lived there to share. He told his mother that it had broken his heart to leave her, but that his father was abusive and destructive and he felt if he did not leave he would either have killed him or been killed by him. He played with Maggie by picking her up and lifting her high into the air as the child giggled with delight. He told Hypatia that the child must not favor the father at all, since she had all of her mother's grace and beauty. On his third visit, this time without Cato, Ankha told Hypatia that his twenty-five year commitment to the Legion would be up in seven years and he would like to know that he had such a household as hers to come home to when the time came. Hypatia told him that he was sure he would always be welcome in the home of his mother, but she withheld the personal encouragement he was obviously seeking.

A couple of weeks after Ankha's third visit, Brutus Gaulinius appeared at their door. Without looking at either Beset or Magdalene, he blurted that he had heard that Hypatia was going to marry Ankha. This, Brutus said, would be a grave mistake, since he, Brutus, was younger, stronger, better looking and came from a more noble family. He explained that he would soon have the means to purchase his freedom from the Legion and would then be able to marry Hypatia whenever she wished. Hypatia thanked him for his generosity but said she could not possibly think of marrying again until she was over grieving for Magdalene's father. She did not know how long that would take.

Nabwenenef himself returned to the house three months after

Maggie's birth. He explained to Hypatia, whom he still called Hathor, that he had been doing more divination and had learned that Ra had not been Hathor's first born, but her second. Based upon his new calculations, her second child would be Ra and would establish a new dynasty in Egypt. Nabwenenef cautioned her to be careful in choosing her next mate, advising that a priest of her cult would be the best prospect. They would not have to be married, he explained, since marriage was not required among the gods.

After Nabwenenef left, without encouragement, Hypatia went outside and saw a short, robed man bent over near her garden. Hearing her, Pachome straightened up and scurried off toward the desert. Hypatia walked to where he had been and found a three small, yellow Acacia flowers neatly wrapped inside a scrap of papyrus pages on which most of the writing had been scratched out.

At night, after she had nursed Maggie and placed her in the cradle Beset had purchased from a local carpenter, Hypatia would light three oil lamps and lay out fresh pieces of papyrus she purchased from a local manufacturer. She trimmed reeds she had picked from the flood basin and allowed to dry in the branches of a fig bush and used a honeycomb-based ink she had commissioned Ankha to acquire from Caneopolis. With great care and a steady hand she transcribed the worn, curled volume she had taken from Eusebius' library onto fresh clean sheets of parchment.

Transcription is the wrong word. Few of the people in Chenoboskion spoke Greek. Her plan was to give away copies of the gospels whenever she found a potential, receptive mind. It was the best way she could think of to honor Timaeus. So, she translated the Greek texts into her native Egyptian language, using the Coptic lettering Timaeus had taught her. She had a gift for writing and the pages she produced were clear and neat and fine.

She started with the *Gospel of Mary*. Hypatia envied the love between Jesus and Mary and the domestic happiness portrayed in the first chapter of the gospel. She knew that it was something that she could not have had with Timaeus. It was as if for all his desire to follow Jesus' teachings, Timaeus had ignored this simple prelude. Most of the remainder of *Mary* consisted of lessons that Jesus gave to Mary to retell to the other disciples. It seemed that doubt and confusion that had burst out among them as soon as Jesus was crucified. They asked basic questions as if they had not been present during his mission in life. What is the meaning of life? What is the nature of God? How can humans become divine? Will the world be destroyed at the end of time? What makes us sinful? To all of these questions Jesus answers serenely and clearly. There is no original sin, only the sin that we make for ourselves. Remember always that the All is within you, that I am within you. Teach what I have taught you, but do not make laws, for laws can only constrain you in understanding what I have taught.

The lessons had to be taught over and over again. It was as if Jesus was a text that could only be read by most in the light that only he emitted. After each vision, confusion followed. Only Mary holds true to his teachings. In the final chapter, the ninth, Peter and Andrew challenge Mary, doubting her words and even that Jesus would appear to her, a woman, and not to them. Hypatia's second favorite part of the Gospel appeared here, when Matthew-Levi rebukes Peter, saying, "Peter, you have always been hot tempered. Now I see you contending against the woman like the adversaries. But if the Savior made her worthy, who are you indeed to reject her. Surely the Savior knows her very well. That is why He loved her more than us."

It took Hypatia two weeks to translate the *Gospel of Mary* into Coptic. When she was finished she had sixteen neatly printed pages of text that she stacked together and put in Timaeus' old sack and placed beneath her pallet.

By the time the torrid days of May arrived, Hypatia had translated a complete copy of the texts she stole from Eusebius into Coptic. The *Apocryphon of John* was a complicated jumble of deities and forces that betrayed the simplicity of Timaeus' life. It consisted of a revelation made by Jesus to John, presumably the disciple. In this book the Earth and mankind are the result of a cosmic catastrophe, the creation of an inferior deity or deities that did not know of the perfect, unknowable one from which all existence flows. Jesus peels back layers of deities and worlds (aeons) to reveal to man how knowledge of this existence beyond the material world can lead to salvation through unity with the pure, true god. Those who do not learn what Jesus teaches will "withdraw to the place to where the angels of poverty will withdraw" and "will be tortured with eternal punishment."

The Sophia of Jesus Christ also told of many emanations and aeons, which Hypatia could not follow or understand. For Hypatia, there were too many riddles, too little direct instruction. For example, at one point Mary asked Jesus how she could distinguish between what comes from imperishableness and what therefore will survive and what comes from the perishable and, therefore, will perish. Jesus answered, "Come from invisible things to the end of those that are visible, and the very emanation of Thought will reveal to you how faith in those things that are not visible was found in those that are visible, those that belong to Unbegotten Father. Whoever has ears to hear, let him hear!" Hypatia failed to see how the answer provided any help at all.

Timaeus' notes on *The Act of Peter* was actually a brief summary of a story in which Peter's daughter was paralyzed by God in order to save her from an unwanted marriage. The point of it seemed to be to praise virginity for its own sake. Hypatia could not reconcile this book with the domestic bliss of Jesus as portrayed in the opening chapter of the Gospel of Mary.

In fact, not much of the remaining three gospels made a lot of sense to Hypatia and she wondered if it had ever made sense to Timaeus. When she had first read the *Apocryphon* and the *Sophia* when Timaeus was teaching her to read, Hypatia had asked Timaeus why he taught that Sophia was the supreme divine essence, rather than the Unknowable One of the *Apocryphon* or the Unnamable One of the *Sophia*. Timaeus had smiled and said, "I studied those books for a good long time before I realized that they are not to be taken literally, the way the Catholics understand their books. It does not matter whether the aeons and deities of those books exist or if they ever existed. The point is to train the mind to see past the visible, to understand the layers of interference between the world we can see and the true existence that is hidden. The teachers who wrote those books did not intend them to be understood literally. They intended to open the mind to a deeper understanding. As for me, I finally decided that since the Unknowable One was unknowable, I would spend no more time attempting to know Him. I decided that what we need to understand is that this world, even the gods of this world, are not where the soul was born and is not where the soul will reside hereafter. Jesus was not resurrected because he did not die on the cross, but ascended to the Pleroma before they crucified his mortal shell. So, of course, Jesus did not promise us a resurrected body, but he did promise us salvation through understanding. I read the scriptures with that thought always in mind." There were now so many other questions Hypatia wished she had asked, but for Gnostic and Christian alike, the grave is the great silencer.

When, by the beginning of May the heat began to rise up from the Earth like leavened biscuits in an oven, Hypatia had finished this first translation of the four texts. She wanted to bind them together, like the Greek codex she owned, but immediately found she had not copied them correctly for the purpose. She would have to recopy them on the four sides of a papyrus sheet that had been folded in half and she would have to determine how many such pages were to be in the text before she wrote them, so that the quires, when placed together for binding, would be in the proper order. After several false starts, she began the writing process over again, this time in a neater hand than her first attempt. After another month she had produced pages written in the proper order to be bound. For a cover, she used raw goatskin that she stiffened using scraps from the pages of her original copy, gluing them to the goatskin and covering the scraps with a clean, piece of papyrus, cut to size and glued over the scraps. The result was not as fine as the Greek volume that was her model, but it pleased her because it was her own handiwork. A book that she had made with her own hands.

Now, in the quiet of a sweltering May evening, by lamplight, with Maggie and Beset asleep nearby in the room, Hypatia remembered the words Timaeus had spoken and appreciated his quest for knowledge. Her work was bringing her closer to Timaeus, keeping him alive in her thoughts. She thought she would never be his Sophia, but she thought she would always be his wife.

If, in the quiet evenings Hypatia thought she would always be Timaeus' wife, the world around her had other plans. By mid-May Ankha had heard from his mother of Brutus' proposal of marriage. He hastened to Chenoboskion with an offer of his own. Combing his helmet-matted, coarse brown hair with callused fingers, he expressed horror at any thought Hypatia may have had that he had not intended marriage in the first place. He would never presume improper relations with such an obviously virtuous, nearly virginal woman such as herself. He could warn her, however, whatever she felt for him, be it love or indifference or something in between, to be wary of Brutus Gaulinius. He came from a wealthier family, to be sure, and Ankha was not so proud as to deny that Brutus was the handsomer of the two as well as younger by five years. But, Ankha said in a conspiratorial whisper, Brutus was a notorious frequenter of brothels who spent all of his pay and whatever additional money his family sent to him on expensive girls and cheap wine. Any proposal of marriage that Brutus made, Ankha said, must therefore be measured against his character and the fact that the proposal was probably made only because Brutus knew such beauty as Hypatia possessed could never be found in a whorehouse.

Cato Plutonious also returned. A fight had broken out in the barracks between Ankha Aegyptos and Brutus Gaulinius and Cato was consulted by their commander regarding the proper punishment. Cato listened to the competing stories. Both were in love with the same woman and each thought the other unworthy of her affections. When Cato heard that their common love interest was Hypatia he felt a hot flash of jealousy burst like a dam and flow through his body like a coursing river, spurred by the thought that he might lose in a competition he had not until that moment known existed. He resolved at once to travel to Chenoboskion to resolve the matter in his favor. He sentenced them to one month's confinement to barracks.

Upon arriving at Hypatia's house, Cato Plutonious immediately explained his purpose in coming. He thought she might have come away from their last meeting with some misunderstanding of his intentions which, he solemnly assured her, were entirely honorable. While he could not marry her because he already had a wife and three children, what he had proposed was a more or less official position as his consort. He admitted that his wife would object to the arrangement, but being of humble birth, she was not in a position to raise too much trouble and, in any case, would have no say in the matter. He would provide Hypatia with a residence and clothes and an allotment and soon even his wife would come to see how the arrangement would redound to everybody's greater happiness and enjoyment. In any case, Cato explained, whatever her decision, she must not marry either of the two soldiers who had accompanied him to Chenoboskion in February. They were common soldiery, without prospects and without much breeding. Ankha Aegyptos, in particular, was a person of very low breeding and was entirely dependent upon his monthly wages. There could be no happiness for her in such a union, Cato said, blissfully unaware that the source of Ankha's low breeding was listening to every word. Once again Hypatia explained that she was still in mourning for her late husband and was not ready to contemplate any future relationships at this time. Cato Plutonious promised to return in two months, at which time he would insist upon her concurrence in his proposal.

The final straw came when a dingy-bearded Pachome appeared at her door with a bouquet of camel hoof tree flowers. Unlike in February when he burst inside without warning, on this occasion he refused all invitations to enter the house. He was wearing his traditional brown cassock, but had obviously made some effort to give shape to the unruly mat of hair that normally raged atop his head like tongues of black flame shooting from a fire.

"I don't know whether you are a gift from Heaven or a curse from Hell," he said from her doorway. "It doesn't matter to me anymore. I can think of nothing else. I can think of no one else. I have forgotten my prayers. I renounce my vocation. Join me in holy matrimony so that I might retain some slight chance at eventual redemption." As he spoke, sweat gushed from his hairline and coursed down through the mottled beard, terminating in a steady stream that leaked out from below his chin.

Hypatia spoke kindly. "Pachome," she said. "I accept the flowers as a gift from your heart, as I have accepted the other flowers you have left for me to find. I can assure you that the devil has not sent me. Nor am I an agent of God. I am a widow and a mother. Nothing more. I urge you to see only that when you look at me. You are far too good a man to abandon your vocation, to breach your vows, on my account. I pray that you see me for what I am and nothing more. For reasons that neither of us understands, I have become a distraction and a temptation to you. Overcome the temptation. Put me out of mind. Go back to your monks. They need you. Tell them that you have been tempted, but have prevailed against temptation. I will not punish you by consenting to your proposal."

Pachome looked at her in befuddled silence. Without further word, he thrust the flowers into her hand and scampered off.

That evening Hypatia resolved to move to the other side of the Nile.

Chapter Twenty-Four

Sheneset

June 326 – May 327 – Sheneset

The Soul is produced out of a certain essence, not matter, incorporeal itself, just as its essence is. Every thing that is born, must of necessity be born from something. All things, moreover, in which destruction follows on birth, must of necessity have two kinds of motion with them: that of the Soul, by which they're moved; and that of the body, by which they wax and wane. On the former's dissolution, the latter is dissolved. This is the motion of bodies corruptible.

Thrice-Greatest Hermes

Hypatia, Beset and Magdalene moved across the Nile suddenly and without notice to anyone. Hypatia had conducted reconnaissance two days before the move, crossing the river in a barge propelled by poles and oars that landed about five miles further down river from where it started. She wore loose-fitting Egyptian robes with a cowl that covered her hair and shaded her face. Finding a man who would even discuss property rental with a woman proved difficult. Although she had selected the dwelling and negotiated the terms of the rental in Chenoboskion from Cannus, having Philippus with her had facilitated the process. Now, on her own, her demur inquiries about a renting a place to live were met either with an angry spit or dumbfounded silence. She had to admit that there were times when she needed a man.

She walked through the eastern outskirts of the settlement that appeared in all fundamentals – people, housing, manners, and economy – to be Chenoboskion's twin. The settlement on the eastern bank of the Nile was administered by the Romans as

Chenoboskion, the same as its western counterpart. But the older residents still called it by its Coptic name, Sheneset. After a half-dozen rebuffed inquiries she observed a matron simultaneously beating rugs and barking orders to two teenage boys. Something about the woman's controlled ferocity drew Hypatia's attention and she approached her cautiously.

"Excuse me, madam," Hypatia said as she approached.

"Madam indeed," the woman shot back. "If I was a madam I'd not have to work half so hard." There was an intelligent hardness to the woman's features. Her skin was darkened and cured by many years in the Egyptian sun, so it was surprising for Hypatia to see a pair of muted grey eyes examining her with a horse trader's intensity.

"I beg your pardon, please," Hypatia said cautiously. "I meant no offense. My name is Hypatia, from Alexandria. I am looking for a dwelling place for my child and me. Just the two of us and my friend who helps keep house. I was hoping you might know of a place."

The old woman pushed the end of her beating stick into the ground and rested upon it, stabilizing herself as she undertook a closer examination of her young inquisitor. Streaks of long grey and black hair had come free from her scarf and she pushed them back under it with her right hand.

"Senmonthis," the woman said.

"I apologize," Hypatia replied.

"You are full of regrets, aren't you, Hypatia?"

"Ma'am?"

"'Excuse me,' 'I beg your pardon,' 'I apologize.' You're full of regrets today."

"I guess I am, though I do not mean to be. It's just that I did not understand what you said."

"Senmonthis? Why, it's my name for Ra's sake. You told me your name and I was returning the courtesy." Senmonthis had not ceased from intensely examining Hypatia.

"Oh, I'm sorry, Senmonthis," Hypatia continued. "But might you know of a dwelling place for my daughter and me?"

"I might," Senmonthis replied, "if you can refrain from apologizing."

"Yes. I will try, Senmonthis."

"Are you single with child?"

"Widowed."

"How old is the child?"

"Four months."

"Boy or girl?"

"Girl."

"Name?"

"Magdalene."

"And your friend?"

"She helps me keep house. Helps care for Magdalene."

"Your servant then?"

"She is my friend. I pay her wages."

"Her name?"

"Beset."

"And you say you are coming from Alexandria?"

"Not directly. I have been living in Chenoboskion, on the west bank, for almost a year."

"And why do you want to move to Sheneset?"

"Change of scene, I guess."

Senmonthis smiled at this. "It's pretty much the same scenery here, love. Valley and crops surrounded by desert hills. Pretty much the same."

"I would like to move. For personal reasons."

"A man?"

"Not exactly. None that I want."

Senmonthis nodded. "I can understand that. But it is pretty difficult in these parts for a young woman to get by without a man."

"We have managed."

"But you need to move."

"Yes."

The two teens Senmonthis had been prodding to work, her sons in point of fact, had stopped and were closely watching their mother and the young woman she was talking to. It was approaching mid-day and heat was beginning to rise from the earth in convected blasts. The boys, lightly dressed, wiped their brows. The two women, heavily cloaked, made no visible concession to the sweltering conditions in which they transacted their business.

Senmonthis broke the brief silence. "I take it from your child's name that you are a Christian?"

"I am not sure," Hypatia replied. "I guess so."

"Well, I keep to the old ways. Would I have a problem with you?"

"No. Everyone must worship as they chose."

"That's not very Christian of you."

"I'm sorr… No, I guess not." Hypatia smiled. "Now you are teasing me."

"Yes, I guess so," Senmonthis said.

After another brief silence, Senmonthis said, "I know who you are, you know?"

"What? How?"

"Hathor?"

"I am not Hathor."

"No, but Nabwenenef thinks you are. I was rather hoping you would have a son. Get rid of the Romans and all that."

"You know then why I must move. Too many people pay attention to me. Would it be the same here?"

"No, I don't think so. Oh, there's plenty who've heard the tale, but not many who followed it so close as me, I guess."

"Could you keep it to yourself?"

"It would be a point of honor to do so."

"Would your sons know?"

"Them two?" Senmonthis laughed. "Not a chance. They got their father's brains, I guess."

"And your husband?"

"He couldn't have figured it out when he was living. Even less likely to now that he's dead."

"So you have a place to rent?"

"I do. But not generally so. I have a small house my husband used to keep his whores in. One at a time, I mean. I'll give him that. The whore's house, I call it. I made him build it two hundred feet from the main house. Far enough for some privacy for you and your little girl. Close enough for me to keep an eye on your comings and goings."

"And space for a garden? It's important to us to have fresh produce."

"All the space you can use, I guess, though the soil is poor."

They quickly agreed upon a price. It took Hypatia a day to arrange their passage and plan the subterfuge of their departure. Two days later, as the sun was entering its evening quarters, Hypatia, Magdalene and Beset arrived at the new house. Nobody knew they were leaving until they were gone. Hypatia had acquired not only a new place to live, but a new friend as well.

This was Hypatia's first summer in Chenoboskion, or Sheneset as she soon learned to call the settlement on the east bank. The heat rose day by day as inexorably as the floodwaters rushed over the banks of the Nile. Yet while the rising of the Nile brought life in the form of fresh water from mountain glaciers and rich silt from fertile forests, the implacable sun drew life out like a leech draws blood from a bruise. The Nile Valley was the green gut of the Egyptian and Roman Empires. It was a long, drawn out intestine that digested the river's intake and provided nourishment in the form of bread and beer and many other staples to the body of those dominions. But though the valley was long and rich it was exceedingly narrow, it was packed on all sides in brown and red, shifting sands and hard, cave-filled hills of sandstone. The river fed the expanse of vast, aggregated regions, but had no surplus for its own limitless borderlands. The fertile soil and life-giving water that was so abundant throughout the heart of the valley had to be augmented with compost and irrigated by hand in those inhabited regions on the edge of the basin. So it was that when, in October, the Nile receded and the temperatures began to ease, Hypatia took to the hills northeast of Sheneset.

This time Hypatia intended from the beginning to sell the surplus guano. Once she had made a few forays into the hills and had discovered ample supplies, she bought a donkey and saddle baskets, planning to make the treks once or twice a week to bring down the fertile bat dung from the caves. She told both Beset and Senmonthis her plans. By the next day, when Hypatia returned, the two older women had obviously been talking and staged an insistent intervention. She could not continue with her plans, they both insisted. It was unbecoming and against all of the customs of the region for a woman to engage in such toil and commerce.

"Don't get me wrong," Senmonthis said, "these folk around here would see a woman worked to death and praise the man who worked her, but what you are doing now, going up into the hills, digging out dung, hauling it down by donkey and setting up shop to sell it, well, if you think you drew attention on the other side by resembling some ancient statue, you've not seen the kind of stir the likes of which what your doings will cause."

Senmonthis said that if Hypatia needed the money and was set on earning it in this way, her sons could do the digging and the selling and she could keep most of the profits. Not as much as doing it all herself, Senmonthis admitted, but most of it and with a lot less aggravation. Beset simply said, "Think of your child, think of poor Magdalene," as if whatever she meant by that was obvious to all.

Senmonthis admitted that her sons were two of the laziest

boys she ever knew and did not take orders as well as some, but it would be better than the alternative. After a half hour contest, Hypatia gave in and hired Bakare and Seti to perform the labor for her project. She did not care about the diminishment in revenue, but bristled over the loss of control. She still had over forty-eight solidi of the fifty Timaeus had left to her and was not likely to run out anytime soon. But the boys were lazy and indolent. They went up into the hills when they wanted, not when they were told or even when the supply had been entirely sold off. And this was a problem because Hypatia turned out to be a subtle, but effective marketer. By the time her first vegetables ripened, she had such a surplus that she was able to sell fresh melons and greens in the market. Her wariness of the public meant that Beset was the one who actually took the produce to sell, but each sale was accompanied with a small square of papyrus on which Hypatia had drawn a picture of a bat. Her produce was prized and people wanted to know how such full fruit and abundant greens could be grown in the poor soil of the outskirts of Sheneset. Beset directed all inquisitors to the northeast part of Sheneset where Senmonthis' boys, if they were in the mood and could be found, would sell the dung for twenty denarii a basket, basket not included. In front of the whore's house, Hypatia had erected a small sign, about four feet square, bearing a larger image of the bat drawing that accompanied the produce. Sometimes Hypatia would cover her face and venture outside to conduct a sale when the boys could not be found, but the demand always far exceeded the boys' willingness to procure the product.

As the months passed Maggie grew. She sat up, rocked, crawled, took her first hesitant steps. She cooed, gurgled, laughed, mumbled, exclaimed incoherent syllables emphatically and stumbled upon her first words. Her first word was "Mama." Her second word was "Beeeh," which everyone agreed meant Beset. She smiled incessantly, cried occasionally, and ate heartily.

In short, she was enjoying the kind of happy childhood that should be every infant's birthright. Senmonthis quickly became part of the family. Four women (if you can count Magdalene as a woman) providing strength and joy and happiness to each other.

In the evening, Senmonthis would bring over an elaborately carved and inlaid Hounds and Jackals board and dice and they would play a round robin tournament while they teased each other and talked about anything and everything. Hypatia learned that Senmonthis claimed descent from high priests from the Thirtieth and Thirty-First and the Ptolemaic Dynasties. Originally priests of the cult of Toth, they had become priests of Serapis shortly after Ptolemy I declared himself Pharaoh and brought Serapis (or a statue of the god) by barge from Sinope on the Black Sea into the harbor at Alexandria. "I am an Eumolpidae," Senmonthis declared one evening, though what she meant neither Hypatia nor Beset had any idea. She explained that the Hounds and Jackals board, made of ebony inlaid with sycamore and ivory, had been passed down through "I don't know how many generations." Senmonthis would also tell stories of the old and newer Egyptian gods and of a modified version of Eleusinian Mysteries in which Osiris, Isis and Nut replaced the Greek deities Hades, Persephone and Demeter as the central characters. Senmonthis seemed to know a good deal about all of the old gods, but did not place them in any particular hierarchy. Eventually, Hypatia told her about gnosis, Sophia, the Ennoia, the Pleroma, the unknowable god, the lesser aeons and Yaldabaoth, Adam, Eve and Seth. On hearing this, Senmonthis said, "It's all the same. Yaldabaoth is Osiris. Sophia is Nut. Eve is Isis. It's the same, world over, by different names, so there must be something to it. The point is to elevate the mind, stand in the dung heap and reach for the stars, understand ourselves to be more than ourselves. Am I right?" To which Hypatia said she wasn't sure.

Senmonthis told Hypatia that there used to be an active

community of Gnostic Valentinians in Sheneset, before the Catholics ran them down with their Roman chariot and that she still knew some who probably still believed all that nonsense.

By the end of 326, conflict arose between Hypatia and Senmonthis' sons. When she made a sale, she would promptly turn over to the boys ten denarii out of twenty. But as time went on the boys provided her less and less. At first they said that someone was obviously stealing the guano. But soon they took to open defiance.

"Why should we pay you," Seti asked, "when we do all the work?"

"You're a woman," Bakare said, as if that was argument enough for the boys keeping all of the profit. When Hypatia protested that it was her donkey that hauled the dung and her vegetables that attracted customers, the boys simply shrugged their shoulders. Hypatia talked over the situation with Senmonthis and she tried to intervene, ordering the boys to pay Hypatia her due. "They outright refused," Senmonthis told her. "They're more like their father every day." Hypatia suggested a complaint to the civil authorities, but Senmonthis said that under Roman law a woman would not be heard if she brought suit, unless the matter involved her own marriage. In the case of a marriage dispute, Senmonthis explained, they would hear a woman out as long as she amused them with tales of her husband's depravity, then would dismiss her claim as not meeting the requirements of law, requirements which were never explained. Hypatia got the distinct impression that Senmonthis was speaking from direct experience.

"Best not to let them boys know there's nothing you can do," Senmonthis said. "Just make as many sales as you can and keep all you take in. That's my advice."

So that's what Hypatia did until the boys decided in protest to stop procuring dung from the caves. Hypatia was left with an ass to feed and nothing for it to do. The ass, which Hypatia had named Alexander the Great, settled down into one of the more comfortable lifestyles in Sheneset.

"There's sometimes you just need a man to live," Senmonthis said. "But marry a stupid one, is the best advice. But, then again what do I know? I married a stupid one and suffered every day for twenty-eight years."

At Hypatia's urging, Senmonthis took the bound translation of the book she had taken from Eusebius' library and gave it to one of the old Valentinians she spoke of. Hypatia did not know and did not want to know the beneficiary of her gift, though was pleased when Senmonthis reported that upon realizing what he had been given, the man threw himself face down on the ground and praised Sophia (the goddess) for the blessing.

In February 327, Hypatia turned twenty. On the last day of February, Magdalene turned one. By the time the summer heat began to rise again in May, Hypatia had begun to think about a long life. She wanted more than what she had. She loved the three women in her life, but she slowly realized that what she had was not enough. She needed more life, more excitement, more struggle. Naturally for one who came of age in a brothel and took her first independent actions as a wandering missionary with Timaeus, her vision of a fuller future took the shape of a man. She did not want any of the men who had pursued her before and after Maggie's birth. Nor did she want a man like Timaeus, who would pursue an unobtainable goal into the mouth of a lion. Her move to Sheneset had accomplished her main purpose. Only Ankha, with whom Beset remained in touch, and Pachome, who seemed to have her scent, had discovered that she had moved less than five miles. Ankha had come to realize that Hypatia would not be his wife. Pachome had resumed leaving the occasional flower for her to find, but she learned that he was busy founding new monasteries on the east bank around Sheneset and seemed to have his obsession at least partially under control. Neither one of them would do. Hypatia was beginning to understand how difficult it was to be an independent woman in the Roman Empire. No laws protected her. Marriage, she understood, was not necessarily the answer. She did not want to be a mere appendage. Ideally, she thought, she wanted a man who would bend to her wishes as often as she bent to his. Someone who could read and write, but who would respect her opinions. Someone who, without suppressing her, would give her standing in the event of disputes like those she had with Seti and Bakare and someone who would shield her from the unwanted attentions of men like Cato Plutonious and Nabwenenef. During some of these ruminations the thought of Philippus would come to her as a candidate. She had liked him, she had to admit and, if he was not bound by the vows of a priest, might make the kind of husband she needed. But she quickly dismissed such thoughts about the young priest because, after all, he was a priest, bound by vows of celibacy and it was unlikely she would ever see him again. So, as her desire for a husband took shape in her mind, she despaired of ever realizing it, especially since she assiduously avoided the attention of men altogether and had no man in her family who could arrange a marriage. Even if these obstacles could be overcome, she wondered whether such a man even existed outside of her imagination.

Still, life was not bad. Better, in fact, she told herself, than she had any right to expect, especially after Nicaea. She would live on, oversee Maggie's delightful growth and in the evenings play games and talk with her friends Beset and Senmonthis. Then, in the middle of May, a brown robed priest showed up at her door. His beard had filled out a little and the hair on his head had thinned a little, but she instantly recognized the anxiously grinning Philippus.

Chapter Twenty-Five

Philippus

327 A.D. – Sheneset

Great is the mystery of marriage! For without it the world would not exist.
The Gospel of Phillip

"Philippus!" Hypatia exclaimed when she saw the expectant countenance of the young priest in her doorway. "What are you doing here?"

It was mid-afternoon with the 100-degree heat as unmoving as an obstinate mule. Philippus' brow glistened and he slumped slightly under the weight of the cloth bag slung over his shoulders. Behind him, Hypatia saw a heavily laden grey and white she-ass tied to a palm tree. Alexander the Great could be seen straining to the end of his long tether to inspect the new arrival.

Philippus daubed at his brow with a cotton cloth that was more mottled grey than its original white. The grin did not leave his face. "You weren't expecting me, then?" he replied to Hypatia's exclamation.

"Should I have been?"

"I wrote that I was coming?"

"You wrote to who?"

"To you, of course. Hypatia of Chenoboskion."

"By way of Imperial post?"

"Yes."

"Oh Lord."

"'Thou shalt not take the Lord's name in vain.'"

"What were you thinking? I never received it. Anyone could

have read it and learn where I live."

"You probably never received it because it turns out I did not know where you lived."

Hypatia shrugged, then hugged Philippus in the most casual of manners. "You may as well come in," she said. "You've travelled this far. Does your ass need tending?"

"She could use some fodder and water."

"Come in then. I'll have Beset tend to her."

Philippus bowed his head and followed her inside. After instructing Beset as to the care of the animal, Hypatia brought Philippus a cup of water and bid him to sit on some cushions arranged on the floor. Philippus removed his brown pileus and began massaging his scalp with his left hand. Soon his smile had reappeared as he looked shyly, but expectantly at Hypatia.

Finally he said, "It was a good bit of trouble to find you. You have moved from the house I found for you."

"I have," Hypatia replied, not bothering to correct his memory of which of them found the house on the west bank. "I like it here in Sheneset much better."

"I don't blame you for not writing to tell me. Still, it was a good bit of trouble to find you. I went to where I left you and spoke with the landlord, but he had no idea where you had gone. He said you had slipped off in the middle of the night." Philippus paused to await an explanation. None was forthcoming.

"I started asking around if anyone knew where a Hypatia or a Sophia of your description lived, but nobody did."

"You asked for Sophia?"

"You used to go by that name."

"Jesus! The whole aim in moving here was to banish that identity."

"Please do not swear, Sof — Hypatia." Hypatia did not acknowledge his rebuke and Philippus continued. "It should be of no concern, because though I met several who said they had known a Hypatia meeting your description, they had not seen her in several months and knew not where she had gone."

"If I was so well hidden, you would not have found me."

"I nearly did not. Night was coming and I sought shelter in a community of monks founded by a good Christian named Pachomius. The man himself was there, though he calls himself Pachome and speaks only in the Egyptian tongue. We needed a translator. He asked what brought me to Chenoboskion and I told him that I was seeking a young woman named Hypatia who probably had a small child with her. When I said your name, he started and stared back hard at me, but hastily denied knowing any such person. He asked me why I sought this woman and I told him. He seemed to consider me and my purpose for a few minutes before finally telling me that he knew where you lived. See, he would not tell me he knew who you were until he determined my purpose, then he said he would take me there in the morning and he was good to his word. So you see, you have a protector here."

"I do not want a protector. I want to be unknown."

"Pardon my boldness, but with such beauty as yours, you cannot be unknown."

Hypatia frowned and said, "What did you tell Pachome your purpose was?"

"The truth," Philippus answered with another smile.

"And what is the truth, Philippus?"

"To bring you your fortune, of course."

"My fortune?"

"Yes. Timaeus' estate. Eusebius managed to secure your inheritance. Timaeus' brother was helpful and cooperative. You know, for someone who dressed and travelled as a beggar and proclaimed to care aught of this world, Timaeus surely owned a big piece of it. Over two thousand gold solidi is what it all came to!"

Rather than the expression of delight Philippus expected his news to evoke, Hypatia grimaced and frowned as two thousand new terrors raced through her mind. The attraction of her appearance and the dangers it engendered were nothing to the attraction of such an amount of gold if news got out that it was in her possession.

"You told all this to Pachome?" she asked.

"Not the details. Not the amount."

"I guess there's some solace in that."

After a few more moments Hypatia asked, "How is it arranged? How am I to access it if I need to?"

Philippus smiled an even broader smile. "By reaching into your purse, I suppose," he said.

"You mean to say you brought it with you?"

"It's packed on the donkey."

"Jesus Christ!"

"I don't remember you being so profane, Sophia."

"I never had such cause. And my name is Hypatia."

Gathering her wits, Hypatia instructed Philippus not to say a word to anyone else about the money he had brought. Even though she trusted Beset completely, it would be best if she knew nothing about it so there could be no chance of an errant word slipping out. Hypatia had never even told her about the small fortune she already possessed. "I wish there was some plausible reason we could give for your visit, other than its actual purpose," Hypatia said.

"We could say I brought you books," Philippus replied.

"What?"

"It would be the truth. I brought you some volumes from the Bishop's library. Gnostic texts. He said it was getting too dangerous to hold on to them and directed me to take them to you."

For the first time since Philippus entered the house, Hypatia smiled. "It's a pretty sorry excuse for such a journey, but that's what we'll say then," she said. "But let's not say Gnostic texts. Let's just say duplicates of Christian texts from the North."

"One more thing, Philippus," Hypatia said. "Can you stay for a while until we get everything sorted out? I'm not sure what to do."

"The bishop said I can stay as long as you need me," Philippus replied.

Hypatia tried to think of what should be done. It was clear to her that she could not keep so large a sum with her. Nor would she trust it to a banker. It was not simply that, having no experience with such men, she could not bring herself to believe they could be trusted; it was more worrisome that the mere act of placing the funds with someone else would serve to advertise their existence to the world at large. Being a single woman was one thing. Being a rich single woman, without any protection or rights at law, was exceedingly dangerous.

More terrifying was the news from Philippus that Athanasius had not ceased his search for Timaeus' companion. With Alexander, the old Bishop of Alexandria, in failing health, the twenty-seven year old Athanasius seemed to be consolidating power, though whether this was with or without Alexander's endorsement was uncertain. Philippus joked that since a bishop had to be at least thirty years of age, Athanasius must be praying daily for old Alexander's recovery, for another three years at least. Philippus was but one year younger than Athanasius, yet while it seemed to him that he was still at the commencement of his vocation, Athanasius acted as if he was born to command and was seizing all the power that Alexander, in his weakened state, let slip free. Athanasius had written a formal letter to all the other major Sees in Alexander's name, proclaiming that it was of the utmost importance that the young woman who, impersonating a scribe, had attended the Council at Nicaea in the company of a famous heretic, be found and brought before the bishop to be questioned concerning the heretic's followers and sources of support. The letter said that she had been known to go by the names Sophia, Sophocles, Adama and Hypatia. The letter said that she was a skillful impersonator of a young man, but that her slight build, soft features, and lack of beard gave away the disguise. It was believed that she might be hiding out in Cappadocia, where the heretic was from, or around Antioch or Alexandria, where she was known to have lived. The letter stated that she was a known prostitute and may have returned to that profession to support herself. The letter finished with a screed against Gnostic thought. That such a well-known Gnostic heretic could have infiltrated the council of bishops at Nicaea testified to the strength and continued vitality of that heresy. It was now time, once and for all, to put an end to all persons and writings that, under the name Christian, adhere to and promulgate this devil's deception. All Gnostic texts were to be burned and all Gnostic adherents were to be excommunicated and punished to the full extent of the Church's ability. All bishops were asked to reply by letter articulating what steps to accomplish these ends had and would be taken and to certify that all known Gnostic texts had been destroyed.

It troubled Hypatia profoundly that Athanasius knew her by Hypatia and that she had once lived in Alexandria. Could it be that he remembered her and knew her name? As far as she remembered, he had paid attention to her in Alexandria only once when she was twelve and for no more than two minutes. In that time he did not ask and she did not say her name. He simply cupped his hand over her mouth and forced his heaving body onto hers. She referred to the rape as her baptism into Christianity, but she did not think he knew her as anything other than just another street waif who sometimes found shelter in the shade of the church walls. This was disturbing news indeed.

Hypatia herself carried the leather bag containing the gold in from Philippus' ass, waiting until Beset had gone to market. She marveled at how twenty pounds of gold could amount to more than most people could use in ten lifetimes. She sold five pounds of bat guano for twenty denarii. She would have to sell several tons of guano to earn one solidus. Now she had more than two thousand of them without having to lift a finger. Without telling Beset, she placed the bag under her bed mat, digging a hole in the earth for the purpose. She knew it could not stay there long.

Beset remembered Philippus and greeted him with an indifferent politeness that betrayed her displeasure at this male interruption into the muliebrous household. At first, the fifteen-month-old Magdalene shared Beset's qualms. When she awoke from a nap to find him seated on a cushion in her house, her round face elongated into an exaggerated frown as if pulled down by gravity. The frown was soon followed by a full-on wail as she scampered on unsteady legs to the arms of her mother. Philippus awkwardly attempted to win the child's favor. He clucked his tongue and smacked his lips and blinked his eyes, but every effort at conciliation only resulted in louder howls of anguish. She pointed at Beset, demanding that she join her mother and her in united defense against this strange intruder. The efforts Hypatia made to assure Maggie that this man was a friend were instantly undermined by Beset's intense hugs and determined patting of her hair. It was a full fifteen minutes before Maggie calmed down enough for any further conversation to be held and that only came after Philippus had left his cushion and stood in the corner of the room farthest from the little girl. Magdalene continued to glower at the stranger with unamused and suspicious intensity.

Before evening Senmonthis appeared. She had seen the priest arrive on his ass and wondered at the meaning of this remarkable occurrence. Hypatia had told her that she guessed she was Christian, but in the months she had known her she had given no indication that she was interested in anything other than those Gnostic texts she studied and even that without much passion. She was also surprised that Hypatia had said nothing to her about expecting a visitor, let alone expecting a priest. As she came over to the old whore's house to satisfy her curiosity, she surmised that Philippus must be a long lost brother. He must be long lost because she remembered Hypatia telling her she was an orphan and a widow, without family. She was determined to satisfy her curiosity as soon as possible.

Hypatia introduced Philippus to Senmonthis as her "old friend." She said that he had come down to Sheneset to deliver some old books of the same kind she amused herself by copying into Coptic in the evenings. He was tired from his travels and would be staying with her for a few days until he was rested and ready to return.

"Oh no he isn't," Senmonthis exclaimed when she heard this plan. "You will not be having a man under your roof at night; I don't care if he is a monk or some such."

"What do you suggest?" Hypatia asked. "He must stay somewhere."

"Why won't he stay with that desert monk I keep seeing?"

"I'd rather he didn't. Not every Catholic is my friend."

"He can sleep with Bakare and Seti if he's got nowhere else to go. But he's not staying here." Philippus' countenance fell, but he did not argue. Senmonthis' emphatic reaction brought home to him in a surge of disappointment that it would not be proper for him to stay under the same roof as Hypatia.

Over the next week a pattern developed. After an uncomfortable night squeezed in with Bakare and Seti, Philippus would rise with the stink of the boys' smell of dung and sweat heavy in his nostrils, where it would remain all day. He would wash at the ass trough, but for the first week found himself unable to bathe or properly scent his body in the manner to which he was accustomed. Hypatia and Beset fed him morning and evening, except on those saint's days and other occasions on which he fasted.

For the first two days he mostly slept, keeping himself awake only long enough to finish his extensive prayers twice a day. On the third day he rose, refreshed and full of life. He said he wanted to help in any way he could. Hypatia told him about her troubles with Bakare and Seti over the sale of bat guano. People still came around to the house to buy it, but they had none to sell. Philippus asked Hypatia why she would want to engage in such labor now that she was rich. She scowled at him and told him that nobody must ever know about her fortune. She told him that it would probably have been much better and certainly much easier if he had never brought it. She told him it would be dangerous for her if word got out that she was worth anywhere near such a sum.

"I am a single mother. As long as I live within modest means and appear to have the need for a small income, I believe I can get by here in Sheneset. But if word gets out that I am wealthy, there will be no end of trouble, for me and for Magdalene."

"You need a husband," Philippus said.

"I do."

"Any candidates?"

"None come to mind."

Philippus smiled and felt a pang of relief, the cause of which he refused to acknowledge to himself.

So it was that Philippus agreed to accompany Hypatia into the hills with their two donkeys to dig guano and bring it back to the yard.

On their journey into the hills, Philippus told Hypatia that it had cost Eusebius almost three solidi to arrange Timaeus' will, buy the ass for Philippus, and pay for Philippus' travel expenses, which included a former legionary to accompany him for most of the journey. Hypatia told him she would give him twenty of the gold coins if he would promise to hire the soldier to keep him safe on his return. He told her more about the politics swirling around the church. The Trinitarians claimed a great victory at Nicaea and, emboldened by the Emperor's apparent support, were aggressively working to stomp out all divergent thought.

Eustathius of Antioch was avidly pushing the bishops to excommunicate Eusebius again, saying that his admiration for some of the writings of Origen betrayed Arian, and perhaps even Gnostic, sympathies. Hypatia was not familiar with Origen, but followed enough to understand that men fixed in their faith were fighting over things that they could not know.

"I think you said you knew Eustathius?" Philippus asked.

"I met him."

"In Antioch?"

"Yes."

"At the brothel?"

Hypatia did not answer but gave a look that signaled to Philippus that his inquiry had gone far enough.

Although they had left before light in the early morning, by the time they reached the first hills of the red land the sun had pulled itself up over the horizon and laid upon them with all its smothering weight. When they reached the first of the caves, the dank smell was as refreshing as the scent of hibiscus because with it came cool respite. The caves were arid (the smell of moldering bat dung providing the dankness). After drawing the donkeys inside, they poured water from a vessel into bowls for the beasts and into a cup, which they shared.

As they filled baskets with accumulated centuries of bat ordure, Philippus prattled on in the nervous manner Hypatia remembered from their earlier journey together. The dark brown bodies of Trident bats hung from the ceiling of the caves like clusters of grapes from a vine, tolerant of, if not grateful for, the housecleaning the two were engaged in several feet below them. Philippus told Hypatia that he was as certain of his vocation as ever, sure that he had chosen the correct path in life for himself, but that it came with regrets. For example, he said, seeing her with her young daughter made his heart long for children of his own.

"I know she doesn't like me much," he said, "but I am determined to bring her around by the end of my visit." He finished with, "I can be charming, you know?"

Hypatia smiled, but did not give him the verbal reassurance he was seeking. Another thing, he told her, was that younger priests, those with a better education, seemed to be rising above him in the Church. He knew that Eusebius trusted and liked him, but it hurt that he was never asked to help Eusebius with his research (he was currently engaged in writing an extensive biography of Emperor Constantine) and had not assigned him to a parish of his own, although several priests younger than himself had been entrusted with such responsibility. He was beginning to wonder, he told her, whether he was the owner of some deficiency of mind or spirit or faith that held him back. "'Patience and prayer,' Eusebius always tells me," he said. "And I pray constantly and I have patience, but the Lord has not yet revealed my place in the world to me. I must pray some more."

"Philippus," Hypatia answered him, "I have known two truly kind men in my life. I married the first one. I am happy to call you my friend. I would surely have perished without you. I am not ignorant of the risks that you and Eusebius have taken for my sake. If to be Christian means to be good, then you are the most Christian of men. Do not trouble yourself about these things. You are on the right path, you just cannot see yet where it leads."

Philippus smiled so broadly at her words that Hypatia could see the expression even in the faint light that eluded the shade of the cave.

When their baskets were filled, Hypatia told Philippus that she wanted to explore caves a little further away from the city as new sources of supply. They left the filled baskets at the entrance of the cave they had been working in for later retrieval and led the asses with them further up into the desert hills. Although they saw several obvious openings among the rocks, this was not what Hypatia seemed to be looking for. Finally, she spied a slight crevice, with a small vertical mouth barely wide enough for her to slip through. She directed Philippus to wait outside the entrance and to call to her if she happened to lose her way once inside. The caution was unnecessary. The cave was shallow. Unlike in the last cave, where the bats remained somnambulant, her movements here disturbed them in great numbers, rushing about above and around her, but never flying into her. Her feet crunched and sunk into the semi-hardened guano. She felt her way to a recess and followed it back a few paces. She wanted to say something, just to hear her voice echo in the cavern, but nothing came readily to mind. She thought of Philippus' fretful account of his doubts. She thought of Timaeus, how that strange and wonderful man had so mysteriously entered her life and led her even here, to this cave above Sheneset, with a kind and worried priest as her companion. She thought that, like Philippus, she could not see where her path would lead her. And thinking these things, she said in a crisp and clear voice, "I give my life to God," and laughed.

"Hypatia," she heard Philippus shout into the cave.

"I am returning," she called back.

When she re-entered the world, the light blinded her and she covered her eyes with her dung-stained hands. Without speaking she led Philippus and the asses away from the mouth of the cave to a distance where she could barely make it out from its backdrop of rock, about fifty paces. She looked around, noting landmarks, the shape of the surrounding hills. A lancet of rock pointed vertically toward the sky, an obscure wind-carved Egyptian face with two distinct eyes and an oval mouth stained into a boulder perched precariously above the opening of the cave. Yes, she could find this place again.

"It is a good place," she told Philippus. "We will come back here in a few days."

"Don't you have enough dung for a while?"

"I have something else in mind," Hypatia replied, and would say no more.

They returned to the first cave and placed the laden baskets on the backs of the asses.

On their way back down to Sheneset, Philippus asked her if she remembered their first meeting, when she and Timaeus came to the church in Caesarea. Yes, of course she did, she replied.

"But do you remember me at all from that meeting?"

"You answered the door and brought us food. That is really all I recall. Timaeus thought he smelled you in the manger where we slept, but we were fearful, being heretics in a Catholic church. I think he imagined it."

"Did he think I meant him harm?

"Yes. He thought you might be intending to cause trouble for us or for Bishop Eusebius."

Philippus gasped. "I would never have betrayed you … or the bishop." His face soured as if he were about to cry.

"I told Timaeus that I thought he was wrong."

They walked on in silence. A trace of white brushed the sky, useless clouds, decorative at best. It was approaching evening as they entered Sheneset. Hypatia realized again that she was fond of Philippus. His proclivity to prattle aside, she found him pleasant and amusing. She liked him.

Breaking an uncharacteristic hour-long silence, as they entered Sheneset, Philippus suddenly resumed with the same subject that had driven him to silence. "Would you like to know why I entered the stable that night?"

"If you would like to tell me."

"I wanted to see you, to look at you one more time before you left."

Hypatia's brow knotted. "To look at me?" she asked.

"I had never seen anyone so beautiful in my life. I needed to check that my eyes were not deceiving me."

"And what did you decide?"

"My eyes did not deceive me," he said. And then, "Do you think such thoughts are sinful for a priest?"

"If so, I forgive your sin as far as it is in my power to do so. Thank you, Philippus."

That evening Senmonthis scolded Hypatia for being away so long in the company of a man. "People will talk, if they know," she said.

"Then you'll be sure not to tell them," Hypatia replied as Senmonthis clucked her disapproval. "And beside that," Hypatia continued, "Philippus is a priest, a man of God."

"Some of them's the worst ones," was the reply.

Despite her disapproval of their outing, over the next couple of days Senmonthis came to like Philippus, to the extent of teaching and allowing him to join in the games of Hounds and Jackals. Magdalene was a little slower to come around, but by the end of Philippus' second week in Sheneset, she was allowing him to hold her and to play games of hide and seek, where the only things hidden were his eyes.

On the Sabbath he wanted Hypatia to go to mass with him, but she refused. She asked him not to attend, being fearful that he might be asked about what brought a priest down to Sheneset and, through further inquiry, lead to the discovery of who she was and why she had moved there.

"I have already said I would never betray you. But I must attend mass, confess my sins and take communion."

While he was gone, Senmonthis came over and huddled a while with Beset while Hypatia fed and played with Maggie on the floor. After several minutes, Beset came over and scooped the child up into her arms. Hypatia looked up to find Senmonthis standing beside Beset, arms akimbo.

"Beset and I have decided that you must marry Philippus," Senmonthis proclaimed.

"That is very unfair of you," Hypatia protested. "I have done nothing improper."

"I know that and it is not likely that you will do so. That is why we must tell you to marry him."

"I don't understand."

"You need a husband. Have you not said so many times yourself?"

"It would make my life easier."

"And you like Philippus, do you not?"

"Yes. I am fond of him."

"He is a perfect husband then. You must marry him."

Hypatia could understand their logic. Perhaps she did not love Philippus, but she did like him and found pleasure and comfort in his company. He would, she thought, bend to her wishes without being completely her slave, just as she sometimes specified to herself. But he was a priest. He would not renounce his calling to marry her. She said this to Beset and Senmonthis.

"He is a priest," she said. "He has taken a vow of celibacy. He would not give up his vocation."

"He is a man first," Senmonthis said. "If flour comes to pudding, let him keep his vow of celibacy, if he likes. That's not what you need a husband for."

Beset laughed at this. "Unless I can't read men no more, that one would follow you into Duat without a guide. He'll make new vows for you I reckon." Her use of "Duat," the name for the Egyptian underworld, instead of Hades or Hell, betrayed Senmonthis' growing influence upon her.

"Well," Hypatia said, "this is all very interesting, but I will not be asking him to marry me and he will not ask me, so that is an end of it. He will go back to Caesarea in a few days and we will likely never see him again. So, that's that."

That may have been the end of it, except that the women would not let the matter drop. When Philippus came to Senmonthis' house that night to sleep with Bakare and Seti, Beset came with him, ostensibly to return the Hounds and Jackals board that Senmonthis had intentionally left behind. When they entered the house, Senmonthis immediately stopped Philippus and said brusquely, "You must marry Hypatia."

"What?"

"She is pretty, is she not?"

"She is beautiful beyond words."

"And you are a good friend to her, are you not?"

"I hope that I am. I would do anything for her."

"And she has told you that she is in grave danger here in Sheneset, has she not?"

"No. She has said nothing of the kind."

"Why do you think she moved from the west bank to here?

"She said she liked it better here."

Beset placed a hand on Philippus' shoulder. "You should know what happened last year," she said ominously. "Them's was bad times and not likely over."

"What? What happened to Hypatia?" Philippus' voice quavered in alarm.

Beset's voice was conspiratorial and full of fear, some of it real. "Just afore the little one was born an Egyptian high priest started coming around, claiming that our young miss was a goddess reborn. Hathor, he said she was. He set up a temple in our yard and had many followers come to worship and camp around the house. They was waiting on the birth of her child. The priest said the child would be a boy and would be Ra himself and would expel the Romans from Egypt. His doings and sayings got the Romans' notice down in Caneopolis and they sent up some dandy consul to come have her killed, rather than risk there being a Ra born. And they'd have killed her too, if the two soldiers that come along with him hadn't fallen in love with her at first sight. I should know, 'cause one of them soldiers was my son, which I hadn't seen in twenty years. Even then the consul said she could live only if she gave birth to a girl child, which our clever miss was able to do. After that both of the soldiers, including my son, proposed marriage to her, the consul come back and want to make her his mistress, the priest come back and want to father a male child with her. Even that monk you stayed with, Pakimas I think, he proposes to throw all he's been doing away if she'll marry him. Now, none of them are suitable for her and if she marries or carries on with one, the others are going to hold a grudge. So she moved over here and so far it's worked to throw them off the scent, except for Pakimas and my son, who won't tell nobody, but how long before the others find out? And I don't know how she supports herself. She's got some money packed away, I guess, but it can't be much. And what can she do to keep herself and the little one? She can't sew or weave, though I've tried to learn her on that. She tries to sell that bat dung, but Senmonthis' boys sell it mostly and keep the money. There's many who think she's a kept woman, but just who would keep a woman without ever seeing her, I guess I don't know. And meanwhile, she can't go nowhere, for fear that all that nonsense from last year will start back up all over again."

Philippus stood with a stupefied expression cemented to his face. He meekly said, "I had no idea."

"So you see," Senmonthis said. "You put her in the stew pot, bringing her down here and no mistake about that. And as a Christian, you're supposed to do good by others, isn't that right? And the best thing you could do for our young Hypatia is to marry her."

Philippus removed his pileus and began to rub at his thinning scalp. This was shocking news and a genuine dilemma. His heart raced at the prospect of what these two women were proposing, but his mind stumbled into complete disarray. From childhood forward he had mapped out a direct and ordered life. The thought of marriage to the beautiful Sophia, as appealing as he found it, shattered those plans.

"I'm a priest," he said quietly. "I have taken a vow of celibacy. I cannot marry."

"Well," Senmonthis replied, "you just removed your priest cap to rub your noggin and I take that as a good sign. Let me ask you this: would marrying Hypatia make you happy?"

"My happiest times in life are when I am with her."

"And does your Jesus want you to be unhappy?"

"No. I don't believe that He does. He wants us to accept Him as Savior and to know that He died for our sins so that we may have everlasting life."

"And can't a married man do that as well as a priest?"

"Yes, but the priesthood is my vocation."

"Can't a priest be married?"

"Technically it is not forbidden, though Eusebius would not allow it among his congregational priests. No, I would have to renounce my ordination in order to marry."

"Well, you must do as you must I suppose, but know you that if Hypatia is not properly married and soon, it is likely she will be killed or suffer an even worse fate."

Philippus continued to rub at his scalp and could be seen visibly thinking over all that the women had said to him. Finally he said, "She would not have me. She would not marry me."

Beset replied, "How do you know? You ain't asked her yet, unless that's what you were doing up in the caves a few days back."

"No, I have not asked her, nor would I presume to, because she would say no."

Senmonthis said, "Don't be so sure before you ask."

The next morning when Philippus went over to Hypatia's house he looked for signs that she knew something about the conversation he had with Beset and Senmonthis the night before, but there was nothing in her speech or conduct that gave away any such knowledge. To test her further he said that he would have to be returning to Caesarea in the next few days, but would miss her and Maggie and Beset and the hospitality they had shown him. Hypatia did not react with any alarm at this news, but did say that he hoped Philippus would stay long enough to help her perform one more task.

"Of course," Philippus replied. "What would you have me do?"

"I would like you to go to the market and purchase a strong iron box with a secure fitting lid and a lock." There were at least two blacksmiths from whom she was sure such a box could be purchased. "If they do not have one ready for sale, commission its manufacture. It must be large enough to contain all of what you brought with you to Sheneset."

"The books as well?" Philippus asked.

"No, not the books. I'll keep them here. The other materials you brought."

Philippus smiled in complicit acknowledgement of the task she gave him. And returned that very day with an excellent iron chest about two feet square, with a secure lid and a lock.

Upon its delivery to Hypatia, Philippus said, "Since you have found the chest suitable, will there be anything else, since I must return soon?"

"I would have you accompany me into the hills tomorrow, to place the chest in the farthest cave I entered last week."

"You are going put the gold in a cave?"

"It will not be found and only you and I will know where it is. It will be much safer there than here."

"You should give it to the Church if you are not going to use it."

"I do not think that is what Timaeus would have wanted. He could have given it to the Church himself, when he was a bishop. No, I think I will hold on to it for now."

"And once you've hidden the box, may I return to Caesarea or will you have further need of me?"

"No," she said. "Once we have placed the box in the cave, you may return, with my many thanks and with my anxious prayers for your safe journey."

Try as he did, Philippus could read no hope into anything she said or did.

The next morning, leaving Maggie in the care of Beset, she asked Philippus to tote the sack lying on the floor next to her pallet and told Beset and Maggie that Philippus would be returning to Caesarea in the next couple of days, but had agreed to help her bring down more baskets of dung from the caves before he left.

"I don't know why you bother," Beset protested. "Them no good ones next door have been selling it right along and I bet you ain't seen a single denarii from it."

"All the more reason to fetch more," Hypatia replied. "That way I'll have something to sell to support us after Philippus leaves."

There were thick clouds in the sky this day, which was unusual for early June. On their way up into the mountains the clouds opened and let fall a few minutes of warm, but refreshing rain on the companions and their beasts. The journey took them through the black land where millennia of Nile flooding had deposited rich, fertile soil on the face of the earth, and up into the cliffs of the red land, barren and dry. Even though they travelled the greatest distance through black land, the time of their journey was spent mostly in red land. After three hours Hypatia spotted the lancet rock, then the Egyptian face boulder. She bid Philippus to carry the sack containing the box the rest of the way to the vertical mouth of the cave. At its entrance, with great effort she removed the box containing the gold from the sack. She opened the box and counted out thirty gold solidi and gave them to Philippus.

"You promised only twenty," he reminded her.

"I guess you don't have to take it all," she replied. "But I find the box is too heavy for me to carry into the cave unless I lighten its contents a little more than by twenty." She gave no look or word that betrayed the fact that her generosity was motivated by anything other than a desire to lighten the burden. Philippus took the thirty coins, saying he would donate them all to the Church, in her name.

She sharply rebuked him. "Give them to the Church if you like," she said, "but not in my name by Heaven's sake."

She left him again at the mouth of the cave while she struggled to carry the box inside. The cave was not deep, ending perhaps four feet from the entrance. She pushed the chest into the cave and reemerged about five minutes later, empty handed.

On the way back to town they stopped at another cave and filled their baskets with rich excrement. When they continued their journey, the clouds were gone and the temperatures soared so in a short time they sought shelter in the shade of an outcropping. They poured the last of their water out, most for the donkeys, saving only a little for themselves.

"You have been very kind and helpful to me, Philippus," Hypatia said. "I hope you will forgive my harsh words to you on the day you arrived."

"And your taking of the Lord's name in vain."

"I will not ask your forgiveness for that. But I am sorry for the anger I directed at you."

Philippus was silent for a few moments, then asked, "Will you miss me when I'm gone?"

"Yes, of course I will. You have been most helpful to me. You are a good friend."

"Will you miss me as more than a friend?" Philippus reddened at his own burst of sudden boldness, but he did not withdraw the question.

"I do not know what you mean. You are a good friend and I will miss you."

Having taken the first bold step, Philippus now stumbled forward. "Could you miss me as more than a friend?"

"I guess I could, if you were more than a friend."

"Would you be more than a friend to me?"

Now it was Hypatia's turn to redden. "What on earth do you

mean by that?" she demanded.

Suddenly realizing how Hypatia had understood his last question, he stumbled on. "As a husband," he blurted. "Could you miss me as a husband?"

Hypatia stared in wonderment at the young priest. Was he proposing to her? Or propositioning her? She could not imagine it could be either, so she said, "I guess I could, if you were my husband, but I don't see how that would ever be."

Philippus was all earnestness now. "Are you saying you would not marry me, if I asked?" He was visibly crestfallen.

"No," Hypatia answered. "I was not saying that. I was only saying that you would never ask."

"What if I did ask you to marry me?"

"Then I would answer you."

"What would your answer be?"

"No, no, no. You do not get a free look. You must ask if you want an answer."

Heart racing, not believing that he had talked himself into this confusing and uncertain position, Philippus plunged ahead. "Sophia," he said. "Would you marry me?"

"Yes," she said. "And my name is Hypatia." There were no tears of joy. Hypatia concealed the excitement she felt. Her simple "yes" and a smile were enough to propel Philippus into a state of confused, but proud ecstasy.

Chapter Twenty-Six

Happy Life

327-330 – Sheneset

> *I am lust in outward appearance, and interior self-control exists within me.*
> *I am the hearing which is attainable to everyone and the speech which cannot be grasped.*
> *I am a mute who does not speak, and great is my multitude of words.*
> *Hear me in gentleness, and learn of me in roughness.*
> Thunder, Perfect Mind

Philippus had no memory of the first several hours following Hypatia's acceptance of his proposal. His mind soared to the firmament where all good things reside and only slowly descended back to Earth softly, as if delivered on a cloud, white and billowy of a kind never seen in Sheneset. Only in the evening, as he was softly touching down, did he decide that he could not wed unless and until he obtained Eusebius' blessing. He wrote a long letter to his bishop to explain his decision, express his regrets, make his apologies and seek approval of his desire to wed Hypatia. He told Hypatia that he could not marry her until he received the reply and desired blessing. In the meantime, he continued to sleep with Senmonthis' sons. While he awaited Eusebius' reply his mind raced with erotic thoughts of the beautiful Sophia, Hypatia, rather, and the pleasures of the flesh he hoped would soon be his. Yet these thoughts triggered an almost immediate wave of shame. He had believed for as long as he could remember that sexual relations were inherently sinful. The Bible promoted marriage, it is true, but only as a necessary substitute for chastity for those weak in spirit. Had not Paul written, "If they cannot exercise self-control, they should marry. For it is better to marry than to burn with passion"? He burned with passion, so it was better to marry, but having lived so long a life of self-control the shame he felt at his failure to sustain it quickly nipped at the heels of his every carnal thought of Sophia, Hypatia. Philippus' internal conflict manifested itself in an embarrassed enthusiasm for every task that any of the women asked of him and the many unrequested ones he performed gratuitously. He looked closely at Hypatia for signs that she too longed to consummate their marriage, but he found none. She was kind and polite, but reserved. If she was anxious or excited in any way, it was not apparent to him. What he did not know was that the beatific calm she radiated and that he mistook for indifference was the soft joy that came from knowing that she would soon be married to the perfect man or, at least, the man whose likeness she had sketched for herself when imagining the perfect husband.

The period waiting for Eusebius' response was eventful for Philippus as he awkwardly merged with the two households. Even though Hypatia quickly nixed any notion they had about having a ceremony that included anyone beyond the seven souls that inhabited the two houses, Beset and Senmonthis were excited by the betrothal and they began to stockpile and plan the acquisition of items necessary for a small feast when the day came. Senmonthis frequently said to Philippus that Hypatia would certainly enjoy having a strong man around the house and that Beset and she wouldn't mind it either. At first Philippus thought this was a straightforward statement, but the frequency with which it was repeated, the sparkle in Senmonthis' eyes when she said it, and Beset's abashed shuffling when she heard it soon caused Philippus to suspect a lurking entendre.

Bakare and Seti did not possess such subtlety. One night as they laid with Philippus on pallets in their corner of Senmonthis' house, the two boys waited a few minutes until they imagined Philippus was approaching sleep, then softly began to moan.

"Oh, Hypatia," Bakare cooed, "you feel so good to my loins."

"And your breasts are like honey stuck in my mouth," Seti replied.

"Oh. Oh. Your thighs are as soft and warm as cheese curds in my hands," said Bakare.

Finally Philippus said, "Enough," to which Bakare replied, "Never enough, never enough of Hypatia."

The two boys burst into laughter at their clever taunting. After this first occasion, hardly a night went by without a resumption of their nighttime teasing, although their supply of similes was soon exhausted. Philippus learned to suffer the taunts in silence, secretly taking pleasure at each mention of Hypatia and reference to her physical attributes.

Hypatia had insisted that Philippus send at least ten solidi to Eusebius with his letter. He sent twenty. Hypatia added a postscript to Philippus' letter in Coptic, which Philippus could not read. The postscript advised Eusebius that his antagonist in Antioch, Eustathius, had been particularly fond of a married woman in that town. Hypatia named the woman, adding only that she thought Eusebius might find the information useful at some point in time. With the money Philippus sent to Eusebius, Hypatia considered the she-ass that Philippus had arrived on as purchased and named her Roxana, after Alexander the Great's first wife. Roxana and Alexander did not wait for the wedding to consummate their union. Before Eusebius' reply arrived, Roxana, by her swelling sides, was showing signs of Alexander the Great's interest in her.

Even though his approaching marriage to Hypatia would remove one of her objections to others knowing about her wealth, Philippus readily agreed with her that they should not risk Alexandria's attention by suddenly joining the ranks of the wealthy elite. Philippus had made vows of chastity and poverty when he took his orders. Eusebius willing, he would be forsaking his first vow. He was not ready to forsake the second an instant later. For Hypatia, the danger of being discovered as Timaeus' widow was not entirely abated by her upcoming marriage to Philippus and she preferred to keep the cave money secret, at least for now.

After six weeks Eusebius' letter arrived by commissioned messenger, along with another volume of Gnostic texts.

"Dearest Philippus," Eusebius began, "be assured that with one condition only you have my permission and my blessing to marry the love you have found on your journey to Egypt. That condition is that you bring her to Christ, that a Catholic priest perform your marriage, and that you two forever remain in the bosom of Christ's holy church. There. I guess these are three conditions, but they are all to one purpose. If you can do these things, I will not hold you to your other vows. You will be sorely missed, of course, but you leave with my blessing.

"The twenty coins you provided has allowed me to send this reply by private courier. He has already been paid. The rest will go to feed the poor of Caesarea and the surrounding villages.

"I am sending you a particularly heretical text so that you may destroy it far away from here, where there may be those who either attempt to preserve it or unjustly accuse he who seeks its destruction of the crime of ownership. Bishop Alexander of Alexandria weakens with each report and Athanasius asserts more power with each passing day. I thank Father and Son that he is only twenty-seven years old and therefore ineligible to become bishop when Alexander passes from this Earthly realm, which must be soon. In league with Eustathius, Bishop of Antioch, they continue to press a charge of heresy against your Eusebius, who has only ever been true and faithful to our Church and obedient of her commands. They point to words he wrote some years ago in praise of Origen, claim that Origen was an Arian and propose that he must therefore also be an Arian. How foolish is reason when founded upon deceit and fallacy! Origen lived more than a century ago and was thereby spared the sectarian hairsplitting with which men of today must abide. See how it is with such men as Athanasius and Eustathius, where good men, long ago gone to heaven, become bad men in the eyes of those who would turn friends into enemies? There is, however, a little solace to be found in that Eustathius' connection to the wife of a prominent congregant has recently come to light and he will likely be removed from office whenever a synod can be convened for that purpose. In any case, I trust you will destroy the volume I hereby send in the same manner you have done with the volumes you took with you for such purpose. And no more said about it.

"So there it is, my young student. Stay forever in the Church's bosom and may you enjoy all that Christ's love of man provides."

The letter was signed simply, "E."

A week later, in July 327, Hypatia wed Philippus. In attendance with the couple were the priest, Senmonthis, Beset, Magdalene, Seti, Bakare, and the monk Pachome, who brought flowers. The air inside the church smelled faintly of dung, courtesy of the arrival of a camel train from the north that coincided with the ceremony. The benediction was provided by a chorus of flies that had followed the camels into Sheneset and entered the church for reconnaissance. The bride and groom led the processional home on the backs of Alexander the

Great and Roxana.

Philippus took up the trade of his father. He purchased blades, punches, hammers, awls, scrapers and other tools necessary for crafting leather from Isodorus, the smith who had made the iron box he had purchased for Hypatia, and bought a supply of skins from a local tanner. With Senmonthis' permission, he built a shop near the rented house. Once a week he went to the bazaar to display and sell his goods and to take orders on specification. It took more than a year to show a profit, but the craftsmanship and techniques he had learned working with his father in Judea were more advanced than what had previously been available in Sheneset. By the middle of 328 A.D., his future seemed secured when his work came to the attention of the garrison commander at Caneopolis, who placed a standing order of five horse saddles per month for delivery to the garrison.

Philippus insisted that Hypatia give up selling bat guano. It would not do, he said, for his wife to be engaged in such a commercial activity. Hypatia secretly smiled at his assertion of dominance, but was happy to comply. Now that she had a husband who worked, she did not need to continue the ruse of having to have an income.

The sexual relations that Philippus had so avidly anticipated proved more awkward than he had imagined. To begin with, they were never alone. The single room of their house was only about twenty feet square and a sound made in one corner could be heard in every other corner. As they lay together at night, she would face him unabashedly and caress him and kiss him gently. She would take his hands and place them on her breasts. But the effect of this tenderness paralyzed him. His mind worked so hard on the problem of what he should do, how he should respond, that natural instincts could not break through. The first few times that they proceeded to the point of entry, his immediate explosions brought a sudden stop to everything as he slumped back in embarrassment. Sophia (she would always be Sophia to him) was kind and gentle and loving. She never rebuked him in either word or response for the inadequacies he felt, never, in fact, acted as if there was any inadequacy at all. She would kiss him and stroke his face tenderly afterward as if in gratitude for his performance, but this only caused him to feel his inadequacies even more acutely. And, of course, this was not something he could bring himself to discuss with her. He would not know how to begin to talk about such matters. He could not imagine what words he could use that would at once identify the problem and overcome his resistance to the very thought of his own sexuality.

Hypatia knew Philippus' anguish. Even though he would not, could not talk about it, she knew. She did not say a word to him about it, but, wordlessly, she made adjustments. She held him back from entering her whenever she sensed that his excited urgency was on the verge of overwhelming him. Instead, she would put a hand on his chest, ease him gently away from her and begin to kiss his eyes, his neck, his chest, his arms and further down his body. She would not linger anywhere long. She would make him wait, make him relax, and stop the irresistible crescendo toward which he had been building. She would climb onto him and take control of their lovemaking, knowing better than he ever did when to ease up, slow down, pause or interrupt in order to prolong his pleasure.

Gradually, for the first time in his life, Philippus began to feel like a full man, accomplished, strong, complete. He enjoyed the way other men looked at him, assayed him when they saw that he was married to such a beauty. His confidence soared.

In March 328, Hypatia quietly told him one evening that she was carrying his child.

With Philippus engaged in leather working during the day and Beset remaining with them to help with Maggie's care, Hypatia was able to translate the texts that Philippus had brought from

Eusebius. As she worked her way through the many books she understood less and less of Timaeus' religion. She knew that Timaeus taught something different than what was contained in any of those books. She wished he had written his own gospel or guide because what he taught was so much simpler and less confusing than most of what she obtained from Eusebius. Still, as she read and translated the volumes she did begin to understand better the context of what Timaeus taught, if not the substance. For Timaeus, there were two basic forces in the world, one good and one evil. For most who called themselves Christians the principal force was the creator god. To the Catholics he was called simply "God." To the Jews he was "Yahweh." The Gnostics generally called him "Yaldabaoth." To Catholics, even those who did not worship him were bound in his power. His forms, his order was the flesh and gristle of everything we saw and experienced throughout our lives. He may have coveted worship, but worship of Yaldabaoth was not necessary for him to prevail. He required only ignorance. In most of the texts she translated there was a good force opposing Yaldabaoth. Timaeus called this force Sophia, though in most of the books that mentioned her Sophia was the emanation of another, the True God or the Unknowable One. As an emanation, she was wholly a part, wholly an aspect of the unknowable All. And her part was that of pure knowledge or, perhaps, wisdom, which is the literal meaning of the word *sophia*. In some of the books she was a fallen figure, expelled from the Pleroma for emanating Yaldabaoth without permission of the Unknowable One. In some of the books Jesus was Sophia's bridegroom, sent to Earth to bring Sophia back into the Pleroma, to allow Sophia to rejoin the Pleroma. This would somehow also provide salvation to those who understood.

Hypatia had a fight with Philippus over the last volume that Eusebius had sent by courier. It was *The Gospel of Judas Iscariot*. Philippus argued that Eusebius had explicitly directed that the text be destroyed.

"No," Hypatia responded. Reading from the letter, Hypatia said, "He wrote, 'destroy the volume I hereby send in the same manner you have done with the volumes you took with you for such purpose.' Your instructions in bringing the other volumes were to give them to me. Therefore, he meant for you to give this volume to me also."

"If that is what he meant, he could have said so plainly," Philippus replied.

"There is nothing plain about his letter, except for his permission for you to marry. He writes of Eusebius being under attack as if he is not Eusebius. Did you notice that he did not even sign it? Just 'E,' not 'Eusebius Pamphili, Bishop of Caesarea' as he signed the letter Acacius read to us in Caesarea."

"That was strange," Philippus acknowledged.

"It was not strange at all. In spite of the precaution of sending it by private post, he was clearly concerned that it would be discovered and read by those unfriendly to him. Although," Hypatia said as an aside, "if the letter was discovered, it would not have been hard to figure out who the blessings were being bestowed upon and, from there, who was doing the bestowing."

Philippus thought for a moment, then resumed his argument for the book's destruction. "He stated that it was 'a particularly heretical text.' He must want it destroyed."

"Perhaps he meant only to pique my interest."

"You are not as perverse as you sounded just now," Philippus said.

"Am I not?"

In the end, they agreed that Hypatia would be allowed to make one copy and Philippus would then destroy the original.

Hypatia was a determined translator and transcriber and remained true to her decision to honor Timaeus by preserving these endangered texts and ideas they contained. But as she did her work she found that the more she read of them, the less she believed. As time passed, she thought less and less about how

Timaeus would have explained her many questions. Instead she came to believe that they were all blind gropings, works of imagination unbounded by any observable measure against which to test their conclusions. Not that she thought that Philippus' Catholicism or Nabwenenef's Kemetism had any greater hold on the truth. To say, as Philippus did with reference to the father, son and holy spirit, that one times one is three and three times one is one, was something so far detached from her experience of everyday life that it could not be true. To posit hundreds of gods with overlapping spheres and with all-too-human attributes, as Nabwenenef did, was pure superstitious fantasy, the remnants of an unenlightened mind that even learning could not dislodge. That there was a divine force at work in the creation of all things she could easily believe, but it seemed to her that all of the religions of which she was aware diminished the wonder and awe of that creation with nonsensical attempts to explain, proscribe and even contain it.

As she translated *The Prayer of Paul* into Coptic, it occurred to her that the author's plea to be granted special favor from the Lord missed entirely the point of the creation. Everybody, she thought, everything that lived had already been granted special favor, already had a gift beyond imagining. What more could we ask for but the potential to do good, to live a useful life? What mattered is what we did with that gift, how we used that gift to improve the fortunes of those around us. What held people back from realizing this were foolishness, superstition, habit and greed. As she completed the translation of the short text of *The Prayer of Paul*, she wrote in large letters across the top of the page, "It is by such prayers as these that we are diminished."

Pachome became a frequent guest at their house. He had gotten over his temporary madness, as he called his desire to marry Hypatia. But he had become fond of her and enjoyed his conversations with her. He spent most of his time at the monasteries he had founded. There were already two of them nearby, at Tabennisi on the west side of the Nile and Pbow on the east. He had established rules for living a monastic life, many of which were to become standards in the centuries to follow. There were already eight hundred souls residing in the two monasteries and more were arriving each month. He told Hypatia and Philippus that the worldly needs of the monasteries required occasional forays into the secular world and that while he left the monastery on each occasion with regret for the disruption of peace and contemplation, he enjoyed his conversations with their Christian family. His conversations with Philippus were through Hypatia since Pachome spoke no Greek and Philippus no Coptic. They talked about religion and he found Hypatia to be at least Philippus' equal when they discussed the meaning and hidden meanings of scripture. Pachome told them that, after his several conversations with Hypatia, he had come to believe that there should be monasteries for women as well as men because they were quite as capable as men of understanding scripture and could benefit as well as men from the contemplative spiritual life of a monastery. To this Hypatia said that he was the first Catholic she had ever heard express an opinion about women that went beyond asserting that they were inferior and subservient to men in all things on Earth and in Heaven.

Pachome told them that he was born a Kemite in Luxor. When he was a young man he was conscripted into the Roman Legion to suppress an uprising of Christians who were rebelling against their harsh treatment in Thebes. By the time he arrived in Thebes, things had calmed down and he did not have to fight or slay another man, but the troops were stationed there against a resurgence of the rebellion. While there, the local Christians would bring food to the impressed troops, tend to them during times of illness and show them the greatest of kindness and solicitude. They spoke blissfully of their Jesus, his suffering on the cross, his resurrection and God's gift of everlasting life to all who followed him. He became a fervent Christian almost immediately. The message the Christians brought instantly found solace in his pagan soul and gave refuge to his troubled existence. A few years later he met a Christian hermit named Palaemon. He stayed with Palaemon for seven years, living mostly in the desert, reading, praying, and meditating. He explained that while he loved Palaemon as a brother in Christ and felt deeply the spiritual benefits of the life they lived, he missed the society of others, conversations and the sharing of thoughts and hardships. So when Palaemon died, he set about building a dwelling where other dedicated Christians could come to live a shared ascetic life. He was amazed at how many had flocked to Tabennisi, where Hypatia had come across him in the desert three years earlier.

When Hypatia asked him if he was a priest he said no, and did not desire to become one. "A priest's mission is different than ours. Our mission is both more selfish and more selfless than a priest's. We will minister to local shepherds, but the role of a priest is not consistent with the contemplative life we desire to live for the glory of God."

On one of his visits, when Philippus was away at his shop, Hypatia confided in Pachome that she was also interested in scripture that the Catholic Church did not accept. She showed him some of the volumes that Philippus had brought from Caesarea and confided that she was translating them into Coptic to better learn and perhaps preserve them. Upon hearing this, a slight smile emerged from beneath Pachome's flecked beard and he asked her if she believed that the texts she translated were true.

"I believe they contain some truth," she said. "I cannot make sense of much of what is written, but I believe they are useful in raising questions about Jesus and his mission on earth, the attempt to answer which, I believe, brings one closer to God."

"But you believe Jesus was both God and the Son of God?"

"That is what the Church teaches and I accept its teachings."

This seemed to satisfy Pachome, but he shook his head in wonderment at the mind of this woman. Finally, he said, "We keep such books at our monastery in Pbow, not five miles from here. And our monks also have translated some into Coptic. Coptic is the only language I know. We do not honor them as we do the true canon, but, like you, I think they are helpful in promoting contemplation. It is very strange and amazing to find you, a woman so far removed from the centers of civilization, by chance and independently engaged in the same work as my monks. I will spend many hours in silence devoted to contemplating the meaning of this."

John was born on Philippus' birthday, January 1, 329. Philippus was twenty-eight. Magdalene was almost three. Hypatia was not yet twenty-two years of age.

As she had with Maggie, Beset midwifed the delivery, wiped Hypatia's brow, held her hand, sang old songs, issued words of comfort and pulled the slippery baby from his mother's womb. During this time Beset was the head of the house, the essential person. She ordered everyone about, especially Philippus, whom she advised to "Sit over there in your little corner and don't be pacing or fretting about or you'll upset the mother and make a bad child of it." In the early hours of labor she told Maggie to bring towels or gourds of water. When the strong pains began, Beset ordered Senmonthis to take Maggie out for a long walk. This order was based upon Beset's enlightened view that a child should not have to witness her mother in pain. Beset had grown stronger and younger since Maggie's birth and her command and confidence reflected and augmented the joy she had found with Hypatia. As she placed young John on his mother's breast and ordered Philippus over to admire his creation, Beset thought of the amazing turn of events that had taken her from a homeless, friendless widow to an important part of what she considered the best home in Egypt. She had been reunited with her son. She was respected in her home and in Sheneset. She had friends. She was loved.

Nabwenenef learned of Hypatia's pregnancy from a Hathor worshiper in Sheneset. The informant had not attended the vigil in Chenoboskion three years earlier and had never seen Hypatia before she moved to Sheneset, but he knew the stories and knew that Nabwenenef had predicted that this woman, Hathor who called herself Hypatia, would have a second child and would give birth to a male-child who would be Ra. When Nabwenenef learned that this woman, whom his informant told him was "the most beautiful creature I ever witnessed," had given birth to a boy, he lost little time in finding her out.

Nabwenenef found Hypatia at home on a market day, while Philippus was away. He was pleased when he learned that the father of the boy was a priest who had left the Christian church to marry her. But he went away crestfallen when Philippus came home, listened to his phantasmagorical theories and predictions, saw his wife's annoyance and promptly ordered the silly robed priest to leave immediately.

"John will be baptized a Christian on Sunday," Philippus proclaimed. As he watched Nabwenenef depart, Philippus felt as proud as Alexander must have felt in defeating the Egyptians in 332 B.C. He was unaware that upon conquering Egypt Alexander had had himself declared the son of Amun, an Egyptian deity most often associated with Ra and during later kingdoms, often called Amun-Ra. Nabwenenef did not return during the remainder of the family's stay in Sheneset.

Two years passed as Hypatia translated her books and raised her children, Philippus prospered as a leather-worker, and Beset grew younger and stronger. Day by day Hypatia's fondness for Philippus grew until, without knowing exactly when, she found she loved him more deeply than she had ever loved Timaeus. By the start of 329 Bakare had found a wife who came with a meager dowry and moved into Senmonthis' house. By 330, Seti followed his brother's lead and Senmonthis found herself spending more and more time under the roof she rented to Hypatia and Philippus because, she said, "Consuming too much foolishness is like drinking too much wine: you soon lose all of your sense and may never get it back." The "whore's house" became the center of the property, switching roles with the house Senmonthis had lived in for thirty-one years. From the start Magdalene looked upon John as someone to be nurtured and mentored. She often found herself amazed at his inability to do things or say words or grasp concepts that she mastered with the greatest of ease. Her mother would remonstrate with her, reminding her that John was three years her junior and could not be expected to do all she could do. But it pleased Maggie to feel superior to John and it pleased Hypatia that the girl took such tender interest in her brother.

It was a happy life that all who lived it might have wished could go on forever. It would not last.

Chapter Twenty-Seven

Athanasius

328-330 A.D – Alexandria

> *If you are oppressed by Satan and are persecuted and you do the Father's will, I say that He will love you and will make you equal with [Jesus] and will consider that you have become beloved through His providence according to your free choice. Will you not cease, then, being lovers of the flesh and being afraid of sufferings?*
> The Apocryphon of James

Saint Mark's great Basilica in Alexandria was in a state of somber anxiety. Alexander, the 19th Pope of Alexandria who wore the tattered shoes of Mark the Evangelist, had died. Mark, reputed author of an eponymous gospel, had founded the church in Alexandria in 49 A.D., just nineteen years after Jesus' crucifixion and fifteen years before St. Peter would found the church in Rome. Alexander had been pontiff for fifteen years. It had been a time of great change and he had presided over the affairs of his See with grace and resolve. Before becoming pontiff, Alexander had lived through the persecutions of the Emperors Galerius and Maximinus Daia during which he was forced into hard labor in the expectation that his body, if not his spirit, would break and he would renounce the barbarian religion. He held firm in body and spirit. He came to office in 313 at the age of forty-four, just as the co-Emperors Constantine in the east and Licinius in the west issued the Edict of Milan, making religious tolerance the law of the Empire. With Rome's acceptance of Christianity came many challenges to the Church. First, there was the issue of when Easter should be celebrated. His writings and efforts on behalf of the current formula were adopted at Nicaea. Then there was the matter of Meletius, who refused to recognize Alexandria's superiority in ecclesiastical matters, ordained as priests some who had renounced their faith during the persecutions, and went so far as to ordain priests to serve within the Alexandrian territory, including Arius. This issue, too, was resolved at Nicaea, with Meletius remaining bishop of Lycopolis, but acknowledging Alexandria's supremacy in ecclesiastical matters. Finally, there was the rising popularity of the heretical doctrine of Arianism tirelessly promoted by the priest Arius. Alexander ordered that Arius be forever banished from receiving communion and, with the help of his young secretary, Athanasius, energetically penned essays and letters opposing the creed. It was to his great consternation that this controversy remained in full vigor as he approached Heaven's gate.

Athanasius' rise to become Alexander's chosen successor as bishop of the city had been remarkable. Alexander had first discovered Athanasius in 313 playing with other children on a Mediterranean beach. They were not playing Romans and Barbarians, as children often did. Instead, Athanasius was leading the other children in a game of baptism, with himself as the priest. Alexander watched as Athanasius, draped in a tattered grey cloak, scooped water out of the Sea with his hands and pressed it upon the heads of his playmates. As Alexander approached the group he could hear the small, flame-haired leader saying, "Εγώ, σοι βαφτίσει στο όνομα του Πατρός και του Υιού και του Αγίου Πνεύματος." ("I baptize thee in the name of the Father, and of the Son and of the Holy Spirit.") As the bishop entered their company, the boys stood up and bowed.

"You look as if you know what you are doing," Alexander said to Athanasius.

"I have witnessed the rite performed many times, your holiness. These boys have not been baptized, but I have taught them the love of Christ and they are ready to follow. I know that they must be baptized by a real priest, but I am preparing them."

"Have you been baptized?"

"I have."

"How old are you?"

"Thirteen, your Excellency."

Alexander smiled and said something to his companions that Athanasius could not make out. Turning back to the boy he asked, "Where is the sacred salt? The baptism cannot be complete without sacred salt."

"The sea provides it."

"Yes, of course. In that case, it is complete." Making a cross with his hands, Alexander intoned solemnly, "In the name of the Christian Church of Alexandria and in the name of the Father, Son and Holy Spirit, I recognize these souls as baptized in the name of our Lord." Turning to the several boys, all of who appeared to be older than Athanasius, he said, "You must still study the catechism and be confirmed, but you are Christians now. I expect you to behave as such and to attend mass."

Taking Athanasius aside, Alexander asked if he could read and write. "Yes," said the boy.

"Coptic, Greek or Latin?"

"All three."

"Would you like to become a priest?"

"It is my only wish."

Alexander decided to take Athanasius into his house and under his wing. Athanasius told the bishop that his parents had died and he lived with his aunt. He was a burden upon her and she would be happy for him to find such a position.

Over the next fifteen years Athanasius rapidly rose from student to scribe to Alexander's secretary to priest to deacon. His modest upbringing deprived him of a classical education. His parents had been pagans, but his aunt was a devout Catholic and provided most of his education before he came to the bishop's household. He learned rapidly and believed zealously, but his education was limited to what the Church taught. His physical stature remained that of a child, never reaching five feet in height or a hundred pounds in weight, but those who dismissed him based on his stature made a grave mistake. He knew more than anyone else about how the See operated, how it was funded, who were its priests and who were its parishioners. He wrote many of the letters and Papal bulls that were issued under Alexander's seal. He became Alexander's favorite and Alexander often said that the only reason he wished to delay his ascension to Heaven was to live long enough that Athanasius could succeed him. By Church law, a bishop could be no less than thirty years of age.

Alexander's decline was evident when he returned from the Nicaea Council in 325. By the middle of the next year, talk of his succession began in earnest. One day in 327, Alexander said to Athanasius, "I do not believe I can live three more years, for you to succeed me. You must wait your turn."

"May you live much longer than that, my bishop. But why three years for me, may I ask?"

"You must be thirty. You were thirteen when you joined us. That was but fourteen years ago. That makes you twenty-seven."

"I do not know how old I was when we met, but I was born in 296."

"That makes you thirty-one."

"Yes."

After that it was decided in Alexander's mind that Athanasius would succeed him. Other ecclesiastical authorities in Alexandria had other plans.

In early 328, Alexander's health improved greatly. For the first time in two years he did not seem on the edge of death. His recovery came at a good time. The Royal Court had moved and Eusebius of Nicomedia was ascendant. As Constantine's bishop he had Constantine's ear and the Emperor was fast becoming more sympathetic to the Arian viewpoint. The agreement forged at Nicaea, that God and Jesus had the same homoousios, proved ephemeral. The Arians readily agreed that Father and Son were of the same essence, but argued that this did not make them equal. While glorifying Jesus, they again asserted that God's majesty was greater and that Jesus was God's offspring, not God himself. The Emperor had gone so far as to order Pope Alexander to receive Arius back into the fold at Alexandria and to cease withholding communion from him.

Alexander responded by dispatching Athanasius to Constantinopolis to plead the case for Arius' continued heresy. Then, in April 328, while Athanasius was away on his mission, Alexander died. The bishops of Egypt hastened to Alexandria to appoint a new metropolitan bishop — a new pope. Athanasius rushed back by fast ship to claim the position.

It turned out that while Athanasius had enough support to prevent anyone else from being elected, there was sufficient doubt about his age and temperament for him to carry the day. The conference continued for over a month when Athanasius convinced four of the Egyptian bishops to come with him to the Church of Dionysius in Alexandria to consecrate him bishop behind closed doors. In doing so he relied upon a decree at the Nicene Council that a minimum of three bishops were needed to consecrate another bishop, provided it was with the consent of the other bishops. Of course, the other bishops had not consented. To overcome this obstacle, Athanasius procured a decree from the Alexandria City Council to the effect that he was the people's choice for bishop of the city. He sent this decree with a letter to the Emperor, written in his own hand, asserting that the bishops of Egypt had unanimously agreed to his consecration. The Emperor accepted his assertion without further investigation and Athanasius moved into the bishop's suite.

It may be that the militant gang of supporters that Athanasius already commanded and the ready mob that appeared to be ever at his disposal tempered the other bishops' desire to challenge his ascension.

It was often said that Athanasius burned against all heresies. With his scarlet hair he was the walking embodiment of flame. Lacking a classical education, learning only what the Church taught, burning with ambition and guided by a genetic predisposition toward certainty of all things at all times, Athanasius' theology was grounded on the bedrock knowledge that the creation was the "Word" of God and that Jesus was the Word made manifest in human form. "He made all things out of nothing through His own Word," Athanasius wrote. After making the world through His Word, his favorite creation, mankind, fell into sin. As a result, "It was our sorry case that caused the Word to come down, our transgression that called out His love for us, so that He made haste to help us and to appear among us. It is we who were the cause of His taking human form, and for our salvation that in His great love, He was both born and manifested in a human body."

He disproved all heresies with reference to scripture. His scripture — the four canonical gospels first selected by Iraneus 150 years before and supplemented by ancient letters selected and edited for their fidelity to the needs of the Church. To the Arians he said, "I refuse to believe that the Jesus that I know as my redeemer is less than God." He pointed to the passages in scripture where Jesus can only be understood as saying that He and His Father are one. He often noted that Jesus was reported to have said, "The Father is in Me and I in the Father." What more proof did one need? It was not our right to demand explanation. Athanasius argued, "We are speaking of the good pleasure of God and of the things which He in His loving wisdom thought fit to do. It is not our right to question these things." He answered the great Gnostic heresy with citations to the Gospel of John. Quoting John, "All things became by Him and without Him came nothing into being," he asked, "how then could the Gnostic god be anything other than the Father of Christ?" Athanasius' circular arguments began by mischaracterizing his opponent's position and always ended with a citation to scripture as if scripture were not simply another construct of man.

What made Athanasius so formidable was not his reason or logic, but the force of his personality augmented by a growing force of lieutenants loyal to his person and the force of the Alexandrian mob ever at his disposal. He fought many battles and many were fought for him.

By 330, Athanasius had consolidated his power in Alexandria for the meantime, but Eusebius of Nicomedia's influence with the Emperor remained strong. The Arian heresy was gaining strength in the east. In Athanasius' eyes the difference between Arianism and orthodoxy was oceans wide and, worse than this, opened the gates to the uncontrollable passions of the Gnostics which made every believer, be it male or (most heretical of all) female, a priest, every priest a bishop and every bishop an apostle entitled to write gospels in whosever name he or she chose. To Athanasius there was only one legitimate faith and only one system of beliefs — his faith and his beliefs.

The Arian controversy occupied most of Athanasius' time and attention. Through sermons and encyclicals, conferences and councils, letters and lectures, pleas and presents, Athanasius assembled and directed his alliance. To him the dispute was not some trifling issue of theological nuance, but the cornerstone of Christianity's future. If Jesus was merely the son of God and not God Himself, the entire faith was sure to crumble. If the Arians had their way the Church would be confronted with the unanswerable either/or question of whether Christianity embraced polytheism where men could become gods (as the old emperors claimed) or whether Christ was a mere mortal man. It had to be one or the other. Either way left the road open to people to pursue the largely defeated doctrines of the Gnostics and set the cause of the Holy Church back by two centuries. For if Jesus was not God or if he merely became God, then what, fundamentally, was wrong with what the Gnostics taught? Then what was true about the Gospels? No, for the Church to survive, Arianism must be defeated.

It was a war of many fronts. The biggest threat was Eusebius of Nicomedia, who was always in the Emperor's ear. Frontal assaults on him were dangerous and counter-productive. So Athanasius turned his efforts on Nicomedia's allies, most notably Eusebius of Caesarea. A straightforward assault based on the claim that he was an Arian suffered from the same inherent weaknesses as attacks against Nicomedia, so other stratagems were adopted. With his young ally, Bishop Eustathius of Antioch, Athanasius wrote that Caesarea was a devoted adherent of the third century theologian Origen. Origen was an adapter of the reasoning of Plato, which was enough to earn condemnation from Athanasius and his cohorts. Worse, before the Arian controversy had germinated, Origen wrote that Jesus was the son of God, not God Himself. This made him the father of Arianism. He wrote that people who lived before Jesus had come to hear the word of God and that among these was Plutarch. He was even rumored to have lived for a time with a wealthy woman who had come from Antioch to Alexandria and who was known to have also housed a famous heretic under the same roof. Origen's thoughts and presumed conduct were posthumously deemed heretical and Eusebius of Caesarea, who had written approvingly of Origen's bravery in the face of Christian persecutions, was tarred with him. Athanasius was tireless in his efforts to bring down all who allied themselves with Arianism. He penned his own attacks on the proponents of Arianism and ghostwrote letters for others, including Eustathius, to issue under their own name. No attack was too personal, no evidence too tenuous for Athanasius to use as a weapon in this war.

But even with Arianism as his main focus of enmity, Athanasius never forgot about the greater long-term threat presented by the Gnostics. Gnostic portrayals of Jesus had threatened to overwhelm and undermine Christianity in its infancy and it had taken three centuries to put it in its present, beaten down state. And he never forgot about the heretic who had infiltrated the Council at Nicaea, whom he had dispatched, and the young woman who had accompanied him, who lived still. Through spies and informants he had compiled a dossier on Adama, as he called her. He knew that Ammianus had taken her from Alexandria to Antioch in 321. He knew that she had worked for three years, between the ages of fourteen to seventeen, in Ammianus' notorious brothel in that city. He knew that Timaeus had purchased her from Ammianus in 324. In 325 she arrived in Nicaea with Timaeus, her hair shorn and dressed as a scribe. Somehow she had escaped Nicaea. Timaeus' landlord in Nicaea had earned the tip Sophia gave him for his discretion by refusing to divulge anything about when or where she had left, but Athanasius strongly believed that Eusebius of Caesarea had facilitated her departure. From Nicaea the trail grew cold until, in 329, he sent an agent to Caesarea to confirm the destruction of any Gnostic texts that may have found their way into Eusebius' collection. Eusebius was away at the time, but Acacius naively told the agent that all of the Gnostic texts had been taken by a priest to Chenoboskion for destruction and that the priest who took them, one Philippus, had found and married a widow in those parts. This news piqued Athanasius' interest, but his conclusion was not fixed until, in April 330 he learned from one of his See's regional administrators that the monk Pachome had spoken of a wedding of a former priest, Philippus of Caesarea, to a beautiful woman named Hypatia of Alexandria.

Athanasius had a reason beyond her heresy to seek out this Hypatia of Alexandria. He remembered her. He remembered how, as a twenty-year-old priest, he would often watch that beautiful girl from behind the curtains of the basilica. He remembered how that witch had infected him with unwanted, carnal desires of the flesh. He remembered coming upon her one night curled up for warmth against the church wall and how, powerless to resist, he pounced upon her and pounded out his hated passion upon her flesh. The shame of his behavior, the sinfulness that called into question his every ambition, his every conception of who he was and for what he was intended served for a long while to break the fever of lust with which she had infected him, but he lived for a long time in fear of his act being discovered, of the siren making accusations, of hell's fire leaping from the ground to consume him. When a year had passed he began to overcome these thoughts and fears. There were even days in a row when he did not think of her or his actions. But when he saw her two years after his sin, more developed, more beautiful and more temptingly wicked than before, the old desires began to take hold of him again. He knew he must act to rid himself of this satanic temptation. He remembered forging the documents that enslaved her to Ammianus. She had been his only carnal sin. Hypatia, Adama, Sophia, and her very memory must be erased from existence.

Chapter Twenty-Eight

An Army of Priests

May 330 A.D. – Sheneset

Listen, my son, to my advice! Do not show your back to your enemies and flee, but rather, pursue them as a strong one. Be not an animal, with men pursuing you; but rather, be a man, with you pursuing the evil wild beasts, lest somehow they become victorious over you and trample upon you as on a dead man, and you perish due to their wickedness.
The Teachings of Silvanus

In early 330, Hypatia and Philippus returned to the cave where they had hidden the Roman coins three years before. They did not go there for the money. They still had most of the fifty solidi Timaeus had left for Sophia to find when he left for Council on the last day of his life and the ten that Philippus had not sent to Bishop Eusebius. Philippus' earnings through his leather trade were almost always sufficient to provide for the simple life that they enjoyed together. On the rare occasions that they needed something more they dipped into the cache that they kept at home, hidden in a deep hole under their sleeping mat, but its rate of depletion was small enough that they might never have exhausted it. Philippus did not claim any right to the money they had hidden in the cave. In fact, they never discussed it at all. So the money stayed in an iron box in an obscure cave four hours' walk from town.

The reason for their return to the cave was that the small house was filling up with the books Hypatia had spent the last three years copying. She had purported to save the *Gospel of Judas* for last, knowing that Philippus would insist on its destruction of the original once she finished with it. She never told Philippus that it was a Coptic text that she had no intention of copying. It was so different than anything else she had ever heard or read about Judas, presenting a view of him as hero rather than villain, that she found she could not bring herself to part with it. In the meantime, she had accumulated copies of twenty-one Gnostic tracts that she stacked in a corner of the house and that served as a constant, if minor, source of irritation to Philippus. Although she gave the Greek originals to Senmonthis to give away, she could not bring herself to part with her translations that she bound by hand.

At Philippus' insistence, the family attended mass every Sunday and he continued to observe most of the fast days he had observed as a priest. The priest in Sheneset, Father James, had been ordained in Alexandria and, like most Alexandrian clergy, was a strict Trinitarian and an intense hater of heresy. When he would come to the house to call upon the family, Philippus would hide Hypatia's texts under covers. On one such occasion, the priest told Philippus that he had recently received correspondence from the bishop in Alexandria telling him to expect a visit in the coming months. Athanasius wrote that he was coming down for the particular purpose of ordaining Pachome and his monks as priests, but that he also had reports of dangerous heretics, including Gnostics, who were reported to live in the area and a secondary purpose was to investigate these reports. Bishop Athanasius instructed Father James to be on the lookout for such heretics, but failed to provide any kind of description or other means to identify them. Father James asked Philippus to inform him if he came across anyone who was promoting Gnostic ideas or any other heresy. Father James did not speak to Hypatia on the occasions of his visits except about the health and training of her children and to ask what might be for dinner.

When Father James left after warning Philippus about heresy in Sheneset, an argument broke out between Philippus and

Hypatia.

"This is very bad. Do you think he is coming for you?" Philippus asked.

"It has been so long," Hypatia said. "And we have been such good Christians, attending mass each Sunday and other church services and events. We affirm every Sunday that Jesus and God are one. I cannot imagine that we are suspect."

Philippus frowned at her response, thinking to himself that after three years he was not sure what she really believed. He said, "These blasted books have to go. Every one of them. If Father James should ever see them, I'm not sure what would happen."

"It pleases me to copy them. I feel like I am honoring a commitment to Timaeus."

"Do you believe in them?"

"Not at all. No more than …" she stopped mid-sentence, then continued. "No more than any of the other nonsense that seems to make up most religions."

"Except the Christian church, you mean."

"Of course," Hypatia said, but her casual tone irked Philippus. He mused for a moment, and then voiced what he often thought, but had never before spoken. "Sometimes I think you are still married to Timaeus."

Hypatia's brown eyes flashed anger. "That is absurd."

"But you still love him."

"I love his memory. He is dead."

"I want these books out of here. They must go."

"You are ordering me now?"

"I am the man."

"And I am the woman. So where does that leave us?"

Philippus thought of the angry response he should make to such effrontery. He thought of quoting the Bible, asserting that God gave dominion to man over woman. But he thought better of it and returned to the subject of her books. "It is dangerous," he said. "Think of John. Think of Magdalene."

Hypatia walked away, signaling to Philippus that she was done discussing the subject. He knew better than to pursue her. He thought he would raise the subject again when she calmed down.

He did not have to. Less than an hour later, Hypatia came to him with a proposal. She would put the texts she had copied into something for storage and take them up to the cave where they had stored the money. "That way I can feel like I have honored Timaeus. They will just be there. That is enough."

"What about the originals you copied from?" Philippus asked.

"I have already given most away through Senmonthis.You can burn the rest yourself, if you have the heart for it. Will that satisfy you?"

"Yes," Philippus said. "Thank you, my love."

The day after they had this discussion, Pachome paid a visit and brought with him two codices. Catching Hypatia at home while Philippus was away, he did not stay long. He too had heard that Athanasius was coming down to Luxor Province. He betrayed no knowledge of Athanasius' intent to search for heretics. His concern, he said, was that the bishop wanted to ordain his monks as priests. He said he would have to lead his men into the desert to escape detection. Pachome handed Hypatia the two codices, one beautifully bound with an engraved calfskin letter and one bound more crudely, like the three she had produced. He told her that he and his monks would have to abandon their monasteries temporarily and he was afraid that if Athanasius came across these volumes, it could mean trouble. He asked her if she would hold on to them until Athanasius left.

Hypatia considered telling Pachome that Athanasius was also coming from Alexandria to search for just these kinds of texts and for her as well, but thought such knowledge might increase the danger to both of them. She accepted the books, but told Pachome that she was going to hide them in a cave, along with the volumes she had produced. He told her that would be fine, so long as they were removed from the monastery and could be retrieved. With that he departed. Hypatia did not tell Philippus of Pachome's visit or of the two books he had entrusted to her safekeeping.

A few days later she acquired a large, reddish earthenware jar that was more than twice as large as was needed for the texts she had translated and the two volumes Pachome had given her. She did not have time to read all the texts that Pachome brought, but she noticed that they contained different versions of some of the same texts she had translated. In two particular texts she read more of what she believed was closer to what Timaeus taught: "The Nature of the Rulers" and "On the Origin of the World." Versions of the story of Noah and Norea that Timaeus had so long ago told outside of Tyre were contained in these books. But although she liked these books better than some of the others because they seemed to more closely adhere to what Timaeus taught, she had come dismiss all of the books as the work of man, flawed with the desperate effort to explain things that could not be understood. There was a time, when she was on her travels with Timaeus, that she thought there were people who knew the Truth and that she, too, could learn it. Timaeus' certainty of his own path and his faith in her had taught her to believe this. But as much as she enjoyed the work of translating and copying and trying to understand what she read, she found less and less that she could believe as true.

She was equally skeptical of Philippus' Catholicism. She attended mass with him and their children. She read the four gospels that he accepted as true and several others that Philippus said were dubious, including "The Acts of St. Paul and Thecla" and "The Protevangelion." But she had seen the Church in action at Nicaea and could not bring herself to believe that an institution so evil in action could be good in spirit.

They spent all day taking the texts up to the cave. The five codices fit easily into the brick red earthenware jar, with plenty of room to spare. Using leather straps that he had fashioned, Philippus lashed the jar to the back of Alexander the Great. They packed some food and two smaller jars of water to the sides of Roxana and the two couples ambled north toward the cave by the lancet rock. They told Beset that they were going to get two baskets of bat guano for their own use in the garden.

May's usual robust heat was tempered by a sweet breeze that slid down from the north and eased their journey. They talked of their children. Philippus never said so, but John was his clear favorite. Although at seventeen months, John had yet to utter much that could be understood by others, he chattered endlessly in the pre-human, uninhibited language of the cosmos, which is chaos to the adult ear. Hypatia and Philippus had learned some of these sounds by heart and had even ascribed meaning to a few, but as of yet John inhabited a world that was largely off limits to them. In the beginning was the Word, but the Word was yet in a language they could not speak or understand. Magdalene, four, continued to dote on her younger brother but was clearly the brighter of the two, even adjusting for their ages. To Philippus' concern but with Hypatia's instruction, she had begun to read. When Philippus objected to her learning from the Gnostic texts her mother translated, Hypatia quickly relented and began teaching her from Philippus' copy of the Greek gospels of Mark and John. Hypatia also wrote simple stories on her own, including parables of Jesus and fables of Rome and Egypt.

Philippus expressed concern about the books Hypatia wrote for Maggie. "You know, sweet love, in writing your stories, you do not seem to distinguish between the truth of the living Christ and the myths of the superstitious."

"Is not truth self-evident from fiction?"

"Yes, yes, but perhaps not so much for a child."

"That is why we take her to service, is it not?"

"Of course you are right," Philippus replied, but without satisfaction. As they made slow, but steady progress toward the cave he thought again, as he had many times in the past, that he still did not know what she really believed. Not really. She attended mass, read the Gospels and seemed to know at least as much as he did of their contents and of the Church's rituals and dogma. She was more knowledgeable about the Church's teachings and the nuances of its faith than any woman he had ever met, a fact on which even Father James had once remarked. For all outward appearances she was a good Christian. But there were hints, such as her last response, that, while not rebellious, suggested ambivalence. For all her knowledge, she displayed little outward passion for the faith. It was of little consolation to Philippus that she displayed no greater passion for the Gnostic texts with which she spent so much of her time. As he always did he tried to let the feeling pass, schooled in the knowledge that further inquiry would lead nowhere and that he was not her equal when it came to discussing such matters.

An hour passed as they ambled through sand and stone. Philippus spoke of his work. Saddles and purses, sandals and sacks. The instructions he had given to a couple of local tanners concerning potions and techniques were beginning to show in the quality of the leather with which he was able to work. This contributed to a better quality of product and a growing demand for his goods. He told her that he could foresee a time, not too far off, when he would need to take on an apprentice to assist him in his labors. As she always did when Philippus spoke, Hypatia listened attentively and asked careful questions that showed her genuine interest in his work.

Eventually they fell into silence. Each held the reins of one of the donkeys. Hypatia held Alexander and Philippus, Roxana. It had been two years since they had travelled to the needle-eyed cave and the winds had changed the landscape in both subtle and dramatic ways. She studied the surroundings closely, trying to extrapolate from their present appearance what she had so closely observed two years earlier. Eventually she made out the lancet rock and, opposite, the wind-carved Egyptian face. The face had changed substantially. One of its eyes had practically collapsed or spread into a slit, as if the face was now winking at her. The mouth, too, had changed. Instead of the oval shape of wonderment it had had two years earlier, it had elongated into a crooked sneer. Even with these changes, she was confident she had found the right spot and proceeded to search for the cave's narrow entrance. This too, was problematic, since sand had blown to cover most of the opening for two-and-a-half feet from its base. Philippus and she dug at the sand to expose it again.

"I will go in alone," Hypatia said.

"The books are heavy. I should bear them," Philippus replied.

"I will go in and you will push the jar through the opening." Her words were a command, leaving no room for further debate. "The cave is shallow. I will only have to slide the jar a few feet and our task will be done. Wait until I call for the jar." With that she turned sideways and entered through the narrow mouth.

Once inside she felt her way toward the recess where she had slid the metal box containing the coins. Finding it, she opened its lid and felt its contents. It had not been disturbed. She carefully removed ten of the gold solidi, counting them separately and placing them into a cloth she had brought for that purpose. She tied the cloth closed with a strip of leather and slid it over her arm and under her tunic. There was no particular reason for her removal of the coins, but it pleased her as if it were a gift from someone close.

"Are you alright in there, my love?" She heard Philippus' voice calling and knew what he was asking even though she could not distinguish the muffled words.

"You can slide the jar inside the cave now," she replied. "I am ready." She closed the lid on the metal box and repeated the words she had spoken when she placed it in the cave two years earlier. "I give my life to God," she said. She said it more quietly but she felt the weight of the words more deeply than the last time she spoke them. She did not know who or what God was, but she felt that there was some measure of truth in the assertion that her life was His. Or Hers.

Philippus had pushed the earthenware jar through the opening. It barely fit. She could see his face in the light of the opening, peering in at the cave. She leaned over the jar that was now blocking the entrance and kissed him on the lips. His face illuminated, seemingly casting a little more light into the darkness.

"What was that for?" he asked.

"I'll just be a moment more," she replied.

The jar, filled with books and sealed with waxed cloth, was heavy and difficult to slide. She first pulled, then, getting behind it, pushed it several feet into the recess. "Finished," she called out and promptly reemerged into the bright sunlight of the desert.

Once outside the cave she straightened the folds of her garments and asked Philippus if he was happy now that the books were safely hidden. "Raptured," he replied, still glowing from the kiss Hypatia had bestowed upon him. "Let us go home now," he said.

"We must first fill the baskets with dung. That is why we came, after all." Hypatia smiled at their shared ruse.

"Oh, yes," Philippus said, and they headed back toward Sheneset.

They stopped long enough at a larger cave to fill two baskets with guano, then resumed their journey homeward.

On the way into town Philippus lost the resolve he had formed not to ask Hypatia anything further about her true beliefs. A resolution can sustain a thousand temptations but if it once gives way, its holder must be judged irresolute. So it was with Philippus. A thousand times he had resisted the impulse to get to the bottom of what she believed. Each hour she spent copying the old Gnostic texts was an hour of moral anguish for him as he wondered how one who professed to be a true Christian could spend so much time studying heresy. And each hour of moral anguish was also an hour of mortal jealousy as he witnessed by the moving shadow on the dial face the hold that her first husband continued to have on her. On the descent the dam broke and he poured out his heart to her. Nothing he said surprised her. At some level that she refused to recognize she already knew of his doubt and jealousy. But she was surprised now that he gave voice to them.

"Do you believe in God?" he asked.

"Of course I do," she said in the same matter-of-fact voice that had served to calm him on prior occasions. He pressed on.

"Do you believe in Jesus Christ our Lord?"

"Yes. I do."

"Do you believe that Jesus is our savior?"

"I believe that Jesus has saved many souls."

"Now, you see," Philippus said. "It is that kind of answer that troubles me. You do not say that Jesus is your savior."

"I cannot say yet whether I am saved." Philippus frowned. Her answer was precise and, in a way, appropriate. He, too, had doubts about whether he was saved; in particular about whether forsaking his vows had been an act beyond forgiveness. But he accepted Jesus as his savior despite these doubts. He wished Hypatia could do the same.

"Do you believe that Jesus is the Son of God?"

"I believe we are all children of God."

"Your answers trouble me, Sophia," he said. "You may face an inquest when Athanasius arrives and you had better be able to deliver better answers than these."

"Do not be troubled, husband," she replied. "I am speaking truth now to my husband. If I speak to Athanasius I will know how to answer him. And my name is Hypatia, not Sophia. You cannot forget that." They were near a Jatropha tree with its long leaves and red blooms. Hypatia gently led Philippus to the shade of the tree, then rested with her back against the trunk. She drew him toward her and kissed him tenderly on the mouth. Reaching down, she felt his excitement rising. She turned away from him, raised her tunic over her hips and placed the palms of her hands over her head upon the tree trunk. He could not resist such an allurement. He had never taken her in this way before. She had always faced him. But there was something so unspeakably urgent and vaguely sinful in her simple action that within seconds he was inside her, thrusting out his life and love in unmeasured rhythms. She could hear him climax and feel the pulsing shots of his semen as it filled her. He began to slump slightly and slip away, but she reached her arm behind and grabbed his neck, holding him tightly against her. She could hear him gasping as she whispered, "You are my husband, Philippus. Never doubt that I would do anything for you."

Philippus passed the rest of the descent in a sublime reverie. As they approached their little house he told her that he had to see the tanner about some skins he had ordered. He told her he would be back shortly. She kissed him again, for the third time that day, and told him suggestively she would be waiting for him when he arrived.

Hypatia led Alexander to the makeshift stable near the house. She removed the two baskets of dung from his back and placed them outside next to some small bushes near the stable. She drew water from the well for the beast and placed fodder at his feet before entering the house.

Her children accosted her immediately: Maggie assailing her with stories of her brother's antics and misbehavior and John latching onto her right leg and riding it forward as she walked toward the table where Beset was washing dates and kale for their repast. "Mama, where have you been all day?" Magdalene demanded. "John has been so bad today. He ate four figs, went to the bathroom in his cloths and knocked over the pyramid I was building."

"That sounds about normal for John," Hypatia reassured her daughter. "Perhaps not so bad for a one-year-old."

"And a boy," Maggie added.

"Yes, a boy," Hypatia agreed. Satisfied that she had done her duty, Magdalene returned to her wooden blocks. Hypatia picked John off the floor, sat on a pallet and began to nurse him.

"Will the master be along soon?" Beset asked.

Hypatia smiled and replied, "Yes, Philippus will be along shortly."

Two hours passed with no sign of Philippus and Hypatia began to wonder what had delayed him. Just when she had resolved to walk to the market to inquire about him there came a soft, continuous knocking at the door. When Hypatia opened it she was startled to see the unkempt monk Pachome standing there with his arm still rapping at the air of the open doorway. Before she had time to say anything, he quickly grabbed her wrist and pulled her outside. Beset, ever protective of her mistress, followed Hypatia out the door.

As disheveled as Pachome usually appeared, Hypatia had never seen him in his present state. Even on the occasion of their first encounter in the desert he had not seemed quite so wild or distraught.

"They have seized Philippus," he blurted once she was outside.

"Who has seized him? What are you talking about?"

"Athanasius. He's come down from Alexandria with an army of priests." Pachome's eyes darted to and fro. His feet appeared to be ready to take to heel on a second's notice. "They will come for you soon. You must leave."

Confused, Hypatia demanded to know where they had taken Philippus.

"They have taken him to Father James' house behind the church. Athanasius believes you are a great heretic and that your husband has been harboring you. He will force repentance, whether your body can bear it or not."

"I must go to him," Hypatia asserted. "I will demand that they release him at once."

"It is impossible. Athanasius has jurisdiction over all Christians in Egypt. He will not release Philippus until he is done with him. And they will seize you as well. You must flee."

"I have nowhere to flee to. I have children. Where would I go?" After a short pause, she asked Pachome what they were doing with Philippus.

"Questioning him."

"About what?"

"Heresy, I guess. I am not sure."

"There is no heresy here. Philippus knows nothing of heresy. His answers cannot hurt him."

"It is not the answers that will hurt," Pachome replied. "Rather, it is the manner in which the questions are posed."

Now firmly resolved to go to her husband, Hypatia instructed Beset to take herself and the children to Senmonthis' house. "Stay inside and make sure the children do as well. Pack their clothes and leave this house as if we have quite gone away." Turning to Pachome, she said, "Take me to him. Surely a good monk like you will have some influence with Athanasius."

Pachome shook his head. "I cannot go with you. Athanasius is searching for me as well. I must lead my brothers deep into the desert to escape him."

"Why on Earth would you need to escape from him? Surely he would not harm you."

"That depends on what you mean by harm," the monk replied. "He wants all of us to be ordained as priests and is demanding we be so. That is not the vow we have taken. We want no part of Athanasius' battles with other Christians. You see, I too must flee. I beg you to come with me. We will hide and protect you and your children. But you must come with me now, for I go."

"I will go to my husband," was Hypatia's reply.

Pachome shrugged and ran off in the direction of the desert.

After repeating her instructions to Beset, Hypatia grabbed a shawl to cover her head with and rushed out toward Father James' residence adjacent to the church in Sheneset.

The little church in Sheneset was set amidst a grove of cypress trees about 300 passus from the Nile. In the next fifty years it would be replaced with a twelve-pillar basilica to honor the grandeur and glory of Christ, but for now the rapidly growing congregation worshiped in the increasingly cramped confines of the humble church. Father James' house was a structure of mud, planks, and brick on cypress timbers adjacent to the church. Long before the basilica was built, the house would be replaced by a fifteen-room rectory and convent, but the present, modest complex provided little evidence of the institutional might that the church was rapidly accumulating.

By habit or instinct, Hypatia first entered the church instead of the small house. The only congregants were spiders and their prey and the only movements were the resigned shutters of flies trapped in the sticky embrace of certain death. She heard nothing, not even the buzzing of entrapped flies. Yet the church was not silent. So slight that she did not at first notice it came a muffled, unidentifiable sound, faintly that of wooden machinery laboring, without lubrication. She did not recognize the sound. There was no humanity in it. Yet somehow it triggered her deepest fears and sent a shudder through her slim body down to her bones. She followed it past the cedar cross at the fore of the church, through the small sacristy and out the back door that faced Father James' house. As she followed the sound, it became louder, with intermittent parabolas of intensity. When she left the dim shade of the church and stepped into the bright afternoon sunshine a sudden shriek tore apart the calm and she recognized the sound as the dire, agonized strains of her husband.

At the door of the house stood two men in priestly garb but, with horn-handled pugios sheathed on the outside of their cassocks, they were unmistakably serving as guards. Her instinct was to rush at them in fury, to break through them by force and rush toward the sound of Philippus' screams. But the futility of that course was apparent. She needed help. The guards had not noticed her, so she slipped back into the church and out the front door.

She slouched quickly, furtively back toward her house, but as she approached she could see a similarly armed priest standing in front of it. Another man was approaching the door of Senmonthis' house. She hunched down behind the shrubs and dung baskets near the stable to await an opportunity to slip past the men. Agonizing minutes passed, but the priests hovered about, apparently on station against her approach. Relief came in the unlikely form of Seti, Senmonthis' younger son. He came from who knows where, ambling toward his home with an aimless stroll. Hypatia threw a clod of dung toward him and it burst and splintered at his feet. He looked up and saw Hypatia, hunkered down, motioning toward him with one hand and with the index finger of her other hand pressed hard against her lips. He strolled up to her casually, his black eyes and heavy brows showing some mirth but no indication of surprise at finding the object of hours of his idle imaginings crouched down in such a manner.

"Hypatia," he called, only to be immediately and firmly shushed.

"Come over here," Hypatia sternly whispered. The urgency of her voice and her hidden posture suddenly awoke the normally somnambulant mind of Seti and he approached her with an unfamiliar alertness. When he neared her she commanded him to stop. "I need you to listen carefully now and do exactly as I say. Nothing more, nothing less. Do you understand?"

Seti nodded.

"Good. Those priests by your mother's house and mine are looking for me and I fear them. Go to your house. If they ask you if you know where I am, tell them you do not. When you are sure they are out of earshot, tell your mother where I am and ask her to come to me if she can do so without attracting notice. Tell no one else. That is all."

She pointed toward Senmonthis' door as a command for Seti to go and he went.

Her lair was a good place to hide, with the brush both obscuring disclosure and providing shade. Once one of the priests came and searched inside the stable, but did not notice her. The sky was darkening when she heard Senmonthis' voice rising from outside the doorway of her house. "I will not stay put," she exclaimed in response to a command that Hypatia did not hear. "Beset here is going to feed and water her mistress' donkey and you'll not interfere with her. I am not a Christian. You hold no sway here." With that, Beset emerged from the doorway carrying a wicker basket. The priest at the door reached for the basket, but Senmonthis slapped his hand away, saying, "Don't touch that basket unless you want to feed the ass yourself." By sheer force of personality Senmonthis caused a retreat. The priest quickly withdrew his hand and allowed Beset to pass.

As Beset approached the stable, Hypatia whispered for her go through the motions of tending to Alexander while they talked.

"How are John and Magdalene?" was the first thing Hypatia asked.

"Oh them two think we're having a party. Senmonthis gave them honey soaked twisted bread so them thinks it's a holiday."

"Good. Tell them that mama and papa have gone on a little

trip and might not be back for a day or two."

"We've already told them as much. They'll be fine."

Hypatia sighed, then said, "They are torturing Philippus. I heard his screams coming from Father James' house."

"You are not to go near that place," Beset ordered. "We feared that would happen. And don't think they won't do the same to you, if they catch you."

"I know, but I cannot think what to do."

"You must save yourself. You must leave now. Get word to me where you've gone and I will follow with the children."

"I cannot leave Philippus to suffer like that. And because of me. No, I will turn myself in to spare his life."

Beset was frantic. "Not tonight, I beg you. I will leave this basket next to the stable. There is food and a blanket in it for you. Eat. Find shelter for the night. If you go to them now John and Maggie will have no father and no mother. Promise me. We will think of a plan tonight. You will think of a plan. Senmonthis is a clever one. She will think of something. I will come here in the morning. Do not go to them before then. Please. Give me your word. Think of your children. Think of your poor Beset, who will perish without you. I beg you."

Hypatia looked up at Beset's agonized face, then over to the priests still standing guard outside the two houses. The little stable blocked the priests' view of Beset. Hypatia tossed seven gold solidi toward Beset where they landed with a soft thud at the old woman's feet. "Take these. Use them to flee with the children. Consult Senmonthis. She will know how to trade them for spendable coin. Change them one at a time so that the money-changer does not learn of the fortune you now have. If Philippus and I do not return, find a way to raise our children with love. Provide for their education." Great sobs clutched Hypatia's throat and she could not continue. Through her tears she now saw one of the priests signal to the other and the other began to approach the stable. Hypatia waved her hand at Beset, who remained frozen, staring at the gold coins littered about her feet. She had long believed that her beautiful mistress was capable of all great things, but she had not thought her capable of casually producing such wealth. Beset stared at the coins as if they were an illusion, a trick her eyes were playing upon her simple mind. Hypatia found her voice, "You'd better get back now," Hypatia commanded. "One of the priests is coming."

Awakened by this command, Beset stooped to gather the coins. "I won't go until you promise," she said.

"Alright then. I will wait until morning. Go now."

Beset tucked the coins into her dress, adjusted it, turned and headed back toward Senmonthis' house. She passed the approaching priest wordlessly. The priest continued on to inspect the stable, finding only a well-fed and watered he-ass. From her vantage behind the shrubs Hypatia prayed he would not notice the basket of food and blanket that Beset had placed against the outside wall of the stable. For once her prayers were answered.

Chapter Twenty-Nine

Inquisition

May 330 A.D. – Sheneset

And now [Sophia] reaches the point where hemmed in by evil, She knows no way out. Misled, She has entered a labyrinth. Then Jesus said, "Behold, Father, She wanders the earth pursued by evil. Far from thy Breath She is going astray. She is trying to flee bitter Chaos, and does not know how She is to escape."
The Naassene Psalm

No plan revealed itself to Hypatia during the night. She removed Beset's provisions from the basket, ate a little and spent eight sleepless hours among the bushes, using the blanket more as protection against the stiff branches than to fend off chill air that never came. Just after the sun left the sky she saw Seti leave the house and walk jauntily past the priests. She did not see him return. Morning's first light found her already sitting upright, looking at the two armed priests who slept facing in opposite directions, backs against an olive tree in Senmonthis' yard. Several times she resolved to slip away and go to Father James' house where she would demand the release of Philippus. She had kept three solidi and thought she might be able to use them to secure her and Philippus' release, but she doubted that Athanasius was corruptible in that way. In the end, her promise to Beset and the hope that she might first get a glance of her children before departing settled her down and she waited for Beset to come.

Shortly after first light Beset emerged from Senmonthis' house and headed toward the stable. Hypatia heard one of the priests say to Beset that her donkey would get fat and lazy with so much food as he was given. Beset said nothing in return and continued to the stable, not looking back. The priests did not follow, but watched her closely. Arriving at the stable, Beset immediately set about drawing water from the well. From within the bush, Hypatia told her to take Alexander's tether and lead him about so that they could talk without notice.

Hypatia spoke first. "I have thought of nothing," she said. "I must go myself and attempt to obtain Philippus' release."

"Clever Senmonthis has thought of something," Beset replied. "She sent Seti to Caneopolis to beg Cato Plutonious to intervene. She said that surely the church had no right to imprison or torture people. You are to remain hidden until Seti returns. With the gods' grace, he will return with help."

"Caneopolis is half a day's ride even on a good horse, and how does Seti even know how to arrange such a travel? No. It is too long. I must go to Philippus."

Continuing to lead Alexander around in circles, Beset's face betrayed her fear. "Senmonthis told Seti to seek out Isidorus, the smith. He has horses and is friends with Philippus. He will surely help. She gave Seti money from her own purse. She said a coin such as you gave me would get the boy killed or lead him to foolishness of some sort. But you must wait. At least until tomorrow. It will do no good if you go to them alone."

Hypatia brushed at her hair with her hand. She instructed Beset to tie up Alexander and return to the house and bring the children out into the yard so that she could look at them. Beset took this as acceptance of her entreaties and did as she was told.

A few minutes later Hypatia saw the small forms of Magdalene and John rush out of Senmonthis' door, followed closely by Beset. She saw Maggie follow closely beside John, lifting him when he stumbled and pointing out insects and rocks and other things to him for his presumed amusement. *She will look after him,* Hypatia thought to herself as she crept out from behind the bushes and made her way toward Father James' house.

This time Hypatia did not approach through the church but went directly to Father James' house where two armed priests stood guard at the door.

"I am Hypatia," she announced. "You have my husband. I have come to demand his release." Wordlessly, the priests seized her, each taking an arm and pulling her into the house. She did not resist.

The front room was about twenty feet square, with plank floors and walls. Athanasius sat on a bench with a portable writing table on his lap, while two more armed priests stood before him, giving a report of some kind. Athanasius looked up to see the two guards escorting Hypatia into the room. He placed his writing reed horizontally on the desk as a slight, and to Hypatia, sinister smile curled into being.

Without rising, Athanasius said, "It is the great heretic herself. The famous Sophia. Brought here in answer to my prayers. God is truly great."

Hypatia replied calmly. "My name is Hypatia. I came here of my own free will. You have illegally and immorally seized and tortured my husband. I demand his release."

Athanasius instructed the four priests to leave. He told the two who brought Hypatia into the room to return to their post. To the two he had been talking to when Hypatia entered the room he said, "Go back and find out where Pachomius and his flock have gone. Someone must know. Report back to me after evening prayers. I will go to them when they are found."

When they were alone, Athanasius placed his desk on the bench and rose. Hypatia could barely repress a look of surprise when she saw that, fully erect, he stood well under five feet tall. He had always loomed larger in her memory. She was almost a foot taller than him. He was thirty, perhaps thirty-one years old and looked even younger. His slight stature and almost juvenile visage gave his presence a dress-up quality. With his raging red hair and his brocaded white vestment he seemed almost mythical, like something out of a children's story, at once comical and sinister.

"I have been searching for the heretic Sophia for three years and now God has delivered her unto me. You will now atone for your sins."

"I will atone for the sins you say are mine when you release my husband."

"Your sins are many. Atonement will be difficult."

"Then we should get started. But first release my husband."

"Yes, your sins are many. Perhaps we should start with prostitution."

"We can start wherever you like, but first you must release Philippus."

Athanasius scoffed. "There is nothing I must do. You and Philippus avow yourselves as Christians. I am the Church's lord Bishop over all of Egypt and as such have complete jurisdiction over all spiritual matters involving our faith. I will release him or bury him as I deem right. The same as I will do with you."

"And what sins does Philippus have to atone for?" Hypatia demanded.

"He married his sins. You are his sins."

"And what are my sins?"

Athanasius stared at her, but she could not read his look. Hostility and hatred abided in his eyes, but there was more than this. He seemed confused and, perhaps, amused as well. What Hypatia could not read was the cascade of definite, but conflicting thoughts and emotions that began to flood over and through him the moment he recognized her as the twelve year old waif from the churchyard in Alexandria. In his mind she embodied his one mortal sin. It was not the act alone or even primarily it that tortured his soul. He had prayed for forgiveness many times and was sure that his account for the act itself had been washed clean by the blood of the lamb, Lord Jesus. But there was so much more to it than this. He had coveted her from the moment he first laid eyes upon her, when she was little more than a child. Dressed in rags, scampering for scraps, sleeping wherever she could find a night's shelter, he knew that he should have pitied and had compassion for her, not lust, not covetousness. She should have repulsed him as the physical embodiment of lust, but she had such a face, such a natural grace and bearing that he alternately thought of her as God's perfect creation and Satan's greatest forgery. He had resisted her by night and by day. He had avoided walking past her, giving her food or even attempting to save her soul because he feared that even such contact as this would send his mind spiraling off into obsession-filled hours of worldly desire and carnal imaginings that would have to be flogged out of his body until his weary arm sank from the weight of the lash and sleep overtook him. And flog himself he did. His back bore her scars. And yet, even with all this, a chance sighting of her exhausted body resting against the wall of the church triggered an uncontrollable act of carnal knowledge that he had solemnly vowed to never experience. The existential sin he had committed was not that act itself, which could be forgiven, but in the wanton thoughts and desires that preceded the act, which the act did not extinguish. He thought he had amputated that sin by arranging for her to be sold to a brothel owner from Antioch. Nobody arose as a new object to replace her as a trigger for wicked desires and he was able to dedicate himself to his faith such that now, at just thirty years of age, he was the most powerful bishop in the entire Catholic Church. But when she boldly entered Father James' house and just as boldly demanded the release of her husband, it all came flooding back to him and he was washed with the twin desires of killing and raping her.

Breaking his ruminations, Athanasius replied. "As I said, your sins are many indeed. Prostitution, fornication, impersonating a priest in the most holy of conclaves and the promotion of heretical doctrines, just to begin with."

Hypatia fixed her eyes on the little bishop and balanced her weight before replying. "I can defend myself on all counts," she replied.

"Oh, I suppose you deny being a fornicator?"

"I was a virgin until you raped me."

Athanasius' face reddened but his voice remained calm. "That never happened and you know it, although I will not deny that you are a sorceress who has sought to lure me to sin every day of your life. I shall add slander to your list of sins."

"So you are the one appointed by God to determine what is a sin?"

"I am God's agent on Earth for such purposes. Upon your death, God Himself will decide your fate."

"And yours," she replied.

Athanasius did not take the bait. He merely folded his hands together and continued. "Prostitution. I suppose you have an answer for that as well?"

"I was a slave."

"You should have given your life to save your virtue."

"You had already taken my virtue."

"Another lie. You compound your sins."

"I have prayed to Jesus for forgiveness. He forgave the adulteress, something that I have never been. Surely He has forgiven me."

"Do not presume to know what Jesus does. Christ alone, using common speech and through the agency of men who are not clever with words, has convinced the world to despise death and attend to things that do not die, to look past the things of this world and to gaze on things eternal, to think nothing of earthly glory and aspire only to immortality. He forgave the adulteress because he had not yet taught the world these things. You have no such excuse. In fact, you have conspired to undermine His teaching by promoting the heretical doctrine of the Gnostics.

What have you to say to that charge?"

"That I am no Gnostic."

"You attended the great Council at Nicaea in the company of the Gnostic heretic Timaeus so that he could seek tolerance and expansion of a doctrine that holds common men equal with Jesus. Even if you do not believe in this heresy, you helped to promote it, which makes you a heretic."

"You yourself wrote to Macarius that Jesus assumed humanity that we might all become God."

"And how would you know such a thing?"

"Eustathius was a caller of mine in Antioch. He tried to convert me while breaking his vows, the hypocrite. Apparently you or Macarius shared your correspondence with him."

"Such a slanderous tongue this whore has! I have had enough. Be quiet now."

"I will not obey the man who killed my husband."

"Yet another lie. Philippus lives."

"I was referring to Timaeus, my first husband."

"Timaeus was your husband? Then his sins were even greater than I thought. But I did not kill him either. He burst asunder in the midst as punishment for his heresy. Just like the Judas that he was."

"How does it harm God for people to find their own way? Is that not what we are always left with?"

"Before Jesus lived, that was true. No longer. Now, men all over the world are forsaking the fear of idols and taking refuge with Christ. The objects of worship formerly were varied and countless; each place had its own god. Nobody worshiped his neighbor's god. But now Christ alone is worshiped and through him the Father, throughout the world. Man must worship something; he cannot worship nothing. Jesus has commanded that we worship His Father, who we come to know through Him. It is finished. It is decided once and forever. No more imaginings and inventions. It is done."

"So says the murderer."

"I have had enough. Mark! Luke! Come in here! Seize this harlot! Take her below to be with Philippus! And gag her so that you do not hear her venomous words."

The two priests entered the room. Hypatia stepped back and removed three golden solidi from her tunic. "I will pay for Philippus' release. Do what you will with me, but release my husband."

Athanasius stepped forward and grabbed the money. "Attempting to bribe God's agent in the commission of His offices. I will add that to the list of sins for which you must atone. The sin of Simony, named, appropriately, for Simon Magus, the first heretic." Athanasius put the coins in his writing desk as Mark and Luke seized Hypatia and bound a cloth around her mouth.

The basement of Father James' house was simply a hollow of earth and mud with a few timbers around the perimeter upon which the upper floor rested and which mostly prevented the collapse of the earthen walls. When she saw Philippus' limp body on a table, face down and covered in blood-stained cotton Hypatia produced a shriek that the gag could not suppress. She threw her body toward him and momentarily wrenched herself free of the clerical henchmen. They quickly recovered their grip and pushed her down on the table adjacent to Philippus.

"Satan speaks," Athanasius said. "He reveals himself through her voice. Good. Good. He will be easier to vanquish now that he has made himself known."

Hypatia was strapped to the table, face up, using leather straps that Philippus himself may have cut from hides. Her gag was not removed. She turned her head and stared over at the motionless form of Philippus, looking for signs of life. He did not move and she could not see his face because it was turned away from her. The blood on the cotton sheet that covered him was concentrated in the area above his back, two broad riverbeds of darkening red from which a hundred small rivulets ran in random directions. The two priests Mark and Luke reascended the steps, leaving behind Athanasius and another large, cassock-clad man who was standing next to a third table, arranging metal instruments that Hypatia could not see.

Without removing her gag, Athanasius began to speak to Hypatia. "We have learned quite a bit from Philippus, but not everything. Your husband loves you very much, that is clear. In fact, we have determined that he loves you more than he loves Jesus, which is a sin. For did not Jesus say, 'He that loveth father or mother more than me is not worthy of me: and he that loveth son or daughter more than me is not worthy of me?' That sin will require additional atonement, but that is not why we are here. And even though he seems to love you more than life itself, it is apparent that you do not love him half so much for you have not told him all. You have not told him what you did with the texts he brought to you from Caesarea. From our good friend Eusebius. You have not told him this, else he would have confessed it to me, as he confessed everything else."

Athanasius draped a red vestment stola over his white cassock and adjusted it so that it hung evenly, uncrossed, to both sides of his shoulders. He pulled on white gloves and lifted a black, leather covered codex from the table where the other man remained busy with his housekeeping. Athanasius' pause was deliberate. He thought that what he had said about Philippus was actively at work in Hypatia's imagination, causing her to first envision, then dread, what would soon happen to her. This was not Hypatia's response. Instead, she hung on the fact that Athanasius had talked about her husband in the present tense, giving her hope that he was still alive and that she might still be able to save him by sacrificing herself.

With his accoutrements in place, Athanasius returned to the table on which Hypatia lay. "Philippus told me that you made copies of the wicked texts and disposed of the originals. He said he burned a few, but was less than clear on the method of disposal of the others. All he could say of the copies is that you and he removed them to a cave that he did not believe he could find again to save his life. We put that assertion to the test and it appears he was being truthful. So, I am going to need for you to clarify his answers to those two points of inquiry. If you do so, we can consider his penance sufficient and it will go some far distance in convincing us of the sincerity of your desire for redemption."

Athanasius lifted the black codex and held it above Hypatia's face. "This," he said, "is the book of the Christ. It contains four gospels and can contain no more and no less for, as Iraneus wrote, 'since there are four zones of the world in which we live, and four principal winds, while the Church is spread over all the earth, and the pillar and foundation of the Church is the gospel, and the Spirit of life, it fittingly has four pillars, everywhere breathing out incorruption and revivifying men. From this it is clear that the Word, the artificer of all things, being manifested to men gave us the gospel, fourfold in form but held together by one Spirit.'" As he quoted the words from Iraneus, Athanasius' altered his voice slightly, lowering both tone and volume as if in reverence to an ancient spirit whose truth could not be challenged.

He continued. "The texts that you had or have in your possession cannot be true because they are not contained in this book. Your Timaeus taught that his doctrines were as old as this and that his teachings were passed down from Christ Himself, but this cannot be true. There is no record of any of the disciples or apostles holding Gnostic beliefs. Did not Mark the Evangelist himself found the church at Alexandria? Did not Simon the Rock found the church at Rome? It is the same everywhere and nowhere will you find a Gnostic among the original followers of Jesus, among those who knew Him and witnessed His ministry upon Earth. The writings you protect are the invention of men who could not understand or accept the simplicity of God's love and tried to make Heaven an exclusive club, open only to those who had acquired knowledge of spheres of heaven and layers of diverse deities. It is and always has been folly, as their disappearance from the world attests.

"You may be asking yourself, what harm do you do by harboring these ideas, by copying and preserving these heretical texts. I told you a few minutes ago that man must worship something, that he cannot worship nothing. We know this because for as far back as history goes, man has sought out God. Without the clear guidance of His Son, mankind always erred, finding multiple gods in the multiple facets of God's creation or imagining a God that loved some of his creations more than others based on the circumstances of birth or geography. In the greatest act of love the world has ever known, God Himself became a man and sacrificed Himself so that once and for all, all people everywhere in the world could know the one true God and the righteous path to life eternal. But just as man cannot worship nothing, nor can he worship everything. God must be seen through a lens, not a prism. The lens of Jesus. If we allow people to believe anything they want to believe, Jesus' message will be diluted. Faith with doubt is not faith. Belief is possible only with certainty. People must be given the one true path. They cannot be given options. If certainty is lost, faith dissolves. This is why God destroyed Timaeus at Nicaea and why I must destroy the texts that you protect. Jesus' return is imminent and as long as these ideas exist on the face of the Earth, mankind will not be ready to greet Him."

Athanasius returned to the table where the large man continued assembling and cleaning his instruments and placed the black codex down. He kneeled and prayed in Latin, then rose and returned to Hypatia's table. "We are going to begin with a flogging," he said casually. "Flagellation cleanses the flesh and focuses the mind so that the forgiveness that is sought is more easily given. Afterward, you will ask forgiveness for your sins and tell me where to find the heretical texts, originals and copies."

The large man now moved toward her, carrying a leather whip of eight or nine tails with pieces of ox bone tied to the end of each tail. He placed it on the table where she lay and undid her straps. He lifted her off the table with one arm, as if she was a sack of kale. He looped her hands, still bound, around an iron hook that had been inserted into one of the support timbers. The hook was placed high enough that her toes, outstretched, barely touched the earth. Then, using both hands, the large man peeled her tunic back over her shoulders, exposing her breasts to the wall and her back to the open air. Her mouth remained gagged.

Athanasius muttered another prayer, again in Latin, then asked, "Do you know why the hook is placed so high on the timber?" Of course, she could not answer, but this did not concern Athanasius. "I have found that the submission required for complete sincerity in the request for forgiveness is more difficult to attain if the supplicant is allowed to brace himself on his feet. This way, submission is complete and the prayers for forgiveness are more easily answered." Athanasius walked in a semi-circle behind Hypatia. "You really are a great beauty," he said. "Women such as you cause much destruction and much evil. Eve was the first example of this. The Greeks write of a Helen whose beauty brought the downfall of two great civilizations. You think your beauty is a gift, but such beauty in a woman can only be the work of Satan himself." Athanasius stepped back and lifted his arm and the strong man began to rain down steady, rhythmic lashes upon her back.

Hypatia screamed with each blow. With the first scream the gag came loose and her voice pierced the dank air. With the second, her toes lost their place in the dirt and her weight of her body hung full upon her shoulders as the straps dug deep into her wrists. Three ... four ... five. Her screams piercing in syncopation with the lash. Six ... seven. Upon the eighth blow Philippus raised his head and weakly commanded, "Stop." The strong man, the whip man, looked at Athanasius, who responded by lowering his hand. The blows stopped.

Hypatia's sobbing continued, but took shape as a word, repeated over and over: "Philippus, Philippus, Philippus."

"I am sorry, Sophia," Philippus said.

Athanasius returned to the table and again picked up the black codex. The book, he called it, "in biblia," the Bible. "This is really very touching," he said as Hypatia's sobbing eased and she sought to reestablish her toes in the dirt to ease the strain on her arms and shoulders. She accomplished the footing, but was too weak to take the weight off her sagging body. "Yes, very touching, but your husband betrays you by naming you Sophia. It is clear now that you are both devoted Gnostics. Forgiveness will be much more difficult."

Athanasius removed his robe and vestment stole and hung them on another hook, near the strong man's table. As Athanasius ascended the stairs, the strong man lifted Hypatia from the hook and carried her back to the table from which he had removed her. He used two hands this time and gently lowered her, face down on the table. He bound her legs around the table. He placed one hand to dangle on either side of the table and bound them together under it. He took a lightweight cotton sheet and draped it over the bleeding wounds on her back. He removed the gag that had slipped down around her neck. Then he ascended the stairs, leaving Hypatia and Philippus on adjacent tables facing each other.

Two hours passed without Athanasius' return. After the flogging he had not asked a single question. He had simply departed. Hypatia was too sore, too exhausted and too relieved to wonder if his conduct was part of some stratagem. Allowed to face each other and left alone, husband and wife stared into each other's eyes. Slowly words came. At first Philippus spoke only delirium.

"I am sorry, Sophia. I am sorry, my love."

Hypatia recovered her wits more quickly. "Hush, my husband," she said. "You have nothing to apologize for to me. You have done me no wrong. It is the lash that speaks, not my husband. It is I who brought the lash and the devil from Alexandria. It is only the lash that causes you to speak such things."

Gradually Philippus reclaimed his consciousness. Slowly, with a clenched throat, he defended his apology, saying he had admitted to Bishop Athanasius that his wife had copied forbidden texts and may harbor heretical beliefs. "I condemned you with my words. I am the reason you suffer now." His voice was weak and halting and clenched with great pain.

Hypatia told him that she loved him more than ever and that it was not his words that caused this trouble, but her stubbornness in refusing to honor his wishes by burning the books immediately. "I was so obsessed by what I lost that I did not think enough of what I had and could lose," she said. "What you said was no more than what is true, though I am not Gnostic. You said what you said because of the pain of the lash. I would have said anything to stop it. You did me no wrong. It was the lash."

"Yes, the lash is painful, but ..." He could not continue. The words he had spoken had so exhausted him that he fell silent and lost consciousness. Some time passed as Hypatia listened to his breathing. Listened to the footfalls on the floor above. Listened to voices muted by the wooden planks of the floor. The dank basement became their world for the two hours they were left alone. They were given neither food nor drink, but thought nothing of the deprivation. Several candles cast a faint light through which Hypatia could see the dust stirred up during the lashing drift in random wafts and settle slowly. To take her mind off the pain, she studied uneven contours of the earthen walls that she could see in front and beside her and could see that entire worlds existed there. She wondered if the worms, beetles, pill bugs and millipedes that inhabited those walls ever came to conflict over the meaning of their surroundings, the creation of their universe, or the correct interpretation of what they found. She thought not. Mostly she looked at Philippus as he slept and wondered where he was, where his mind had gone to and what thoughts he had there. She knew at least that he did not blame her, that he loved her and that she loved him.

When after thirty minutes or so he again opened his eyes, he looked at her and smiled.

"Philippus," Hypatia asked, "where is Father James? I have not seen him."

"Athanasius." The name stuck in Philippus' parched throat. He began again. "Athanasius sent him away. He protested what was being done, so Athanasius put him on the search for Pachome." His eyes closed and Hypatia thought she would lose him again, but they opened again and the smile returned and he said, simply, "I have the most beautiful wife in the world. Me. Philippus of Joppa."

He asked about the children. Hypatia told him that she left them in the care of Beset and Senmonthis. Philippus nodded. "I fear you will have to raise them alone. Promise me they will be raised as Christians."

"What nonsense is this?" Hypatia asked. "You will raise them with me. If one of us is to perish here, it will more likely be me. Surely you will recover from the whipping you received."

"It is not the whipping," he said, but again did not continue. After a few more moments he sighed and said, "No, it will be you who survives."

"I will tell him everything he wants to hear," Hypatia said. "We will both survive."

The door from the upper room opened, casting a bright stream of light into the basement below. Athanasius descended alone and closed the door behind him, leaving the basement again in shadows. Hypatia took some heart at the fact that the strong man did not follow Athanasius down the stairs. Athanasius' mood seemed to have changed. He began by asking how each of them were doing and told them that he would soon send Luke down to tend to their wounds.

"The purpose of what is done here is not cruelty, but kindness. It is being done primarily to obtain obedience to the Word of God with the object of atonement for sins committed. I have flogged myself many times while saying prayers. I think you will be amazed at how cleansing it is once its object is attained. Of course, a second purpose is to obtain information regarding the heretical texts and to raise our confidence that the information obtained is trustworthy. But this, too, is a merciful object, since by finding and destroying these texts we will prevent other good Christians from going astray and missing the opportunity for salvation that our short sojourn in this world of sin provides."

As he spoke, Hypatia saw him emerge from a corner of the room carrying a heavy, damp cloth. She heard him place the object on the table and strike at it with an iron instrument. She thought then she heard a sound that she had not heard since her days in Antioch, the sound of ice clinking into cups. This could not be, she thought to herself, since ice was an unspeakable luxury. It had to be transported from mountain glaciers and heavily packed with straw and cloth against melting. Even thus protected, most was lost by the time it reached its destination or shortly afterward. She was sure that Father James had never kept it and the cost of acquiring it simply for Athanasius' visit was, she believed, prohibitive. But then she heard water being poured into the cups and the ice tinkling against the cups' sides as they were filled. All doubt was removed when, with the greatest solicitude, Athanasius placed his hand on her chin to lift her face and pressed a chilled chalice to her lips. "Drink, my daughter," he said gently. She felt the cold, refreshing water on her lips and took a measured sip before abruptly stopping to say, "Philippus."

"Yes, yes," Athanasius said, his voice filled with feigned kindness. "Philippus, too, must drink. But you finish first." Hypatia took a long draught and again said, "Philippus."

"Are you quite sure you have had your fill?"

"Yes. Philippus."

Athanasius turned to Philippus' table and held the cup before his face, but Philippus could not raise his head high enough to get his lips to it. Athanasius sighed, then roughly pulled his face up and poured the remainder of the contents into his mouth. Philippus could not swallow it fast enough to prevent much of the water from spilling onto the table. When the cup was empty, Athanasius lowered Philippus' head into the pool and returned to the strong man's table, poured some water for himself and took a long drink. He returned to Hypatia's table and pulled the cotton down from her back, emitting a clucking sound as he did.

"Those scars will last," he said. "Your physical perfection is no more. I have done you a great service. Vanity is a sin, something of which these scars will remind you for the rest of your life."

"Something you said above stairs has been troubling me. You claimed that you saw Eustathius in Antioch. I know this is a great lie, but I cannot presume your claim to be coincidental to Eusebius' recent claim that Eustathius has been having relations with a married woman. It is a slander made by a desperate supporter of Origen and Arius against one who has ever been faithful to the one true faith. But he has pressed these claims and is demanding a synod for the purpose of a trial against the good bishop. So, in addition to the location of the heretical texts, I am going to need you to tell me everything you know about this matter and to admit that Eusebius' accusations are based upon your testimony."

Athanasius paused for a moment, and then said, "Speak!"

Although she had told Philippus that she would tell Athanasius everything he wanted to know, this new question made her hesitate. What were the implications if she admitted telling Eusebius about Eustathius' affair? Could such an admission be used to harm Eusebius? The answer was surely yes. She avoided the subject. "The originals of the books you seek were given to a trusted friend. I will retrieve them. The copies are in a cave about four hours from here. I can lead you to them."

"Yes, yes. I knew you would cooperate. Your path to salvation is before you. Now, all you must do is admit that you are the one who fed the slander to Eusebius. Swear to it and sign your name to the testimony and I will give absolution to you both."

"I will tell you the truth," Hypatia said. "I told Eusebius nothing of the kind. But I will sign whatever you wish."

"You once again betray your dishonesty. I want the truth. I need details. You must write the statement yourself."

"Tell me what to write and I will write it."

Athanasius shook his head. "I am going to go up the stairs and retrieve my assistant. You have that much time to reconsider your deceit."

Athanasius ascended the stairs and departed, leaving the door open and the light streaming down. Hypatia looked over at Philippus, intending to seek guidance, but he was unconscious again, face down in the small pool of spilled water. She tried to think of what to do. The truth was that she had written to Eusebius, providing him the name of a woman whom Eustathius was fond of. While this might be enough to make trouble for Eusebius, it would surely not be all that Athanasius wanted. She dreaded the blows that would rain down upon her if he was dissatisfied, but did not know how to satisfy him.

As Hypatia was struggling with what to say below, she heard a commotion above. It started with voices. There was a male voice, vaguely familiar. She heard Athanasius ordering the newcomers to leave immediately. She heard another voice, one that she knew, that of Senmonthis, telling someone to get out of her way. Then she heard the clanking of metal, groans and shrieks. She heard steps rapidly retreating and fading away. Looking up into the light, she saw an extended steel blade, dripping with blood, coming down the stairs. A tall, helmeted man dressed in Roman mail carried the sword and was coming down the stairs. As he reached the bottom step she recognized the soldier as Ankha Aegyptos.

Chapter Thirty

Flight, Again

330 A.D. – Nile Valley

[And Jesus said to Judas]: You will exceed all of [the disciples] for you will sacrifice the man who bears me.
The Gospel of Judas Iscariot

Ankha Aegyptos descended the stairs to Father James' basement and shouted in anger. "It is worse than I thought." He dropped his sword heavily onto the ground, untied Hypatia's bonds and sought to raise her, but she stopped him, telling him to attend to Philippus instead. Hypatia lifted herself from the table, pulled her torn tunic back over her shoulders and turned in time to see Ankha pulling the cotton sheet away from Philippus' back. As he pulled, Philippus came fully awake and howled in pain. The sheet was glued to his back by dried blood, and Ankha stopped pulling almost as soon as he started.

Senmonthis came down the stairs with her voice preceding her. "What is taking so long? We must get moving. They will be back. We must return home and retrieve Beset and the children." When she saw the blood seeping through Hypatia's tunic and Philippus lying in blood-drenched rags the cascade of words stopped. She rushed toward Hypatia, but Hypatia pointed at Philippus and Senmonthis diverted to his side. Taking a look at the blood on the sheet and the small portion of his back that Ankha had exposed, Senmonthis exclaimed, "By Isis above, they've skinned him."

"What?" Hypatia asked urgently.

"They've stripped the skin off his back. This is serious. This is severe." Turning toward the stairs, she hollered, "Seti!" The young man's face appeared above them. "Take the money you've got left and buy a horse cart. Isidorus will sell you his. If he wants more than you've got, tell him I'll be along directly to settle with him. Put some fresh straw in the bottom of it. Take Ankha's horse to pull the cart and get you back here before I count ten. Go now, boy." Seti bounded out of view.

Senmonthis looked about the room, inventorying what she had to work with. She went over to the strongman's table and returned with a pitcher of water, an earthenware jar and several sheets of cotton. Laying them down on the table next to Philippus she said, "Now then, we are going to try to replace your bandages, sir. It will likely hurt more than you can stand but I'll be as gentle as I can be." Hypatia had risen to stand beside Philippus, hold his hand and wipe his brow.

Senmonthis doused Philippus' existing bandage with the water then said to Ankha, "Help me pull this back now. Slowly."

As they peeled the cotton from his back, Philippus' body tensed and he gripped Hypatia's hand with all the strength he had left in him. The removal of the sheet revealed two even and parallel strips of bare, red muscle from which the skin had been methodically peeled away. Hypatia began to weep when she saw this and leaned over and kissed his forehead tenderly. Philippus' grip on Hypatia's hand eased as his breathing regained a regular rhythm.

"I'm going to put some salve on you now," Senmonthis explained. "I don't know what it is, but you need some unguent to be sure. Try to bear it." She tore a piece of cotton, dipped it in the earthenware jar and began to daub the salve on Philippus' raw back. "I should have held on to the little red jerboa for you to run through," she said to Ankha. "Instead I let him scamper off with only a slap to repay this cruelty. A slap weren't nearly enough. If there's a next time I'll kill him myself and sing my own praises over his severed head."

When she had finished applying the salve, Senmonthis told

Ankha to help her wrap Philippus in fresh cotton, of which there was still an abundance. Athanasius had come prepared. They accomplished the wrapping by Ankha lifting first his torso, then his legs as Senmonthis and Hypatia, who was able to help, wrapped the cloth around him, three layers thick, top and bottom. Philippus had on no other clothing. As they were completing the wrapping, Seti reappeared. "I've got the cart, all hitched up," he shouted from above stairs.

"We have to be off," Senmonthis said. "We're not out of the grove yet. We've got to get Beset and the children and get out of Sheneset before that red jaculus regroups with his men. Ankha, can you carry Philippus up the stairs?" Ankha picked his sword off the earthen floor and sheathed it. He lifted Philippus up, laid him over his shoulder and slowly and carefully climbed the steps into the bright afternoon sunlight. Hypatia was able to climb the stairs on her own, but before ascending, she found Athanasius' ice wrapped in cloth in a dark corner of the basement and carried it up the steps with her. Philippus hung down from Ankha's shoulder. Climbing the stairs behind Ankha, Hypatia looked into Philippus' eyes and he looked back into hers. Wherever they were going, whoever was going with them, with their eyes they told each other they would go together. Senmonthis gathered up the unguent and remaining cotton and followed the others up the stairs. Once above stairs, Hypatia unwrapped the ice and put it on the floor of the house where it immediately began to melt and pool.

A tableau of gore greeted them at the top of the stairs. Mark was sprawled, face down in a pool of blood, with his pugio just out of the reach of the last movement of his outstretched arm. Luke lay face up, curled, still clutching his pugio, his free hand futilely planted on a stomach wound that had stopped gushing and now only oozed blood. The strong man sat with his back against the bench where Athanasius had been seated when Hypatia entered the room a few hours earlier. His neck had been hacked at a slightly downward angle and his head tilted away, exposing the tendons and empty veins and arteries of the neck. Athanasius' writing desk was still on the bench next to the former strong man. Hypatia opened it to find a Bible, a book filled with Greek symbols and formulae, some pages on which Athanasius had written, several sheets of blank papyrus, five styluses, four bottles of ink and three gold coins.

"Those are mine," she said to herself as she closed the desk and carried it with her out the door. Outside they found Roxana, Philippus' mule, tethered to a post. Ankha Aegyptos laid Philippus face down on the straw in the cart Seti had just acquired and helped Hypatia onto the back of the donkey. With Ankha at the head of the procession, the party of five made its way toward home. They did not know what they would find there.

Later, Hypatia remembered the trip to Senmonthis' house and the adjacent whore's house that she called home only in fragmentary pieces, played out in staccato rhythm. It was the same with her memory of the flight north and east out of Sheneset that led them after a full day's journey near the cave where she had hidden her money and books.

She remembered that John screamed to be fed the moment he saw her and that somehow she satisfied him while thinking he would have to be weaned soon. She remembered Beset and Magdalene crying when they saw her and Maggie wailing when she saw the condition Philippus was in. She remembered trying to comfort the child as best she could. She remembered Senmonthis and Beset making all the preparations, gathering water and provisions, hitching Alexander to the little, rarely used garden cart she owned. She remembered that the priests who had been standing guard when she left in the morning were no longer there. She remembered entering what had been her happiest dwelling for the last time, looking around and gathering clothes.

The house had been ransacked, but she found the forty-seven solidi remaining from what Timaeus had given her on the last day of his life still hidden in the dirt under the pallet where she and Philippus had slept. Under the sack containing the coins was the book containing *The Gospel of Judas Iscariot,* which she had forgotten to include among the books she had hidden in the cave the day before. She grabbed the coins and the book and loaded them into Alexander's cart along with the clothes she had gathered. She remembered Ankha standing tall, on guard, outside the two houses, while the women readied for the trip. She remembered Seti standing proud just outside the house, bragging to his new wife and Bakare about the role he had played in the affair. She remembered that she was the one who determined the direction they went, but she did not remember discussing the reason for Senmonthis going with them.

It was late in the day after their rescue that the little band found rest in the shade of the cliffs, a steep mile from the cave that Hypatia and Philippus had visited two days before. The going had been slow, due largely to the many stops made to attend to Philippus' needs. He was not doing well. He had to be transported in the horse cart, face down. There was no established road, only paths that often ended abruptly or turned off into cliffs that could not be climbed. They travelled slowly, but even at a slow pace the cart bounced and Philippus would awake in pain and the women would attend to him as best they could. The children mostly rode in the donkey cart, with the burden of pulling it falling on Alexander. Often John would demand to be carried and Hypatia was not recovered enough from the flogging to lift the child. He was, however, happy to ride on Ankha's leather shoulders. The goods they packed for their journey were mostly borne by Roxana. So, here was the procession most of the time: Ankha, armored and armed, with John on his shoulders; Senmonthis leading the horse by its reins and Philippus riding face down in the cart; Roxana, laden with clothing, food, water and other provisions, following behind the horse cart; Beset leading Alexander the Great; Magdalene in the donkey cart surrounded by other possessions the company had packed; Hypatia following behind, in pain and weakened by the beating she had received from Athanasius' henchman. They navigated by the sun and stars, heading generally north, without any discussion about the why or wherefore of their direction. By the end of the first full day they were running low on food. Decisions would have to be made.

They pulled off the little path they were on and set up camp as best they could. The meal consisted of dried lamb, bread, dates and figs. They had come across a spring along the way and had refilled, so they had plenty of water for the animals and themselves, but in their haste they had neglected to bring forage for the beasts. There were a few desert plants that the donkeys found palatable, but the horse would not eat any of it and had to be given the last of their bread. They would have to head back toward the Nile the next day, which could be dangerous. Ankha emptied the donkey cart and turned it on its side so that Philippus could sit up by holding himself on to it. He smiled at the children between the grimaces, but could not support himself very long, and soon had to be returned to his bed on the horse cart. Hypatia told the children the story of Jesus feeding the multitudes with loaves of bread and fish. The children were exhausted from the travel and the sun and were soon asleep.

Sitting in the shade of the cliffs as the sun declined, the remainder of the group rested and talked. Hypatia wanted to know how and why Ankha had come from Caneopolis to rescue them. It was the purest of luck, Ankha told her. He just happened to be on guard for Court Day when he saw Seti come into the building. Seti was immediately overwhelmed by his surroundings. The white marble pillars of the consul's palace and the spectacle of legionaries in dress, fine citizens in robes and the immaculately dressed Cato Plutonious, who was now full

Consul, sitting like a wrathful god in judgment stole Seti's tongue. He was asked what he wanted, but could not speak. If it were not for the fact that Ankha had recognized him, he would have left without even attempting to accomplish his mission. But Ankha did recognize him and was given leave to follow him out of the hall to ascertain his purpose. After Ankha had broken Seti's trance and gotten out of the boy what he had come for, he lost no time in marching the youth back into the palace where, with much help and prompting from Ankha, Seti was able to explain his mission.

Ankha could not tell whether or not Cato Plutonious knew that the Hypatia of whom Seti spoke was the same Hypatia he had sought as a mistress three years before, but he thought not. What Cato said was, "That is Church business; it does not concern Rome. Away with you before I have you flogged for wasting Rome's time." At that precise moment, Ankha made a decision that, two days later, was causing him great concern. Without asking for or obtaining leave he walked out of the palace with Seti and directed him to take him to where Philippus was being held. They rode together without stopping on the back of Seti's horse. They went first to Hypatia's house, hoping to find her still in hiding. When he saw the priests standing outside the houses of Hypatia and Senmonthis, he told them to disperse under the authority of Consul Cato Plutonious. He did not know where they went. He went inside Senmonthis' house and ascertained where Hypatia was. Senmonthis went with Seti and him and his mother stayed with the children. Upon entering Father James' house, a ridiculous little red haired man told them to leave. Senmonthis told him to get out of the way, slapped his face and proceeded toward the open door to the cellar. The two priests with pugios pulled their blades and rushed at Senmonthis. Ankha cut them down in two strokes. The big man had been seated on the bench, but rose and grabbed a roman sword, much like his own. Ankha struck a blow to his neck, virtually severing it. The big man appeared to simply sit back down and died. The little red haired man ran away muttering something about the vengeance of God.

"I cannot thank you enough," Hypatia said to Ankha. "You saved both our lives, I have no doubt." Ankha looked over at Philippus in the cart and frowned, but did not contradict her. Instead, he said what had been troubling him for the past thirty-six hours.

"I am glad I made the decision I did, but it is not without consequences. I have deserted my post. That offense alone is punishable by death. Perhaps even worse, I have killed three priests acting in their official capacity, sanctioned and directed by the bishop of Alexandria. Now that you have escaped from the bishop, I think I may attract more danger than I avert."

Hypatia considered what Ankha said and analyzed it based on the facts that she knew. The directness of thought that Timaeus loved in her was never more apparent. "You told me once that your commitment to the Legion was twenty-five years, is that true?"

"Yes."

"And you have what, three, four years left?"

"Four."

"Your friend, Brutus Gaulinius, told me that he could purchase his way out of his commitment. Is the same true for you?"

"Yes, but the cost is a solidi per year remaining. Four solidi. It is impossible."

"Let us take inventory." Hypatia retrieved the three gold coins from Athanasius' writing desk. Then, taking the sack she had retrieved from below her pallet, she returned to the little circle of friends. She laid a cloth down on the ground and poured out the contents of the sack. A pile of solidi and pieces of solidi spilled out onto the cloth. Hypatia added the three retrieved from the desk to the pile and began to count. It added up to a little over forty-nine solidi. Senmonthis leaned in and dropped four more solidi on the pile. "I gave three to Bakare and Seti, for them to live on, since I'll not be returning."

Fifty-three solidi. The band of exiles was rich beyond the imaginings of any of them but Hypatia and Philippus, who slept. Even Hypatia, who had always feared and hidden her wealth, felt a sudden giddiness at its open display. She did not say anything about the two thousand more that was hidden less than a mile from where they sat.

"I think we have quite enough to buy your freedom," Hypatia said, "although how it can be arranged, I am not sure."

"I can arrange it at any town where there is a garrison. I carry my enlistment papers on my person." Ankha paused. "If they have charged desertion," he continued, "it may complicate matters."

"A complication that I venture to guess can be unraveled with a little extra coin," Hypatia said.

"Yes, but there is still the matter of the slain priests."

"I could be wrong," Hypatia replied, "but I do not think Athanasius would want what happened in Sheneset to become widely known. If he presses charges, we will publish the true events and certain other things I know about him and post them throughout Alexandria. No, I do not think he will want widespread knowledge of the affair."

"Alexandria!" Senmonthis exclaimed. "How are we to post anything in Alexandria?"

"Because that is where we are going or, at least, where I am going."

Until the moment she said the word 'Alexandria' Hypatia had not known where they were heading. But once spoken, the destination became logical, necessary, inevitable. It came to her as a revelation. Where better to be safe from Athanasius than in his own capital? She would not wait for Athanasius to press charges against them. She would go to Alexandria to bring charges against him, to humiliate him, if possible to bring him down. Alexandria was not a Christian city or, at least, was not controlled by the Christians. It was the melting pot of the Roman world. Every language was spoken there, every religion was observed. Any action Athanasius took against her there could be made known to a wider world. She could find shelter among others there who did not share Athanasius' beliefs or cower to his authority. "I will be safest in the pit of the viper," Hypatia said.

The others discussed it. Senmonthis said that she might be able to find family there. The Hounds and Jackals game had come from Alexandria, or so family lore had it and she had always wanted to go there to discover her stock, which she had always believed must be made of better stuff than the relatives she remembered. She said she would gladly go to Alexandria with Hypatia.

Beset said she would follow Hypatia to the ends of the earth and she meant it. Ankha said he would stay with them for as long as he was needed. Philippus remained asleep.

Hypatia smiled in satisfaction over the decision. She had been hiding for five years since Nicaea, since she was eighteen years old. No more hiding. No more fear. She would confront the beast, whatever the consequences. In a moment of exultant spirits Hypatia told the others: "One more thing. From this moment on, I am Sophia. That is what Athanasius calls me. That is what Philippus calls me. That is what Timaeus called me. I will not run from it. I am Sophia."

The following day they turned west, toward the Nile. They passed through settlements along the Nile Valley and were easily able to acquire the food and other provisions they needed along the way. In Panopolis Kemmis there was a legionary outpost where, after two days of negotiations, Ankha was able to buy his release from the legion and dismissal of the charges of desertion of post for four and a half solidi. Ankha sold his mail, armor and shield, but kept his sword. He had been in the Roman Army since he was sixteen. At age thirty-seven, the civilian clothes he purchased could do little to disguise the mien and bearing of a soldier. He would always bear the distinctive scar on his chin, cut by the helmet he wore during his years in the Legion, not to mention the battle scars on his chest and left shoulder. His mien and bearing, together with the sword he carried on his hip was sufficient to dissuade any who may have thought of accosting the little band. One person Ankha talked to in Panopolis had heard that three priests had been killed in Chenoboskion, but nobody had issued an alert for Ankha, Philippus or Sophia. It appeared they were not being hunted.

Sophia was Sophia again. As she had been with Timaeus, she was an itinerant, a traveler on the Roman viae. This time she was not seeking out the symbols and landmarks of religious knowledge, but hoping to avoid the knowledge of religious authorities. But as she had been with Timaeus, she was pleased with her traveling companions. By day they would walk beside the horse and donkeys and talk of life and hopes and expectations. The children treated the travel as an adventure. To them, they had lost only a house and a yard. The people they loved and who loved them were all with them on the exploit.

This feeling of adventure was entirely subsumed by the anguish the travelers, and Sophia in particular, felt over Philippus' condition. As the days passed he spent longer and longer periods of time awake, but his back did not heal. He was made aware of the plans to travel to Alexandria, but whether he agreed with the decision or not was less than clear. During the two days they spent in Panopolis Kemmis he was taken to a physician, who applied dried aloe to his back and ordered his bandages to be changed at least twice a day. For a few days Philippus appeared to improve, but the two strips on his back darkened. He would let the children ride in his cart with him and would tell them stories of his father and mother and brothers and sisters in Joppa and of Eusebius, whom he called Uncle Eusebius, in Caesarea. When they stopped for a rest, he could climb out of the cart and sit among the others for a time, but the pain of the effort showed on his face and he quickly tired and had to lie down again. Once, when he heard Senmonthis talking about looking for long lost family from among the Egyptian priesthood, he objected.

"Sophia and I are Christians and must live as such," he said. Sophia did not contradict him or argue with him, though she was determined never again to place herself or her family under the jurisdiction of the Church. She spent hours attending to him and she read to him from Athanasius' Bible, which he said brought him comfort. She did not tell him that, buried in the straw of the donkey cart was the Gospel of Judas Iscariot, which, in the haste of their preparations for flight, she thought would be better taken with them than left behind for discovery by Athanasius or his men.

The group decided not to travel by river boat because of the lingering fear that church or state authorities might be looking for them in connection with the Chenoboskion priest killings and detaining them on board a boat would be considerably easier than chasing them down along the road. They passed towns large and small: Antaeopolis, Hieracon, Pesla. They crossed to the west bank of the Nile at Antinoe. By the time they reached Antinoe, the raw stripes on Philippus' back had turned black and the surrounding tissue a raging red. He ran a fever that could not be contained. The physician they consulted in Antinoe exclaimed "gangraena" when he saw it.

"The usual treatment," he told Sophia, "is amputation of the infected limb. But this is not a limb, but the trunk. Make him comfortable is all you can do. He will soon die."

Sophia wanted to take rooms at an inn to give him rest and as much comfort as she could, but Philippus insisted that they keep moving. He was nearly out of his mind with fever and little else he said made sense, but so firm and sure and almost violent was he on this subject that Sophia and the others relented and they continued on northward.

They travelled slowly for the next week. Most of the time Philippus was delirious. Sophia sat beside him on the horse cart, held his hand, combed his hair and wiped his brow with a wet cloth. The only coherent word to pass his lips during the times of delirium, repeated over and over, was "Sophia." Sophia would bring one or both of the children on the cart with him and tell them what a good and gentle father they had. She said that someday they would understand how rare a man their papa was, possessing kindness to the core of his being. Magdalene earnestly told her mother that she was praying for papa and that she knew her prayers would be answered. "Jesus is good and papa is good so I know that Jesus will save papa," she said.

Three or four times during the week his fever broke and he would sit up and talk. At such times he talked about his burial. He knew they were not at home and that Father James could not preside, but he wanted a Christian burial. Sophia told him that he should not talk of such a thing, that he was going to get better and they would live many years together in Alexandria. They both knew better and the last time she told him this he said that he was ready to be judged and thought he would not be found wanting.

While the party rested at night Sophia would light candles and read the Gospel of Judas. Timaeus had never spoken of this particular gospel, but while the reversal of roles for Judas from villain to hero was surprising, the message of the text was much in line with some of the other texts she had translated. The book took place during the last week of Jesus' life on earth and purported to be a secret account of a revelation from Jesus to Judas Iscariot. Unlike in the three synoptic gospels and Acts of the Apostles, with which Sophia was familiar, here Judas was not the evil betrayer, but alone among the twelve disciples Judas understood or at least recognized the true nature of Christ. Jesus laughs at hearing his disciples say a prayer of thanksgiving. When they ask Jesus why he laughs at them, he says he is not laughing at them, but that their prayer does not flow from their own free will, but because they think it pleases their god. They protest that he is the son of their god, to which he replies that none of them know him and that "no generation will know me among the people who are with you." Jesus then challenges the disciples: "Is there any of you who are strong enough to bring forward the perfect person and stand before my face?" The other eleven protest that they are strong, but only Judas stands. Judas could not look Jesus in the eye, but he says, "I know who you are and from what place you come. You have come from the immortal realm of Sophia, and I am not worthy to pronounce the name of the one who sent you." Jesus asks Judas to step away from the others and proceeds to confer upon him truths that the others are not capable of understanding.

The narrative of Judas is not linear. At times Jesus appears to his disciples as a dancing child. After an absence, Jesus tells the twelve that he spent the night in another realm. The disciples tell Jesus about a dream they had of priests sacrificing animals in the Temple. Jesus tells them that the dream is about themselves, that they are the priests and that the sacrifices are one of the ways they are misleading their followers. Judas tells Jesus that that he had a vision of himself being stoned by the other disciples. Jesus tells Judas that he has seen a vision of his own fate. He teaches Judas mysterious truths that no one has ever known. The truth that Jesus describes is much like the Apocryphon of John, which she had translated while still in Chenoboskion. Essentially, Jesus explains to Judas that this world is not the creation of the one, true God, but of lesser gods who are foolish and murderous. People, such as the other disciples, who worship a lesser god, are worshiping the wrong deity. People must not worship the gods who brought this world into creation, but the true goddess

Barbelo (Sophia). Jesus says some people have the divine spirit that will transcend the world and have eternal life even after the creation itself is destroyed and that Judas will be prominent among these: "You will exceed all of them, for you will sacrifice the man that clothes me."

The Gospel of Judas, then, was like several of the other texts that Sophia had translated in that it turned orthodoxy on its head. Judas was not a betrayer, but an enabler, the necessary instrument of freeing Jesus from his earthly body so that he could return to the divine realm from which he came.

The codex that contained the Gospel of Judas contained other writings, including the letter from Peter to Philip and the First Apocalypse of James, that she had already copied, but the translations were different than hers had been. In reading how other, presumably more educated men had treated the texts, she realized the deficiencies of her work. There was also a text identified as the Temptation of Allogenes, concerning a divine or semi-divine figure that could communicate with other realms and aeons.

Philippus died just outside of Oxyrynchus.

The children took their father's death as young children often do, with grief alternating with forgetfulness. Magdalene asked several times where papa had gone. The answer that he had gone to heaven seemed to satisfy her each time she asked and she was soon telling the others, in all earnestness, that papa had gone to heaven because Jesus loved him too much to leave him with her. For John there were a few days when his silences were longer than usual. A young child soon gets over the loss of a parent and reoccupies himself with the people and events of immediate life. But more and more as time passes, the loss weighs in, again and anon at unpredictable times and places and the pain of loss is constantly renewed for the rest of his life.

Sophia separately asked Ankha, Beset and Senmonthis whether they thought it safe to contact a local priest to preside over the burial rites. They all said no. It turned out that even securing burial in a Christian cemetery was impossible without alerting Catholic authorities. So, as it was Ankha secured a place for burial inside a cave outside of Oxyrynchus. Acting on Sophia's instruction, Ankha purchased a concrete vault for Philippus' body. He returned from this task with a story the vault maker had told of a Christian massacre of hundreds of Gnostic ascetics near the town fifty years earlier. Their bodies and their books had been thrown into a dump for refuse.

Sophia wrapped Philippus' body in new robes and Ankha laid him gently in the vault. Sophia did the best she could to conduct a Christian burial. She led the group in three hymns that she had often sung in Church with Philippus. She passed bread and wine to the others, asking each to take a bite of bread and sip of wine in Jesus' name. She knew there was something missing. She was overcome with a forlorn sadness at the thought of him being buried alone, so far from where they had lived and so far from where she was heading. She took the codex containing the Gospel of Judas and put it beside Philippus in the vault, to keep him company. Then, thinking that he would disapprove of such Gnostic texts going with him to the grave, she took the Catholic scriptures and the algebra book from Athanasius' desk and placed them on the other side of his body.

"Goodbye, my sweet love," she said. "You have been the best of husbands, the best of fathers, the best of men. The world will know who killed you. I will always love you."

Ankha placed the lid on the vault and the group resumed their travels toward Alexandria.

Chapter Thirty-One

Alexandria

June 330 A.D. – Alexandria

Jesus said, "If your leaders say to you, 'Look, the (Father's) kingdom is in the sky,' then the birds of the sky will precede you. If they say to you, 'It is in the sea,' then the fish will precede you. Rather, the (Father's) kingdom is within you and it is outside you.

"When you know yourselves, then you will be known, and you will understand that you are children of the living Father. But if you do not know yourselves, then you live in poverty, and you are the poverty."

The Gospel of Thomas

In the summer of 330 A.D., Alexandria was more than 660 years old and over 400 years past its glorious apex. Yet even in its deliquescence, it remained the most cosmopolitan, diverse, educated and sophisticated city in the Roman Empire and perhaps of all time. Laid out with barley flour by Alexander the Great in 331 B.C. and built in the following years by the Ptolemy Pharaohs, Alexandria quickly rivaled, then surpassed Athens as the intellectual, scientific and cultural capital of the Roman world.

Ptolemy I had been one of Alexander's childhood friends and later one of his generals and closest advisers. Growing up, he shared Alexander's famous tutor, Aristotle. After Alexander's death, Ptolemy acted quickly to separate Egypt from the rest of Alexander's sprawling, ungovernable empire, built Alexandria to be Egypt's new capital and arranged to have himself proclaimed Pharaoh. Neither Constantinople nor Babylon nor Damascus had surpassed the splendor or glory of Alexandria.

Whether status is gauged on the basis of art, music, architecture, monument building, wealth, commerce, scientific achievement, scholarship or any other standard, Alexandria excelled. Only Rome rivaled it. The Pharos Lighthouse, one of the seven wonders of the ancient world, rose 400 feet to beacon flotillas of merchants into the harbors. It was a city of science. Euclid did his work in Alexandria. Herophilus first described the linked functions of the brain, spinal cord and nervous system there. Aristarchus was the first to attempt a calculation of the relative sizes and distances of the Earth, moon and sun. Although he was widely inaccurate, his attempt was based on the belief that there was no need for divine explanations of the universe, that it was only nature and that anything natural was subject to observation and explanation. Aristarchus also theorized that the earth and planets revolved around the sun, but even the tired old gods of Rome and Egypt shook off their slumbers to rise up against this particular assault on their centrality.

Eratosthenes, working in Alexandria, posited that the Earth was round and calculated its circumference to within 200 miles of modern measurements. Archimedes studied in Alexandria. Hero was a great builder of automatons in the first century A.D. His constructions included a wind engine that powered organs and vending machines, and once staged an entirely mechanical play with moving scenery and sounds brought forth by a series of ropes, weights, pulleys and cogwheels. Philo attempted to bridge the gap between Greek and Jewish philosophy. Claudius Ptolemy created a workable, geocentric model of the universe that stood until Nicolaus Copernicus and Johannes Kepler turned the cosmos upside down over a thousand years later. The list goes on. Whatever the field of study, Alexandria nurtured and attracted the best minds and gave them the economic and religious freedom to pursue their studies. Aristotle's greatest student, Demetrius, moved there to oversee the collection of books and knowledge aimed at accumulating all of the world's knowledge in one place. Early Alexandria represented one of those rare moments in history where inquiry and study was allowed to compete openly with superstition and religion in defining the world and its meaning.

Perhaps the city's famed library should have made the list of world wonders. Said at one time to have contained the original or a copy of every book ever written, regardless of language, by the time Sophia and her companions entered Alexandria, it was gone after suffering several destructions. It was partially destroyed by the forces of Julius Caesar in 48 B.C. In recompense, Marc Anthony presented his lover Cleopatra with the 200,000 books from the library of Pergamum in Anatolia. Rebuilt and enlarged after Cleopatra's death in 30 B.C., the library was severely damaged by the Roman Emperor Aurelian in 273 A.D. in the suppression of a revolt led by Queen Zenobia of Palmyra. Further damage was done by Emperor Diocletian in 297 A.D. while suppressing a Christian and Jewish revolt. Much of what survived Aurelian and Diocletian's forces was removed to the Serapeum, and to various warehouses scattered about the Greek quarter.

Officially, the Serapeum was a temple to the god Serapis, whom Ptolemy reinvented for his own purposes. Having both Greek and Egyptian attributes, looking like Zeus crossed with Osiris, Ptolemy's purpose was to unify the religious beliefs and destinies of Greece and Egypt, so that the Greek Ptolemy could legitimize his desire, for himself and his descendants, to become Egyptian pharaohs. Serapis was given many powers, including powers over life and the afterlife. Ptolemy was able to cajole the dynastic priests of Egypt and bribe the Eumolpidae, priests of the Greek temple of Demeter and Persephone at Eleusis, to jointly declare that Serapis, as represented by his enormous statue, had decided to move to Alexandria and bestow his blessings upon the fledgling city. (Senmonthis was distantly descended from a line originating in a marriage between priests of these two religions.) Plutarch wrote that Ptolemy stole the statue from Sinope on the Black Sea. Serapis is rumored to have arrived on a barge in Alexandria's new harbor where it received the joint blessing of the Egyptian and Greek priests. Eighty years later, under the reign of Ptolemy III, Serapis was moved inland to stand astride the opening of his new temple. The arm span of Serapis was said to be large enough to reach from one side of the temple to the other. It is a tribute to the success of the Ptolemys and Alexandria that the cult of Serapis expanded into Greece and Rome over the coming centuries. Its cult, centered at the Serapeum, still existed in Alexandria in 330 when Sophia and her band entered the city.

Yet the Serapeum was more than a temple. In 330 it housed what was probably the world's greatest existing collection of books and still attracted some of the world's greatest mathematicians, philosophers, physicians and astronomers. In modern terms it was a university, a think tank, a temple, a library, a museum and a cultural, commercial, religious, and intellectual center. Sophia had seen the Serapeum in her youth and, as all young Alexandrians did, heard grand stories about the discoveries made there and the men and women (yes, women) who populated its halls. So it was not a coincidence that when the little band arrived there in the summer of 330, she sought about finding housing as close to the Serapeum as possible.

Alexandria was not what it had been. An age of discovery and invention was followed by an age of commentary and explanation, which was itself followed by an age of religious awakenings and re-awakenings. The city was built as an attempt to merge the philosophy and religion of Greece with the philosophy and religion of Egypt but from the start was also home to thousands of Hebrews, Kemites, Hellenists and Roman polytheists. As long as religious tolerance was the norm, all worked out as well as can be expected in a human world. But as the fortunes of first the Ptolemaic and then the Roman empires sank, tolerance was gradually replaced by insistence and fervor. The work at the Serapeum continued, but surrounded by growing suspicions and hostility. By the middle of the third century, religious wars and riots between the Christians, polytheists and Jews had become a common feature of Alexandrian life.

Sophia's group moved into housing that had been built after the Aurelian's sack of Alexandria, 150 years earlier. The apartments were on a busy street where workshops and street front stores also competed for space. It had three rooms, including a room dedicated to food preparation. The building, which housed four similarly sized apartments and a bakery, had its own cistern fed by water from the nearby Lake Mareotis. Of the new tenants, only Sophia and Ankha had known such an amenity existed anywhere. The apartment was located in the area where the old Egyptian town of Rhakotis had sat before Ptolemy I built Alexandria around it. Originally considered the Egyptian quarters, it was now largely populated by Greek speakers. It was about halfway between the Paneum (a man-made hill which provided a spectacular view of the entire city, harbor and lighthouse in the distance) and the Serapeum, about a thousand yards from each. From their streets they could hear Egyptian, Greek, Latin and Hebrew voices, sometimes merged into a polyglot language that only long-time residents could understand completely. Sophia quickly remembered most of it from her youth.

Even if Alexandria was centuries past its heyday, it remained spectacular. A short walk south from Sophia's apartment led to Pompey's Pillar, a 99-foot-tall monolith, principally carved from a single piece of red granite and erected just outside of the Serapeum to commemorate Diocletian's suppression of riots in 297 A.D. It stands there still, in lonely vigil to a bygone age. The Serapeum stood in a grove of palm trees next to the pillar. Near the shores of Lake Mareotis was the chariot stadium with its

1,000-foot oval track. A half mile to the north was the Heptastadium, a 4,000-foot-long road built on a break-wall that connected the mainland to the Island of Pharos, home to the Posidium (Temple of Poseidon), the Temple of Isis, the great lighthouse and many of Alexandria's wealthiest inhabitants. To the east was the heart of the city, including the Caesareum, a theater and the long-since shuttered mausoleum of Alexander the Great. A little northeast of this was the gated and heavily fortified entrance to a man-made peninsula that stretched out into the Eleusinian Sea and housed the royal palace where Cleopatra had lived and died and where, in 330, Eusebius of Nicomedia's brother-in-law, Julius Julianus, served in the secular capacity of prefect of Egypt. South and east of the palace was the Jewish quarter where there had always been tensions with the pantheistic authorities and where many of the consequences of Christian ascendency in Alexandria were being played out. There were shops and street vendors throughout and every kind of goods available anywhere in the Roman Empire could be purchased. Preachers and proselytizers of every religion, including some of the preacher's own invention, could be found along the streets and in public places where their reception ranged from the gathering of a small crowd to the hurling of stones, to, worst of all, utter disregard. Water was everywhere. The Mediterranean Sea to the north of Pharos, the harbor waters, Lake Mareotis south of the city and man-made canals that channeled Alexandria's portion of the Nile's effluvium through the city and into its harbors. The Mediterranean cooled Egypt's desert climate so that even during summer months the average temperature was only in the high seventies. In the winter months the temperature was often in the mid-60s and the lows were rarely below 45 degrees. Alexandria had a pleasant rainy season between November and February, but was never cold and never too wet. It was a resort city, industrial center and intellectual haven rolled into one. The city was a paradise to the band of migrants from the south.

After settling in, furnishing and equipping the new apartment, Sophia got started on a project that had been gestating since before Philippus' death. She intended to cause as much harm and embarrassment to Athanasius as she could manage. To start with she needed new and suitable clothing, more ink and an abundance of papyri. Alexandria had all that was needed, including an Empire-wide monopoly on papyrus. She purchased simple children's clothing for John and Magdalene. Beset and Senmonthis bought clean, modest robes. Beset's clothing was either white or dull cream; Senmonthis went in for a little more color, but stayed within respectable bounds. Ankha, too, stayed within the normal range, with white robes worn around and over a pocketed tunic.

Sophia thought a good deal about how she should appear when she went public with her attack on Athanasius. She eschewed the more elaborately embroidered stolae of the wealthier class. She could afford these and the workmanship on some of the stolae for sale in the shops was extremely fine. There were silk embroidered patterns of leaves and of palm trees and even one of gazelle running heel-to-toe up one side and down the other of the garment. She was after something more restrained. She selected solid colored tunics of muted greens and blues and white stolae made of finely woven Egyptian cotton.

She wanted to be presentable, respectable. She wanted to be taken seriously. She dared to hope to become known in the city, thinking that the better known she was, the more effective her attack on Athanasius would be. She was not sure where this would lead. She expected that Athanasius to retaliate. But she had reached her limit. She moved to Athanasius' home city with the intention of harming him in any way she could.

She spent a few days composing a letter, writing and rewriting until it said everything she wanted to say. When she was done, she gathered Ankha, Beset and Senmonthis together and read it to them. At the top, in large Greek letters she wrote:

Κατηγορώ Αθανασίου, Επίσκοπος Αλεξανδρείας
(I Accuse Athanasius, Bishop of Alexandria)

I am Sophia. Formerly, I was Hypatia of Alexandria. I am nothing. I grew up on the streets of this city. I did not know my mother or my father. As far back as I remember I spoke both Greek and Egyptian and could understand some of the Hebrew spoken in the Jewish Quarter, but I do not know who I am. I am insignificant. And yet for the past eleven years the great Athanasius, Christian Patriarch of this city, has taken notice of me and has brought to me and those I love great hardship, suffering and anguish.

I bring the following accusations against Bishop Athanasius, the Red Devil. I make them in the bright light of day, with my head unbowed. I make them to the good people of Alexandria, the Christian, the Greek, the Roman, the Egyptian and the Hebrew, so that they might know the kind of man who resides among them, who has much power over many and much influence on the affairs of this city.

First, in 319, when I was but twelve and an orphan on the streets, the Red Devil, then a young priest under Bishop Alexander, came across me while I slept against the wall of a church on Serapic Way. He fell upon me while I slept, beat me, violated me, took my virginity and left me dazed and bleeding as he rushed off for the shelter of the church.

Second, in 321, when I was fourteen, the Red Devil forged papers and had me sold to a brothel owner from Antioch. From age fourteen to seventeen I was forced to entertain any gentleman who paid the brothel owner to have me. I became pregnant three times in three years and was forced to end each pregnancy by the drinking of a vile potion that left me weakened and sick for weeks at a time. I stayed at the brothel until a kind, former bishop of Kaymakli purchased my freedom without condition, an act of love and compassion by a true Christian. A year later, I married that Christian. His name was Timaeus.

Third, in May 325 I traveled with Timaeus to the great church council at Nicaea, called by the Emperor Constantine. At the Council, Timaeus asked the bishops and the Emperor to uphold and preserve the religious freedom that this city and the Empire hold dear. In payment for his words, the Red Devil poisoned him and Timaeus died a horrible death on the steps of the Emperor's palace in Nicaea. Afterward, the Red Devil came for me, but I was able to escape with the help of a good and kind Christian priest named Philippus. I took exile in Chenoboskion, near Thebes along the Nile. Two years later Philippus returned on an errand. He proposed to me, was released from his priestly vows and we were married in the Catholic Church. Philippus and I were good and faithful Christians for the next three years.

Fourth, in May of 330, this year, the Red Devil came with his army to Chenoboskion, pursuing rumors that I had in my possession certain Gnostic gospels and texts that the Catholic Church has rejected. I do not deny this charge. I do not believe in all the Gnostic writings have to say, but I found them interesting. Some are older than the Church's Gospels, yet give a very different account of Jesus' life and his teachings. I believe that studying and contemplating all available evidence is the best way to facilitate wisdom and understanding. The Red Devil Athanasius does not agree.

Upon arriving in Chenoboskion, he first seized Philippus, who had nothing to do with these books and always begged me to destroy them. I went to the Red Devil and offered up all of the books voluntarily. The Red Devil ordered continued torture. He had me flogged with a bone-barbed lash. The lash was not the worst for poor Philippus, my beloved husband. The Red Devil had Philippus filleted like a rabbit, peeling two wide strips of skin from his back. With help from friends we escaped, but Philippus' poor body could not recover and he died in Oxyrynchus, after suffering for several weeks. We provided Philippus with the Christian burial he desired, even after all the Red Devil had done to him in Jesus' name.

I, Hypatia of Alexandria, Adama of Antioch, Sophia of Nicaea, have come to Alexandria, to the very home fires of the Red Devil, to bring these accusations in my own name. I call upon the Red Devil, Athanasius, to answer them, in public, for I have proof of all I say. Let us be judged together. Let justice follow the result.

Sophia of Alexandria

When Sophia had finished reading silence gripped her small audience like a cold hand. The initial response was expressed in frowns by Ankha and Senmonthis and a dumbfounded stare by Beset. Senmonthis broke the silence. "And just what are your plans for this fine piece of writing?"

"I am going copy it and post it throughout the city."

"For what purpose?"

"People should know that the bishop is a monster."

Senmonthis clucked her tongue. "In my experience," she said, "when you tangle with one of the big people you get what they deserve." Having deposited her wisdom, Senmonthis departed the room.

Ankha asked, "What makes you think he will not retaliate?"

"If he does, we will make his actions known."

"What makes you think people will care?"

"This is Alexandria. People care about everything."

"And you want me to protect you?"

"If you are willing."

Ankha nodded and left.

Alone with Sophia, Beset began sobbing. "I had no idea, mistress. I knew there was a history to you, no doubt I knew that. But all this? The rape? Selling you into slavery. Those beautiful babies never born. And two husbands killed by the same man. I trust you to do what is most right. Whatever it means to me, I trust you."

"Thank you, Beset," Sophia said. "I know you think you owe your life to me, but it is not true. Rather, it is I who owe my life to you. My life, my children and all the happiness I have had, I owe to you. Please, I am not your mistress. I am your friend, as you are mine."

Beset stopped daubing the tears from her eyes long enough to hug Sophia. Sophia felt a frailty that she had not noticed before. In the five years they had been together, Beset's hair had turned from a streaked grey and black to a fine silver that framed the blunt, but noble features of her Egyptian face. But before now she had not thought of Beset as aging. Perhaps it was the recent travails and the hard journey north, but now, in her embrace, she felt the diminishment that comes with age. Beset gradually pulled away from the embrace to wipe some more tears. "Mistress," she said.

"Sophia or, if you like, Hypatia. Please."

"Hypatia. I will say it but I am not comfortable saying it. Please let me call you mistress."

"How about friend?"

"I cannot promise not to slip. But mistress, friend, you say in that letter there that you can prove everything you write. How is that? How is it not your word against his?"

"If he denies any of it, it will be his word against his words." Sophia pointed at the little writing desk that she had taken from Father James' house on the day they fled. "It is all in there," she said. "His writings, his notes, his journal. He prays for God's forgiveness for his uncontrollable desire for me. Before I read those papers, I could not have proved that he poisoned Timaeus. I did not know how I came to be a slave in Ammianus' possession. He does not ask forgiveness for those things. He writes that he is on the verge of obtaining the heretical Gnostic texts from the evil witch Sophia. Senmonthis and Ankha are witness to his treatment of poor Philippus and me. I can prove every word."

"Don't that make him even more dangerous? That he knows you have such?"

"Probably," Sophia answered. "But I am through being his victim. Or, if I am to be his victim, everyone will know about it."

"Alright," Beset said. "I will be with you. I trust you."

Over the next two weeks, Sophia copied her letter a hundred times until the copies comprised a thick, brownish column. Each was about ten inches by sixteen inches, large enough to contain what she had written in the neat, steady hand of her Greek lettering. When they were finished she announced that she was going out to post them throughout the city. Ankha said he was going with her. He slung his sword by its sheath over his shoulder and picked up the heavy stack of paper. Sophia laughed when she saw him.

"Doubly armed," she said. "With word and blade."

"Why do you laugh?" Ankha was not accustomed to being laughed at.

"Because it occurs to me that the sword won't be much good with the paper in your hands."

What followed was a bit of comedy. Sophia lifted the stack,

but only with some difficulty. She would not last long with its weight in her arms. Ankha suggested going out multiple times, taking only a quarter of the pages at a time. Sophia said she did not want to be coming and going, since once Athanasius got word of what she was up to, she had no doubt they would be followed. Her plan was to post them all in one tour of the city, then return home as secretively as possible, hopefully without being followed. She wanted Athanasius to be aware of her, she said, but she did not want him to know where she lived with her children. She asked Beset to sew pockets onto the inside of a green tunic, using fabric from the old garment she had been wearing on the day she was beaten. When Beset pointed out that it was blood stained, Sophia assured her that the fabric would not be seen. Sophia asked Beset to cut the tunic down the middle and add hooks so it could be fastened back together.

So, Ankha removed his sword as Beset sewed. When she was finished, Sophia divided the papers into two stacks and placed one stack in each of the new pockets. With Beset's help, she put the tunic on, but quickly realized that she would not be able to retrieve them from a tunic worn inside of a stola. Her solution was to wear the green, pocketed tunic outside, over the stola. She then decided that the pocketed tunic was too long and asked Beset to shorten it, so that it was just long enough to cover the pockets and hung only down to her hips. The result was a vest. It was odd looking to Beset, Senmonthis and Ankha. Maggie, when she saw her mother so attired, said, "Mama, what are you wearing? I want one like that." Sophia was pleased with the arrangement. Ankha redraped his sword and they headed off.

They started north, toward the harbors, stopping at trees and kiosks to tack sheets up with the hammer and brads that Sophia brought with her. They turned east along the hundred-foot wide Canopic Way, toward the ruins of the great library and the damaged Museum. They posted a page, the "Katagoso," Sophia called it, at the docks and outside the grand theater and the forum, outside the royal center, and in front of the Emporium Caesareum. They posted one notice prominently at St. Mark's basilica in the Baukalis District near the Jewish Quarter, where Athanasius lived and worked. Then they headed south, posting several Katagosos on the Paneum hillside and along the remains of the southern wall, just north of Lake Mareotis. Then they turned west, posting along until they reached Pompey's Pillar near the steps of the Serapeum. They posted a Katagoso near the pillar and in front of the steps of the Serapeum.

By the time they reached the Serapeum they were being followed by a group of about twenty men, dressed in brown robes of vaguely clerical nature. Several of the men held copies of Sophia's Katagoso, which they had obviously ripped down from where they had been posted. As she was tacking a copy into the mortar base of the statue of Serapis, men from this group began shouting at her, escalating with each successive charge, each shouter attempting to outdo the one before him.

"Liar."

"Whore."

"Witch."

"Sorceress."

"Mathematician."

Ankha turned and, placing his hand on the hilt of his sword, faced the group. This action silenced them for a moment, but soon a rock was thrown and then another. The group was quickly getting larger as young men came running down the streets to join in the action and share the outrage. The mob started surging and retreating, attempting to summon the collective nerve to rush at Sophia and Ankha, despite the danger presented by Ankha's bearing and well-displayed weapon. From the rear of the crowd someone yelled, "Beat her. Kill the heretics." More rocks flew and the crowd surged closer.

Rescue came not from Ankha's sword or fear of it, but from a group of men, mostly young students running from the

Serapeum armed with clubs and daggers. The two groups had obviously clashed before. Some members of the opposing groups knew certain members of the other group by name. The obvious leader of the group from the Serapeum was a man approaching forty years of age, hair still black, with thick brows framing a square face and a straight, Greek nose. This man, arriving a little behind his group of armed scholars, was not armed, but he walked to the fore of the group to stand beside Sophia and Ankha. He carried with him an air of authority, apparent not only to the students, since he was their master, but to the clerics as well. Their rocks were held and their surging stopped. When he arrived at the side of Sophia he said in a loud, amused voice:

"Is that the best insult you can hurl, Macarius? Mathematician? Surely your Jesus has lower stations in hell for more deserving occupations."

An averaged sized man of about thirty, with a face and nose too long for the body on which it sat, a full beard and long brown hair parted in the middle and drawn back, stepped forward. "Being an esteemed mathematician yourself, Pappus, you know that the practice of your faith inevitably leads to attempts to explain the earth and the stars above and to the study of the demon arts of divination and astrology."

Pappus laughed. "Demon arts," he said, "that is a new one to me. I guess attempting to understand how God structures and orders the universe is devil's work?"

"Exactly so," Macarius said. "For Jesus has told us how the universe is structured. It is structured with the faithful above, in heaven, and all others, like you, Pappus, burning in the fires of hell, below."

Pappus laughed again and changed the subject. "Tell me, Macarius, where is your Tiro? Macarius the Younger. Where is he?"

A second man stepped forward, taller than the first, with a long face more proportioned to his body. He wore his hair and whiskers in the same manner as the other Macarius. In fact, most of the clerical mob wore their hair and, if they could manage to grow them, beards, in the same manner, in the manner they imagined Jesus had worn his, three hundred years earlier. "I am not younger," the new Macarius said. "We are the same age."

"And may your lives be equally long," Pappus said. "But I must have a way of telling you apart when you appear at our steps here at the temple of learning and seek to debate my scholars with rocks and weapons, so you are Macarius the Younger."

"We did not come here to fight you," Macarius the Younger said. "We came to stop this woman and her protector from spreading heresy."

"Heresy, is it," Pappus asked, mockingly. "Well, that is a serious charge." Addressing Sophia he asked, "Young lady, are you a Christian?" His eyes stayed fixed upon her as he became aware of a beauty unlike any he had ever seen.

"No," Sophia answered. "I am not Christian."

Still looking at Sophia, Pappus said to the clerics. "There you have it then. She cannot be a heretic because she is not a Christian."

Macarius the Elder answered, "She is a Gnostic, which has been heresy since the time of Iraneus."

Pappus never took his eyes from her. "Is this true, are you a Gnostic?"

"No," she said firmly, "I am not."

"She says she is not. Indeed, I am not sure there are any Christian Gnostics remaining. You Christians are more effective at wiping out faith than the Romans ever were."

"She is spreading great slanders against our bishop," Macarius claimed. "Here. Right here in this paper."

By the calmness of his voice and his humor Pappus was subtly and gradually changing the mood of the mob. He had seen this kind of confrontation escalate into full-scale riots. In the legalized

Church's teenage years, Alexandria had become one of the world's all-time hotbeds. Most of what remained of its grand intellectual heritage were the few students of the Serapeum and the fact that the city's many battles and riots often started over theological or philosophical disputes. The newly liberated Christians fought everybody. One target were the Hebrews in the Jewish Sector. Having only recently been legalized and enshrined as the Empire's favored religion, the Christians immediately claimed the right and power to oppress others, just as they had been oppressed. They fought the civil authorities, for what right did a governor have to supersede God's law? But their favorite targets were the pagans and particularly the pagans who studied at the Serapeum. As far as the Christians were concerned it was a two-for-one bargain: the scholars were mostly citizens of Rome so an assault on them was in some small part retribution for three centuries of persecution by the Romans and, more importantly, they worshiped false gods and had the audacity to try to discover and explain God's ineffable creation. So the tone Pappus took from the beginning was a studied improvisation aimed at defusing the passions and avoiding bloodshed. He now took a Katagoso from Sophia's outstretched hand and pantomimed reading it, watching to see if the Christians would tolerate this delay. Surprisingly, they did.

When he had taken as long with the pantomime as he felt he could take and as voices from the Christian mob had begun again to urge action, Pappus lowered the Katagoso and turned to Sophia. By this time the Christian mob had grown to over a hundred.

"These are serious charges you make against the head of the Christian Church in Egypt. If not true, they are surely slander. You write that you have proof. What proof do you have?"

Macarius the Elder, his voice metallic with confidence, said, "There can be no proof in support of lies."

"Indeed, indeed," Pappus said. "So you see, uh, Sophia, you

must tell us what proof you have or I shall have no further defense for you."

If the scene intimidated her, Sophia showed no sign of it. If she had never before spoken in public, her voice did not betray it. She reached over and placed her hand on Ankha's muscled arm, tense with readiness, and spoke.

"I have Athanasius' own writings, which admit the truth of what I say." Her voice was firm but not deep or loud and did not carry as far as the mob of Christians. A murmur went through the mob. From among them someone yelled, "She has nothing."

"She says Athanasius has condemned himself with his own written word."

"Proof! Proof!" the mob shouted.

"Have you the writings on your person?" Pappus asked.

"I have secured them and will produce them when Athanasius appears in any fair forum to challenge the accuracy of my accusations."

Pappus smiled. This, he saw, was no ordinary woman. Her beauty was evident to anyone. She had the grace of a Muse. But there was more to her than this. There was a confidence to her that was rare. More than this, in insisting on a fair forum, she was displaying a strategic intelligence that was more pleasing to him than her other qualities. To the mob he said, "Her proposal is fair. Why don't we reconvene in one week's time and see if she has the proofs she claims? Why don't you consult with your bishop and see if he consents."

"No good," yelled Macarius the Elder. "She must present some proof of her claims here and now. Elsewise we demand you surrender her to us."

"I don't presume you brought any proof of your claims with you?" Pappus said to Sophia.

The mob was in no mood to wait. Shouts rang out. "She has nothing." "She is a liar." "Give her to us."

Sophia raised her right arm in the air, momentarily quieting the crowd. They watched as she unhooked the green tunic, removed it and handed it to Ankha. Facing the mob and away from Pappus, she drew the stola over her shoulders, and, clutching the front of it to her chest, let it slide part way down her back, allowing Pappus to see the top portion of her back. She then slowly turned her back to the mob and, removing her hand from the front, allowed the stola to fall to her waist. She did not speak a word.

Her back was a jagged map of burnt red river beds, some deeper than others, still mottled and swollen. Even the angry mob gasped at the sight of such marred beauty, the physical residue of extreme cruelty.

Pappus spoke as Sophia drew her stola back over her shoulders. The humor in his tone was replaced with anger. "Have your bishop refute her charges, if he will," he said to the mob. "If he refuses, the people will know that her charges are true." To Macarius the Elder he said, "If he consents, we will post notices and meet at the top of the Paneum, so that any who has ears to hear can hear."

The Christians, bewildered, disbursed, departing in different directions. Sophia thanked Pappus, re-hooked the green tunic over her stola and left with Ankha, assuring herself several times before they reached their home that they were not being followed.

Chapter Thirty-Two

To The Paneum

June 330 A.D. – Alexandria

> *I came from First Who Was Sent, that I might reveal to you Him Who Is from the Beginning, because of the arrogance of Arch-Begetter and his angels, since they say about themselves that they are gods. And I came to remove them from their blindness, that I might tell everyone about the God who is above the universe. Therefore, tread upon their graves, humiliate their malicious intent, and break their yoke and arouse my own. I have given you authority over all things as Sons of Light, that you might tread upon their power with your feet.*
>
> The Sophia of Jesus Christ

Athanasius had returned from Upper Egypt in a bad temper. He had come back without three of his most trusted assistants. He told the clerics of his household that they had been set upon by a group of rogue legionaries and robbed. The villains had gotten away with only a little gold and his favorite writing desk, Athanasius told his staff, but had killed Mark, Luke and Gregory. This setback, he told them, had prevented him from accomplishing either of his goals: the ordination of the Pachomian monks and the suppression of Gnostic heretics. Both projects had failed, he told them, due to an act of random thuggery perpetrated by a band of disgruntled Roman deserters, Mithrians or Kemites, no doubt. Athanasius had returned to Alexandria to address many episcopal concerns. On the day after his return he presided over the mass for the Nativity of St. John the Baptist. Two thousand Alexandrian Christians attended. Athanasius gave his homily on the centrality of charity in the life of a good

Christian.

When the service ended, he swept out of the sacristy and into his office. Young men were waiting to take his vestal robes and to drape him in his workday garb. A meal was placed before him. There were many pressing matters and the young bishop attacked all of them with characteristic zeal. As he picked at the meal, he wrote. He sometimes commented that the life of a great bishop consisted primarily of the reading and writing of letters. Most of the letters sought his blessing for something or someone: a church, a relic, a shrine, a new order of ascetics, a city, a family, a person. Some were from parishes in his episcopate seeking guidance of one kind or another, others were from job seekers, still others were from admirers simply wishing to bask in the glow of his holiness. From the volume of correspondence he received it seemed scarcely conceivable that less than ten percent of the Egyptian congregation was literate. He received and replied to letters in Greek, Latin, Hebrew and Coptic, all languages he had mastered. He took time to answer them all and shouldered the great weight of knowing that Church history, his legacy, and, more importantly, the salvation of many souls, depended upon the clarity and nuance of his words.

Most important of his tasks was suppressing the spread of heresy, which seemed to abound everywhere.

Principally, there were, of course, the Arians, led by Arius, the pernicious former bishop of St. Mark's Church, the very church where his episcopate was now headquartered. Athanasius had left Nicaea believing that the controversy had been put to rest. All but a few of the priests and bishops in attendance had signed the Creed, which stated in no uncertain terms that Jesus shared the same spirit as the Father, was begotten solely from the Father, not from woman, and that there was never a time when he was not. That should have ended the matter, yet Arius and the two Eusebiuses had never stopped agitating in favor of heresy. Nicomedia was but a stone's throw from New Rome and Bishop

Eusebius of that city had the ear of Constantine and his beloved sister, Constantia. It was Constantia who converted the Emperor to Christianity. In 330, as she was dying, attended to by Eusebius, she beseeched her brother to order Arius reinstated to the bosom of the church and allowed to return to his ministry in Alexandria. Arius himself was in exile in the house of Eusebius of Caesarea and, upon hearing of Constantine's decree, had petitioned Athanasius in arrogant terms to honor Constantine's orders. Athanasius bridled at the meddlesome interference of a mere catechumen into the solemn and sacred affairs of the church. What was more, there was to be a synod in Antioch in a little over a month. Eusebius of Caesarea had charged Pope Eustathius with (of course) heresy and with immoral conduct, including having had sexual relations with prostitutes and, over a period of several years, with a local congregant's wife. Constantine had ordered Eustathius to attend the synod even though, as bishop of that city, he should have been allowed to stop it. The ignorant Emperor was meddling in Church affairs. The charge of heresy was absurd, since Eustathius was charged with no more than believing in the Nicene Creed, but the morality charge was more troubling. Athanasius had hoped to secure evidence that the charge was a disgraceful slander while he was in Sheneset, but the harlot had escaped before he could do so. He now resolved to travel to Antioch himself to give the great weight of Alexandrian authority in support of the beleaguered bishop.

Almost as pernicious as the Arians were the followers of Meletius, former bishop of Lycopolis. The Meletians did not believe that those Christians who had renounced their faith to avoid persecution or death should be readmitted into the clergy or allowed to receive Holy Communion. Athanasius took a more tolerant view, as had his predecessors Alexander and Peter, who had deposed the Meletian clergy from their posts. Athanasius had believed that this controversy had also been resolved at Nicaea, with the Church readmitting the Meletians to their positions provided that they swore allegiance and subservience to Pope Alexander of Alexandria and his successors. Upon Alexander's death and Athanasius' succession, they had lapsed back into heresy and, as a result, in western Egypt many good and faithful Christians were being denied access to the Church and its redemptive authority. Since his letters of reproach had failed to achieve obedience, Athanasius resolved with a heavy heart to send his loyal clerics to compel it by whatever means necessary.

What others did not understand was that he, Athanasius, spoke directly to God. God did not appear to him as He had Moses or Isaac. He had not heard God's voice as had Rebekah and Balaam. He had prayed fervently for these things, but they had not happened. Yet from a young age Athanasius knew that God spoke to him through certainty. When an issue of Church doctrine or Christian conduct arose he would study it, think about it, examine every facet of it from every angle. He was trained not only in the texts of the Torah, the gospels and the epistles of the first disciples, but had also read Greek philosophy, and studied the Socratic method and the logic of Plato. He would apply all his knowledge and considerable intelligence to an issue, often without resolution. Then he would pray. He spent four hours or more each day in prayer. Silent prayer, as Jesus counseled. It was through prayer that certainty came. When he knew, really knew, the answer God would give him certainty. That is how he knew the answer to the relationship between God and Jesus and how he knew that the Arians' attempt to separate the two was heresy. Once God gave him certainty on a question or a course of conduct, Athanasius could not be deterred. No means of accomplishing God's purpose was off limits. Had not God killed the men of Bethshemesh for looking into His ark? Had He not smote entire cities and armies to accomplish His will? God's will must be obeyed. And God gave to Athanasius certainty so that he would know God's will.

Two weeks after his return and just three weeks before the scheduled Antioch Synod, Athanasius learned that the Gnostic heretic Sophia had arrived in Alexandria and was accusing him, publicly and in writing, of a shocking list of crimes including rape, murder and selling her into slavery. The two Macariuses brought the news to him less than an hour after their confrontation at the Serapeum. Handing him a copy of Sophia's Katagoso, Macarius the Elder recounted the events of the day and the challenge to rebut the woman publicly in a week's time.

"You should confront the whore and prove that every word she writes is a lie straight from Hell," the Younger Macarius said.

"That is why I am Bishop and you are not," Athanasius replied. "A bishop cannot jump at every dodge or he would be jumping at shadows from sunrise to sunset."

"Do not acknowledge it. Do not dignify it," counseled the Elder.

"Who knows about this?" Athanasius asked, holding up the Katagoso to the men's faces.

"The entire city by now, I expect," said the Younger. "She posted these everywhere and they were being read. People ran off with some of the copies before we could pull them down. You must rebut her lies."

"I choose a different course," Athanasius said.

"What course?" the Younger asked.

Athanasius pulled at his beard and looked up at the two men. Pointing at them, he said, "Go to Pappus. Tell him that, of course, the Episcopate denies the slanderous accusations. Use those words exactly: 'the Episcopate denies the slanderous accusations.' Tell him the Episcopate is prepared to refute all of the heretic's allegations, but that the Episcopate requires that the heretic present whatever proofs she claims she has in advance. Do you have all that, word for word?"

The Elder said that he had it down, word for word. Athanasius proceeded.

"I want you two to discover where the heretic lives. She stole my desk, journal and personal papyri with which she could construct every manner of forgery. Before we deign to respond to her absurd charges we must know what evidence she intends to produce and my property must be returned. Do you understand?"

When the two Macariuses had left the room Athanasius stood, agitated. He knew very well what proof Sophia possessed. She had his raw journal. He was accustomed to writing in it several times a day. Every few days he would remove entries that were not suitable for preservation. These he would destroy by fire. What he did not destroy was preserved for posterity, the history of the Church. He was keenly aware of himself as an historical figure. During the sixteen hours, from the time his men captured Philippus until Philippus' escape with the witch, Athanasius had written angrily of all the evil this woman had done to him. He wrote of the poison he used on Timaeus, his method of delivering it to him and the precautions he had taken to avoid ingesting any himself. He had written that his act was just, given the damage that Timaeus was attempting to do to the Church everlasting, but that blame for his death was properly placed at the feet of the whore who had no doubt seduced Timaeus to do the Devil's work for her. He had written of the purgative treatment he had prescribed for Philippus and the whore. He had written at length about his moral lapse with the Devil eleven years earlier, hoping that the pen could explain to him what he could not explain to himself. He did not covet women. He did not covet girls. He did not long for carnal relations. It was just that unique and unspeakable pull that this one woman had — has — upon him and the fleeting moment of weakness that overcame him once, only once in a lifetime of virtue. And he had written of how he had managed to get the girl out of Alexandria so that he would never be tempted again. This is what he was writing when the Roman soldier burst in and caused him to flee for his life.

Athanasius was a great man. He knew he was a great man. His position in this place and at this time required greatness and he was certain he was the right man for this place and time. He was certain that if Christianity was to survive in this new and perilous period, to survive true to Christ's Word, true to God, it must not be shaped by the shifting expediencies of political concern. Doctrine must be set by great men such as himself. Men who were certain of what is right, certain of what must be done and strong enough to do it. He was such a man. Now, for a second time in his life, this nobody, this witch, this whore, this Devil, this woman, jeopardized all he was and all he had been certain he would become.

Three days after the confrontation at the Serapeum, Senmonthis came into the apartment carrying a page of papyrus. Neither Sophia nor Ankha had left the house since they posted the Katagosos. Sophia did not want the bishop to know where she lived — where her children lived — at least until after she had publicly confronted him. She was undecided what she would do then. Move perhaps. Leave Alexandria perhaps. It depended upon what happened when they met. She thought she might even be killed by his mob, in which case Beset and Senmonthis had agreed to take the children and flee Christendom. Ankha, if he wasn't killed, had promised to go with his mother. In those three days, Sophia spent most of her time with Maggie and John. John was now a year and a half and was just beginning to make intelligible sounds. Words like "give" and "mine" had entered his vocabulary to keep company with Mama, Bessa, Meega and Monka. He had no word yet for Ankha, but when he walked, John would try to emulate the soldier's erect bearing and he wanted Ankha to carry him everywhere he went. Magdalene had become more solemn. She asked about her father in heaven, what was he doing, who was he seeing? Did he see her? On one occasion after a period of silence, Maggie said to her mother, "Papa was not my real papa, was he?"

"He was as real a papa to you as could ever be. He loved you and cared for you as much as any papa could love his daughter."

"My real papa is in heaven too, isn't he?"

"Yes, Maggie."

"I guess my papa and my real papa like each other in heaven."

"I think they must," Sophia said, but she no longer believed in any heaven, Catholic or Gnostic.

In the evening Sophia copied Athanasius' journal onto fresh papyri pages, writing the Greek words in a cleaner, neater hand than Athanasius had managed.

Senmonthis came in with the page and said, "I can't read a word of this except the first one. 'Sophia,' plain as day, right at the top. I guess that's what you're calling yourself these days, isn't it? It's posted about and I brought one here for you to see. More trouble is what it means, I have no doubt."

Sophia read the page.

SOPHIA

Bishop Athanasius has accepted your challenge, with conditions. Your accusations will be heard at the peak of the Paneum on Tuesday next, one hour before the decline of the day.

To discuss the conditions set by Athanasius, you must contact me at the Serapeum as soon as possible. Ask for Pappus as I am,

Pappus of the Serapeum

"Where did you find this?" Sophia asked Senmonthis.

"They're posted everywhere, love. I saw people reading them too."

Sophia put the copied pages of Athanasius' journal into his desk, made sure the amount of ink and the number of writing reeds was approximately equal to what was in the desk when she took it. She put the desk in a cloth sack and tucked it under her stola. She walked to the Serapeum on her own, rejecting Ankha's insistence that he escort her. She wore an old, drab tunic and undyed, hooded stola made of coarse cotton, pulled the hood up over her head and walked hunched over, traveling directly south. As she approached the Serapeum she saw several women wearing shortened green tunics over white stolae, just as she had done three days earlier. She wondered if, quite by accident, she had that day adopted and recreated a fashion of the day.

The Serapeum was a combination pagan temple, university and library. A contemporary of Sophia, the historian Ammianus Marcellinus, gave the following description of the Serapeum:

> The Serapeum, splendid to a point that words would only diminish its beauty, has such spacious rooms, filled with life-like statues and a multitude of other works of art, that nothing, except the Capitolium, which attests to Rome's venerable eternity, can be considered as ambitious in the whole world.

In many ways the Serapeum represented the last, grand stand of the dream that was Alexandria. The most brilliant minds still flocked there from throughout the empire to study and learn from masters who were the intellectual descendants of Aristotle, Euclid, Ptolemy and so many more. Surrounded and supported by thick, granite pillars, upon entering the temple Sophia was overwhelmed with the majesty and awe that the great architect Parmeniskos intended when he designed it 600 years before. The entrance hall was at least a hundred feet wide and longer even than that. She understood immediately why the scholars here were referred to by the Christians as pagans. Statues of many Greek, Roman and Egyptian gods, each carefully carved by gifted sculptors, lined the hall or gazed from alcoves that lined the perimeter. Isis, Osiris, Toth, Apis the bull god, Zeus, Demeter, Achilles, Priapus, Athena, Juno and Bacchus were all represented. Before each statue was an altar and at least one priest or priestess in attendance to facilitate the sacrifice appropriate to their particular cult. When, out of curiosity, Sophia paused for a few moments to look at the fifteen-foot tall statue of Hathor, the priest looked at her and fell to his knees. Sophia walked on. When she reached the end of the hall she began to ask where she might find a man named Pappus. She was directed to a large anteroom in the southwest portion of the temple. The room was shaped in a semi-circle, elevated in the back, descending to the center, with granite benches at each elevation. There were about thirty young men and three young women seated on the benches. All three of the women and about half of the men were wearing green tunics over what traditionally was outer garb. At a podium in the center stood Pappus, arms gesticulating and lecturing in a voice registering a mixture of wonder and amusement. He was remarking upon the hexagonal forms of the honeycomb and saying, "Here again, we see the residue of the divine mind of creation working mathematically through the insensate industry of the common bee."

Sophia stood at the back of the room, listening unobtrusively. Pappus noticed her standing there and paused. "Sophia," he said, "would you like to sit in on our discussion today? You may be unfamiliar with the subject, but I believe you are quite up to the task of understanding us." With this, the heads of the students turned and looked at her. Soon they were rising from their benches, standing and snapping their fingers in approval of their unexpected guest. "You have quite captivated the imagination of the students here at the Serapeum," Pappus said.

"Look, many even attire themselves in homage to you."

"I do not understand," Sophia said.

"Why, Sophia," Pappus said, "you have struck a blow against a dangerous theocrat. He wants this temple destroyed and the students disbursed. He thinks we worship many gods or no god at all, even though we welcome students of all religions. In this very room we have Christians, Jews, Kemites, Zoroastrians, and Neo-Platonists, among others. We seek understanding and knowledge, regardless of our individual faiths. Anyone who challenges the authority of ignorance is a friend of the Serapeum."

Amidst a fresh wave of finger snapping, Pappus said, "My fellow scholars, Sophia has come to see me on a matter of some urgency. I fear we must interrupt our discussions for today. I will pick up where I left off on the day after tomorrow."

The students rose and began departing the room. As they did so, a line formed in front of Sophia. The students wanted to grasp her hand, embrace her, tell her they would be at the Paneum to support her, fight for her if they must. Pappus made a faint attempt to move them along, saying he was sure Sophia needed to be about her business, but Sophia said she wanted to meet all of them and the procession continued. She asked each their name and where they were from and thanked them individually. By the end she was crying, saying she had never expected the support the students had so spontaneously expressed. When the last had departed she said to Pappus, "I feel loved."

"You are, Sophia. Yes, I believe they love you." He paused a moment, then said, "Who could not?"

Sophia and Pappus met in a large room below the ground level of the Serapeum. "This is my office," he told her. There were codices, scrolls and scroll vessels lying about. In one corner was a fully erect skeleton mounted on an alabaster pedestal. Sophia stopped and stood shock still when she saw it. Noticing her reaction Pappus said, "Don't mind old Herophilus. He's been hanging about here for almost 600 years, at least that's the rumor. We think it really is Herophilus, but there have been interruptions of custody a few times over the centuries, so we can't be sure. In any case, he won't stick his nose into our business, if for no other reason than that he has no nose."

Sophia sat on a stool from which Pappus had removed some codices and slid over to her.

"You wanted me to talk to you about conditions the Red Devil has set for his hearing. Is it customary for the criminal to set the conditions for his trial?"

Pappus chuckled. "Come now, Sophia. You know this is not a criminal proceeding. And we both know why you have not charged him to the Roman authorities. You would be the one to be punished." Pappus smiled. "Sometimes I think what you have done is very clever. You want to get the truth out in a very public way, in a way it would never have come out if you had gone to the civil authorities. I think you will get your way. So in that way I think you have been clever. But I am not sure if you have thought this through altogether. There are numerous difficulties in getting to the day of reckoning, if you will. But what happens after that will be more difficult, I think."

Sophia did not want to speculate on what might happen after the event, so she stuck to its antecedents. "What difficulties in getting from here until then?" she asked.

Pappus nodded. "Well, getting home from here is the first, I suppose, though I believe have a solution to that problem. In any case, you cannot just walk out the way you came in. No doubt by now, without intending to, some of the students have betrayed your presence here. I would be very surprised if word has not already reached Athanasius that you are at the Serapeum. I am assuming you do not want him to know where you live."

"No. But what is your solution to this problem?"

"Well," Pappus said, "this basement that you are in now, this very basement, is connected by a tunnel to the great catacombs of this city. There is a circular staircase up to the ground once you get past the Hall of Caracalla. Some people find death preferable to the sight of death, but I suspect you are not one of those. So, if you don't mind the passage, I think we can get you home safely. I will escort you myself, if you like."

"You can guide me through the catacombs to the staircase," Sophia said, "but I will take myself home from there."

"Very well."

"What other difficulties are there?"

Pappus did not immediately answer. He sat opposite her, staring at her as intently as if she was a problem he was trying to resolve in his mind. Perhaps it was because he had just mentioned the catacombs, but Sophia could now smell a dank, moldering odor in the not-quite-still air of the basement. This smell was merged but not improved by the smell of incense, both fresh and stale, that she had noticed immediately upon her descent. She could pick up the odors of myrrh, cedar, and frankincense. Separately and in faint traces, such odors were pleasing, but the mixture of smells from various sources and times collapsed upon themselves to create an almost impenetrable barrier to breath. She breathed lightly and through her mouth and tried not to show her discomfort to Pappus, who appeared oblivious to the malodorous assault.

"The next difficulty," Pappus said, "is that Athanasius has conditioned the confrontation upon the return of all that he claims you stole from him in Sheneset and he says he must know all the evidence you intend to produce. If you really want your day of reckoning, I fear you will have to comply with his demands."

From beneath her stola, where she had pinched it between her left arm and torso from the time she left home, she removed the sack containing the finely hewn writing desk that she had taken on her day of flight from Father James' house. She placed it on

Pappus' lap. Pappus looked at it from all sides before opening it. Inside he saw papers, both blank and inked, reeds, sharpened and unsharpened, and three small bottles of ink. He began reading the pages that had been written upon, frowning more severely with each page. After several minutes he placed the papers back into the desk and said, "He really is a monster, isn't he?"

Sophia did not respond to the question. It was a conclusion that she had long since assimilated.

"What makes him so horrible, so inhuman," Pappus continued, "is his Goddamned certainty that everything he does is ordained by God."

Again, Sophia did not reply. Pappus looked into her face for consent in his judgment, but she just looked back at him as if his observation was so obvious it did not need to be said.

"Tell me," he finally said, "if you are giving me this to return it to him, then what proof will you have of your accusations?"

"The pages are copies I made from his hand. I have kept the original pages."

"Is this everything you took from him?"

"There were three gold solidi in the desk when I took it," she said. "But it was money I gave to him to purchase my husband's release. He took the money but did not free Philippus. The bargain was not kept. The money is properly returned."

"You had so much to offer?"

"Yes. There were also texts, scripture and algebra. I buried them with my husband."

"Athanasius owned a book of mathematics? I am surprised."

"Yes."

"Well," Pappus said, "I think you have fairly met his conditions of combat. How shall I get in touch with you to make the final arrangements?"

"I will come here with Ankha on Tuesday, two hours before decline of the day. You and your students can escort us to the top of the Paneum, if you will."

"Come to the entrance to the catacombs, which you will see when you exit. I will be waiting for you there at the appointed time. There might be a crowd of unfriendly Christians to greet you if you come directly to the steps of the Serapeum."

"Alright." Sophia focused a keen look on Pappus. "Do you know," she asked, "if there is much interest in this affair? Outside of your classroom, I mean?"

"The entire city talks of nothing else, I'm told. There will be a great crowd."

Sophia smiled slightly, but otherwise did not comment on this news.

Pappus smiled back, then roused himself suddenly. "I have been a bad host," he said. "Can I offer you something? Tea or wine, perhaps?"

"No, thank you. You have been a very good host and I will be forever grateful to you, whatever happens."

"Can I show you around? We here at the Paneum believe we have the largest library in the world. Can I show some of it to you?"

"I would like to see it sometime," Sophia replied. "But now I must return to my children and family. They will be worried about me."

"Well, anytime you can, my offer to show you the library remains open. And the rest of the Serapeum, of course." Pappus took a lamp, turned up the wick and rose. "Follow me," he said.

He guided her past a small, stone door and through a narrow passageway into the caverns of the catacombs. Grand pillars held up the ceiling. On the walls in bas-relief were carvings of a solar disk, serpents, and many Egyptian deities, including Horus, Toth and Anubis. Pappus explained to Sophia that the catacombs had been built by a single, wealthy Alexandrian family over two hundred years earlier, but were now available to all for a fee. He said there were two more levels below where they walked. In recesses that lined the walls were skeletons and shrouded remains in various states of decay. In the largest room, the Hall of Caracalla, were the skeletal remains of over 20,000 Alexandrians and many of their animals, slaughtered by Roman troops on Emperor Caracalla's orders and thrown randomly into the great chamber. Alexandria's offense? Staging a satirical play that mocked the Emperor's belief that he was Alexander the Great incarnate. Their bones lay scattered, as they had fallen when they were thrown into the largest chamber of the catacombs, 215 years earlier. In other rooms, here and there, were expensive sarcophagi containing among the last mummified remains that Egypt produced.

"I hope to be buried here myself, when the time comes," Pappus said. "I think it would be wonderful to lie among such company."

They climbed a spiral staircase to ground level. There was a large room at the top and a large door to the outside at the end of the room. Pappus led Sophia to the door and explained that, for obvious reasons, the door could be opened from the inside, but not from the outside without a key. That is why he would meet her just inside the doorway next Tuesday.

In parting, Pappus said, "You are an interesting young woman, Sophia. I hope I can get to know you better when this is over."

"If I live," Sophia said.

"Yes, if you live."

Sophia and Ankha left their apartment about fifteen minutes before the appointed time for her rendezvous with Pappus at the entrance to the catacombs. The rest of the household was to stay home, with bags packed, ready to flee. Sophia wore a white stola over a plain, black tunic. She covered her head in a colorful scarf purchased in the Egyptian Quarter. Ankha wore an expensive white robe, under which he carried his sheathed sword. There was no hiding his height or military bearing. Great gusts of wind surged from the north, heralding shipwrecking storms at work out at sea. The winds chased cascading waves of billowing clouds that tumbled over and collapsed upon each other above the city. The sky was filled with sea birds seeking shelter from the storm. Waves of gulls, albatrosses, small storm petrels, and storks merged and separated on the wind in conic movements in the sky.

It was not far from their home to the entrance of the catacombs, but almost as soon as they stepped out, they could sense that excitement coursed through the arteries of Alexandria. It was not only the winds and the clouds and the movement of birds that caused the excitement. Shops were being closed early. Small groups of people huddled and talked, all looking north at the sky and all looking south toward the Paneum. Several of the men and women they saw wore green tunics over their outer garments.

Pappus was waiting for them just inside the entrance to the catacombs. After introducing himself to Ankha as a teacher of mathematics, he ushered them through the catacombs into his office below the Serapeum. "We have a little time before we must go," Pappus said. "Do you mind if we talk?" Pappus offered them seats and sat beside them.

Rather than answering his question, Sophia asked, "Does Athanasius still come?"

"I have heard nothing further since I delivered his writing desk. I did not see him on that occasion. I gave it to the Macarius I call the Elder. I said, 'Sophia has met the Episcopate's conditions,' as I handed him the desk and he said nothing in return. Not even a thank you. But word of rejection has not come down from St. Mark's, so I am presuming we are on. In this opinion, my students and, it would appear, much of the city, Christian and non, agree."

"Much of the city?" Sophia asked.

"I told you the last time we met that the city talks of nothing else. In the three days since then the excitement has grown. There is likely to be a great crowd."

"Will Rome intervene?"

"I do not believe so. There has been no indication of riot or fighting, and Rome, or New Rome these days, is accustomed to these curricular activities in Alexandria. No, the weather, I think, poses more of a threat than the authorities. Let us hope that the winds turn east, as they seem to be doing."

After a moment or two of silence, Pappus asked if she had a strategy.

"The facts," she answered.

"The truth, then, is to be your case?"

"The truth is whatever someone chooses to believe. I will present the facts. I will go through each of my allegations and ask him if he denies any of them. If he does, I will read from his own hand. When it comes to the condition poor Philippus was in when we were rescued, I will call upon Ankha to provide details."

Ankha had not been told of this part of her plan and shifted uncomfortably on his seat when he heard it for the first time. But he did not demur. He simply nodded.

"A good strategy. A fine strategy," Pappus said. "A winning strategy perhaps. But what will you win, Sophia? Have you thought what is the contest?"

"To humiliate the Red Devil."

"In that case, you have already won. Outside the Christian community he was already disliked. After the posting of your Katagoso, dislike has grown to repugnance. Even some of the Christians who study here have begun to ask if these things can be true."

"If fortune smiles, then after today even the Christians will know his character."

Pappus led them up some stairs to the main floor of the

Serapeum where a crowd of about seventy-five supporters awaited, some armed and most wearing the outer green tunic that had become the symbol of support for Sophia. The group began to snap their fingers when they saw Sophia arise from the basement with Pappus and Ankha. A handsome, square-faced man of about twenty emerged from the group, holding a green tunic, cut down the middle and with fastening hooks sewn on the front. It was similar to what Beset had fashioned for her to wear a week earlier when she posted her Katagosos. The young man held it out to her and asked if she would put it on. Sophia looked at the young man's face. Alone among her supporters he had drawn a cross over both eyes in black kohl.

"We are calling ourselves 'Sophites,'" he said. "Some suggested 'Sophists,' but that word applies to someone who teaches only those who can afford their fees and you have taught Alexandria about the cruel nature of Athanasius only at a steep price to yourself. We would be honored if you would wear this vesta in solidarity with your supporters, as your supporters wear them in solidarity to you."

Sophia took the tunic. "What is your name?" she asked.

"John, from Jerusalem," was the answer.

"I met a boy named John in Jerusalem," Sophia said. "He would be about your age. He was a carpenter, the son of Marsanes. Do you know of him?"

"I am that John."

Sophia embraced him. "How is your father, Marsanes? And your mother, Ephedra? And Thomas and Magdalene?"

"Father is dead," John replied. "Last year, in Jerusalem. He died when the scaffold he was on was pulled out from under him. The killer escaped, but we believe he was sent by the Bishop Macarius. Such accidents and outright killings have become common among those who adhere to Gnostic beliefs. Father would never be silent about his quest for gnosis."

Sophia held John tighter as tears fell from her eyes. She had known Marsanes and his family for only one day, but their meeting had made a lasting impression on her. She had named her first child Magdalene, and her second, John, partly in honor of the memory of Marsanes' family.

"I am so sorry," Sophia said to John. "When Timaeus and I left your house those five years ago, Marsanes told me that I could always find haven with your family. It was the first time that I ever felt that I belonged to something, rather than to someone. My heart breaks at your news."

Sophia released John, whose eyes had also begun to fill with tears, and draped the tunic over her stola. "Are you a student here, John?" she asked.

"No," he answered. "I am here to honor father's pledge to you. I paint my eyes to honor Timaeus."

Sophia's throat contracted at hearing this and a sob clutched her throat. Ankha's strong left arm wrapped around her and kept her from swooning. The group of supporters gathered about them had followed the conversation and their mood turned from youthful exuberance to somber anxiety as the gravity of the occasion sunk in.

When she had recovered herself, Sophia asked John, "Word of this has travelled as far as Jerusalem?"

"As far as New Rome, I have heard," he replied.

Summoning her strength and resolve Sophia said, "Thank you for coming, John. We have Macariuses here in Alexandria as well." She turned to the rest of the group and said, "Thank you all for supporting me. You are my strength. But there will be no martyrs today in my name. If matters take a turn, Ankha will protect me. If he cannot and we are overwhelmed, run. Do not fight. Do not come to our aid. Your numbers are our strength. If that is not strength enough, flee. Even if they kill me, with your help we have already won. I want no other deaths to diminish our victory."

Finger snapping and shouts punctuated the group's approval

and excitement, if not their agreement with Sophia's admonition. "We must go now," Pappus said.

The group emerged from the Serapeum with Ankha, Pappus and Sophia at its center and began their progress along the streets, east toward the Paneum. The streets to the Paneum were crowded with people, all moving in the same direction. Most of the people were from the Greek Quarter, which included many Romans, but there were many native Egyptians as well. Quite a few of the Greeks and a few of the Egyptians wore green tunics over their outer garments. It was evident that among non-Christians. Sophia's attack on Athanasius had found footing. The winds that had gusted when Sophia left home had consolidated into a steady force blowing from the north. The clouds, too, had congealed and darkened to form a grey and black firmament above buildings and towers of the city.

When they reached the base of the Paneum, the crowd thickened and progress through it became slow. Men at the fore of Sophia's escort shouted, "Make way, Sophia arrives," and slowly the sea of bodies parted and they made their way upward. Half way up the ascent they heard shouting from the north as a group of several hundred Christians, led by the two Macariuses, made their way toward the top. Sophia could not see above the heads of her group to ascertain what was happening, but Ankha, at over six feet in height, told her he could see the black and brown robes of many clerics pushing their way up the hill.

"Is Athanasius among them?" Sophia asked.

"I do not see him, but I can see little else but the robes."

In a circle surrounding the top twenty feet of the Paneum was a fence of Roman soldiers, armed with swords and shields and the stoic look of professional non-participants. Stretching down the hill from the circle of soldiers like spokes from a hub were lines of additional soldiers standing at arm's length distance from each other and dividing the grounds of the Paneum into six wedges. As they approached the circle of soldiers, a commander stepped forward and, after a brief conversation, allowed Sophia, Ankha and Pappus inside the circle.

It was now one hour before the decline of day. The time for the contest had arrived. From inside the circle of soldiers Sophia could see just how great a gathering the day had become. In his official report to Constantine, Julius Julianus, Prefect of Africa, wrote that over 40,000 persons made their way to the Paneum to observe or root for a side or to participate in any melee that arose. Every kind of Egyptian, Roman, Greek, Hebrew and Semite in every kind of garb lined the hill all the way down to its base until by sight they merged into a great sea of humanity. On the south side of the incline amidst the sea were several large pools of green, undulating, as those who wore their tunics out moved and pushed for position.

After a few minutes a surge of brown and black clad clerics pushed their way to the circle, led by Macarius the Elder. Macarius argued with the commander, asserting that Rome had no authority to intervene in a clerical matter. The commander ignored Macarius and, in a stentorian voice read from a scroll that a soldier unrolled before him:

"I am Amnius Anicius Paulinus, Commander of the Alexandrian Garrison of the Second Roman Army. By order of Julius Julianus, Prefect of Africa, I have been charged with maintaining order here today and with preventing riot among the several tribes of this city, as so often occurs." As Paulinus spoke, his words were repeated in loud voices by designated soldiers stationed in the lines that ran down the Paneum. He paused, then in a voice loud enough to topple trees, proclaimed, "There will be no disorder today."

Paulinus adjusted his scarlet robe and helmet, which had slightly skewed from perfection with the effort of the last sentence. He continued. "The adversaries will each be allowed two assistants with them in the circle. The accuser is one who calls herself Sophia of Alexandria. As the accuser, she will proceed first. The accused is Bishop Athanasius of Alexandria. He will be given as much time as needed to respond. I have forty-two Echoes stationed in descent from the top of the Paneum. They are instructed to repeat what the principles say verbatim so that all may hear what is spoken. This is not a trial. There will be no verdict. There will be no vote. When the adversaries are finished, the crowd will disburse or they will be disbursed."

As Paulinus spoke, Sophia looked at the sky. She feared the sound and volume of his voice would unleash the torrents, but the cloud firmament remained fixed above the hill, darkening more in the east, and held its rain. Paulinus turned to Macarius and asked, "Where is Bishop Athanasius?" Macarius turned and faced the crowd and unfurled a scroll of his own.

"Bishop Athanasius," he read, "rightful spiritual heir to Saint Mark the Evangelist, composer of the Gospel, companion of the disciple Simon Peter whom Christ loved above all others, Athanasius through whom St. Mark speaks, declines the invitation to degrade his name, his office and the glory of God by deigning to respond to accusations that cannot in the Lord's good name be true. The accusations are made by an infamous prostitute, a deceitful impersonator and an admitted protector of heresies and heretics. Slanderous accusations made by such filth against the apostolic successor of Simon Peter and Mark the Evangelist must be met with reprimand, not response. I call on the Legion to arrest her for trial." As the Echoes repeated his words down the hillside, the crowd on all sides began to surge and was pushed back on all sides by the soldiers. A din arose as shouts of "*deilos*" (coward) and "*saura*" (lizard) arose in Greek from the south, west and east sides of the Paneum, to be met with "*porne*" (whore) and "*airetikos*" (heretic) from the west and north. Paulinus remained static, gaving no order to carry out Macarius' demand for an arrest. Just when it appeared that the number of soldiers was insufficient to restrain the crowd's frenzy a poly-veined flash of golden lightning blazed through the eastern sky, followed quickly by an explosion of thunder that tailed off to a series of rumbles that rolled on for over a minute. As the thunder faded, Macarius said, "God has spoken. The apostate is silenced."

Led by Macarius the Elder, the Christians began to push their way down from the top of the Paneum. Sophia held up her hand, as if to ask a question, then addressed Paulinus. "May I respond?" she asked. Paulinus nodded and his soldiers stopped the egress of the clerics.

"Thank you, Alexandrians," she said, "for giving hark to my accusations. I set forth my grievances in writing and offered to prove them. Athanasius has refused to respond. You, Alexandria, you, Rome, be the judge. Thank you."

Her words bounded down the hillside on the voices of the Echoes until replaced with silence. She clasped Paulinus' hand and proceeded down the Paneum, trailed by her followers. In his report to Julius Julianus, Paulinus remarked with satisfaction that only four bodies were found littering the Paneum once the crowds had disbursed. Forty thousand Alexandrians gathered together and only four dead! Despite the officials' fears, the gathering had been remarkably peaceful.

That night at the Serapeum there was wine and the playing of flutes and lutes and lyres and tympana. There was dancing and singing and boasting and speeches. Sophia stayed off in a corner with Ankha and Pappus, but stayed nonetheless. Partiers would come over to talk and she would take their praise and congratulations and answer their questions and thank them again and again. As the evening progressed, the revelers became more gregarious and bolder, more fulsome in their praise, first of her heroic actions, then of her beauty. She smiled and returned their praises, but declined all of the many requests to dance. She talked a little more to John about how the other members of his family were doing and promised to visit them if the occasion ever arose. The students of the Serapeum were about her age, but she felt much, much older, as if she could have been a mother to most of them.

A pretty young Egyptian girl in an unhooked green vesta came over and, speaking to Ankha, said, "Greetings. I am Arsinoe. I command you to dance with me." Sophia was surprised when Ankha assented and handed off his sword to her. She was even more surprised when she saw how adeptly Ankha performed the geronos, a circle dance imported from Anatolia. She stayed late, talking mostly to Pappus, who had a seemingly endless list of questions.

After fielding many questions, Sophia began to demure, saying, "I am accustomed to being a mystery."

"I am accustomed to solving mysteries," Pappus replied. Finally, exhausted, Sophia pulled Ankha away from Arsinoe and asked him to accompany her home. They left by the front steps of the Serapeum and walked unmolested to their door.

It had been a very good day.

Chapter Thirty-Three

The Rest of Her Life

330-391 A.D. – Alexandria

I am the staff of his power in his youth,
and he is the rod of my old age.
And whatever he wills happens to me.
Thunder, Perfect Mind

Except for a few short sojourns, Sophia spent the rest of her life in Alexandria, a city without equilibrium. The one constant was conflict. For much of the century, as the Arians fought the Trinitarians, the Christians fought each other almost as much as they attacked the Hebrews and the pagans, and all whom the Christians attacked, attacked in return. Riots, looting, battles, murders, massacres, and serial attacks on temples and people seasoned the life of the city and gradually undermined the civic calm necessary to achieve great accomplishments. Each side buried the bodies of their own fallen as the catacombs filled with the corpses of pagans, church yards expanded to accept the internment of the Christian dead and the Necropolis to the west of the city accepted everyone else. There were times when one knew what section of the city to avoid or knew not to leave one's home at all. Roman Consuls of Egypt were replaced so often that most of their names have been lost to the erosion of time, but nobody could maintain order in the city of Athanasius and his successors. In Alexandria, as in the rest of the Empire, what remained of the Gnostic faithful were hunted down, killed or otherwise quieted, their books burned, the remnants of their faith destroyed. When it came to the Gnostics, there were no great battles, no large massacres. There were not enough

Gnostics remaining to require such an effort and the Gnostics' interest in this world was insufficient to inspire any organized defense of their faith. A killing here and there was enough to drive most of the others into silence, which was completely compatible with the esoteric faith many continued to hold. The destruction of their texts and fear of association was enough to cause this early root of the Christian tree to wither and rot unseen.

Sophia drew more completely away from all religions and abhorred those who, on the basis of faith, felt compelled to kill and be killed. Publicly she pursued a course of studied neutrality in religious matters and managed to stay on the sidelines of the secular wars for most of what remained of her long life. Privately, she came to conclude that matters of faith should be kept to oneself and that skepticism toward almost everything men concluded on the subject was the most enlightened attitude.

The obscurity, which Sophia so fervently desired following her triumph on the Paneum, eluded her. Two weeks' time found her in Antioch with Ankha, sponsored by Bishop Eusebius of Caesarea to give testimony against Bishop Eustathius at a synod of bishops. Although young Athanasius of Alexandria and ancient Alexander of New Rome successfully defended Eustathius on the charge of heresy, Sophia's testimony and the testimony of others she identified condemned him as unchaste and ribald and unworthy of his office. When it came to Sophia's time to be heard, Athanasius left the hall and did not return until her testimony was over and she departed. Although he did not attend the synod, Constantine was in Antioch and confirmed the decision to depose Eustathius. Eusebius was offered his position of Pope of Antioch, a major elevation from Caesarea, but he declined. His friend and fellow Arian Paulinus was installed in his stead.

In the succeeding years in Alexandria, Athanasius followed the same approach to Sophia he had taken in Antioch: avoidance, not confrontation.

Her visit with Eusebius before the synod convened was short and bittersweet. Eusebius wept over the death of Timaeus and again over the death of Philippus. He told her that he had arranged for Timaeus' burial in a plot outside of Nicaea and had conducted the ceremony himself, with Eusebius of Nicomedia and the gravedigger the only other persons present. The bishops prayed for God to make an exception for Timaeus' soul, for even if his faith had wavered, his heart remained pure. Never had the funeral of a heretic been performed by such august Christian company. Sophia told Eusebius about the manner of Philippus' treatment and death and said he had received a Christian burial in Oxyrynchus, according to his wishes. She did not tell him that it was she who presided over the rites, nor did she mention that she buried Philippus with the *Gospel of Judas Iscariot* that Eusebius had sent to her. Eusebius asked her if she had found Christ during her time with Philippus. "I found Him," Sophia answered, "but I have lost Him again." Eusebius counseled her to examine her heart from time to time, as she was sure to find Him returned.

As Sophia and Ankha were preparing to leave the inn in Antioch, two Praetorians arrived and ushered them into the presence of the Emperor. They travelled by foot over a bridge to an island in the Orontes River where Constantine maintained a large palace of impressive stone and glasswork. He met them in a spacious common room, accompanied by only two guards and a scribe. The room was decorated with tapestries and flowers. A large bowl of fruit, dates and pears, stood on its own pedestal near the table at which Constantine sat.

Constantine had aged since Nicaea, developing jowls that kept his face largely free of lines, but he had gained weight and his aging body sank slightly with the burden. Still, he remained an impressive figure. He commanded Sophia to sit and she sat, but made no such offer to Ankha, who remained standing. He studied her intensely before speaking, then handed her one of the Katagosos that she had written and posted in Alexandria.

"Is this of your doing?" he asked.

"Yes," she replied.

"And you say you have evidence of your accusations?"

"Yes. When we escaped from Sheneset, I took his desk that contained his diary. He wrote of all these things."

"Do you have the writings still?"

"Yes. They are in Alexandria."

"You will provide them to my Prefect, Paulinus. Not our new bishop in Antioch. The Prefect in Egypt. Same name. Quite different persons. You will take them to him." It was not a question.

"Yes," Sophia replied.

Constantine smiled and turned his palms upward in a sign of giving grace. "I remember you," he said. "In Nicaea at the Council. You were dressed as a scribe or a priest. There under false pretenses, I guess?"

Sophia felt a passing fear. Was the interview turning suddenly dangerous? She said, meekly, "Yes," without explanation.

Constantine smiled. "Well, let us say no more about it. You have paid enough, I think."

"Thank you, Emperor."

"Yes, yes. And Timaeus dead at Athanasius' hand. It is a greater transgression than yours, I think. I will be most interested in reading his account of how that happened. I remember the man, Timaeus. His suggestion, which he said came from you, was most helpful. The same homoousios. We thought that solved the problem, but alas… I asked Timaeus to bring you to me, so that I could thank you, but he died and you disappeared."

"I did not know of your request," Sophia replied.

"Well, we meet now at last and I have new cause to thank you."

"New cause?"

"Your evidence against Athanasius. He causes much trouble, you see. We thought your solution would work. The bishops agreed on a creed that said so. But some, Athanasius first among them, have no tolerance for the slightest variation in belief. I had hoped to unify the Empire under the Christian banner, but I find the bishops, for all their solidarity in adversity, cannot agree upon anything in peace, nor tolerate divergences in practice. There may come a time when Athanasius must be knocked from his high pedestal in Alexandria. I will not act now and hope I will never have to, but if the need arises, and I fear it will, I will know where to start."

Speaking against her better judgment, her fragile voice betraying the cold fear she felt in this man's presence, Sophia chanced a question. "But you remain dedicated to Christianity itself, do you not?"

Constantine smiled enigmatically. "Of course," he said. "Jesus must be our savior." He signaled to his scribe and then whispered something in his ear. The scribe left the room. While the scribe was out, Constantine smiled at Sophia in silence and Sophia worried that her question had aggrieved the great man. The scribe returned half a minute later and pressed something into Constantine's palm. Constantine took a bright, new coin between his fingers and held it out to Sophia.

"I almost forgot to give you one of these," he said. "They were minted in honor of the consecration of Constantinopolis in May. I want you to have one from me, in gratitude." He handed the coin to her face up and she saw his image, in profile, helmeted, with what appeared to be a lance, half cross, half weapon, resting against his left shoulder, symbolizing, perhaps, both his success in battle and his fealty to Christ.

Constantine rose and signaled Sophia to do likewise. "You are a remarkable beauty," he said. "I am happy we finally met."

"Thank you," Sophia replied.

Addressing Ankha for the first time, Constantine commented

that he looked like a soldier. "You have the legionary's scar on your chin. Did you see any action?"

"Some, sir."

"Come now. Do not hold back. Which battles?"

"Adrianople."

"You fought with me at Adrianople?"

"Yes, sir. And at Chrysopolis and Mardia. I was injured at Chrysopolis and was allowed to return to Egypt, where I was born, as a consul's guard."

"Three of Licinius' attempts to destroy me?"

"Yes, sir."

"Many of your company have solicited me directly for favor. And I always try to accommodate. Is there something you desire of me? Do not overreach, soldier, but if there is something in my power to grant, just request it."

Unsure of how to take this turn, Ankha answered with, "I received my wages. I ask no more."

Constantine smiled. "Well then you, my son, really are a hero. You have my undying gratitude." Constantine seemed to consider Ankha a moment longer, then asked if he could see his battle wounds. Ankha cast a shy or wary look toward Sophia.

"Sophia," Constantine said, "could you please wait outside? We old soldiers wish to compare battle scars. We won't be long." It was phrased as a question but, after all, it was the Emperor of the united Roman Empire who asked it. Caesar himself. Escorted by one of the guards, Sophia retired to an anteroom.

A few minutes later Ankha joined her, holding in his shaking hand a piece of unfolded parchment, which he immediately handed to Sophia. Although she knew he could read at least as much as was required for a Court guard, she read it aloud, judging that either the words on the paper or, more likely, the moment itself, had rendered him incapable of discerning the letters.

TO ALL CONCERNED. TAKE PARTICULAR NOTICE THAT THE BEARER HEREOF, ANKHA EGYPTOS OF ALEXANDRIA, HAS THE PERSONAL COMMENDATION AND FAVOR OF FLAVIUS VALERIUS AURELIUS CONSTANTINUS AUGUSTUS, IMPERATI ROMANII

The parchment was signed by Constantine and sealed by his own hand.

Sophia never asked to see Ankha's scars and never learned that much of the freedom from danger she enjoyed for the rest of her life was the result of a letter Constantine wrote to Athanasius later that day, informing the bishop that if any harm should come to her in Alexandria, whatever the circumstances, Athanasius would be held personally responsible.

Some time after they had left the Emperor's palace, Sophia made a closer examination of the coin he had given her. It was a nummi, made of copper. In contrast to the cross-bearing Constantine on the front, the back was graced with an image of Tyche, the Greek goddess of fortune, good or bad. Constantine, it seemed, was still hedging his bets.

They returned home through Jerusalem and spent a night with Marsanes' family. Magdalene was now eleven years old. John and Thomas were grown. Ephedra was diminished, saddened and sunk by the death of her husband. None of them still practiced their old religion. "It is too dangerous," John explained. Seeing Maggie made her miss her own children, who had stayed behind with Beset and Senmonthis.

Jerusalem was much changed. In late 325, the year Sophia and Timaeus had passed through, Emperor Constantine's sainted mother Helena had undertaken a pilgrimage to the city and claimed to have discovered the actual crosses of St. Dismas, Gestas and Jesus hidden in the foundation stones of the Temple of Venus. The crosses were said to have been constructed from the timbers of a bridge into Jerusalem built by Solomon for his wife, the Queen of Sheba, to cross one thousand years before, the bridge timbers, in turn, said to have been planed from the famous tree of Eden, the fruit of which Adam and Eve so tragically ate. Upon the discovery of the True Cross, Constantine ordered the demolition of the pagan temples and the construction of a modern, Christian city. The temple of Venus on the site of Golgotha had been demolished and a glorious basilica was being built in its place. There was little left of the Hebrew city Christ had known.

When the pair arrived in Alexandria, Sophia showered Maggie and John with kisses and hugs and presents. She promised she would never be gone another night and would always be there to tuck them in when they went to sleep.

Sophia broke her promise two months later. The occasion was a request that Ankha made solemnly to Sophia.

"I have been seeing Arsinoe," Ankha said after securing a private audience with Sophia. He was clearly nervous. "And I was wondering, well, if you have any objection to me asking Arsinoe to marry?"

Sophia was surprised. Since Ankha deserted his post to rescue her and Philippus, and particularly since Philippus' death, she had half expected Ankha to renew his addresses to her. She had thought quite often of what she would say to him. She did not want to remarry. Certainly not soon, while the pain of the loss of Philippus still burned. But he had saved her life, had gotten her family safely to Alexandria and had stood by her when she stood up to Athanasius. And she had become very fond of him. She thought of him as she thought a sister might feel toward a close and strong brother. Now he was asking if she had any objections to his marrying another. She would have been lying if she denied any pang of jealousy or regret. Yet that was not the strongest feeling. The strongest feeling was intense happiness that Ankha had found someone he wanted to marry and the prospect that he had a chance at the happiness and fulfillment of a wife and children.

"Ankha," she answered. "You do not need my permission to marry."

"But do you have any objection?"

"No, you have my full blessing and best wishes. I would however, ask one more service of you."

"Anything you ask, Hypatia." Alone, he still called her by the name by which he first knew her.

"It is a big request, but if you will do this thing for me, I shall be able to provide you with a handsome wedding gift."

"What is it? I say yes before you answer."

"Accompany me back to Sheneset. I have left something of value there that I must retrieve."

"Yes. Of course I will go. Do you think it will be dangerous?"

"Danger seems to always be on my heels, doesn't it?"

"And catches you sometimes too," Ankha replied.

Before the two departed Alexandria, Senmonthis told Sophia that she wished to return home. "I know those boys aren't good for much," she said. "But as much horn of Pan as those two have I'm bound to have grandchildren soon and I'd like a go at raising young ones without the interference of one so unloosed as my husband was when he was alive." So, before they left, Sophia hired an Egyptian teenage girl named Isis to help Beset with the children and chores while she was away.

The three travelled by hired carriage south. Sophia had, with great regret, sold Alexander the Great and Roxana shortly after arriving in Alexandria. The horse Seti had purchased from Isidorus, which Sophia had never named, had been sold as well. With the inevitable breakdowns and horse and carriage changes, the trip took ten uncomfortable days.

During the trip Ankha talked of his plans for the future. He had been talking to paper makers who had complained about interruptions in the supply of papyri reeds that they needed for their production. They were reluctantly considering whether to set up their own supply system and, as "green vesters" in attendance at the Paneum, had witnessed Ankha's size and bravery. They had made inquiries about whether he would consider establishing security for large volumes of reeds to be transported north from the Nile Valley. Ankha told Sophia and Senmonthis that he thought the work would suit him, even though it would take him away from Arsinoe for weeks at a time several times each year. Senmonthis expressed the opinion that such separations were good for a marriage and the wish that she had been accorded more of them while her husband was alive. Sophia asked if perhaps the work might be made more profitable and his schedule less arbitrary if he set up the supply business himself. "You say the paper makers are reluctant. That is no doubt because it is not the trade they know. But if they were to agree to purchase from you, the business could be undertaken by contract."

"I do not have such funds as would be necessary," Ankha replied. "I would have to be able to purchase the reeds, transport them, probably with a boat I would have to purchase, and have a place in or near Alexandria to store what is not sold immediately."

"I could invest as your backer," Sophia said. "We could agree on, say, twenty percent of profits going to me as return on the investment."

"There may not be any profit. If a shipment is lost, the business and investment is lost with it."

"Then I would be taking that risk with you. You would owe me nothing. But I trust you to bring the reeds in safely to Alexandria."

"It will require more than the forty solidi we have left for your household."

"You leave that to me. Will two hundred do?"

"It is more than enough."

"Some for you and Arsinoe to live on then, until the profits start."

"More than enough for that as well. Should a new business take on so much debt?"

"I told you, it is not debt. It is an investment. Any you need beyond what is necessary to start the business will be my wedding present to you."

"It is too generous."

"It is not nearly generous enough, for what you have done."

When they arrived in Sheneset late summer was in full oppressive reign. Temperatures rose to over 100 degrees by day and cooled only to the high 80's by night. Bakare and Seti and their wives came out to greet Senmonthis like she was a conquering hero. They had managed to spend and lose the three gold coins she had given them so that while the house had a few additional objects such as furniture and an elaborately carved abacus, which neither boy knew how to use properly, the four had begun to worry about how they would feed themselves and the babies that now bulged their wives' wombs.

Ankha and Sophia took up rooms at the only inn in Sheneset. The innkeeper recognized Hypatia, but did not object when she called herself Sophia of Alexandria when checking in. On the day following their arrival they rented an ass from Isidorus and, because of the heat, laid by provisions for a two-day trip into the red land cliffs. Sophia still had not told Ankha the purpose of their journey.

During the day Sophia received a visit from Pachome. He had somehow learned that she had returned to the area and where she was staying. For an alleged hermit, he was able to keep himself well informed. He brought with him Father James, who stood behind Pachome at her door. Sophia called for Ankha to join them before admitting the two Christians into her room.

Pachome said first that Father James wished to apologize for his role in what happened to Philippus and her. He nudged James forward. Father James kept his eyes down. He could not look at her. He said, simply that he was sorry and followed the apology with a justification. He did not know what Athanasius intended and he left his own home when he saw what was happening to Philippus. "I should have done more," he said.

"Yes, you should have," was Sophia's reply.

Pachome stepped forward. "I should have done more as well," he said. "I could have led my monks against the cruelty. I suspected what the Bishop might do and yet fled for my own purposes. Athanasius is no Christian."

To Pachome Sophia said, "I forgive you. You gave me warning, at least."

"Thank you," Pachome said. He then turned to Father James and said, "Run along now. She has forgiven us." Father James accepted Pachome's interpretation of Sophia's words and left.

Once James had left, Pachome produced a slim, well-bound volume from under his robe. "I have heard of your triumph in Alexandria. To show the world the Bishop's true nature is a remarkable accomplishment."

"It does no good," Sophia answered. "He remains bishop."

"Athanasius now spends all of his time trying to undo the harm, which means he does no further harm, for the time being. That alone is something for which my monks and I are thankful."

Pachome handed Sophia the codex he had produced. "We found this after the visit by the Bishop. Whether he saw it or not, I don't know, but our library had been gone over and yet, when he left and we returned, it remained. Whether or not he saw it, this book remains too dangerous for us to keep. Athanasius has strict ideas about what is orthodox and what to do about those who are not. Would you take this and place it with its sisters?"

"I will hide it where I hid the others," Sophia said.

"Hypatia," Pachome said, "you have ever been a revelation to me. I wish you a long life." With that, he departed.

Sophia and Ankha left the inn four hours before the first light of day. As the sun began to ascend, the cliffs became familiar.

Sophia eventually recognized the needle rock. The Egyptian face rock above the entrance had continued its transformation into a plain boulder. What had once appeared to her to be two eyes and a mouth now looked like mere blemishes in stone. How rapidly the wind did its work, she thought.

Once she was sure she had found the right cave, she told Ankha, "I am going to go into that cave and drag out a locked chest. Inside the chest is all the money we need to start your business and more. All you have to do is get me and the box safely back to Alexandria."

She came across the earthenware jar first and pushed it outside the opening. "Could you pull this away a little?" she asked Ankha. She went back in, found the metal chest and drug it out. Taking a key that hung from her neck, she undid the lock and opened the box. The gold flashed in the bright sunshine. "You see," she said to Ankha, "we have quite enough to get you started."

Ankha stared in wonder at the box and its contents. He thought to himself that perhaps Nabwenenef had been right; perhaps Sophia was, indeed, a goddess. She could certainly produce miracles, for here was another miracle, blinding him with the reflected sun.

The wax that Sophia had used to seal the earthenware jar had begun to sink and crack in the middle of the opening. Borrowing Ankha's knife, she cut around the perimeter, removed the wax and placed the volume Pachome had given her on top of the others. She had examined the codex before they left the inn. It contained only two texts, both of which were already contained in the earlier books: *The Apocryphon of John* and *The Holy Book of the Great Invisible Spirit*. She did not read the texts in the newest codex and did not know if they differed in any way from the earlier texts that were already in the jar. When it came to resealing the jar, Sophia sought to improve upon her method. She found that the bowl she carried fit the mouth of the jar exactly. She put the old wax in the bowl and melted it in the sun, then put the bowl over the mouth and shaped the wax with the knife to form a seal. When she was done, she pushed the jar back into the cave.

They spent the brutal hours in the shade of the rock that once bore an Egyptian face and headed back to Sheneset in the early evening. The next day they visited Senmonthis. Sophia wanted to give her 200 solidi, but she would accept only twenty. She would die long before the twenty was spent, she explained, and if, upon her death, the boys came into possession of one tenth of such a sum, it would surely be their ruination. Sophia cried when they parted, thinking she would never see her friend again.

To return to Alexandria they booked passage on a ploion hellenikon, a large riverboat with oars and sails used for river travel on the Nile. Moving with a current that travelled at about five miles per hour, their journey took under one week. Sophia had packed the iron chest in a wooden clothing trunk and covered it with garments.

Ankha and Arsinoe married two weeks after their return. Their pagan wedding was held in the Serapeum, presided over, at Arsinoe's request, by Pappus. Afterward Pappus played an expert lyre to accompany the wedding dancers.

Although he and his followers proclaimed victory over Sophia and cited as proof God's verdict of thunder and lightning, the events at the Paneum had long-term consequences for Athanasius. The rate of conversions to Christianity from among the Jews and, particularly, the pagans, slowed to almost nothing and remained stagnant for several years. This in itself was embarrassing since, with the Emperor's embrace of Christianity and the passage of laws designed to promote its expansion, the faith exploded in almost every other region.

Athanasius responded by consolidating his power among his clergy. Years of struggle followed for Athanasius. He fought with all who offended him: Arians, pagans, Meletians, Kemites and others. He sent the two Macariuses out into the Nitrian Desert just to the west of Alexandria to form monasteries and recruit young men to join them. Macarius the Great (or Elder) founded the Paromeos Monastery. Macarius the Younger (or Macarius of Alexandria) formed The Kellii, a monastery located just a few miles from Paromeos. The black robed monks of these monasteries would become known as the Nitrian Monks and Athanasius used them as his personal army, dispatched at his command to forcibly expel, beat or kill opponents for years to come. Athanasius' successors would continue to use the Nitrian Monks as their muscle for over a century after Athanasius' death.

On Athanasius' orders the Nitrian Monks burned houses and destroyed churches and Eucharist chalices. He was called before Synods and Emperors. In response to demands that he appear to account for his actions, he fled into Gaul or into the desert. He once appeared in rags before the Emperor pleading for mercy and, as always, accusing his accusers of slander and dishonesty. He was exiled five times, but each time returned to resume his rule as Pope of Alexandria.

Temporarily out of exile, Athanasius was present in Constantinople in 336 when, with Arianism again in ascendance, Constantine ordered Athanasius' ally, the ninety-seven-year-old Alexander of New Rome, to give communion to Arius. Pope Alexander wept and claimed he would not give communion to the inventor of heresy. The Emperor did not relent and the old bishop was faced with the dilemma of either complying with the Emperor's orders or being exiled himself. The night before Alexander was to be forced to conduct the service, Arius suddenly became ill and died within minutes. In Athanasius' preserved written account, Arius, "falling headlong, burst asunder in the midst and immediately expired as he lay, and was deprived both of communion and of his life altogether." The Trinitarians claimed it was God's judgment. Constantine, in possession of Athanasius' confession to having poisoned Timaeus in the same manner eleven years earlier, sent Athanasius into exile again and he remained banished until Constantine's death in May 337.

Over the course of a forty-five-year papacy, Athanasius was banished by an emperor on five occasions, each time finding refuge in quarters away from the emperor's reach. During these exiles he spent over seven years in the Egyptian desert, seven years in Rome under the protection of Constans, the Emperor of the western part of a re-divided empire, and four months in a tomb. Even when he fled Alexandria, his forces remained behind. In both 345 and 361, successors to Athanasius as Pope of Alexandria were killed by mobs loyal to Athanasius. Athanasius returned from each of these exiles in triumph.

Athanasius' exiles and returns were accompanied by "force, murder and war," as a statement by the bishops at the Council of Serdica in 343 put it. Whether he was present or absent from the city, his supporters, the Nitrian Monks at the fore, would paint Alexandria red with the blood of his enemies. He died seated as Pope in Alexandria in 373 at the age of seventy-three, even though he was officially seventy-seven. Seventeen of his forty-five year reign had been spent in exile. Like-minded men, first Peter, then Timothy, then, in 384, Theophilus, succeeded him. His successor, Peter, took Athanasius' last confession. In recounting his sins, he did not mention Timaeus or Philippus, but did confess, as a transgression, "The Gnostic yet lives. I had not the strength to destroy it." Peter attempted to console him with assurances that nowhere was the Gnostic faith practiced, that no adherents remained.

"You have triumphed over that heresy," Peter assured him.

"She lives," were Athanasius' last words.

What Athanasius could not accomplish during his life, the defeat of Arianism, was accomplished by others in later years, but Athanasius, through his persistence and certainty, was given much credit and has been remembered down the ages as the Father of Orthodoxy.

Sophia's friend and one time suitor Pachomius died in 348 at the age of fifty-six, having founded eight monasteries in the Egyptian desert. Saint Pachomius is remembered as the father of Christian monasticism. One of the many miracles attributed to him is that although he never learned Greek, he could miraculously speak it on occasion. The reality was not so miraculous. The Greek he knew and occasionally spoke had been learned in Hypatia's house in Sheneset.

Sophia married Pappus in 333. It was a slow courtship, the pace dictated by Sophia's reluctance to marry again after the death of two husbands and Pappus' distraction with his other obsessions. Pappus was persistent and pleasant and learned and, importantly to Sophia, able to find humor in almost everything and everyone. After Ankha's wedding to Arsinoe, Sophia did not see him for almost a year. She thought little about Pappus except for the occasional urge to take him up on his offer for a tour of the Serapeum and its great library. She was happy to be with her children again, to reestablish the routine and order in her family that makes for the happiest childhoods. She kept Isis on after her return from Sheneset and for the first time in her life Beset had someone whose tasks and movements she could direct. Six months after returning from Sheneset, with Ankha married and his business established, Sophia bought a spacious seven room house in the Greek Quarter on The Serapic Way, a wide thoroughfare that ran northeast-southwest past the Serapeum. An entire room was dedicated to food preparation, with wood stove, tables and a cistern. One room contained both a tub for bathing and a toilet into which water could be poured to discharge the contents through buried clay pipes into the channel that ran from Lake Mareotis to Cibotus Harbor. There was a dining area, two sleeping quarters, a pantry and a parlor.

She spent almost 500 solidi on the house, had invested 200 in Ankha's business and had given away or spent another 70 between the time Philippus had arrived with Timaeus' inheritance until Ankha's business began to make a profit. That left over 1300 solidi on which to live out her days. Ankha turned out to be a good businessman and, within a year, owned his own boat and had twenty men in his employ, many as buyers stationed along 500 miles of the Nile River. He supplied up to fifteen paper manufacturers at a time and although some of those businesses came and went, Ankha's ability to supply manufacturers with a reliable source of raw materials remained constant. The letter of commendation he received from Emperor Constantine tamed the customary capriciousness of the tax collectors. Ankha himself became wealthy and Sophia's reserves never dipped below 1300 solidi. She was by no means one of the rich elite of Alexandria, but she was comfortable and the lifestyle of her family reflected it.

Although the excitement surrounding her confrontation with Athanasius soon faded, to be replaced by other daily and weekly crises mostly involving Athanasius, Sophia remained a person of renown in Alexandria, particularly in the Greek Quarter where she lived. She was not the kind of person who could just blend in to a crowd without recognition. As a result, to maintain her privacy and reclaim at least a measure of anonymity, she rarely strayed from her comfortable abode. But one day in 331 when it was Isis' day off and Beset was ill, Sophia ventured out along the Serapic Way to purchase provisions from grocery merchants. From across the Way she heard a voice calling her name and saw Pappus dodging the traffic to make his way to her side. He greeted her with a hug and smiles and reminded her of his promise to show her around the Serapeum. They set a date and time a week hence for the tour.

At the appointed time Sophia passed under the outstretched arms of the 650-year-old statue of Serapis and up the stairs into the temple. Pappus greeted her at the top of the steps.

"Sophia," he smiled, "it is so pleasant to meet you in the open, in the mouth of the Temple." Pappus had a strong, square face, a full head of hair and a Jovian beard. The hair and beard were black, streaked with grey. The internal lamp that lit his dark brown eyes reflected the intelligence of their owner. In the fear of the few days following the posting of the Katagosos, Sophia had not noticed how pleasing a face Pappus presented to the world.

He first escorted her to the statue of each of the gods, gave an account of their history, when people first recognized their divinity, their personality changes over the years and their current status in the pantheon. Whether it was an Egyptian god, such as Osiris, or a Greek god such as Zeus, or a Roman god such as Bacchus, Pappus, like a natural born Englishman who can identify the precise class and status of every person he meets, was able to place them in their proper hierarchical order. "Now Jesus," he said, "is not to be found here at the Serapeum. If he were, these older gods would hide their eyes in shame. Gods, you see, are like the dead heroes in Homer's Hades: they require libations of blood to bring them to life. And more blood is spilled for Lord Jesus than all of the other gods combined."

At the statue of Hathor, Pappus commented, "You bear a remarkable likeness to the statue."

"I've heard that before," Sophia answered.

The library was contained in ten separate rooms of the Serapeum. Each room was dedicated to different subjects. On that first visit they made it only into the first of these rooms, the one dedicated to literature. "We have all eight books of the Epic Cycle. Five different versions of The Iliad. Seven of The Odyssey. Scrolls and codices in forty-seven languages. We managed to save most of what was in the old Library and Mouseion when Diocletian's forces sacked Alexandria and set fire to the city," Pappus commented. "Not all of them are here. Some are stored in warehouses elsewhere, but we have access. Three hundred thousand volumes, at least." Sophia walked through the room and remembered back to the night in Eusebius' library with Timaeus. She had never seen so many books before. Eusebius had perhaps two thousand in his personal collection. She was now in a room that could contain ten of Eusebius' library. And there were nine more rooms like this one in the Serapeum. And warehouses that contained even more. A profound sense of awe overtook her, brought on by the almost physical presence of other humans in other times, each in their own way trying to make sense and order of their lives and of the world. Civilizations gone, except for their remnants on the pages of scrolls. Things lost to memory, but preserved to be discovered, relearned and advanced by future generations. She picked up scroll boxes with the contents noted by lettering on the box, sometimes in symbols she did not understand, but usually also in Greek. Some eighty plays by Aeschylus. Over a hundred by Sophocles, including several originals in his own hand. Her tour was prolonged by her inability to pull herself away from simply reading the titles of the books in this one room. She finally consented to leave the first room of the library only after Pappus, with apologies, explained that he had a class to teach and had to end the guided tour. They set a date for her return.

By the time six weeks later when she had finally been shown eight of the ten rooms, Pappus had decided he wanted to marry her. He had been married once before and had a sixteen-year-old son named Hermodorus who was a student at the Serapeum. His wife had died ten years earlier and he had thought never to remarry. He devoted himself to his studies, writing and students. Yet, as so many men had before him, he fell under the spell of Sophia. For Pappus, it was not her beauty, which at age twenty-five remained unrivaled among the women of his acquaintance. Yet he convinced himself that it was her mind and soul that so drew him to her. Her conduct, poise and tactical intelligence during the confrontation with Athanasius had impressed him from the start. Now, as she moved from room to room of the museum, asking surprising, intelligent questions as she went, it dawned upon Pappus that he had rarely met anyone, man or woman, with such instinctive wisdom, such native intelligence, such broad curiosity as Sophia obviously possessed.

"You say you subscribe to the philosophy of Plotinus and have explained some small part of it to me," Sophia remarked in the religion/philosophy room of the Serapeum. "How does Plotinus' 'the One beyond being' differ from the 'Unknowable One' of some early Christian thinkers, of which I have read?" In the astronomy room Pappus gave Sophia a basic introduction of Ptolemy's system, to which she replied, "I have come to believe that men are almost always wrong when it comes to their own importance in the universe. Why must the sun and stars revolve around the earth? Why can't it be the other way around or why can't they be revolving round each other? Would we even notice a difference?"

As they walked together, he answered her questions as best he could. In the mathematics room she said, "I understand nothing of this religion." Pappus told her it was not a religion, but a science.

"Does it require assumptions and faith?" she asked.

"Well, to a certain extent on some problems," he answered.

"On the most difficult problems, perhaps?"

"Yes, generally."

"Does it try to answer the unanswerable questions?"

"Sometimes it succeeds."

"Then it is a religion," Sophia said.

Sophia did not immediately agree to marry Pappus. His method of asking was peculiar. "I think we should marry. It would be a good match, I think," was how he proposed. She said she would think about it, but she didn't see him again for another two weeks. She only saw him on that occasion because she returned to the Serapeum for a tour of the Astrology room of the library. He began the tour as he always did, pointing out books that he thought she might find interesting, explaining the authors, their methods and discoveries. Neither one raised the pending question until the tour was over and he asked, "Have you thought about it?"

"Yes," she replied.

"Yes, you will marry me?"

"Yes, I have thought about it."

"And?"

"I am still thinking."

After that it occurred to Pappus that he ought to make more of an effort, so he started making unscheduled visits to her home. He would stay for an hour and attempt to engage Sophia in conversation. The wit and keen intellect that he observed at the Serapeum was mostly absent at her home, as she focused her attention more on her children than on her visitor. The seven-year-old girl was obviously very bright. She could read and write and engage in adult conversations, though she largely ignored Pappus in favor of her mother.

"What is this man doing here?" Maggie asked Sophia on one occasion.

"He is courting me."

"He doesn't bring gifts, does he?"

"No. He's a philosopher."

After that, Pappus brought gifts, first for Sophia, such as flowers, then children's scrolls for Maggie and John. The scrolls delighted Maggie, but the four-year-old John was unimpressed and discarded his scroll in favor of the wooden blocks he incessantly played with. On the next occasion Pappus brought a mechanical toy soldier that would march when wound. From that point on, John was his friend and sought to bring him into his play activities. It was the gift of a finely thrown and crafted ceramic serving bowl to Beset that seemed to clinch his acceptance into the family.

Shortly after this Sophia said to Pappus, "I am leaning in your favor, but I would like to meet your son. If it's a bad match for him, then it's a bad match for you as well."

Dinner with Pappus and Hermodorus was a scheduled event. Sophia, who was learning to cook, prepared the partridge in scallions and garlic, which turned out well, and the baked gourd and date pottage, which did not. Beset made a dessert from boiled papyrus tubers sweetened with honey. Egyptian beer was served to the adults and Hermodorus, tea to the children. Hermodorus was a student at the Serapeum, but had not decided on a field of study or whether he might want to pursue a trade, such as engineering or seafaring. He got on well with Sophia's children, especially John, with whom he played as if something of the four-year-old still remained within him.

After the dinner, Sophia said yes. They were married a month later. Pappus and Hermodorus moved into Sophia's home on the Serapic Way.

When she married him, Sophia did not know that Pappus was perhaps the foremost scholar of his age. The work for which he is primarily remembered today, the Synagoge or Collection, was an eight volume work that explained and expanded upon earlier works in the fields of mathematics, geometry, and mechanics. He wrote on hydrostatics and created an instrument that accurately measured liquids. He dabbled in astronomy and astrology, which, at the time, were intimately related fields of study.

With his marriage to Sophia he became ever more sociable and within a few years the soirees held at Sophia's house on the Serapic Way became one of the highlights of Alexandrian intellectual life. Beset, Isis and Sophia would spend a full day preparing food and procuring fruits and nuts. Wine and several varieties of Egyptian beer were served. Students and scholars from the Serapeum and from other schools would often attend. Mathematics, astronomy, mechanics, physics, geometry, biology and religions were discussed until the wee hours. Over the years the attendees included Antoninus from nearby Canopis, and Serenus, Philometer, Maximus and Himerius from the Serapeum. Asclepiades the Cynic from Antioch was an occasional guest, as was Dexippus from Syria. At first Sophia would serve simply as the beautiful hostess, lost, as she had been when she first left the brothel to travel with Timaeus, in a mysterious world of thought and language that she struggled to comprehend. But over time she picked up the language and could follow the thoughts and began to contribute her own thoughts and observations. By the time her third child was born, in 340, she had become one of the main attractions of the parties. Guests would copy down some of her sayings and would pass them around to others, such that by the time Pappus died in 350, she was quite as famous as her celebrated husband throughout the eastern Roman Empire.

The seventeen years she was married to Pappus were the longest of her three marriages. One day married to Timaeus, three years to Philippus and seventeen to Pappus. After a respectable period of grieving she would joke that with her growing success at marriage, the next one might just last her the rest of her life. She was only forty-three when Pappus died at age sixty and in time would receive several other proposals of marriage, mostly from younger men caught up under Sophia's spell as some came to call it, but she was never again tempted to accept.

The marriage to Pappus was a good one. They were happy. She studied enough geometry to follow the rudiments of what he had to say on his favorite subject. She was interested in his religious views, which he denied constituted a religion. "Throughout man's time on Earth, for as far back as we have any record," he told her once, "we have looked for an answer to the question: what is our existence? If we look to nature and look to causes and principles, we see certain patterns repeated over and again. The designer of those principles and patterns is The One, the source and destination of all things. The fact that man can discern the One through the One's patterns suggests that the human soul, which is separated from the One, may, through understanding, return to eternal existence." When Sophia said that this sounded a lot like her first husband's Gnostic beliefs, Pappus rejected the comparison. "The old Gnostics sought understanding through mysticism, whereas the One is to be understood only by the study of nature and its works."

"I am not sure whether you are selling the Gnostics short or pricing yourself too high," Sophia replied.

They were happy at home and, as the children of previous marriages grew and left home, happy at the Serapeum where Sophia spent more and more of her time among the scrolls and codices of the library.

Hermodorus left home first, in 336, to become an engineer building the new world capital in Constantinopolis. As John grew he became increasingly interested in his real father, an interest that only increased when, in 340 at the age of twelve his mother brought forth a new child with a different father. Thereafter, he took more and more of an interest in Christianity, an interest that, because it enlivened and pleased John, Sophia did not discourage. In 345, to Sophia's unspoken anguish, he left home to join the Kellii Monastery under the guidance of Macarius the Younger. He was back home three months later when he refused to participate in the killing of Pope Gregory and slipped out of his black cassock and back into his mother's house. Athanasius' frequent resort to surrogate violence convinced him to leave Alexandria, but did not dissuade him from the Church. Within three months he left for Rome to work for the Roman Bishop as a translator and clerk. He did not take vows. He wrote home only occasionally; once, in 355 to inform Sophia that he had married and had two sons and two daughters.

Magdalene grew up as bright and beautiful as the promise of

her youth. When old enough, she studied at the Serapeum, taking a particular interest in the Greek classics and Epicurean philosophy. She put off marriage until she was twenty-three and had decided to never wed, but her heart was won by a determined and wealthy scholar from Mesotopa, a Manichaean by faith but not practice. After the wedding she moved with him to his home in Ctesiphon. Although she corresponded by post, Sophia saw her only rarely after the wedding and saw the four grandchildren who were born to Maggie only twice.

Beset died in 340, ever grateful to Sophia for the life she had given her, including the supreme blessing of grandchildren. To Beset, grandchildren were a gift that could not be imagined until received and she welcomed the two girls and two boys into her world as the unexpected fulfillment of a life that was ending far happier than its beginnings had portended. Ankha, Arsinoe and her four grandchildren were with her in the final hours, but it was Sophia who wiped her brow, Sophia who told her stories of the great unknown, Sophia who sang her old, forgotten songs, and Sophia who held her hand and eased her passage into whatever comes next.

Pappus died in his sleep in 350 at the age of sixty, enjoying a death that was as gentle as the life he had lived. As master of the Serapeum and one of the most esteemed scholars of his age, there was a large funeral attended by the famous and the obscure, as Sophia had him laid to rest in a sarcophagus placed among other sarcophagi in a recess in the second level of the catacombs. For over a year after his death, Sophia continued to receive letters of condolence and praise from people whose lives Pappus had touched and inspired, including many from people he had never met.

Pappus' death left her alone in the big house with servants whose names and identities changed every few years and with what she came to realize as her greatest achievement in life, her son with Pappus, named Theon.

Theon was ten when his father died. He adored his father and felt the loss deeply, but he was a brilliant child, with innate abilities in music and mathematics, and his devotion to developing these talents filled some small portion of the vacuum in which his father's departure left him. For a time after Pappus' death, Sophia stopped hosting the soirees that had become famous in Alexandria. This was a loss felt deeply, particularly by the community centered around the Serapeum and only a little less so by the rest of Alexandria's non-Christian professionals and intellectuals. Sophia resumed hosting parties four years after Pappus' death, in 354, when Theon was fourteen. By this time the child had surpassed most of his teachers in his understanding of Euclid, Pythagoras, Epicurus, Ptolemy, Plato, and Aristotle and was beginning to study *The Enneads of Plotinus* with a seriousness of spiritual quest that Pappus had never shown. With a vast knowledge at his ready recall and his excellent abilities at several wind and string instruments, Theon became a valued contributor to and participant in these gatherings. Yet more than ever, as time went by, it was Sophia who drew the most interest. In her late forties, she retained much of her youthful beauty, but it was her grace and, foremost, her wit, that attracted so many acolytes. It was not an obtrusive wit. She was happier to listen than to speak. So much of her attractiveness to the people who attended was ineffable, since it resided in the underrated ability to listen with interest and understanding and intelligence communicated through expression, as effectively as with words. Yet it was her words, usually a short comment or an apt question, that would send men to their pens and paper to record for future reference and inflamed the regard in which her guests held her. Lyric poems were written about her and passed around among sympathetic people throughout the Empire. An invitation to her house became a highly valued honor and prize in the intellectual community of the city.

After Pappus' death, Sophia spent more and more time studying at the Serapeum, if only to try to keep up with Theon so that she could remain interesting to him as he grew in understanding. She attended lectures on philosophy and religious studies. She did not venture very far into what were for her the more arcane world of mathematics and geometry. Mostly, she read.

Homer was a particular favorite, but in that she had much company. She loved the adventures of the clever wanderer and the life force of the man Homer so sympathetically portrayed. But it was the *Iliad,* with its relentless march to an inevitable conclusion and its loving portrayals of humanity captured between the crushing forces of its own nature and divine will that proved Homer's eternal genius. She read other books of the Epic Cycle, including *Aethiopis* by Arctinus and *Cypria* by Stasinus, but they did not compare to Homer's work. Homer's world, with gods divine, malign and capricious, mankind's craft and nobility spent in pursuit of destructive and self-destructive ends, and ephemeral glory the highest purpose of life, was, to Sophia, as plausible an explanation of mankind's existence as any religion had achieved.

After Pappus' death she studied Latin, primarily so that she could read in the original Virgil's *Aeneid,* which Pappus had so often praised. Whether it was the fault of her limited ability with the language or the poem itself, she decided that it did not measure up to the works of Homer. Latin, she thought, was like working stone with chisel and mallet: there was weight and depth, but only spare beauty. Greek added brush and pigment, capable of so much more color and nuance.

Her opinion of Latin improved in 360, when she fell in love again, this time with a man who had been dead for 400 years. Titus Lucretius Carus' long poem, *The Nature of Things,* came to her as a revelation. Ostensibly a paean to the Roman goddess Venus, it was a frontal challenge on the power of the gods. Beginning with the story of Agamemnon's sacrifice of his daughter Iphigenia at the bidding of priests who claimed it was necessary to satisfy a god's blood lust, Lucretius pronounces that "if men but knew some fixed end to ills, they would be strong to withstand religions and the menacings of seers." He lamented that mankind, "lays miserably crushed before all eyes beneath religion." His solution is to look to nature. Rather than trying to find meaning in the minds of elusive and unseen gods, Lucretius advised men to try to see how nature works to understand the whys and wherefores of existence. He posits the existence of "procreant atoms," so small they cannot be seen and which can neither be created nor destroyed: "Once we know from nothing still nothing can be created, we shall know more clearly those elements from which alone all things are created and how created by no tool of the Gods." He proves the existence of these invisible particles by the movement of the winds and other natural phenomenon that cannot be explained except by the existence of substance that cannot be seen. The soul, no less than the body, consists of procreant atoms of their own nature, which, like the body's atoms, do not die with the death of their holder, but are ever moving, uniting and dissolving and uniting again. For the rest of her life, Sophia would read and reread Lucretius and wonder why he had not succeeded in chasing religion and superstition from the earth.

Because of Theon's teenage obsession with Plotinus, Sophia read *The Enneads*, Plotinus' lessons on his philosophy. The six *Enneads* consisted of fifty-four discussions on various topics, with each *Ennead* comprised of nine such discussions. Organized by Plotinus' student, Porphyry, from lessons taught by Plotinus, the discussions began with subjects related to the conduct of everyday life. By the final *Ennead*, the discussions center on the causes and principles of existence. For Plotinus, the world was not the deliberate creation of something out of nothing, but does prove the existence and absolute transcendence of the One. The Universe is the consequence of the One's existence. Emanations of the One include the divine mind, order, thought and will. Nature is a lower level of the divine soul. Below that is the human soul. It is through recognizing what is intrinsically good and beautiful that people can recognize the One, first in material things, then in its eternal forms. Plotinus, or at least Porphyry, required devotion to these teachings and concepts with the goal of attaining a sort of ecstatic union with the One. Plotinus' philosophy was called "Neo-Platonism," because Plotinus derived his thinking from Plato's *Republic* and *Timaeus* dialogues. She could see in the *Enneads* threads that entwined it with the Gnostic search for the Unknowable One through knowledge, wisdom and contemplation. She began to understand that Neo-Platonism was part of a broader rejection of the polytheism of the ancients in favor of a single god or, for the Neo-Platonists, single entity or existence whom they did not name "God". While reading the *Enneads* she again wondered why, more than thirty years earlier, Timaeus had convinced himself that she possessed some unique or special knowledge of these matters. All she experienced were nagging questions and doubts concerning all of the religions with which she was acquainted. She had taken the name Sophia, first in obedience to Timaeus and, later, as an act of defiance against Athanasius, but she was not, she knew, the Sophia whom Timaeus had sought.

On finishing the *Enneads*, Sophia made her way through Plato's *Republic* and the *Timaeus* dialogues in an attempt to see if she could discern the origins of Plotinus' discussions and conclusions. In the *Republic*, Sophia could see Plotinus' process, but not his result. Still, she was fascinated by how Plato, through the Socrates character, could introduce uncertainty into every confident and seemingly logical pronouncement of his companions. She thought that, if truth was their goal, every religion would be well served to have a Socrates among its leaders. She also liked Plato's attempt to outline the ideal form of government, one whose avowed purpose was to provide happiness to its citizens. This was far removed from Roman and local governments of her time. So taken with the *Republic* was Sophia that she purchased her own copy of it from a cypher house that, in 356, was still supplied with papyrus by Ankha and his sons.

After studying Plotinus and Plato, Sophia read several other religious texts but found little in which she placed any faith. She read Philostratus' book about Apollonius, a first century prophet whose birth was said to be divine, who taught that people should not be concerned about their earthly lives or material goods, who performed miracles, including raising the dead, who ascended into heaven after his death and was seen by at least one follower afterward. Instead of a Jew preaching in the remote regions of Galilee, Apollonius was a Greek polytheist who travelled throughout Cappadocia and Crete and Syria, but Sophia could not help but see the parallel to the life Christians now claimed for Jesus. She read a Greek translation of Mani's *Fundamental Epistle* and spoke to several who called themselves Manichaeans who described a cosmos in which the forces of good were in eternal conflict with the forces of evil. The Manichaeans' purpose on earth was to free the forces of light that were imprisoned by forces of darkness, which for the elect basically meant not doing anything to help themselves, not even sowing grain or picking fruit. They had to be kept alive by keepers whose only spiritual reward was the possibility of returning as one of the elect in a later life.

She read the *Septuagint*, the Greek translation of the Hebrew Torah, reported to have been commissioned by Pharaoh Ptolemy II. The stories of the creation, Moses' miracles, the Flood, Sodom and Gomorrah, and Jonah and the fish struck her as so ridiculous that only a fool could believe them. This thought contrasted with her observation that some of the wisest and most profound people of her acquaintance were practicing Jews.

Rather than providing enlightenment, the religious books she read were a sort of inoculation against established religion of any kind. She became more and more skeptical about all of it.

In 363, when she was fifty-six years old, she found reference to the existence of a collection of Gnostic texts that were purported to belong to the library. Acting on an urge that she did not bother to analyze, she decided that she must read them. It took her three months to discover their location, not in the library itself, but in a mostly forgotten warehouse where some of the books that had once belonged to the old Alexandrian Library had been stored after Diocletian's torching of the city, sixty-five years earlier. It took Sophia another three days of breathing dust and shifting about unorganized piles of scrolls and codices before she found the Gnostic collection, or most of it, in the eastern quarter of the building, under several hundred pounds of other manuscripts.

Some of the books, those written on scrolls, were almost 300 years old. Others were in folios and codices. Virtually all were written in Greek. There were some thirty texts in total, some fragments, some full treatises or gospels, some books of sayings and some instructional or liturgical guides. She had not read or translated a Gnostic text in over thirty years, yet almost by instinct or as if by gravitational pull, as she sat down with the Greek texts she prepared reeds and papyri and translated as she read. The information that they were Gnostic texts was not quite accurate. They consisted of a variety of texts written by a variety of people with a variety of beliefs for a variety of purposes. She saw little unity among many of the texts.

Some of the texts were "Sethian," meaning by Gnostics who believed that Seth was the first child of Adam and Eve and that Cain and Abel were the descendants of Yaldabaoth. There were Valentinian texts, one perhaps written by Valentinus himself, that taught that salvation came through knowledge of God. There were texts that revered Hermes, the Greek god responsible for guiding souls into the afterlife. In these texts, Hermes was reconstituted as an Egyptian divine teacher and guide. These texts, too, taught that salvation comes through wisdom and knowledge.

Despite their divergences, Sophia saw patterns in the text that she could not have discerned when, in her late teens and early twenties, she had read the earlier volumes. It seemed to her that what held the divergent strains of Gnostic thought together was the notion that the physical world we inhabit was at best an illusion and, at worst, a prison. In this light, attaining gnosis meant peeling away the layers of sight, sound, smell, touch and taste to attain an understanding of an existence independent of and superior to the everyday reality of the senses. The Gnostics sought an individual religious awareness that could not be experienced by following the rules of any religion, regardless of what those rules were. With this understanding, she saw Timaeus' quest in a brighter light. Sophia came to believe that by the time he found her in Antioch he had largely completed or abandoned his spiritual journey and that his mission with her was not a continuation of that journey, but a return to the world of the senses in which he was endeavoring to assure that the pathways to gnosis that he had explored would remain open to future generations. And, understanding this, she was saddened by the thought of what an abject failure she had been as his Sophia. Of course in believing this she was forgetting that he claimed to attained gnosis and to have entered the Pleroma only with his full engagement to the physical world.

By far Sophia's favorite of the "Gnostic" texts was named, simply, "*Thunder*." It was written by a woman who identified herself as Sophia and consisted of a series of contradictory statements concerning her nature and existence: "I am the honored and the scorned. I am the whore and the holy one. I am the wife and the virgin … I am the barren one and many are my sons and daughters … I am the bride and the groom … I am silence that is incomprehensible … I am the voice whose sounds are many … You who hate me, why do you love me? You who tell the truth about me, tell lies about me and you who have lied about me tell the truth about me ... I am judgment and I am pardon. I am sinless and the root of all sin ... I am perfect mind and perfect rest. I am the knowledge of my search and the discovery of all who seek me." To Sophia, this book came as close to how she felt about religion and faith as anything she had ever read. Every time you think you know something, the opposite appears as truth. Every nature contradicts itself. Kindness and cruelty, ignorance and knowledge, faith and doubt exist as companions in the human soul. Knowing not the contradictions themselves, but the existence of the contradictions was the beginning of understanding. When it came to the great mystery of existence it seemed that nothing was true without its opposite co-existing in truth with it.

It took Sophia over a year to translate the thirty or so texts. More than anything, the exercise took her back to her time with Timaeus, when Adama became Sophia. She thought of how Timaeus had changed her life and, in fact, liberated her from a predictable existence that would predictably end with her discharge from the brothel for a short afterlife on the streets, followed by an ignorant and ignoble death. He had given her a life richer and fuller than she could have ever expected. She was not the embodiment of wisdom, she was not the keeper of gnosis for the ages, but she was grateful to the odd man with stars for eyes that had rescued her. She was certain that she was not his Sophia, but he was hers.

When she was done, she had her translations bound and placed the codices on a shelf in her house. By accident, her copy of Plato's *Republic* was bound together with the Gnostic texts in one of the codices. She returned the originals to the Serapeum where they remained until that great temple was destroyed in 391.

For the next twenty-seven years she did not look at them again. From time to time she would think of them and remember the texts she had hidden in a cave in 330. In Alexandria she never came across anyone who identified himself as a Gnostic Christian. Their faith had vanished from the world. The books she had translated would stay in the jar and on her shelves. They were of no use to anybody living.

By his early twenties Theon had become a master at the Serapeum and was fast becoming one of the most renowned scholars of his day. He became known as "Theon of the Mouseion," referring to the temple of the Muses that had been an institution of learning adjacent to the library for 600 years. But the Mouseion, like the Library, had been repeatedly gutted over the centuries and, in 365, its remains had been washed away by a tsunami caused by an earthquake in Crete that devastated much of the Mediterranean coastline of the Roman Empire. The Empire would never fully recover. Alexandria was particularly vulnerable and was especially hard hit. The remnants of the Library and Mouseion were washed away. The remains of Cleopatra's royal palace and the Temple of Artemis on the Lochias peninsula fell off into the harbor. The Christians attributed the disaster to God's wrath against the Empire in retaliation for Emperor Julian's attempt to reinstate the pagan gods and suppress Christianity. But the timing was all wrong, since Julian had died in 363 and was succeeded by the devoutly Christian Emperor Jovian. Theon's association with the Mouseion came about because he often insisted in calling the Serapeum "the new Mouseion." By the fourth century, the word Mouseion had taken on a secondary meaning as a place of learning and its original association with the Greek Muses had been largely forgotten. In referring to the Serapeum as the new Mouseion, Theon was anticipating that the increasingly Christian Empire and city would find the designation less offensive than a temple named in honor of the Greek-Egyptian god Serapis.

His mother's relative wealth freed Theon from any concerns

about having to convert his knowledge into income and he flourished in his intellectual pursuits, which were many and diverse. In 362 he married a beautiful orphan who had been taken in and raised by a Roman governor named Flavius Itulimius and his wife. The wedding was attended by most of the city's dignitaries and by many citizens who came from other cities of the Empire at the invitation of Flavius. Among the most famous of the attendees, however, was Sophia herself. At fifty-five years old, Theon's mother remained beautiful. Any of her physical beauty that the years had stolen had been compensated for by grace and the wisdom for which she had become renowned. Only the bride, Bassilina, attracted more praise and attention.

Bassilina came to live with Theon and Sophia in the house on the Serapic Way. The first year of their marriage did not correspond to the most productive year of Theon's academic career. Sophia woke up to, went to sleep with and was serenaded by the sounds of their lovemaking. Sophia herself had had no lovers in the twelve years since Pappus died and had never experienced the insatiable lust that infused the entire household with the tender, comic, annoying, and prickly-sweet omni-presence of their love. Above all the petty annoyance she felt at times, Sophia was happy for her son and new daughter-in-law, but it made her think of her own, strange carnal career. From the ages of fourteen to seventeen she had a few dozen callers, some of whom believed they had fallen in love with her and many of whom believed they had brought her to ecstasy. But for Adama they were intruders. She felt pleasure at times, she remembered, but was always completely aware of the transactional nature of the relationship. There was never any love or real passion. Then there was Timaeus, for whom she felt a profound love and affection, but who seemed to drift away from her during each of the three times they made love. Toward Philippus she felt an abiding tenderness and desire to please. She was sure she did please him and the gratitude he showed pleased her in return. She expected no more.

Finally there was Pappus. With him all the studious concentration of the scholar was abandoned when he wrapped her in his arms. His kisses were as tender and gentle as a warm southern breeze in winter. His touch relayed back to her the excitement he felt. His eyes rarely closed and he looked at her with such devotion that the sexual climaxes that she experienced seemed inevitable from the start. Pappus did not stop with kisses and touches and loving gazes. He was an energetic lover, who explored all of her, body, mind and soul, in every way his inquisitive mind could imagine, always keen to pursue what pleased her and to abate anything that suggested otherwise. Kisses were not reserved for her mouth. He devoted time to every inch of her body, from her toes to the crest of her head. He would kiss and trace the scars on her back with his tongue. After he discovered that his tongue and lips on her vagina brought her particular pleasure, there was rarely a time that he did not devote at least fifteen minutes to the exercise, bringing her such intense pleasure that after three or four climaxes she would tell him that she did not think she could stand another without the pleasure bending over into pain. In the early years, when the time allowed, they would make love through the night, sometimes sleeping for fifteen or twenty minutes, then resuming. Hearing the sounds that emanated from Theon's room, Sophia knew that he and Bassilina had found together the kind of pleasure she had known with Pappus.

Six months into their marriage Bassilina was pregnant. She gave birth to a son, whom they named Epiphanius, which meant divine understanding. A year later, in 364 Bassilina died giving birth to a daughter. Theon never remarried, but devoted himself to his studies and the education of his children. He named his daughter Hypatia, after his mother.

As his father had, Epiphanius excelled at mathematics from an early age. By the age of eighteen he was helping his father with research and writing. Theon's interests were diverse and he published commentaries and treatises on many subjects, including careful elaborations on the works of Ptolemy and Euclid. He wrote original scientific works on optics and the astrolabe. Yet he was also interested in matters that modern readers might categorize as superstitious. He was interested in telling the future, divination. He sought divine truths in the many books of the Serapeum's library. Inspired by a conversation with his mother about books she had translated, Theon wrote books about Hermes Trismegistus (Thrice-Great Hermes) and mystic orphic oracles. He wrote a book entitled *On Signs and the Examination of Birds and the Croaking of Ravens.* He wrote one on the function of the star Sirius and the influence of planets at work in the annual flooding of the Nile. It was an uncertain age as Christian ascendency moved to blot out the Sun shining on all other intellectual endeavor. Theon was not alone in examining alternatives to Christianity in explaining what was, to him, a magical world where omens and suggestions of Platonic forms lay just beneath the patina of the visible. Yet characteristically, Theon went beyond what most others were capable of discerning, depositing gems of brilliant insight even among works that his mother described as utter nonsense.

As advanced as Theon and as promising as Epiphanius were, both were outdone by the beautiful and brilliant Hypatia. It seemed that she started life possessing all the learning and wisdom that took even the most accomplished scholar half a lifetime to accumulate. In face and form, by the time she was sixteen she was the cloned image of Sophia. By the age of twelve she was amazing her grandmother's guests with knowledge and observations far beyond her years. In addition to mathematics and geometry, she took special interest in astronomy, the movement of the spheres, in conic shapes, in the forces at work in the bending and refracting of light. In spiritual matters, she was devoted to and advanced the Neo-Platonists beliefs held by her father Theon.

By 391 A.D., at the age of twenty-seven she had been a master at the Serapeum for eight years and had a growing body of scholars who attended her lectures and, in many cases, sought her hand in marriage.

Chapter Thirty-Four

An Earthenware Jar

391 A.D. – Alexandria and Sheneset

Then the peoples will cry out with a great voice, saying, "Blessed is the soul of those men because they have known God with a knowledge of the truth! They shall live forever, because they have not been corrupted by their desire, along with the angels, nor have they accomplished the works of the powers, but they have stood in His presence in knowledge of God like light that has come forth from fire and blood."

The Apocalypse of Adam

On February 22, 391, Sophia turned eighty-four, still vital in mind and body. The physical beauty that had once been hers had not dissipated so much as been absorbed inward, concentrating into a light that shone upon and illuminated all around her. To celebrate her birthday Theon, Epiphanius and Hypatia invited everyone she knew, everyone still living who had ever attended her soirees. So many accepted the invitations that the location of the party had to be moved to the main hall of the Serapeum. Theon secured an enormous wooden and wicker chair with cushions for the guest of honor to sit upon throughout the evening. When the time came, Sophia refused to sit in it. "I am not a goddess or an empress," she said. She spent the evening circulating among the guests, occasionally resting on one of the granite benches along the perimeter of the hall.

The Serapeum was much changed of late. By 391 most of the pagan temples in Alexandria had been converted to Christian churches or simply destroyed altogether. Even the long closed tomb of Alexander the Great, including Alexander's bones, had been converted to Christianity and refashioned as the tomb of St. Mark the Evangelist. By virtue of the fact that hundreds of the brightest minds of the realm still came there to study and learn and many of the Empire's top administrators and advisors had studied there, the Serapeum had survived intact longer than most. But even the Serapeum was in danger. Although Serapis still graced the entrance, many of the interior statues of deities had been removed. All that remained were covered with drapes, awaiting their removal. Over the previous two years Emperor Theodosius had issued a series of decrees that, among other things, outlawed the worship of the old Roman and Egyptian gods. It was in no small measure a delayed reaction to the fact that, in 360, the last pagan emperor, Julian II, had attempted to reimpose Roman paganism as the official religion of the Empire. He had audaciously rescinded the annual stipends that Constantine had awarded the Christian bishops and had seized property that prior Emperors had given to the Church. After being killed in battle against the Persians (the Christians believed in answer to the prayers of Saint Basil of Caesarea) Julian's successors quickly returned to the Christian fold and began the process of removing the last vestiges, both physical and spiritual, of pagan worship. Under Theodosius, calendar dates that for centuries had been feast days for old gods had been changed into workdays. He had banned animal sacrifices much earlier in his reign. He prohibited haruspicy (the sacred examination of entrails) upon pain of death. To mark the beginning of the year 391 he had issued a decree that forbade anyone from entering any pagan temple "or rais[ing] his eyes to statues created by labor of man." With the other pagan temples in Alexandria having already been destroyed and converted into Christian churches, the masters of the Serapeum, including Theon, ordered the removal of all relics of other religions and were attempting to convert the temple into a secular school of learning.

Over two hundred people attended Sophia's birthday party,

some from as far away as Constantinople. With so much of the old world being ploughed under by the Christian tillers who ruled the realm, the celebration was a respite and, without any encouragement of or participation by Sophia, took on the feel of a pagan celebration, a Bacchanalia of sorts, with wine flowing freely and bands of musicians playing old Roman tunes and dancing breaking out here and there. The guests drifted in and out during the evening. Such had become her renown that many who had never attended her dinner parties and soirees sought and were given invitations to the party. Two of the most notable and surprising attendees were the most powerful religious and civilian authorities of Alexandria: Evagrius, the Prefect of Egypt, who solicited and obtained an invitation, and Bishop Theophilus, who arrived unexpectedly. As if they had coordinated their schedules, their visits did not overlap. Evagrius arrived early in the evening without entourage, dressed modestly in a manner that did not bring attention to his official capacity. He did not mingle with the other guests but seized an early opportunity when he found that the gathering around Sophia had diminished to only a few. He was a stout man in his late forties, with short hair framing a face that had been considered handsome before the added pounds jowled his cheeks. Approaching Sophia, he bowed slightly and asked if she recognized him.

"No, I am sorry, but I do not," she replied in the voice of a woman much younger than her years. "Have we met?"

"Perhaps not," Evagrius said, "but I have seen you before. But then, everyone knows about the famous Sophia."

"Please," Sophia said modestly.

"I am Evagrius, Prefect of Egypt. I am pleased to finally meet you."

Sophia now took a closer look at him, then corrected him. "Prefect of the Diocese of Egypt, I believe it is now called."

"Yes, you are correct."

"Even the governors now must have ecclesiastical titles, it

seems."

"We are a Christian Empire."

Sophia smiled. "Yes. And soon they will rename it the Christian Roman Empire or, if they lack all humility, the Holy Roman Empire, I suppose."

"I haven't heard that."

"Perhaps not. After all, it qualifies as neither Christian or Roman."

"Well."

"Certainly not holy."

"Well."

"What with Rome ruled by Valentinian and the lack of compassion shown by the Theodocian Decrees."

"Perhaps you should not defame the Emperor."

"I am an old woman. It has always been the prerogative of old women to say what they think."

"I suppose you are right. About the prerogatives of old women, I mean."

"Not that anybody ever listens to us."

Despite himself, Evagrius was smiling, which was the response Sophia was seeking. She suddenly held out her hand and said, "I am Sophia. I am pleased to meet you at last."

Taking the offered hand, Evagrius said, "You do not fall short of your reputation."

"You shouldn't listen to gossips," she replied.

"Or old women, either?"

"The same thing, often enough."

Evagrius reached into his tunic and removed a folded piece of paper. He held it, without offering it to her. "There is some truth to what you say about the Christians and the Empire, although if you turn gossip on this subject, I will deny I said that."

"You do not have to say it. Everybody knows it. All the old faiths banished! All the practices outlawed on pain of death! All the temples destroyed or turned to tombs or churches! So many books burned! So many thousands of years of knowledge lost! What folly."

"The Emperor would say that folly is what is being removed. All that is being destroyed is superstition."

"So that the Christian superstition is all that is left."

"But that is not superstition. That is the word of God as set down in the canon of the New Testament."

"Canon that was determined by Athanasius only a few years ago."

"Determined by the most sacred men of our faith. Athanasius was a great bishop."

"No doubt Athanasius was a great bishop. But he was not a good man."

"Are you saying that other books should have been included?"

"What I am saying is that the best way to recognize folly in our own lives is to laugh at those who came before us. If you get rid of all records of the old superstitions, how are you to recognize the same kind of error in the new ones?"

Evagrius frowned but said nothing. He shuffled uncomfortably on his feet, still holding on to the page he had removed from his tunic. Sophia tried to ease his discomfort.

"Come now, Prefect. Surely you did not come here to discuss theology with me. You must have heard I am a great heretic."

Evagrius cleared his throat. "Ah, no. I had not heard that. But I did not come to discuss theology with you either. Except to say, that just as Bishop Theophilus has been busy shutting down temples, his priests have been going through the official records of Roman Rule in Alexandria and removing entries that tend to cast the church in a bad light. I count myself a Christian, but I am uncomfortable with destroying records of past times."

"We share that in common," Sophia said.

"Yes. So, I have been going through some of the records and when I can I remove something that has been culled for the fire and send it away to family in Constantinople or give it away to someone who may have an interest in some particular report and, therefore, might preserve it, for a time at least."

"Not a very effective process, I shouldn't think."

"No, probably not. But I came across a report that might be of some interest to you and I decided to come here tonight to give it to you." He reached the page out to her. Sophia paused before taking it. She had no doubt that it was an account of the Paneum incident sixty-one years earlier. She recalled everything about that time and was not sure she wanted to read the official account out of fear it would contradict her memory. Slowly, she reached out her hand and took the offered page. After looking at it a few seconds she handed it back and said, "My sight is not what it once was. Could you read it to me?"

"I have trouble seeing the words in this light as well," Evagrius said. "That is what scribes are for."

Sophia called her granddaughter Hypatia over to her. She came, as she almost always did, in the fore of a small cadre of young admirers. "Yes, Gya-gya?" she said.

"This is Evagrius, Prefect of the Diocese of Egypt. Bow to him in the appropriate manner."

Hypatia bowed her head slightly and smiled at Evagrius. The smile, as she knew it would, compensated for any deficiency in obeisance. Hypatia was nearly as beautiful as her grandmother had been sixty-five years earlier, when she was worshiped as a goddess of Egypt. In face, form, height and grace, Hypatia could have been Sophia's twin, adjusting for age. The men who had followed her took a step or two back to avoid any danger of being introduced to the Prefect.

"Hypatia, we need you to read this page to us. It is from the official Roman records of this city."

"Certainly, Gya-gya," Hypatia said, and began reading.

"'22 February 1065.' That is, what, 311 of the Christian era?"

Sophia nodded and thought, *So it is not the Paneum incident. I wonder what it could be.* Hypatia read on.

"Report by Titus Proculus, Legion Praefect, Alexandria.

"The Emperors' order to end the persecution of Christians seems to have loosened some Christians to take vengeance upon some of the more vulnerable of the non-Christian community. Today a group of Christians fell upon and began stoning a small group of scholars as they were leaving the Serapeum. Most were able to flee, but two were killed, a young man and his wife. His name was Philatreas, hers was Minerva. Two men of the Serapeum reported that Philatreas was from Pergamon in Anatolia and had come to Alexandria to study philosophy. Both bodies were stoned severely and both were dead before the legionaries arrived. As they were removing their bodies, a girl child, three or four years of age, sprang up from under the body of her mother and fled. The guards were not quick enough to grab her and she has been lost for now. It appears that the father and mother fell upon the girl to protect her from the stones and, unfortunately, gave their lives in the effort. The men from the Serapeum said they believed the child was named Hypatia. Legion posts have been put on notice that if they find her they are to seize her because there are those among the students who would take her in and raise her. With so many orphans these days there is little likelihood of her being found. The perpetrators of the murders could not be identified. This is the third instance this month of Christians killing those they call pagans."

When Hypatia finished reading she looked at her grandmother, who looked back through tear-filled eyes.

"I know a little of your story," Evagrius said. "I know you grew up an orphan, without home and that your name was Hypatia. When I read this I thought it might refer to you and your parents. The time is about right, I think. In any case, this page was removed by Theophilus' priest and is to be destroyed.

If you want it, it is yours."

Sophia took the page from Hypatia's hands and for several minutes was lost in musing. Whether she thanked or even said goodbye to Evagrius, she could not remember, but by the time she thought to do so, he was gone. At eighty-four she had never known who her mother and father were or where she had come from. Was this them? At the dawn of awareness, as far back as she could remember, she knew four things about herself: she was an orphan, her name was Hypatia, she was five years old, and her birthday was February 22. The report was dated February 22, 311. Was that her fourth birthday? Or was the date of the event planted in her mind so deeply that it was remembered not as the day her parents were killed, but as the day of her birth? She had no recollection of her parents being attacked or killed. Hypatia's reading of the report did not trigger any such memory. Could it be that the couple from Pergamon were not her parents and the child was some other Hypatia? There was no way of knowing. There were only possibilities and probabilities. She decided to accept the account as a report on the death of her parents. She accepted it on faith, without certainty, without knowing. Having faith gave her parents. Philatreas and Minerva. Dad and Mom.

Her musings were broken by Hypatia, who had left her side and now returned with another man in his middle forties. This one was thin and bearded and dressed unmistakably in the dingy white robes of a scholar. "Gya-gya," Hypatia said, "this is Eunapius of Sardis. He has asked to be introduced to you. He has brought you a gift."

Socially awkward, Eunapius began by reintroducing himself. He explained that he had been in Alexandria for three months. "I am at work on a great book," he said immodestly. "'*The Lives of the Philosophers and Sophists*,' I call it. To carry on the work of Sotion and Porphyry. Porphyry of Tyre, although he died only a hundred years ago, ended his work with Plato and Sotion of Alexandria, who lived nearly five hundred years ago. Nobody has written of the lives of the philosophers and sophists who lived between Sotion and Porphyry, as their number and many sidedness deserves. Oh, there was Philostratus of Lemnos, I suppose, but his work is at best superficial indeed and even he could go up until only the middle of the last century because he died then. So, I have been gadding about in all the old haunts where I might learn something of the great thinkers whose lives have not been sketched and who might fall into undeserved obscurity. Men like Euphrates of Egypt and Dio of Bithynia and many others. Even divine Plutarch, who wrote many lives himself, has not had his life written. So, I am about correcting these omissions and my work brings me to Alexandria, where many great philosophers have lived, Antoninus among them and your very son Theon. And so I have come here to work and to read and to discuss what is known about the lives of these gods among us and everyone I speak with mentions one name above all others as one worthy of being immortalized in verse as foremost in thought and that one name is Sophia. 'Sophia,' I hear it everywhere. And I had not heard of her, let alone met her, although I did meet the great Sosipatra of Ephesus, whose beauty was exceeded only by her wisdom. And here you are, in Alexandria, and still alive, but you do not count yourself a philosopher, I think?"

Not since Nabwenenef had Sophia heard anyone speak so fast and long without taking a breath. When he paused she did not immediately realize that he had hung a question on the end of his digression. He repeated it. "You do not count yourself a philosopher, do you?"

"I do love wisdom," she said, "but I have found so little and retained even less. So, no, I do not."

"No, I did not presume so, although with what you have said being so profound and befuddling, if you were to call yourself a philosopher I would not argue. But you have no school, I think, that you claim or that claims you and no students and nothing written and you have performed no miracles of which I have heard and do not claim to divine the future or to see events occurring in distant lands, so I think you must be left out of the great book I am writing, although some day, I am sure, someone will write a great book about you. But for now, what I have done is to collect your sayings. Everyone I talk with in Alexandria has one or more than one, it seems, and has been quite willing to share them with me so I have written them down. And when I heard there was to be a celebration for your birthday and that you would be in attendance and that it was to occur just at this time when I happened to be in Alexandria, I counted my good fortune and secured an invitation from your lovely granddaughter, who may be more beautiful than Sosipatra, I think, and I have had a book made, only a slim codex, but profound, such that I had two hundred of them made, and the demand overran the subscription, so the cost is paid for, so do not worry about the expense, and I have come here to present one to you and I would be honored if you would accept it from, as it were, an admirer, on the occasion of your eighty-fourth year."

Eunapius fell into sudden silence and his right arm extended toward Sophia a slim codex bound in green leather. Engraved on the cover were the words *Η σοφία της Σοφίας – The Sophia (Wisdom) of Sophia.* Sophia took the book from Eunapius' outstretched hand. She opened it and turned the pages, glancing at the words without reading. To Eunapius she said, "It is appropriately thin." Then, smiling, "This is unexpected, but I am sure that my words have no more wisdom in them than those of anyone else here tonight."

"The others here have a higher opinion of them, I assure you," Eunapius said. "To what do you attribute that?"

"I was once beautiful," Sophia replied.

Sophia spent much of the evening with Arsinoe, Ankha's widow. Ankha died in 370 at the age of seventy-seven and had left a prosperous trade transport business to his sons. The children had become Christians, but Arsinoe stubbornly adhered to the cult of Serapis. She was three years younger than Sophia and they had remained close since that day in the Serapeum when she commanded Ankha to dance. They spoke of children, grandchildren and, in Arsinoe's case, a great grandson. Sophia said she believed that both John, who had passed, and Maggie, had grandchildren, which made her a great grandmother, but she never saw them. Throughout much of the evening they stood together, talking and smiling, bestowing an aged gentility to the celebration, forming a nucleus while the rest of the celebrants merged and separated and merged again into ever changing clusters, like molecules forming and dissolving in agar as different agents in the form of personalities were added to or removed from the mix.

About two hours into the party, Sophia's eyes fell upon an aged man entering the temple and proceeding with the aid of a cane in her direction. He was accompanied by a younger man and, as he approached, she saw that he had a withered hand that was drawn up toward his chest, supporting some green cloth that she presumed to be a cloak. In their dress and manner, the old and young man were obviously different than the rest of the party. They were tradesmen, not merchants or intellectuals. The little hair that remained on the old man's head was white and his face was withered, but well before he arrived at where she stood Sophia recognized him as John of Jerusalem.

Breaking away from Arsinoe, she rushed toward him, saying excitedly, "John, John, how good of you to come. How unexpected. How many times have I thought of you?" The commotion stilled the cacophony of voices and instruments as the current molecular groups turned to see what had generated so much excitement in the heart of the guest of honor.

John was moving so slowly that Sophia reached him when he was still near the entrance of the great hall. By now all other conversation had stopped. Nobody alive at the time could remember Sophia acting with such excitement or showing so much deference as John's arrival prompted. The rest of the group craned to hear and see what or who had caused this reaction, this utter lack of the restraint that Sophia always displayed.

"Oh, John," Sophia said when she reached the old man, "my celebration is complete. All my wishes are fulfilled." She embraced him with such vigor that she knocked the cane from his good hand and it fell to the floor. The young man he was with bent over to pick it up. As he did so, John spoke.

"I did not think you would remember me, let alone recognize me. We have seen each other only three times, the last time over sixty years ago. Added together, we have spent less than a full day in each other's company. It is I who am overwhelmed and fulfilled." His voice cracked with age and feebleness. When Sophia freed him from her embrace, he staggered and she held him up as the younger man replaced the cane in his good hand. Sophia led him to the enormous chair that she had refused to sit in. Once he was seated, he introduced his grandson to her. His name was Luke. He then told Luke to find other company because he had something he wanted to say to Sophia in private. When Luke departed, John repeated his request for an explanation of Sophia's reaction to seeing him.

"I told you in this very room sixty-one years ago what your family meant to me. I told you that I had named my first born after your sister and my first son after you. Are you really so surprised then, that I would rejoice upon seeing you after so long a time?"

"But how did you recognize me? We are so changed."

"Are you saying you do not recognize me, John?"

"No. I recognize you, sure enough," John said. "But, then, how could I not? You are Sophia. You are the keeper of gnosis for the ages. You were the angel of my youth. I dare say I thought you were the goddess herself, come to Earth. That is what Bishop Timaeus thought as well. You are old now, it is true. But I see you there, I see the goddess lurking beneath the disguise of age."

"I think in your heart you know better than that?"

"I know what I see."

"Do you still keep to the old ways, then?"

"In my heart I do, but we are all Catholics now. Luke is especially devout. We follow what is orthodox and when orthodoxy changes, we follow that too. It is easier."

"I have found shelter from that here, at the Serapeum."

"When I was last here, that was in doubt. We feared for your life."

"Yes, I bit the snake and the snake shrank back into his nest. I was fortunate to have so many friends."

John smiled, then began to cough. Sophia had water brought to him and eventually the cough subsided.

"You are frail, John," Sophia said. "You should not have come. You could have summoned me and I would have journeyed to you."

"I had to come," John replied. "In the sixty-one years since that day on the Paneum I have thought many times about what you did, what that all meant. You weren't just challenging an evil and powerful man, you were exposing his lack of power, his lack of grace, his lack of authority, his absence of holiness."

"Was I?" Sophia asked. "I thought I was just tired of running."

"I think you know better. I think you knew how powerful a single voice could be."

"People have always projected upon me more power than I actually possess."

"Perhaps. But whether you intended it or not, what you did meant all that to me. I am an avowed Christian now, it is true. But I follow the real Christ, the Christ Timaeus taught, Christ the teacher, not Christ the God. What good is Christ the God? You taught me that."

"Did I? I had no idea."

"You did, and I think you know you did. You taught us all."

"John."

"And so I had to come. To repay my debt to you. You see, I have kept this vesta since that day." With his good hand, from under the withered one, he drew the green cloth and held it out to her. "This vesta, which I wore on that day. How many times have I looked at it? How many times have I put it on over the years? And each time I think of you. I think of Sophia. I think of resistance to smug and pious authority. And now that my life is nearly over, I had to come to present it to you, to return it to you and to thank you for all you have meant to me, all the strength you have given me, all the strength you give me still, now, at the end of life."

As John spoke, others in the room gradually became aware that something significant was happening and craned to listen in on the conversation. Most of them had heard something about what had happened sixty-one years before, that Sophia had accused the late Bishop Athanasius of a list of crimes and he had failed to deny them. Few knew the details or the full context, but they knew about what happened in a vague, approximate manner, including that Sophia had worn a green vest. The vest had become a symbol of resistance to church authority, but even that fact had developed numerous interpretations about its purpose and origin. From his chair John reached his outstretched left arm holding the vest out toward Sophia. Chants of "put it on, put it on," arose from the celebrants. With the help of Theon she slipped the vesta on over her stola. The group began to snap their fingers, then to cheer. John attempted to rise to join in, but his knees gave way and he sank back into the oversized chair.

Just then Pope Theophilus entered the hall, leading a procession of priests and black robed monks, thirty or so in number. They swept in like conquerors, surveying the hall with profound disgust, not pausing for anyone in their path to step aside, but moving forward like a battering ram until they reached the center of the room where John sat in the great chair and Sophia stood in her green vesta.

Theophilus was tall and thin and wore long, overlapping robes, red on white and embroidered with gold. An ornate cross hung from his neck and on his head he wore a short, tight fitting white cap pressed down to his forehead. His beard was full and long, but he shaved a few inches beneath his mouth, leaving a gap between his mustache and chin whiskers. In his great work, *The Decline and Fall of the Roman Empire*, Edward Gibbon wrote that Theophilus was, "...the perpetual enemy of peace and virtue, a bold, bad man, whose hands were alternately polluted with gold and with blood."

As Theophilus spoke, his voice, despite his thin frame, was deep and loud.

"We have just come from clearing out the last icons and fixtures of the Tychaeon here in the sacred city of Alexandria. All temples to the Greek and Roman gods must be destroyed. The gold and silver icons will be melted down in service to the holy church of the Christ. The temple stone will be smashed. We have come here having heard there was to be a celebration in honor of a heretic who once was famous. And we are concerned that a pagan temple was chosen as the site of this celebration. So we have come to assure ourselves that this is no longer a temple to the pagan gods. Prefect Evagrius has assured us it is not, but how can a temple dedicated to a false god of Egypt be cleansed of its evil without the presence of a cross?"

Theophilus paused to look around. No statues of gods were visible but he noticed in the center of the room an old man was seated on an enormous chair. He made a gesture with his right arm and several monks in his entourage spread out and headed toward the sides of the great hall. Theophilus pointed at John seated in the chair and said, "What kind of ceremony is this? Who sits on the temple throne as if to symbolize a pagan god?" John attempted to rise but stumbled and sat back heavily in the chair.

"Behold," Theophilus said, "the very site of the cross causes the false god's knees to buckle."

"He is Christian, Bishop. I am Sophia, your heretic. I gave him the chair because he is lame and has travelled a great distance."

Theophilus examined the old woman who stood before him. The sight of her made him want to strike her down. She was the very symbol of paganism, he thought to himself, weak and old. He turned toward the oldest monk in his company, one who appeared even older than Sophia. The old monk nodded his head and whispered something in Theophilus' ear. Theophilus nodded, then said, "You say he's a Christian?"

"Yes," Sophia replied.

"Then he will have no objection to kissing the ring of his bishop." Theophilus extended his left hand toward John. This time, with great effort, John rose, steadied himself and, with Luke's help, went down on both knees. He leaned his face forward and kissed the offered ring. Luke helped John rise again and he remained standing.

"You should be ashamed of yourself," Sophia said. "That was an act of cruelty."

"As a heretic, you cannot understand the healing power of God's grace," Theophilus said. "See, he stands now when before he could not." Theophilus pointed at the green vesta Sophia was wearing. "Old Macarius here tells me that you are wearing the green vesta of defiance to God. When you die, and it will be soon, old woman, it will be the first thing to burst into flames in Hell."

"Oh," Sophia asked, "does our clothing now make it to the afterlife? I will have to dress more carefully now that my time is short."

Theon, watching, recognized the mood his mother was in. He had seen it many times before. He had seen it escalate from the time Theophilus entered the room, exacerbated, no doubt, by memories triggered by the old man from Jerusalem's arrival. He now stepped forward to intervene. Theophilus was a powerful and a dangerous man. He was to be coddled and mollified, not teased and ridiculed.

"Bishop Theophilus," Theon said. "Please excuse my mother, her jokes are sometimes inappropriate. But I can assure you, as a master of the Serapeum, this is no longer a place of worship. The old idols are in the process of being removed, in compliance with the Emperor's edicts. Most are already gone. The remaining ones are covered. We are a school of learning now. Nothing more."

"This place," Theophilus said, "this place is a temple. If it is not to be a temple to the Lord, it must be destroyed."

Theon frowned. "Surely, Bishop, there is a place for institutions of learning. We house one of the great libraries of the world here. Surely there is a place for that."

"The books can add nothing to our knowledge. If what they contain confirms scripture, they are not necessary. If what they contain disagrees with scripture, they are heretical. Either way, they must be destroyed."

Hypatia now entered the discussion. "Bishop Theophilus," Hypatia said, "you cannot be as ignorant as you sounded just now. Clement of Alexandria, Justin Martyr, and Origen, among many other church fathers found wisdom in the philosophy of Plato and the Stoics. Certainly there is something to be learned that is useful to the Church."

Theophilus turned back toward old Macarius the Younger and said, "These pagan women dare to speak to your bishop! Such impudence! Listen to them talk, these pagans. Their hope is gone. Without Christ there is no hope. The old world is to be cleansed in the blood of the lamb. The kingdom of heaven is at hand. His way must be prepared. The old temples must be destroyed."

"We are in compliance with Emperor Theodosius' Edicts," Theon said with a bit of defiance slipping into his voice. "This is not a pagan temple."

"We will see."

Sophia, who had been biting her tongue, now spoke. "Bishop

Theophilus," she said. "Wherever you pursue it, evil will always elude you."

Theophilus sneered. "Are you saying I move too slowly to catch my quarry?"

"Not at all," Sophia said. "It is only that your decisions concerning every important matter in this world are so infallibly wrong, that your chances of identifying evil are nonexistent."

Suddenly, a loud crack and snap was heard coming from one of the alcoves in the south of the hall. All eyes turned toward the sound and saw the white drapery that had been covering the chryselephantine statue of Priapus, a Greek fertility god, fall to the ground. A monk had separated Priapus' oversized penis and, with another monk, struggled to carry the four foot long ivory member toward Theophilus.

Theophilus turned back toward Theon and said, "This proves you lie. We have what we need."

Sophia replied, "I would not think a celibate would need any such thing at all."

Theophilus said no more. He and the other monks followed in a procession behind the monks with the severed penis, who were holding it aloft, triumphantly, and carrying it out of the Serapeum.

The Christian mob aided by the Roman legion laid siege to the Serapeum the day after Sophia's eighty-fourth birthday. It was overrun within three days and was destroyed over the course of the following two months. Theon had urged caution coupled with a written appeal to the Emperor. He was allowed to pen the letter and pay for its delivery to Constantinople by fast ship, but others of the Serapeum plotted a more aggressive defense. Among these were Ammonius, priest of Thoth, Helladius, priest of Ammon-Ra, Olympius, the last priest of Serapis, the twenty-one-year old Claudian, future court poet in Rome, and the poet Palladas, famous for wry epigrams from the point of view of a bemused pagan living in increasingly Christian times. These men became the leaders of several young scholars who volunteered in defense of the Serapeum or, as they saw it, in defense of knowledge.

The morning following Sophia's party, approximately sixty pagans and non-sectarians fled into the Serapeum to escape escalating violence directed at them by roving bands of Nitrian monks who were parading through the city holding aloft Priapus' ivory cock and attacking anyone not wearing a cross. By noon the monks and other Christians had surrounded the building and any pagans who attempted to enter thereafter were severely beaten, sometimes fatally. Theophilus made frequent visits to the front to urge the Christians to fear not the pagans because the kingdom of heaven awaited them. Theophilus also petitioned Evagrius, the Diocese Praefect, to send out the legion to enforce Theodosius' edicts against pagan temples. Like Theon, he wrote to solicit Theodosius' intervention.

The defenders of the Serapeum erected barricades and, when there was a lull in the Christians' stone throwing, would rush out into the outskirts of the crowd, throwing back the stones that had been thrown at them, seizing any vulnerable strays among the crowd, and dragging them back into the temple. They would make their Christian captives sacrifice to the de-membered Priapus and other remaining, now undraped gods. Those that refused were beaten and thrown into the catacombs. Within a week, Emperor Theodosius wrote his reply to the letters sent by Theon and Theophilus. Theodosius' orders were that the pagans inside the Serapeum were to be given pardon, but that the temple itself was to be destroyed. By the time Theodosius' orders were received, they were moot. The fighting was over. Evagrius had sent in the legion. A legionary had climbed the pedestal of Serapis and hacked at his head. After three blows, the head came off and it crashed to the ground. After 650 years, the citizens of Alexandria discovered that Serapis was not made of solid stone, as all had presumed, but of a clever and durable composite, framed with wood, that broke rather easily under the sword and axe. It took the mob less than a day to finish disassembling the god. With the legionaries' support, others from the mob rushed into the building, killing several of the defenders, stealing everything they did not destroy and setting fire to many of the books of the library. Eunapius' account states that the Christian mob, "fought so strenuously against the statues and votive offerings that they not only conquered but stole them as well, and their only military tactics were to ensure that the thieves should escape detection." When it was over, Bishop Theophilus climbed upon Serapis' pedestal and addressed the triumphant crowd. Christ made might and Christ made right. The old gods have fallen. The kingdom of God has come to Alexandria and, soon, to the entire world.

Theon was among the defenders who were killed, ripped limb from limb by frenzied invaders. John died of a heart attack on his way home to Jerusalem.

Sophia, so vital on February 22, 391, was shaken one week later. Her beloved son Theon was dead. Her grandson Epiphanius had fled the city. The Serapeum, the 650 year old symbol of Alexandria, was being taken apart blow by mattock blow. Most of its scrolls and codices were reduced to smoldering ash and charcoal. Her world was upended. Her faith in life itself shaken.

Hypatia stayed with her grandmother at the home on the Serapic Way during the siege. Although, at twenty-seven, she was a confirmed Neo-Platonist, Christianity as a belief system, independent of the actions of Theophilus, the Nitrian monks and the mob, did not offend her. She had several Christians among her students and as long as they attended to their lessons in mathematics, geometry and astronomy, she abided their occasional insistence that their God could bend the rules of nature at his whim. She hoped that this disturbance, like so many before it, would subside and leave Alexandria more or less how it had been. Above all else, she wanted to be left alone to study and teach.

After the destruction of the Serapeum and the death of Theon, Hypatia's father, everything changed. For a time they worried that Theophilus would turn the attention of the mob to their house, which had been a well-known pagan gathering place for many years. After the arrival of Emperor Theodosius' letter, which had commanded that pardon be given to the pagans, Theophilus sent the Nitrian monks back into the desert and urged the celebrating mob to disburse and return to their jobs. Sophia and Hypatia were allowed to claim Theon's body and lay it to rest in the catacombs beside Pappus, his father. A new Praefect was sent to replace the ineffective Evagrius. Upon her petition to Poethus, the new Praefect, and with Theophilus' assent, Hypatia was allowed to bring to her house any surviving scrolls and codices from the Serapeum and the warehouses, provided she allowed periodic inspections to assure that heretical texts were not among them. In the following years, with the wealth she inherited from her grandmother, she was able to procure many additional important texts in her several fields of inquiry. Hypatia's plan was to set up a school in her grandmother's house and try to preserve as much of the intellectual tradition of Alexandria as she could.

When Sophia learned of the conditions set upon Hypatia's plans, she thought immediately of the thirty or so Gnostic texts she had translated and bound over twenty-five years earlier. Her first thought was to destroy them so that Hypatia could carry on as she planned. But she could not bring herself to do this. She thought, instead, of Timaeus and of how all he taught and believed was now thoroughly gone from the Earth. Everything except her, her and these books. And so Sophia resolved, at the age of eighty-four, to hazard a dangerous journey back to Sheneset, to try to find the cave marked by the Egyptian face rock, to unite these texts with their siblings. She knew the plan was irrational, that she likely could not find the same cave, sixty-one years after she had last been there. She knew that even if she could find it and succeeded in placing these books with the others, it was a senseless thing to do since there was no reasonable hope that the texts would be found before turning into dust. She asked herself what the difference was between putting the books in a cave in the desert to never be found and simply destroying them in the comfort of Alexandria. She knew that at her age, she might not even be able to survive the journey to Sheneset or return from it if she did. Hypatia pleaded with her not to go. But at night Sophia could again hear Timaeus' voice, telling the gathering in Jerusalem that she, Hypatia, Adama, Sophia, that she was the keeper of gnosis for the ages and she knew she had to try. Timaeus had made her life possible. It had been a good life, a long life, filled with the love of husbands and children and grandchildren and many, many friends. All because of Timaeus' unexplainable conviction that she was something that she knew she was not. John had spoken of his debt to her. How much greater was her debt to Timaeus? She needed to repay that faith, that debt with this act, this sacrifice. Perhaps the books would never be found. Perhaps Timaeus' faith and beliefs would be forgotten. All that it was within her power to do was to try. She would try, for Timaeus' sake, to be the keeper of gnosis for the ages.

She left Alexandria for the last time in early April, 391. To guide and protect her, she hired a young pagan named Maecius who worked for Ankha's family and knew the routes along the Nile. When Hypatia realized that her grandmother was determined to undertake the journey, she insisted on going with her. Sophia refused to allow it. "Your work is here, in Alexandria," Sophia said. "Your work is the future. Mine is the past. Let us both do our best with what we are given to do."

"But Gya-gya," Hypatia replied, "you are acting on a baseless faith, the very thing you have always ridiculed."

"Sometimes baseless faith is the only thing that makes sense. It has come to that for me. It is not that I believe that any good can come of this. It is the matter of a debt I owe to someone I once loved, a debt that must be repaid."

Sophia enjoyed a splendid evening with Hypatia the night before her departure. They had just received word from Epiphanius that he had escaped the city and was heading toward Greece, the birthplace of modern philosophy, where he would try to carry on. Sophia forbade Hypatia from mentioning the upcoming journey and, with Sophia's encouragement, Hypatia expounded excitedly until midnight about her plans to teach in the house on the Serapic Way. They drank too much wine and Sophia ended up telling Hypatia stories of her youth, from the brothel in Antioch, to the journeys with Timaeus, to life in Sheneset, of Senmonthis and Beset and Pachome and Philippus, whom, she confided, she loved the most. She told of the strange month that she had been worshiped as Hathor by the ridiculous priest Nabwenenef. She showed Hypatia an aged copy of her Katagoso and told her how a crowd of forty thousand had protected her when she stood up to Athanasius. Hypatia laughed and cried at the stories and for the first time in her life saw the full person who was her grandmother and thought for the first time that for all of her own accomplishments and renown, for all the fame won by her father Theon and grandfather Pappus, the old woman she called Gyagya was truly the most extraordinary person she had ever known. Before she departed in the morning, Sophia signed everything she owned over to her granddaughter, her namesake, Hypatia.

Sophia and Maecius travelled south by ploion hellenikon. Tacking and stroking against the rising waters of the Nile, the journey took two weeks, but was safer and more comfortable than traveling by land would have been. Sophia had packed the codices into two leather bags that could be slung over the back of an ass and had put the bags in the bottom of a large clothing trunk. To the texts she had translated twenty-seven years earlier, Sophia added the slim, green codex that Eunapius had given her. With all that had happened since that night, she had never read it. She brought with her two solidi changed into nummi, folli, and siliqua.

As the boat struggled its way against the current, hanging close to the marshlands along the shore, Sophia watched the landscape. She saw many spoon billed ibises wading atop the croplands that would reemerge as the water receded. She saw crocodiles waiting for their dinner to come to them. As they proceeded further south, she saw the nostrils of hippopotami peeking out from the green and brown effluvium. She could feel the Nile's age, its timelessness, how it suffered men to profit or die from its existence and habits with complete indifference. She could almost feel the presence of the Egyptian gods that had grown organically from the river's existence, its annual rituals of flood and drought. Those gods made sense to the ancients. They explained the world in tangible ways that the Unknowable One of the Gnostics or the adaptable god of the Christians never could. The Egyptian world had fallen and the Roman world was falling apart. Christianity, like a fungal growth on a rotting trunk, was replacing as it consumed the remains of the Empire. Perhaps it was inevitable that the old gods had fallen into disrepute. But they satisfied the Egyptian's need for explanation better than an imported god ever could.

Maecius was a good companion on the river. He was in his middle twenties and single and spoke with all the certainty and confidence of his age. He had made the journey many times, he told Sophia. There was nothing to worry about with him as her guide. He would get her to her destination without fail. At stops along the way they would disembark to stretch their legs and Maecius would amble a little away from her so that he could say things that he found amusing to the young women who passed by. He imagined himself clever enough and Sophia old enough that she would not understand the game he was playing.

They disembarked from the boat on the Chenoboskion side of the Nile. Sophia thought about trying to find the old house she had rented from Cannus when she first arrived there in the summer of 325, but decided to save her energy for what lay ahead. They spent the night in an inn and travelled by barge the next day to Sheneset. It troubled Sophia only a little that Maecius seemed unaware of how to go about getting from the west bank of the river to the east.

In Sheneset they checked into an inn and purchased an ass and several water jars and laid by provisions for their journey into the desert. Maecius appeared confused about the reasons for such preparations, but Sophia was excited at the prospect of the morrow.

Sheneset was no longer the somnambulant village she remembered. It had grown to accommodate the many pilgrims who came to spend one, two or four month sabbaticals with the monks of the Pachomian Monasteries. Shops now lined the street that ran along the Nile, selling penitence in the form of habits and robes and incense, blest in advance by the monks.

Sophia roused Maecius before dawn the next morning. He awoke in a surly mood and sharply asked why they had to rise so early.

"We are headed up into the red land. It will be hot. Best to get started early."

"The red land? Why are we going there?"

Sophia sighed. She left him in the room while she drew water into the water jars, packed enough food for three days and loaded the food and the bags with the books onto the ass. She returned to find Maecius asleep again. "We must go now," she said and pulled back his blanket. A huge erection greeted her.

Maecius was unabashed, saying, "I'll bet you never saw one like that."

"It has been a while," Sophia replied. "Get dressed. The donkey awaits. We must go."

While stars still filled the sky they passed the street where the little church made from Cyprus wood and the mud, brick and timber house of Father James once stood. There were enough lamps lit from within for Sophia to see that the church had been replaced with a twelve-pillar basilica made of glass and limestone and the little house had given way to a spacious rectory with adjacent school and convent. The size and grandeur of the buildings attested to the growing strength of Christianity, even at the edges of the weakening Empire.

As they passed through the black land of the fertile valley they stirred up slumbering mosquitoes that swarmed about, biting them on every uncovered inch of their face and hands and through the clothing of covered limbs. Maecius swatted and griped while Sophia drew her hands into her sleeves and covered all but her eyes with a scarf.

By the time Sophia saw Homer's rosy fingered dawn they were in the red land of the desert, ascending into the cliff lands on narrow paths cut by centuries of wanderers and millennia of winds. For Sophia, it was the same landscape she remembered and yet everything had changed. She travelled in the direction she remembered, occasionally thinking she recognized a rock, a cliff or a cave, but never being sure. As they rose into the high ground of the cliffs the sun rose in the sky, covering the travelers in intemperate waves of heat. With the mosquitoes gone, Maecius complained of the sun, the sand, the terrain and the smell of the ass. He drank too frequently of the water and thrice attempted to mount the already overladen ass. Well before they reached the high terrain that Sophia recognized as near the cave for which she was searching he had begun to demand more payment, saying it was a far harder job than the one to which he had subscribed. Sophia paid him what she had left on her person, knowing that most of what she brought remained at the inn in her clothing chest.

The cave was so changed that they circled around it twice before Sophia recognized it. The distinctive needle rock had been dulled to a blunt phallus. There was no face on the boulder that had fallen down in front of the cave. But when Sophia entered the narrow entrance she immediately stumbled upon the red earthenware jar. She used her hands to remove decades of sand and bat excrement that covered the jar while Maecius sat in the shade of a boulder, wiping his brow and drinking water. Sophia made several short trips from the ass to the cave carrying armfuls of books. She instructed Maecius to wait by the ass to make sure it did not run off. The boy lethargically rose, grabbed the ass' tether and pulled it roughly to where he had been sitting, then dropped back down. She doubted he would have done anything more if she had asked him to. He sat beside the donkey, drinking water. When she had carried all of the books from the ass to the cave, she sat and, with a sharp blade, cut the wax from around the rim of the jar. She pulled out some of the codices she had put in the jar in 330, sixty-one years earlier. They were undamaged. She put them back in place and put the new books on top of them.

The last book left out of the jar was Eunapius' gift, *The Wisdom of Sophia*. She opened it and began to read, struggling to make out the letters in dim light with diminished eyes. The volume was slim, only a few pages. As she read the sayings that were attributed to her she was taken back through her years in Alexandria. She remembered some of them, who she said them to and what prompted them. Of others she had no recollection at all. Some she thought were quite wise and perceptive. Some she thought were shallow and foolish. Some were composites, parts of things she had said at different times to different people in different contexts, but combined to make a single saying. All were out of the context in which they had been spoken. They were said lightheartedly at parties, often intended as a tease of either the person to whom she was speaking or a common friend or acquaintance. It is not that she was insincere when she said them, it was only that she had no intention of being taken seriously or of them being reduced to writing. Here, on the page, they came across as contrived and pedantic. The phrasings were too formal, worded in a way that she did not speak, and she was sure that Eunapius had substantially edited the quotes to make them more of what he wanted than what she had actually said. There was one attributed to her that she had no doubt repeated several times, but that she distinctly remembered hearing from Pappus the first time she went to the Serapeum for a tour of the library. Still, the book brought her joy as it rolled back the years on memories of a period in her life that was mostly happy. When she finished reading she placed it on top of the other texts inside the jar.

After spending perhaps half an hour in the cave, she emerged to seek Maecius' help to take the jar from the cave to reseal it. Maecius was gone and with him the ass, food and water. She called for him in increasingly urgent tones, but he was gone and, she knew, would not be returning.

She thought about the prospects of returning to the black land of the valley on foot and without water. Her chances were not good. Her chances had never been that good, but she had made it so far, so much farther than could ever have been expected. She decided she would try, come nightfall. It would be hard to find her way, but there was a moon, and at least the killing sun would be asleep. In the meantime, she replaced the wax-covered bowl on the jar, rubbing the wax with hot stones until it melted sufficiently to seal the mouth. By the time night fell she was parched and tired. She had not made it twenty feet from the cave when she stumbled and fell hard to the ground. There was an intense pain in her right hip and she shrieked into the empty night air. She managed to crawl back to the cave in the dark and, finding the jar, sat against it, resting on her left hip. Once settled there she laughed at the ridiculousness of her predicament, the foolishness of this errand. She remembered that the first two times she had been in the cave she had said, for the sake of an echo, "I give my life to God." She did not say it now. If there was a God, her life was already His to take. If there was no God, the statement was pointless. On the verge of death she did not resign her reason. Instead, she said out loud, "I guess I'll just wait here."

She thought, of course, of her children and grandchildren, especially Hypatia, who would continue the mission of the Serapeum and preserve the tradition of Alexandrian scholarship until it could be fully restored. She thought of Philatreas and Minerva of Pergamon, her parents, and thought that, out of the mist of memory, ever so faintly, she could see the kind, loving eyes of a mother she had never known. And she thought of her husbands, the amazing and clever Pappus, the kind and truly Christian Philippus, and the sweet, naive, but knowing Timaeus, to whom she owed the most. Perhaps, she thought, that debt had been paid. She passed, mercifully, a short time later, still leaning against the earthenware jar. Her last thoughts, it may be presumed, were of the absurdity, cruelty and perfection of this world.

Chapter Thirty-Five

Sophia's Afterlife

391-1945 A.D.

O Egypt, Egypt, of your reverent deeds only stories will survive, and they will be incredible to your children! Only words cut in stone will survive to tell your faithful works, and the Scythian or Indian or some such neighbor barbarian will dwell in Egypt. For divinity goes back to heaven, and all the people will die, deserted, as Egypt will be widowed and deserted by god and human.
Asclepius, 21-29

Sophia spent many years waiting in the cave with her back against the earthenware jar. Meanwhile the procreant atoms that comprised her body, mind and soul disbursed, moved invisibly through the ether and reformed to comprise other beings, things and essences, visible and invisible.

During the years Sophia lived, Christianity was reduced to the Catholic Church and the Catholic Church decided an important issue: Whether Jesus was merely the son of God, or whether Jesus was God himself. It fell to men to decide this question, although if the learned church fathers of the fourth century had consulted the endless comedy of human folly compiled by King Josiah's priests a thousand years earlier to form the basis of what the new church now called the Old Testament, they might have realized the almost certainty of their error. The Trinitarians, those who knew that Jesus was fully equal with God, in fact was God, thought they had prevailed at Nicaea in 325, but there were learned men who refused to cede Jesus' humanity so readily. The original champions of the alternative view, that Jesus was fully human in life and subordinate to God, all died within a few years of each other. Arius burst asunder to spare Pope Alexander the sin of administering the Eucharist to him in Constantinople in 336. Eusebius of Caesarea died in 339, having succeeded in having had Athanasius banished for a second time. Eusebius of Nicomedia, the bishop who performed the death bed baptism of Emperor Constantine in 337, died in 341. They were succeeded by others and the fight went on. For much of the half century following Nicaea, the Arians held the upper hand. But in the end it was the Trinitarians whose views were enshrined in what Christians, Protestant and Catholic alike, subscribe to as the Nicene Creed. It was not, as the name suggests, the creed adopted at Nicaea. It took until 381, at a council held in Constantinople, for a modified creed, and with it the Trinitarian view, to prevail. In between Nicaea and Constantinople, councils were convened frequently in competing attempts to subdue one faction or another. These included Antioch (330), Service (341), Milan (345 and 355), Sirmium (351, 357, 358, 359), Arles (353), Beziers (353), Rimini-Seleucida (359) and Constantinople (360), among others. Today these councils are little remembered. In between and during these councils, the words of the debate were written in the red blood of the citizens of the major cities of the Empire as the populations passionately fought to the death for their respective sides. On the outcome, they believed, depended not simply life and death, but eternal life and eternal death.

The Constantinople Council was convened by Emperor Theodosius in 381 and marks the decline of Arianism as a Catholic doctrine. Henceforth, Jesus was, had always been, and forever would be, God. The Latin bishops, in league with a few powerful Greeks such as Athanasius, had won.

In 395 the Roman Empire was permanently divided, East from West, and was never again stitched together.

Once the Church decided that Jesus was God, another pressing question rose to the fore: What was Jesus' nature? Did he have a wholly human nature? Was he fully and indivisibly God?

Or did he have the nature of both man and God? Which nature predominated? How could God have a human spirit? How could God die? And what about the Holy Spirit? What nature did it possess? The Church fought over these issues for another century and a half. Half of Christendom was lost to the Catholic Church, which settled down hard in Rome as the center of its universe. The Latin bishops had always resented the over-educated Greek thinkers of the Church. The Latin bishops had not tasted the exotic fruit of Greek philosophy, did not admire Plato, Epicurus, or Pythagoras. And whereas Christianity had developed and spread first in the eastern Empire, the Latin bishops were still in the process of conquering the west for the Lord. To the former pagans of the Germanic, Nordic, Gaelic, and Gothic tribes the Latin Catholics preached a Jesus who was God on Earth, easing the transfer of allegiance from belief in gods who sometimes walked the Earth to interfere in the affairs of men to a single god who did so once and only once upon a time. The remnants of the Greek world largely repudiated Rome's vision of Christ and the Church, like the Empire before it, split, east from west.

The decline and fall of the Roman Empire cannot be laid entirely at the feet of the Church. The Empire was in decline when Constantine made Christianity the preferred faith of the realm early in the fourth century. Yet it cannot be denied that the faith imposed, the taxes levied, and the land appropriation ordered by Constantine and his successors to fund the massive growth of the Church and the support of its clergy were unpopular among many people. Nor can Christianity's uncertainty about the identity of its founder and the passionate wars fought between advocates on all sides have provided the peace, unity and tranquility Constantine envisioned when he promoted the Galilean to the head of Rome's pantheon. Part of the blame, too, must go to the almost inevitable failure of so audacious an attempt to graft a new faith onto a civilization whose roots, trunk, limbs and leaves had grown from a much different religious seed. Perhaps all that can be said with any real confidence is that the Empire was breaking when Constantine adopted Christianity and Christianity was unable to mend the breaks. By the time the Roman Catholic Church definitively decided that Jesus, like a schizophrenic, had two natures, one fully human and one fully divine, the Roman Empire no longer controlled Rome and the Roman Church no longer controlled the Eastern portion of Christendom.

With the Roman Church able to impose its view of the Christ in the west, the eastern realms pulled away from the Roman Church. In the east, where Jesus had lived and where his disciples first carried his message, belief in his humanity remained essential. In the Seventh Century, this area of the Roman Empire would begin to rapidly adopt a newer religion whose founding prophet was not proclaimed God's equal by his successors.

With the collapse of the Roman Empire in the west, power fell to or was seized by the Roman Church. The organization that had spent so much time and spilt so much blood defining truth and banishing heresy was not amenable to further debate or exploration of alternative notions and ideas. Independent thought became heresy.

The rigid adherence to orthodoxy imposed by the church in Rome over what became known as Europe may not have been enough on its own to incubate the period of decline in the cultural, scientific and economic health that engulfed Europe for the next thousand years or so. Certainly progress in these human activities was bound to be inhibited in a society that enforced the idea that all that men needed to know could be found in the twenty-seven books identified by Athanasius as orthodox in 373 and later adopted as Church canon. Indeed, the Church so limited the sources of sanctioned knowledge that the Latin word for any book, *biblos,* came to refer to its single, accepted tome: The

Bible. But this alone may not have been enough to stunt the development of humanity for so long a period had the Church not thrown away and forgotten knowledge that had once been discovered. The destruction of the Serapeum in 391 is marked by many as the end of Greek scholarship on a large scale, yet during the next few decades many attempted and succeeded in advancing knowledge in the fields of astronomy, geometry and philosophy. Sophia's granddaughter, the lovely Hypatia, continued to study and teach out of the home on the Serapic Way for many years after the fall of the Serapeum and she was not alone. It is believed that before her death at the hands of a Christian mob in 415 she had begun again to explore an helio-centric theory of the solar system, as first proposed by Aristarchus 600 years earlier. She remained a Neo-Platonist and pagan, but shared her learning with all who sought it. Much of what we know of her today comes to us through letters written by a student named Synesius of Cyrene who later became a Catholic bishop in the city of Ptolemais in what is now Libya. Socrates Scholasticus, a contemporary Christian historian, wrote the following account of Hypatia:

> "There was a woman at Alexandria named Hypatia, daughter of the philosopher Theon, who made such attainments in literature and science, as to far surpass all the philosophers of her own time. Having succeeded to the school of Plato and Plotinus, she explained the principles of philosophy to her auditors, many of who came from a distance to receive her instructions. On account of the self-possession and ease of manner which she had acquired in consequence of the cultivation of her mind, she not infrequently appeared in public in the presence of the magistrates. Neither did she feel abashed in going to an assembly of men. For all men on account of her extraordinary dignity and virtue admired her the more."

Hypatia was killed at the instigation of Cyril, Theophilus' nephew and successor as Pope of Alexandria. There was nothing personal in the murder. Cyril likely had Hypatia killed to retaliate against her friend and student Orestes, the Praefect of the Diocese of Egypt, for his having stood in the way of Cyril's efforts to expel Alexandria's large Jewish population from the city. Hypatia was drug from a street into a church, stripped of her clothes, flayed alive with shards of floor tiles, then burned. Thus died the last great Greek scholar.

The Dark Ages is now disfavored as a name for the period that followed in Europe. To the extent it suggests that there were no significant developments in the arts, literature or science, it is certainly overly broad. People were born, grew, learned, lived and died in much the manner they always have and always will. Certainly advances in the art of cathedral building prove that not everything was stagnant. But with almost all scholarship and even the ability to read and write made the exclusive province of the Church, there can be no doubt that the diversity of experience and education and freedom of thought required for advancing one's own mind and expanding upon the understanding of one's predecessors was absent. The very ideas of democracy and republic, birthed in Greece and which even Rome had kept alive as a kind of puppet show of the ideal, vanished as the Roman Church invested kings with the power of God to rule over its worshipers and circumscribed every station in life as if set in stone by the divine will of the Creator.

To claim that it was the Church alone that preserved much of what was preserved is only to acknowledge that the opportunity for other institutions to play such a role in those times was limited to what the Church allowed.

In these centuries the last remnants of what the Gnostics thought, believed and taught about Jesus was virtually lost entirely and only the anathemas of Iraneus, Justinius and other early Gnostic haters contained the distorted hint of what once was believed by their early brothers in faith. The Gnostics' belief in esoteric knowledge as the source of salvation would bubble up from time to time, such as with the Bogomils, Cathars and Paulicians, only to be promptly suppressed by the very exoteric hands of the Inquisitions. During all this time Sophia waited, her skeletal back against an earthenware jar in a region of Egypt so remote from Europe that it had ceased to exist outside of myth and fairy tale.

The emergence from this dark period came slowly and in fits, followed always by inquisition and suppression. In 1095, Pope Urban II launched the first of several great crusades. Knights, peasants and serfs from many European lands left their homes to fight in the Levant and recapture Jerusalem for Christ. An unexpected consequence was that returning heroes and murderers brought back many Greek volumes that had not been seen in Europe for hundreds of years, including many works of the man universally referred to simply as "the Philosopher," the esteemed, but, in Europe, scarcely preserved Aristotle. It took nearly a century for these rediscovered works to be translated and circulated among the few who were educated enough to esteem them, a process delayed because the language of Greece had long since vanished from Europe. The twelfth century saw its own renaissance, with the first European universities being formed and philosophers such as Pierre Abelard again exploring concepts like universals (that is, whether such things as "white" or "chair" are real in and of themselves or whether the words are simply names of concepts that transcend the things themselves), thus beginning to rediscover philosophical seams mined by Plato more than a millennia before. For his efforts Abelard was excommunicated and exiled.

Each period of intellectual exploration was followed by Catholic inquisitions and secular plagues, in which many saw the hand of a vengeful, angry God.

In 1417 Poggio Bracciolini discovered a fragile, 800 year old

Latin text in a monastery in Germany, surreptitiously copied it and took the copy back with him to Florence. It was Lucretius' masterpiece, *De Rurum Natura,* The Nature of Things. Slowly the text made its way back into the cobwebbed recesses of Europe. Eventually promoted by and inspiring philosophers like Giordano Bruno, poets like William Shakespeare, astronomers such as Galileo Galilei, and other explorers in other fields, it was to have a gradual, but profound impact on European thought. "Fear not death or the gods," Lucretius urged. "Look to nature." These explorations came not without cost to the explorers. The Church imprisoned Bruno for seven years, then burned him at the stake for heresy in 1600 to celebrate the new century. Galileo was accused of heresy, forced to recant his assertion that the Earth revolved around the sun, and spent the last twenty-seven years of his life under house arrest. However, with Johannes Gutenberg's invention of the printing press in 1440 it became only a matter of time before the Church lost the ability to hold the lid down on the stewpot of human curiosity, expression and behavior. We use terms like The Reformation, The Renaissance and The Age of Enlightenment to describe the awakenings that followed, the periods when people rediscovered lessons long lost, often without realizing that they were plowing old fields once tilled by the greats of yore and long since laid fallow by fear, fever and famine, overseen by a church that rose to power in the ashes of an empire and assiduously culled all unwanted seeds from the soil before they could sprout.

As Sophia waited, knowledge of what Timaeus and his predecessors thought and wrote and believed became ever more remote and forgotten. But this, too, was about to change. Beginning in the eighteenth century, Europeans, accelerated by Napoleon's invasion of Egypt in 1798, rediscovered the regions of the Upper Nile and soon vast antiquities markets arose to meet both the supply and demand side of the plunderers' trade. Papyri survived well in the arid climes just outside of the Nile's flood plains and soon scraps of such paper containing fragments of Gnostic texts began to appear in Europe and Great Britain which, in turn, began to spark renewed interest in what some of the earliest Christians believed and how they understood Jesus and the meaning of his life. In the late nineteenth century a single, crudely bound codex was found in what had been a Christian cemetery near the ancient town of Panopolis Kemmis, where Ankha Aegyptos had purchased his freedom from the Roman Legion in 330. This Coptic book, which has become known as the Berlin Codex, contained three gospels and notes on another: *The Gospel of Mary, The Apocryphon of John, The Sophia of Jesus Christ* and notes on *The Acts of Peter*. The Berlin Codex was the first book that Hypatia-Sophia translated while Magdalene slept in 326. Senmonthis had given Sophia's translation away to people who still practiced their Gnostic faith in Sheneset and the book was buried in a grave fifty miles north of there. With the discovery of the Berlin Codex, interest in the ancient Gnostics grew some more, although translation of the full text had to await the passage of two World Wars. Still, Sophia waited, the cave collapsing and filling in, but protected by a boulder whose Egyptian face had long since vanished.

Sophia's wait ended in 1945 when several fellahin, farmers, travelled up into the cliffs and caves to collect fertilizer. They came from eastern bank of the town of Nagaa Hammadi, which in ancient times, before the sweep of Islam into Egypt, had been known as Chenoboskion and Sheneset. Looking behind a large boulder on the slope of cliff debris, the fellahin, led by a man named Muhammad Ali, came across a reddish, earthenware storage jar. Thinking the jar might contain gold or other hidden treasure, Muhammad kicked Sophia's loose bones and other debris out of the way to take a closer look at it. A bowl sealed with wax over its mouth covered the jar. Muhammad and the other fellahin, including two of Muhammad's brothers, took counsel, for although the jar might contain treasure, it might also contain a jinn, or evil spirit, entrapped long ago to secure the world against its evil. They did not consider that the jar might contain both treasure and a jinn. Greed quickly overcame fear and Muhammad's younger brother took his mattock and smashed off the top of the jar. Wonder of wonders, gold dust flew into the air. The fellahins' hearts leapt together as visions of luxury and beautiful wives filled their imaginations. Then they looked inside to find nothing but a bunch of old books stacked together, one on top of the other. The gold dust was comprised of small fragments of papyri that had come loose from the texts. The books would be good for starting fires, but not much else. Muhammad tore apart some of the codices and offered to share them with the fellahin who were not his brothers. They declined and he stuffed torn pieces into intact books and carried them home on the back of his camel.

When he got home, Muhammad threw the texts into the courtyard where his animals fed. His mother mixed some of the pages with straw to make kindling for her stove. The family thought of trying to sell the books for a few pennies each. Some were traded for cigarettes or pieces of fruit. Eventually the proprietor of the Cairo Antiquities Gallery saw some of the pages, realized what they might be, and set about reuniting what remained of the texts.

The Nag Hammadi Library, as these fifty-two texts came to be known, was finally released in English and German translations in 1975. At long last the world could read many of the actual books that those who believed in Jesus as a teacher of knowledge, gnosis, used as guides in the practice of their faith. In about that same year another of Sophia's texts was found in Philippus' burial vault outside of Oxyrynchus. It contained, among other texts, the long lost *Gospel of Judas Iscariot*. The discoveries have inspired many brilliant minds to read, research and write and have prompted many Christians to reexamine the roots of their faith. Philippus' bones, like Sophia's, were of no value to the discoverers of those treasures.

Can a long lost faith be revived? What does it mean to those who believed in a faith that promised eternal salvation when that faith ceases to exist altogether in the lives of men? Does its disappearance disprove a faith once held? Is salvation obtained through such faith revoked when the remnants of that faith are lost? Are the gates of Heaven opened or the Pleroma dissolved to disgorge the souls that entered those realms based on a faith that is no more? There are some today who call themselves Gnostics. There are those who believe that there once existed a faith called Gnosticism and believe they can discern from the rediscovered texts what the ancients who sought gnosis through Jesus believed and practiced. But this, too, is folly. In this world there is no resurrection.

It is unlikely that Sophia would have considered the discovery of her books as fulfillment of Timaeus' faith that she was the keeper of gnosis for the ages. The books were discovered too late to preserve the faith and they will likely be lost again before mankind completes its rampage on the Earth. It was not, however, an anticipated result, but the effort, the payment of a debt she owed to Timaeus, that drove her back into the desert in 391. She knew when she made that journey that it was likely to end in failure. Sophia would have been pleased, however, by the fact that her sayings, compiled by Eunapius as *The Wisdom of Sophia,* upon their rediscovery in 1945, were used to start a fire that provided heat and light, if only briefly.

Chapter Thirty-Six

APPENDIX: Η σοφία της Σοφίας

The Wisdom of Sophia*

**Reconstructed from secondary sources by The Sophia Project, Chair Dr. Richard D. Armentrout, Boston College*

The author has received permission to print as an appendix the entirety of the Sophia Project's reconstruction of the little book compiled and edited by Eunapius of Sardis in or about 391 A.D.. Dr. Armentrout, Chair of the Sophia Project, has cautioned that the following probably bears little resemblance to the book Eunapius presented to Sophia on her eighty-fourth birthday. While it is likely that some of these quotes were in the original, it is equally likely that some were not and that Eunapius was able to include many others that have been lost forever. What the Sophia Project has been able to do is to find fragments in other fourth century sources that attribute sayings to a person identified as Sophia of Alexandria and which appear on balance to reflect what we know of her thinking during the years that she lived in the house on the Serapic Way. What we have is likely only a whisper, a hint of what she actually said to shock, amuse and entertain her guests at her soirees in Alexandria. We cannot know what we have lost.

I am Sophia. I am not Sophia (Wisdom). Men have always projected onto me that which I am not and often cannot see what I am.

What am I? I am a woman and not a very exceptional one, if truth is told. It is just that you men cannot look at a woman without your minds becoming engaged in deciding whether she would be a desirable mate and what she might look like under her robes. I think the inability of men to see what is directly in front of them and to understand, directly, what is said to them, explains most of the mysteries, magic, confusion and nonsense that comprise the religious ideas they generate. I mean, if men are incapable of understanding that babies born from the same womb, with the same number of arms, legs, fingers, toes, and eyes are their equals, but, think that women, by virtue of their superior genitalia, are inferior beings, then what hope is there that they might understand anything else of importance?

The important questions of existence are never answered and never leave us alone. Rather, they are decided then undecided then decided again. Knowledge is gained and lost and rediscovered. We do not live long enough to remember what we have forgotten and we live too long to adhere to a belief once it is formed.

Among human attributes there is nothing more precious nor more pernicious than faith. Life without faith is unhappy and, ultimately, unlivable. Yet faith without reason is folly and faith without doubt is ignorance.

That which we come to know cannot be spoken for words leak knowledge like a wicker basket leaks water. Between the time that words are formed and sent on their way and the time that they are heard or read their intended meaning has mostly leaked out, leaving only the moist trappings of their intent. Sometimes this is enough. For the really important things it never is. Even when the author of those words reads or speaks them back to herself they are diluted and fail to convey their intended meaning, so much so that she must doubt that the knowledge she thought to express was ever in her possession at all.

Lucretius said it best but Lucretius got it wrong, as all men must. Or perhaps my Latin is insufficient. We are made of invisible stuff, procreant atoms he calls them. But there is no reason to stop there and presume that these atoms are not themselves made up of even smaller bits and those of smaller bits still. The important lesson of Lucretius is not whether or not he is right about the existence of atoms; it is the admonition to look to nature for answers and to fear not the gods. Whether or not you see a god's hand at work in nature is entirely up to you.

We do not fear the death of our body or our soul, whatever that may be. We can abide the loss of a limb or an eye. We fear only the loss of our awareness, our consciousness or whatever it is that makes us aware of ourself as ourself. And this is a silly fear since we lose consciousness every night and count ourself blessed if the duration of that loss is extended beyond two or three hours.

Anguish over death is profoundly exacerbated by the hope that death might be avoided if only one discovers the magic formula.

Gods are like the dead heroes in Homer's Hades: they require libations of blood to bring them to life. By this measure, Jesus has certainly been resurrected.

Most people, whatever their religion, know that on some level they do not fully understand the premises of their faith. And so their faith actually resides not in God, the gods or Jesus, but in learned men, such as priests and bishops, who have been appointed to have faith for them. The average person believes that the priest has more knowledge, in fact has actual knowledge of such things as salvation, life after death, and the nature of God. And while the priests play their part, they cannot actually possess knowledge of such matters because such matters are not available for inspection. The Greeks used to trust priests to tell them of the goings-on and intentions of the Gods on Mount Olympus. But men have since scaled that mountain and found nothing there save an extraordinary landscape. One day, perhaps, people will pierce the firmament and will find no heavenly angels there. What will the priests do then? No doubt they will find some other address for God.

As all creatures, we live temporally but exist eternally. Our existence is eternal because it exists, now and forever, in the exact temporal location where it occurred. But we live temporally because we pass each temporal location as ships pass an island in the sea. As the ships move, the island fades, then disappears over the horizon, but the island does not cease to exist. When we die, our temporal lives are over. Our existence continues, as the island remains. The great mystery is whether we retain any awareness of our existence, but it is frivolous to fight over this mystery, for the very reason that our concern centers upon retaining awareness of our temporal lives, which have ended, and not upon our eternal existence, which exists without memory or awareness. Our lives are sensate and our existence is insensate. By demanding immortality, what people really want is the perpetuation of temporal awareness, which is different than existence.

The Christian Gospel John states that in the beginning was the word and the word was God, as if God spoke the world into existence. This cannot be true. The world came into existence, then words were invented to describe and define it. But in the process of describing and defining the world, words inevitably circumscribe and limit what they describe and define. In this way, the word becomes God by setting boundaries on the boundless meaning of the world. God is not the word. Rather, the word is God. John also writes that the Word became flesh and made his dwelling among us. If Jesus was God's word made flesh, then why do not the learned churchmen spend more time studying the words of Jesus, and less time arguing over his place in the firmament, which they can never discover?

It seems most unChristian to punish an eternal soul eternally for sins their inhabitants committed during a brief sojourn on Earth. Shouldn't forgiveness be offered to all souls, regardless of their corporeal status?

If Jesus has two natures, both human and divine, and the

divine nature, as all agree, is unknowable, then why do the learned churchmen spend so much time arguing, fighting and killing over this issue? Why not simply study the human nature of Jesus, for it is not unknowable and there is much to be learned from him?

Jesus did not establish a religion, but a religion was established in his name. The Christians have created the very thing that drove him to the cross. But whereas the Romans are said to have crucified Jesus on a cross of wood, the Christians have crucified him on pages of paper, from which there is no resurrection because each word buries him deeper, obscures who he was more completely. Jesus did not come to be memorized and memorialized, but to be mimicked, to have his example followed. The more godlike he is made, the less possible it becomes to follow his example.

In the years since I started coming to the Serapeum I have heard more and more stories of philosophers for whom it is claimed, as proof of their wisdom and excellence, that they possess the power of miracles or divination and who have disciples who follow them around to witness their supernatural conduct. It is almost as if the pagans are in competition with the Christians and as if wisdom is too feeble to stand on its own legs, but must be supported by claims of divine powers. To my mind such claims diminish the philosopher's discoveries.

The Jews and the Christians have created the worst kind of system. Imagine insisting upon giving all power to one god and denying the very existence of other gods that might have some power to temper, moderate or mollify an almighty deity, living alone and day by day, like a hermit, becoming more cranky, less hospitable, and less accepting of individual variation. Men are fools to entrust all power over them to a single, tyrant god.

It is error to think of people as God's creations. Rather, we are aspects, parts of God. The Pleroma of Timaeus and the heaven of the Christians, if it exists at all, exists indivisible from ourselves.

Perhaps this is what Jesus meant when he said the kingdom of God is inside of you and outside of you.

The world was a better place when people did not know they had religion. Once one realizes that her beliefs form a definable system, she becomes bound to think about its aspects and finds that none of it is certain and most of it is simply made up. It is better not to know such a thing.

It is true. I once worked in a fornicarium. But prostitutes, it turns out, are perfect Christians. They render unto any Marcus, Diophanes or Caesar what they pay for, they love their neighbors, they do unto others what they would have the others do unto them, usually without reciprocity, and they can always be counted on to turn the other cheek.

The concept of eternal life has always been strange to me. Eternity? What does that mean? For ever and ever knowing the same things, seeing the same things over and over, hearing the same songs played by the same angels on the same lyres. Imagine that. It is quite possible that most of us, perhaps all of us, given long enough, would choose mortality over immortality. At least with mortality you have something for which to live, something for which to look forward?

I sometimes think that I am a bigger fool than Athanasius because I am certain I know nothing and he is certain he knows everything. Since we are both certainly wrong, it is perhaps better to know you are right.

Uncertainty is the necessary ally of truth. The person who is certain of truth stops searching for it. There is comfort to be found in certainty, but the path to discovery is closed.

Humans show their limitation by insisting that God is a being. Since we are beings, we insist that God is a being. But what if God is not a being? Is that the same thing as saying God does not exist? And what if God was a being, perfect, complete and lonely and became bored and split herself into infinite fragments such that all the stars and sun and planets and moon and Earth and rocks and water and sand and creatures are but bits of a self-dismembered God? Would it make a difference to us if we knew this? Would we act differently toward each other if we realized we were all part of the same being, fragmented but longing for reconciliation?

Jesus aimed his message at the least among us, the marginal, the itinerant, the whores and the beggars. He had to be killed so the priests could adapt his message to suit the landlords and the lenders. Forgiveness of debts becomes forgiveness of trespasses. Living in poverty becomes being charitable. What Jesus taught could never have formed the basis for the official religion of the Empire because it did not suit the rich and powerful.

My first husband was a Christian Gnostic. He believed that Jesus taught about Sophia in the Pleroma and how to join Jesus in that realm. And he claimed to have found the Pleroma on at least one occasion. What I have always wondered is: What happens next? Timaeus did not stay in the Pleroma, but returned to this world, where he was killed. So, if entry into the Pleroma is based on knowledge, but the knowledge to find it is not sufficient to remain there, then what chance is there to join it later, when you are dead, and your knowledge is gone? In the end I believe it was the seeking, not the finding, that brought Timaeus his greatest joy.

The Mithrians, the Kemites, the Eleusinians, and many other such believers say that they have discovered mysteries that explain the meaning of existence, the secret of life and afterlife, and of the gods, but that can be told only in secret to initiates who have devoted years honoring the premises of their faith. It is good to keep such mysteries a deep secret, I think, since telling them to the wide world would likely expose them as equally absurd to and no more insightful than the explanations advanced by other, less mysterious faiths.

Dramatis Personae

All dates are in the common era

SOPHIA (307-391) – Title character. Sophia grew up an orphan in Alexandria, Egypt, was sold to a brothel owner in Antioch in 321, was purchased and freed by Timaeus of Kaymakli in 324, when she joined him on his journeys as a Christian Gnostic missionary. Birth name Hypatia. Also known at times as Adama, Sophocles and Hypatius.

TIMAEUS (280-325) – Born in Cappodocia, son of a paper and book merchant. Born and raised a Catholic Christian, took priest's vows and worked under Bishop Eusebius of Caesarea from 297-311, left eye put out during the Christian persecutions under Emperor Diocletian, appointed Catholic Bishop of Kaymakli (Cappodocia) in 311, adopted Gnostic beliefs while bishop, removed from office and blinded in right eye under order of Bishop Alexander of Byzantium in 317, wanders throughout the Eastern portion of the Empire advancing Gnostic Christianity from 317-325.

PHILIPPUS (301-330) – Born in Joppa (Judea) to a Christian family. Took priest's vows and worked under Bishop Eusebius of Caesarea from 319-328). Renounced vows to marry in 328, but remains a faithful Catholic.

BESET (c. 265-340) – Born in Chenoboskion, Egypt, married to an older alcoholic circa 280, had nine children, widowed and left homeless in 325, hired by Sophia as housekeeper in 325.

SENMONTHIS (c.285-???) – Born and lived in Sheneset, Egypt. Sophia's landlord and friend from 326-330.

ANKHA AEGYPTOS (292-370) – Son of Beset, left home to join the Roman legion at the age of 16, fought alongside Emperor Constantine in his battles against Licinius (315-324), Consul guard in Caneopolis Egypt, 325-330, left the Legion in 330 and moved to Alexandria in 330, where he became a successful papyrus merchant.

JOHN OF JERUSALEM (310-391) – A Gnostic Christian who is forced by circumstance and violence to adopt the outward appearance of orthodoxy. John shows up at three key moments in Sophia's life.

CONSTANTINE THE GREAT (272-337; Emperor (306-337) – After an extended period of sharing power with Emperors Maxentius and Licinius, Constantine I became Emperor of the united Empire in 324 and made Christianity the preferred religion of the Empire. Constantine called the first great Ecumenical Council in Nicaea in 325 and involved himself in Church governance for the remainder of his life. He was finally baptized by Eusebius of Nicomedia on his death bed.

EUNAPIUS (mid fourth century – early fifth century) – Author of *Lives of the Philosophers and Sophists*, providing the only contemporary account of fourth century Neoplatonists. Collects the sayings of Sophia and presented them to her in book form on her 84th birthday in 391. Wrote a contemporary account of the destruction of the Serapeum in 391.

HYPATIA OF ALEXANDRIA (c. 364-415) – Last great Greek philosopher, mathematician and astronomer of Antiquity. Her death at the hands of a Christian mob in 415 is often marked as the end of classical Antiquity. Daughter of Theon. In the novel she is the granddaughter of Sophia.

PAPPUS OF ALEXANDRIA (290-350) – One of the last great mathematicians of Antiquity, author of *The Synagoge*, a compilation mathematical discoveries through the third century A.D. Married to Sophia from 333-350.

THEON OF ALEXANDRIA (c.340-c. 391) – Also known as Theon of the Mouseion. Mathematician, updater of Euclid's work. Father of Hypatia of Alexandria. In the novel he is Sophia's son.

Catholic Notables

ALEXANDER OF ALEXANDRIA (c. 250-328) – Bishop (Pope) of Alexandria from 313-328. Attended Nicene Council in 325. Opponent of Arianism and fervent Trinitarian. Succeeded by Athanasius.

ALEXANDER OF CONSTANTINOPLE (c. 237-337) – Bishop (Pope) of Byzantium (later named New Rome and Constantinople). Attended Nicene Council in 325. Opponent of Arianism and fervent Trinitarian.

ARIUS OF ALEXANDRIA (c. 250-336) –Alexandrian priest, philosopher, author, poet and songwriter who gave his name to the Arian viewpoint. Attended the Nicene Council in 325 and was exiled by Constantine after refusing to avow the first Nicene Creed. Found haven with Eusebius of Caesarea, was later reinstated to the Church. Died from a sudden illness under suspicious circumstances in Constantinople in 336.

ATHANASIUS OF ALEXANDRIA (c.299-373) – Bishop (Pope) of Alexandria from 328-373, with at least five periods of exile totaling seventeen years. A saint in both the Roman Catholic and Eastern Orthodox churches. Attended the Nicene Council in 325.

EUSEBIUS OF CAESAREA (c. 260-c.339) – First great Christian historian whose *Ecclesiastical Histories* cover the development of Christianity from the days of the disciples to around 314. Bishop of Caesarea from c. 314-c. 339. Sided with the Arians in the Arian-Trinitarian conflict. Attended the Nicene Council in 325.

EUSEBIUS OF NICOMEDIA (c.280-341) – Bishop of Berytus (modern day Beirut), then Nicomedia (Greater Constantinople) then Constantinople. Strident Arian in the Arian-Trinitarian conflict. Attended the Nicene Council in 325.

EUSTATHIUS OF ANTIOCH (c.290-c.337) – Bishop (Pope) of Antioch from c. 325-330. Attended the Nicene Council in 325. Deposed and exiled to Thrace in 330 on charges that he was having an affair with a married woman.

MACARIUS OF JERUSALEM (c. 270-c. 335) – Bishop of Jerusalem from c. 312 to c. 335. Attended the Nicene Council in 325. A saint in the Roman Catholic Church. His skull and other relics are kept in Saint Anthony's Chapel (Pittsburgh, Pennsylvania).

MACARIUS OF EGYPT (c. 300-391) – Also known as Macarius the Elder to distinguish him from Macarius the Younger. Founded the Paromeos Monastery in the Nitrian Dessert west of Alexandria. The "Nitrian Monks" were active as the muscle for Alexandrian bishops from Athanasius in the fourth century to at least Cyril in the fifth century. A saint in both the Roman Catholic and Eastern Orthodox churches.

MACARIUS THE YOUNGER (c. 300-395) – Founded the Kellii Monastery in the Nitrian Dessert west of Alexandria. The "Nitrian Monks" were active as the muscle for Alexandrian bishops from Athanasius in the fourth century to at least Cyril in the fifth century. A saint in both the Roman Catholic and Eastern Orthodox churches.

PACHOMIUS THE GREAT (c. 292-348) – Founder of the first Christian monasteries in Upper Egypt. Although a Trinitarian, fled into the dessert to avoid being ordained as a priest by Athanasius. A saint in both the Roman Catholic and Eastern Orthodox churches.

THEOPHILUS OF ALEXANDRIA (c. 335-412) – Bishop (Pope) of Alexandria 384-412. Led the Christian mob that destroyed the Serapeum and its library. Uncle of his successor, Cyril.

TOP HAT
BOOKS

Historical fiction that lives.

We publish fiction that captures the contrasts, the achievements, the optimism and the radicalism of ordinary and extraordinary times across the world.

We're open to all time periods and we strive to go beyond the narrow, foggy slums of Victorian London. Where are the tales of the people of fifteenth century Australasia? The stories of eighth century India? The voices from Africa, Arabia, cities and forests, deserts and towns? Our books thrill, excite, delight and inspire.

The genres will be broad but clear. Whether we're publishing romance, thrillers, crime, or something else entirely, the unifying themes are timescale and enthusiasm. These books will be a celebration of the chaotic power of the human spirit in difficult times. The reader, when they finish, will snap the book closed with a satisfied smile.